ricochet

Fiona Kidman was born in Hawera in 1940. She has worked as a librarian, creative writing lecturer and teacher, producer and critic, but primarily as a writer. To date, she has published sixteen books, including novels, poetry, non-fiction, short stories and a play. She has won numerous awards and fellowships, including the New Zealand Book Awards fiction category for *The Book of Secrets*, the OBE for services to literature and the New Zealand Scholarship in Letters. She lives in Wellington with her extended family.

For Lauris, with love

RICOCHET BABY

Fiona Kidman

VINTAGE

Vintage New Zealand
(An imprint of the Random House Group)
18 Poland Road, Glenfield
Auckland 10, NEW ZEALAND

Sydney   New York   Toronto
London   Auckland   Johannesburg
and agencies throughout the world

First published 1996

© Fiona Kidman 1996
The moral rights of the author have been asserted.
Printed in New Zealand
ISBN 1 86941 304 0
All rights reserved. No part of this publication may be reproduced or transmitted in any form or by any means, electronic or mechanical, including photocopying, recording, storage in any information retrieval system or otherwise, without the written permission of the publisher.

contents

Acknowledgements	vii
one	1
Family Connections; Roberta	
two	6
Bernard and Orla; The Unclean Box; Sarah	
three	17
Breathing Lessons; Moon Shadows	
four	28
Glass; Orla; The Third Daughter of the Earl of Maudsley; The Cage; Scarlet Ribbons	
five	48
Walnut	
six	55
Life in the Country	
seven	59
Breaking Rules; Turkey; Thoughts About Leaving; At the End of the Year	
eight	72
A Letter to Roberta; Returns; 16 Digglie Street	
nine	79
Clearing Wreckage; Roberta's Baby	
ten	87
Birth Notices	
eleven	92
Regrets; The Water Bearer; Grief; Recognition	
twelve	99
Poultices	
thirteen	102
Roberta	
fourteen	107
Edith; Only the Lonely; The Woman in the Paddock	

fifteen	110
War Woman; Snot; Rockin' Rollin'	
sixteen	116
Renunciation; Correspondence	
seventeen	126
The Counsel of Fools; Roberta; Wallflowers	
eighteen	147
Milking; True Virgins; A Mandelbrot Set	
nineteen	155
Sarah	
twenty	158
Roberta; Cat Twists; Some Aspects of Sexual Desire	
twenty-one	173
Mrs Blue Eyes; Home TIme	
twenty-two	179
Josh	
twenty-three	185
Family Remains; An Application; Unease; Conversations Abroad	
twenty-four	195
Infinite Chaos	
twenty-five	204
Exodus	
twenty-six	212
More Recipies for Disaster	
twenty-seven	215
Exposure; Choosing Truth	
twenty-eight	224
Roberta and Sarah; An Ordinary Gran; Going On; Wendy; Nathan	
twenty-nine	235
Inside	
thirty	238
Roberta	

acknowledgements

I wish to thank Michael Harlow, who has been generous with advice; Themla Puckey and Dr Rob McIlroy, who supported my research into psychiatric care; members of the Post and Ante-Natal Distress Support Group; Elizabeth Smither for helping me to research crop circles; Joanna Kidman and Amelia Herrero-Kidman who advised me about songs; *Holmes* programme staff; Victoria Forgie; and Anna Rogers, for her unfailing patience and good humour while editing. Jane Tolerton's *Convent Girls* and *The Gardens of Russell Page*, by Marina Schinz and Gabrielle van Zuylen, were two particularly invaluable reference books. My thanks, as ever, to Ian Kidman, who makes computer technology work for me.

Permission to use the following songs and poetry is gratefully acknowledged: 'Scarlet Ribbons' by Evelyn Danzig/Jack Segal (Reproduced by permission of Warner/Chappell Music Australia Pty Ltd. Unauthorised Reproduction Is Illegal.); 'Moon Shadow' (Sony).

Victoria University Press for lines for 'Instructions for how to get ahead of yourself while the light still shines', from *Moving House* by Jenny Bornholdt.

While working on this book I was the recipient of a grant from the former Arts Council of New Zealand Toi Aotearoa (now Creative New Zealand).

one

FAMILY CONNECTIONS

WHEN ROBERTA FALLS pregnant her whole family is filled with joy. Fallen is not exactly how Roberta would describe it, for she and Paul have planned the baby and it has been conceived at exactly the time they chose. But that is how their mothers speak of it, as if there is something wanton and abandoned about the conception, and in a way this pleases Roberta. Both sets of parents immediately arrange to visit. We'll have a party and celebrate, they say. Her mother and father drive over the hill from the farm, more than two hours away, and Paul's come from across town.

Fay and Milton, Paul's parents, bring good champagne, with a clean, crisp bite. Edith and Glass bring a bottle of gin. Paul raises his eyebrows in mock astonishment, but Roberta pretends not to notice. Of course you won't be drinking now, they all say.

'I've brought you some silverbeet,' Edith tells her. 'The iron is good for you. Seafood's good, but for goodness' sake be careful. And milk. You never liked milk, but if you can just try to get it down. Six glasses a day? Well, you are taking motherhood seriously.'

'Are you getting heartburn?' Fay wants to know.

'A little.'

'They say it's a sign the baby will have lots of hair. I had it so much you wouldn't believe.'

'I don't remember that,' Milton says. 'Paul didn't have much hair.'

Fay laughs. 'I didn't say it was true.' But she looks uncertain, as if there is faulty recognition in her memory.

Edith has brought the christening shawl that has been in Glass's family for years. 'It needs some airing, but plenty of time for that.'

Her husband's eyes widen. 'Where did you find that?'

Edith looks embarrassed, as if she's been caught in some illicit act. 'It's odd what you find when you're spring-cleaning.'

'So there'll be a christening?' Fay asks, more eagerly than she intended. Paul and Roberta had had a secular wedding in the farmhouse garden.

'If they waited until the summer I could do a mixed pink and blue cornflower border. No? Then I could make it all white, which might be nicer.' Edith is at her sharpest and most charming best, as if everything is decided.

Fay and Milton exchange glances which they think nobody sees.

'Have you told Bernard and Orla?' Roberta asks her mother, hoping to change the subject.

'Time enough for that,' Edith says easily. 'They're so busy, now the season's starting again. You'll have to let Michael know.'

'You know how hard it is to get in touch with big brother.'

They nod, they sigh.

Paul's parents have brought a matinée set wrapped in tissue paper. The pattern is like shells and foam, delicate, precise, not a stitch out of place. We know babies wear stretch-and-grows and all those modern cute little clothes and we can't wait to start buying them, they say, but Milton's mother knitted these before she died. It was her ambition to live long enough to see her great-grandchildren, . . . well, it can't be helped, but it seems a nice way to start your layette.

Layette. It's not a word Roberta has heard since she was at school, when girls still talked about their futures.

The two families move on to prams. One will buy that, the others the bassinet, but who will buy which?

'Shouldn't we leave the pram till the baby's born?' asks Glass.

'Why?' They are all instantly curious.

'Oh, I don't know. Something I heard.'

Superstition. You can feel the unspoken word settle on them, lightly, like an echo dissolving into their laughter. But nobody wants to know what will happen, if they don't follow through, now that the matter has been raised. Once you've stated the possibility of disaster, then everything has to be done to avoid the risk. Besides, pregnant women are unsettled by such talk; there's no knowing how their fancies will stray if they are fed with ideas. The mother is host to the mystery, her child the unknown person in their midst. She must not be disturbed.

'We can wait until the baby comes then,' says Milton, appeasing his daughter-in-law's father. 'As long as we decide on who's doing what.'

They will toss for it. And there in the startling sunlight, the coin spins and twinkles, and rolls down the path so they have to run after it. Heads, they call, tails, and everybody is happy with the outcome.

'We're going to open a special bank account for education,' Milton says. 'You can't start early enough.' Milton is a public servant. He is well placed in the ministry, as he tells them in an easy and charming way.

This day will come to seem like a dream to Roberta. Although it is midwinter it feels like early spring, a day on which their house is suffused with sunshine, and they are able to open the windows to the sea. An early dusting of snow lies on the hills but inside their courtyard it is warm enough to bring tables outside. The trees will grow, the families say, looking at the gums and kowhai Roberta and Paul have planted. We'll be able to sit in the shade of them some day, and this baby will be climbing in their branches. You can build a tree-house for him, Paul. Or her, as the case may be.

You won't find out the sex of the baby, will you? It doesn't matter what this one is, as long as it has all its fingers and toes. Have you thought of a name? And they all look expectantly, hopefully, towards the young couple, then avert their collective gaze, hoping to disguise the naked longing in their eyes. Edith. Fay. Glass. Milton. Well, maybe there is nothing in these names for young people. They will have their own ideas. The parents don't voice their thoughts.

The sky above is as blue as a thrush's egg and the far below sea a dark navy that stains the Wellington horizon. They all feel drenched with blue and gold light and full of hope.

Except that, once during the afternoon, when they have eaten lunch, fresh salmon seared quickly and cooked with a slice of brie and a dash of chablis, and a salad, and soft focaccia bread containing whole grapes, Roberta looks up and sees a dark unease in her father's eyes, as if he can see into the future. This frightens her because she knows that sometimes he does. She looks across at her mother. Something about Edith, sitting in the sunshine, makes her think of a buttery-coloured frog. Beneath the weathered skin lies a pallor as if she is recovering from an illness, which, in a sense, she is. Hers is a chronic ailment.

Later, Roberta opens the bathroom door and finds Fay sitting on the edge of the bath. Her air-brushed, permanently suntanned mother-in-law, arms laden with gold bangles, is crying. Roberta supposes this is the effect of Edith's gin, and that Fay is not used to it in such quantity. When she looks up at Roberta, her face is ugly with grief, but Roberta is mature enough to know that women have regrets as they grow older, regrets that can catch up with them in unexpected moments and go away as quickly as they have come.

In the evening, a sudden storm from the south whips itself up into a frenzy and she and Paul lie in bed with their arms wrapped around each other and listen to the rain and say what a good day it has been.

As Glass and Edith drive home over the hills towards Walnut, the air is thinning with cold, and on the other side, away from the wind, frost settles on the roofs of barns and sheds.

ROBERTA

ALL MY LIFE, I have felt like a person on the move. In all my dreams I am moving.

When I was a child I was a gymnast, my body perfectly tuned to perform on the beam, hovering over space with immaculate poise. It is as close to flying as I will ever come, my body like a machine or an instrument, with an infinite capacity that I was always testing. My medals still cover the wall of my old room at the farm I now think of as home, the place where I grew up from the time I was a small child.

Before that, my mother roamed over one or other of the farms we lived on, across the wide Waikato Plains, holding me buttoned under a man's rough jacket and singing to me as she worked. I'm not sure whether I recall these details exactly, but my mother described it to me once, and I believe I remember. She told me in one of the rare moments when she sought to be close to me, and, I think, at the time, I pretended not to hear her. Or perhaps my father came in and distracted us. There is a certain violence in his eyes which I find quite beautiful and compelling, and so does she. But there is a memory of ineffable joy which comes to me sometimes in the middle of the night when I'm lying awake beside Paul, and I suppose it is this that I'm remembering. Tonight I can't sleep, and I wake him to ask him what he thinks, whether this beating wing of happiness in my heart is memory. I wouldn't do this as a rule, but I've been thinking about today. Already the baby has created a host of new sensations, which are crowding in on me, and I wonder if they have already begun to change my perception of the past.

'You're supposed to know how people feel,' I say. Paul has a degree in psychology. He is what's described as a human resource consultant, meaning he hires and fires people for his company. Communication and skills are his business.

'Go back to sleep,' he groans.

'Interpret their innermost thoughts.'

'You're feeling inadequate again, Roberta,' he says. 'Can't we talk about it in the morning?'

'Why do you say that? Who says I feel inadequate?' I have a half-finished degree in accountancy, which is the only specific thing I might feel dissatisfied about, and that's only temporary, because one day I'm sure I'll finish it. I work as a data processor in the tax department.

'What's the matter? Have you had a bad dream?' His skin is rumpled round his eyes like a premonition of age and I feel remorseful for waking him up. Paul has a shock of brown hair and slightly prominent upper teeth which give him interesting hollows in his cheeks.

'What will it take to put you back to sleep?' he asks, placing his hand gently on my stomach, letting me know that he understands why I'm restless. 'Roberta, honey, I'm really tired. We've both got to go to work in the morning.'

'I just can't stop thinking.'

'I can't stand thinking at two o' clock in the morning.' He puts the light out.

'Paul,' I say, quietly in the dark. 'D'you reckon I'll be a good mother?' For this is what I need to know so badly. The trouble is, I don't know exactly what it means. I'm thinking about Edith and Fay, and neither measures up as the role model I'm seeking, though I can't explain why. My mother can't be so bad; I am her obedient child, and so far I have not done too badly in the world.

Paul is asleep already; it's a trait I envy in him, this ability to drop straight into oblivion. I try to lie very still, staring up at the glimmering dark of the ceiling. I'll come to think of this moment, like the day that has gone before, as part of something nameless. Nobody knows what the most unforgivable act in the world is until they have done it. In the end, I will have to name it.

two

BERNARD AND ORLA

WHY GO ALL the way to New Zealand for a husband, Orla's family said to her. You'll end up a heathen, you mark my words, her mother said. This man you're planning to marry, his father's not even a Catholic, just his mother, if you can take his word for that, and she can't be loyal to the faith and all, if she's married out of the church. The priests are lax and they'll probably let you get away with anything, you might even end up not having your babies baptised in the church. Why is this Bernard walking round and about here in Ireland when he says he has a farm on the other side of the world? Who's looking after his farm, and what is he running away from? You can tell with some men that they have a secret — what's his? You'll get in with the blacks, you'll get contamination.

These are things they said to her, and now Orla knows that all of it was a lie and most of it is true. Which is to say that, ten years later, marriage to Bernard Nichols does not seem such a good proposition to her as it had done in Belfast, where he proposed to her on his one and only overseas trip, the big OE as the New Zealanders called it. And now they hardly ever see her. Oh, it's all very well and all to have aeroplanes that take you here, there and everywhere, but Bernard is not the kind of man to make many trips. It's all up to Orla, who has been home twice, but her mother can't face the idea of such a journey. *Find me a ship*, she tells Orla in her letters, *that's something I could put up with if I had to, if I had to sit quiet on board a boat for months at a time, with the thought that I would see my daughter at the end. But put me inside one of those flying sardine tins with no way out, and not God Himself, hail Mary full of grace forgive me for speaking this way but I cannot say otherwise, could tell me whether or not I would make it there. No Orla, you'll have to come home to me again, that's all there is to it.*

Bernard, her husband, the object of her mother's suspicions, takes off his gumboots and pads into the kitchen in his dank work socks.

'Where's smoko?'

It's his stock phrase, as if it were not waiting for him each day.

'It's ready.' She lays out scones and cream and fruitcake. He is a tall, big-boned man, with shoulders like two legs of ham under his woollen shirt. His dark hair is tousled above the collar of his thick plaid shirt, his sideburns like those of a hillbilly. She has seen pictures of the family of Arthur Allan Thomas, who had been accused of murder and languished in jail while he fought for years and years to prove his innocence. They were country people, with narrow, bewildered eyes, the men sprouting hair on their faces, and this is what Bernard has come to remind her of, only less open.

He didn't always look like that, not as she remembers it. He had seemed a plain man, but rosy-cheeked and strong, with a wide, white smile. He had swept her off her feet and she couldn't work out why he had chosen her. It'll be a comfortable living, he told her modestly. But it is more than that. How can he have come so quickly to this, unkempt and complaining, when there is so little to complain about? They have a house on the farm, made of solid brick with concrete foundations, built up the hill a little way so they can see down the valley and across the river. *I can see the Maori houses from where I live,* Orla writes to her mother, *but it is all right they don't come near us, they have their own ways, they are not like the South Africans . . .*

No, Mother, we do not have to have bars on the windows or anything like that, though I've heard they do up north, some places. The house has carpet in every room, and a kitchen with a microwave and a dishwasher. There are three bedrooms, one for Bernard and Orla, and one for boy children and one for girls. *You would like it here, Mum, we have plenty of room for you to come for a good long stay, and you'd find Bernard's parents would make you very welcome.* The main bedroom has its own en suite. *We have a toilet and handbasin just next to our room, Mum, so you wouldn't have to share the bathroom with us . . .*

Her mother writes back: *Orla, you must do something about that lavatory next to your room, it cannot be healthy. Can you get that husband of yours to do something about it? I knew he had strange ways the moment I set eyes on him.*

But it is not strange ways that have driven them apart into silence broken by occasional bursts of bickering like pattering gunfire. It is their childlessness. That, and the doctor who says there is no reason why they shouldn't have children. Blame and appeasement go hand in hand, but Bernard and Orla cannot enjoy either.

'Are you working at the house today?' Bernard asks. He speaks of his parents' house as if it's still his home and they are camping out somewhere. His mother has a magnificent garden which she opens to the public and hires out to charities for fund-raising functions.

'Did her majesty say if she was expecting me?'

'Don't talk about Ma like that.'

'I'm sorry. What on the good earth could have got into me? Has she had a drink this morning?'

'I didn't see her. I expect she'll need a hand with the thinning.'

'I've got accounts to do down here,' says Orla, and turns away.

Of late, Orla has been thinking it might be safe to carry out a plan she has in mind. In this country, she could perhaps get away without her own mother learning of a mortal sin. She is thinking of leaving the sacred institution of marriage.

THE UNCLEAN BOX

PEOPLE CAN'T TAKE their eyes off Marise. Her hair is the colour of pale grey dawn watered silk, hanging in two curtains, like the wings of an exotic butterfly. She is paper thin and nearly everything she wears is grey. Only a slashing scarlet mouth illuminates the fragile whisper of her presence. She owns a beautiful red Porsche to match her lips.

Marise is Roberta's supervisor in the tax department. She worked for an accountancy firm that went under when one of the partners fiddled a client's money. Roberta is sure Marise could do better than this job, which seems to go nowhere.

Roberta is not sure why she is in the job herself; it is something that filled a gap, a job when there were staff redundancies in the last government department where she worked. It was meant to be temporary but three years have passed and she tells herself it is not bad, some days she even likes it, and she thinks she is good at the work.

'I wouldn't mind being an investigator,' she tells Marise. The best thing she can do is make a go of it, not let the baby slow down her career.

'Why ever would you want to do that?' Marise asks, her silver eyebrows raised. Roberta is sure that the eyebrows aren't real; eyebrows are the last part to go grey, and Marise is only forty. Her scepticism about everything isn't real either, she has decided. Only the way she hangs out for anything in pants is frightening. Marise is married to the most handsome man Roberta has ever met. He has dark tanned skin and white teeth that look as if they have been capped, only Marise says they are not, and crinkly greying hair that he parts slightly to the left of centre.

'Rules are rules,' says Roberta.

'And people who break them get into trouble. How very Puritan you are!'

Roberta flushes angrily. She has pale creamy skin that she doesn't allow to tan and her throat goes bright red when she is angry, like that of an older woman. 'Well it's true, or at least that's what I thought.'

'What a very repressed childhood you must have had, Roberta.'

Roberta is convinced there is nothing wrong with chasing defaulters who owe money to the department. There are always people who moan about taxes and feel they are entitled to get something back, even if it means cheating the system now and then. There is a certain virtue in the idea of keeping people on the straight and narrow.

But today her arguments seem hollow and she thinks doubts may have surfaced since her pregnancy began. The thought comes unbidden that, for some poor families, a new baby may be the last straw. She doesn't know whether she really wants to come back to the job, even though she has been told it will be kept open for her. Her stomach is beginning to swell and the baby moves at night. Some days she will be sitting here and the baby will poke his foot out; she feels him doing this now. He is telling her he is in there and she is distracted by his presence, already in love with him.

'I can't sit still,' she says abruptly. It is ridiculous to be arguing the morality of her job with her supervisor; surely they have got things back to front. Roberta stands and walks around her desk with a show of stretching herself.

Marise says nothing, just sits in front of her computer terminal watching Roberta. 'Time to go home and put your feet up,' she says. Roberta can tell something is really bugging her.

'Don't be silly, I can work for months yet. Besides, I promised Paul I'd make some more payments on the mortgage before I stopped work.' They have one of those mortgages that can be paid off quickly to save some amazing amount like a hundred thousand dollars. She is not sure how much it matters because they are well off, as far as Roberta can see, but Paul gets indignant when she says this. Marise snorts and Roberta thinks that her instincts are right, but she doesn't like the derisory way Marise is reacting, as if nothing she says is of consequence. 'What's the matter with you anyway?' she asks.

'Nothing. I just hate this damn job.' Marise speaks with such vehemence that Roberta believes this is partly true, even if she's also holding something back. 'It's coming between me and Derek. He says the system's iniquitous and everyone who works in it is tainted by it. I sometimes think it's true.'

Roberta says, 'I could ask Paul if he knows of anything.'

'I already have.' Her bright red mouth tightens bitchily into a small flame of disapproval.

Roberta has forgotten, for the moment, that Marise and Paul don't get on. They are two people who apparently cannot bear to be in the same room as each other. She sees again a nasty little scene at a staff party. 'I wouldn't recommend you for any kind of job, you're too unstable,' Paul had said that night. 'If you walked into my office, I'd show you the door.' Maybe they were drunk, but Paul is not a drinker, not one you would notice anyway, and Roberta knows about these things. She sits at her desk again and rolls the chair backwards and forwards as if to make room for her stomach, even though it's not very big. 'I'd like to move this desk, make some space.'

'Oh yes, for the *baby*.' Marise rests her arms on the edge of her desk.

So now Roberta knows what's eating her. They are about to have one of *those* conversations, which follow a predictable course.

'Is it because you're a Good Girl, Roberta?'

'I'm not,' she says quickly, but she knows that, by comparison, she has been very good.

'How come you make a baby so easily? I screwed everything that moved. Count yourself lucky, I wouldn't mind looking like an elephant.'

'I don't. Not yet.'

'No, but I'm sure you will,' says Marise, with vindictive relish.

Roberta tries to concentrate on her screen, but she's not in the mood and, besides, she really likes Marise. All the same, she's trying to imagine what else they might talk about.

'I did it with a Mr Whippy man,' says Marise. 'When he parked in our street after dark.'

'Marise, you didn't!'

'The man from the AA when my car broke down.'

'You're lying. Your car never breaks down.'

'I ran the battery flat. Oh, and there was the man who fixed the washing machine. That seemed like a near thing.'

'You deserve to get the pox.' Roberta doesn't say that other ugly, scary word people use now. She knows how old-fashioned she sounds.

'It was only a baby I was after.'

'Why don't you go on an in vitro programme?'

'Because I smoke and I'm too old.'

'You're like my sister-in-law, Orla, I guess,' says Roberta, thinking that sympathy is the best way to deal with Marise's distress. 'She can't have children either. Well, the doctors say she can, but she can't. They can't. Nobody knows why.'

'How much am I like her? Do we have things in common?' Marise asks eagerly, hungry for clues to her condition.

'You're not remotely like her. She's so holy nobody except Bernard would ever have got through her filtering system.'

'Oh.' Marise is disappointed.

But, Roberta thinks, in lots of ways she really *is* like Orla, in those moments of despair that you see in their eyes, the resignation, the kind of outer toughness that they hide behind. Orla cloaks her sorrow by seeming not to care any more about how she looks; Marise smokes like a volcano all the time and grizzles about the loss of smokers' rights. Since smoking in the office has been banned, she spends her spare moments in the smokers' trough, a concrete fenced area outside the building. She carries a mauve umbrella, hand-painted with pale blue flowers, to keep her silver fall of hair dry while she smokes on wet days.

Orla, on the other hand, neither smokes nor is too old to hope for children. There's still plenty of time for it to happen, but you can tell that it probably won't. Orla wears bloomers. Roberta sees them hanging on the clothesline when she's out at the farm.

'I need a royal stud, Roberta.'

'Maybe you've had one all along and just didn't notice.' Roberta has always liked Marise's handsome Derek. They look like a magnificent couple.

'Tell me, do you know when you conceive? I mean, do you come?'

'This is my first,' says Roberta.

'So did you this time?'

'I don't know when it happened.'

Marise sits back, white-knuckled, her grey pewter earrings gleaming against her cheekbones. 'You'd have to know.'

'I don't see why. Why should I know a thing like that?'

'Because you must know when something like that happens to you,' says Marise. 'Like shadows on the sun.'

Roberta starts to laugh, in spite of herself. 'You're crazy.'

'Like a blade breaking through an egg.'

She stops laughing because this sounds too sinister, too troubling, and she doesn't want to bear the weight of Marise's problems. 'If I don't know, perhaps it's not true.'

She turns to her screen, processing a return for Josh Thwaite, spray painter of Wainuiomata. 'This guy's tax is for two grand and he's sent a cheque for eighty-nine dollars — what does he think he's playing at? Who does he think he's kidding?'

'I expect he got it mixed up with his electricity bill. Dump it in the unclean box,' says Marise.

The unclean box is as hygienic as any other stacked metal tray in their utilitarian open-plan office, mildly refurbished with dim blue carpets and new sets of vertical Venetian blinds. The box gets its name because it holds all the tax returns that have to be forwarded for further examination by Revenue Control, when the person paying tax has deviated from the correct method of payment. Not a good way to draw attention to yourself. Roberta taps in some numbers. Josh Thwaite averages a turnover in excess of fifty thousand dollars a year.

'Business must be down for Mr Thwaite,' she comments. 'He ought to be paying more than this.'

'Make a note of it,' says Marise, suddenly efficient. 'Somebody will pick him up.'

Which, indeed, is quite likely. In the staff canteen, at morning tea, Roberta listens to the investigators recounting their exploits. This guy had cash buried in the garden. You wouldn't believe it, the way they think they can get away with hiding the stuff. Think they can fool us, but we break them, we know when they've been picking up cash jobs. We break them.

Roberta glances at Marise and wonders if she has tried a spray painter. What if Josh Thwaite has three kids already and another baby on the way?

He is a marked man. Marise takes a phone call and while she is not looking Roberta plucks the return out of the box and slides it under her computer pad.

SARAH

'Darling, you will come, won't you?' Sarah Lord tries to disguise the anxiety in her voice. Being in love is supposed to be delightful, even if her lover is married to someone else, but it has begun to feel increasingly like grumbling toothache. If she could get through a day without thinking about him, perhaps things would improve. Or if she saw him just once more, she could say goodbye to him properly. But this is an often rehearsed scenario that never eventuates. At the last moment, just when she's preparing herself for grand exits, he mentions a next time, and she doesn't dare to tempt fate by asking if he really means it. He lives in another town, a man who passes from one place to another in his work, which is collecting rock samples for a university.

The same ordinary, unsurprising dilemma that women like Sarah, who have been abandoned by their husbands, face all the time. The single men who are left are gay and the divorced ones are paying maintenance (including her own husband, but he has just about enough to go round) and love is like living on a railway station waiting for late trains.

Her lover's only son is sick, and he doesn't know if he will be round her way, after all.

'But he'll be all right, won't he? Nothing serious?' she says.

'I can't talk any longer. My wife will notice the phone bill.'

'Don't hang up.' As if his wife paid the bills, although some women do, like ironing socks and taking out the rubbish. Masochistic.

But he has gone.

Standing beside the phone, Sarah considers her house, a 1930s bungalow. Although it's shabby, everything in it has been chosen by her, or given to her by her mother. Some of her belongings have been rescued from storage: paintings, crowded bookshelves, pottery jars, floral pitchers and fat white china hens with their heads on an angle, a chiming clock with an eagle etched on its face, a weathered piano engraved with fire-eating dragons that her mother used to play. The children, Ellie and Jack, have gone to stay with their father, everything is ready for her lover's arrival. A free woman, she is alone in her empty house.

She is still standing by the phone, the receiver quiet in its cradle, when it begins to ring again. Although Sarah picks it up quickly, her voice is cool and remote; she knows he will have found a way to come. But the caller is her mother, Wendy, whom Sarah calls by her name.

'I've decided to pay you a visit,' Wendy says.

'When?'

'Tomorrow.'

'Oh no.' Sarah's voice grows faint. 'You can't.'

'Why ever not, dear? I thought you'd be pleased to have some company.'

'Thank you, but it's not convenient right now. I've got a friend coming to stay.'

Her mother's tone is sturdy but Sarah detects uncertainty. 'I won't get in the way, you know me.'

'You can't do this to me, Wendy.' She feels like an axe murderer.

Wendy is instantly tremulous. 'So you don't want to see me?'

Sarah hesitates. 'I always want to see you, Wendy,' she says.

And in a way it's true, no different from other daughters who love their mothers but just don't want to see them all the time. But Sarah has been adopted by Wendy, and it seems to her that many politenesses and rituals of kindness must be observed which are absent, in a way, from relationships of nature. Reassurances of love that others take for granted. She is her mother's only child, her Sarah. Princess, she whispered to her, late at nights, when she thought Sarah was asleep. Often, Sarah feels it is her responsibility to make Wendy feel guiltless about mothering her, to protect her from the opinion of people who refer to mothers like her as child-snatchers.

So she is trying to be calm and reasonable, as if she might lull Wendy into doing nothing. But that has never really been possible. In spite of their mutual concern, it is Wendy's nature, once she has embarked on a scheme, to be an unstoppable force.

'Can you leave it a few days? There's something happening in my life right now,' Sarah tells her.

Wendy sighs, not asking what it is.

'I'm studying,' Sarah says, which is true, since she is a part-time student taking English the long, hard way. She sees Wendy now, an old woman with rough white curls, wearing a long Indian cotton skirt, amid the incredible clutter of the tumbledown shack she occupies by the sea on the rugged Taranaki coastline. Only this is not strictly correct, at this given moment, because Wendy uses the phone in the camping ground office. There are probably unkempt young men playing pool in the recreation room, the air full of smoke and ragged with their laughter.

'There's something I want to talk about,' says Wendy. 'I don't want to leave it till later.'

'You're not ill, are you?'

'No,' says Wendy, with considerable vigour. 'But there's some putting right to be done.'

'Not that again.' Sarah guesses, at once, that Wendy is again on the track of her birth parents. 'It doesn't matter any more, I don't have expectations. I guess, it's just not a problem.' What her children would say. Not a problem. No way, Jose. Get a life, Ma. This is what children say, this is what Sarah says to her mother.

'Sarah, we could take a garden tour.' Wheedling now. This is the part Sarah hates — Wendy begging.

But gardening is Wendy's passion, even if her passion is more imagination than fact. Outside her cottage stand old wash tubs filled with marigolds and flowering sweet peas, protected from the elements and drifting sand by lengths of sacking. In her head, she owns parks and gardens as large as country estates. After Mac died, she moved from one to another of his brothers' houses, treating them as if they were her own. If people called when her brothers-in-law and their wives were out, she would offer to show them the garden, as if it were hers. Do look at my snapdragons, she would say, in even the meanest of the suburban gardens she periodically inhabited. I'm thinking about spraying the roses, that's if they're not beyond redemption, or perhaps I'll just turn them over. Things seem to have gone to pot. She would laugh at her own joke but nobody else did. None of them allow her to stay any more, only Sarah. Wendy hasn't tried to move in with Sarah, or not until recently, when her daughter has been on her own, as she puts it. But this is coming too close for comfort. My mother is so lonely, Sarah tells her friends and, lately, her lover. I wish I could do more for her.

Wendy is regrouping her energies. 'Did I tell you about my father's conservatory in England?' she asks. 'The loggia we called it, it had these wonderful high arches. Inside, the earth smelled rich and warm, and outside, jasmine grew up the wall, flourishing in the damp air of spring nights. It was romantic and European, in the tradition of Turgenev. My father loved Turgenev, did I ever tell you that? He was a classical kind of man. You would have liked my father, Sarah.'

'Yes, you've told me, Wendy. I wish I'd known him.'

Wendy is resolute and defiant. 'Actually, I've booked a garden tour for both of us. It would do you good to get out for the day.'

'How do you know what's good for me?' Sarah shouts.

Wendy hangs up on Sarah, just as her lover had done. The camp office is closed until the following morning, and by then Wendy will have begun her journey from the coast to connect with the southbound bus.

This is how Sarah comes to be at the bus station the next day, sitting on a vinyl-covered bench, digging her nails into the putty-coloured fabric, trying hard not to cry in public. She sees her mother first, recognises something sharply wistful in her face, before she arranges it to meet Sarah. As she climbs down the steps of the bus, Wendy is carrying a large crushed velvet carry-all, with wooden handles. It bulges with all the belongings she has brought. My God, Sarah thinks, my mother is a bag lady.

three

BREATHING LESSONS

Roberta raises her head, astonished by the pile of bodies surrounding her. Twenty or so women, looking like beached whales, arranged on mats beside all kinds of men. They breathe in and out, in and out, very slowly, taking deep lungfuls of air, then pant together. Alongside her lies her own husband, Paul Vaughan Cooksley, wearing a look of intense, labouring concentration as he pulls his diaphragm in tight and slowly exhales, huuuh, and the susurration of all their sighs melts together and fill the room like a wave. She tries to imagine weightlessness and the featheriness of flesh that is untouched by sex and its consequences, but it is hard not to think that the point of nature is really to trick human beings, through sensations of delight, into this heaving animal condition.

The instructor, Ann Claude, walks around each mound, observing the couples. She wears lipstick that stays on and Italian shoes. Her shoes are about all they can see of her at the moment. They don't know whether she has ever had children of her own; she doesn't let on at pep talk time. Either she doesn't know what she's talking about, or she's holding back some vital information. How much will it hurt, they ask, but she looks impatient and vaguely mysterious. It will hurt, of course, she says, but, no, she can't say how much. These things are individual.

'Remember, hubbies,' she says, and pauses briefly, 'and partners, when you're in the labour room, you're there to help the mother relax. Relax. If her lower tummy is sore, it's best for her to lie on her back, that's right, roll over, then pull her nightie up, no, during the birth, not now, and lightly stroke your finger tips across her lower abdomen, yes you can practise that, no need to feel embarrassed, we're all the same here.'

Of course, everyone can see that they are not. But the women on the floor have one thing in common — they are what Roberta's Presbyterian grandmother would have described as being with child. The men are as different as anybody could imagine; you can tell by their feet, undressed without their shoes. Some wear thick nylon mix work socks with holes, others are clad in fine wool, and all exude, to a greater or lesser degree, the same whiff of bad bananas. Just by looking along their feet, she can tell what their partner will be like — most of them, anyway. She wishes she didn't do this analysing and filing of people. Like, well, like an Inland Revenue clerk, if she is truthful. Besides, some of them fool her, like the woman with close-cropped hair, whose partner is another woman dressed in overalls. Or the girl who is rumoured to be fourteen, so enormous her thin legs can hardly support her body when she stands up. She comes with her mother.

To Paul and Roberta's left lies a woman with a taut, satiny throat, beginning to soften and blur beneath her chin. Helen's clothes are designed to make her look stout and handsome rather than pregnant. Her husband, whose name Roberta never does learn, has bright blue eyes, a heavy moustache, thick, wavy hair streaked with blonde tints, wears a Rolex watch and carries a cellphone which he forgets to turn off. When it rings he gives a small apologetic smile but he doesn't hang up, just excuses himself from the group and walks outside with it clasped to his ear, talking quietly, as if he is in love with it.

One evening Helen had turned to Roberta and said, in a dreamy voice, 'Did you by any chance happen to see the piece in the paper about the ninety-two-year-old woman who carried a baby inside of her for sixty years?'

Roberta admitted that she had not seen this. How could it possibly be, she asked.

'It died before birth and calcified inside her. They call it a "stone birth".' Helen had said it carefully, so that Roberta would not forget, and then repeated it. Stone birth.

After this, Roberta has tried to act as if the couple were not there. She looks for a different position in the room, but Helen and her husband always find a place beside them. Once she found an excuse for them to be late, without telling Paul, because he thinks they are really neat people, but Helen had saved them a place. 'Helen gives me the shits,' Roberta tells Paul, but he says ssh, she'll hear you.

Mr Blue Eyes, as Roberta calls Helen's husband, is out of the room on a call, when she whispers to her. 'Did you hear about the woman who left her two children in the car while she looked in the shops?'

'No,' Roberta mutters, trying to look as if her breathing is everything. She knows she will hear something horrible. It is worse than she imagines.

'The car went up in flames, blazing from end to end, and her children were burned. To death.' Helen's beautiful fine throat is working. She has a problem, Roberta thinks. Why doesn't she tell the people on the other side of her?

But she can see why she wouldn't. The man has SUCKS tattooed on his forehead, and snakes coiled down his arms. His partner is a woman with dishevelled hair and a broken tooth. She wears a zipped-up bomber jacket that turns her belly into the shape of a soccer ball. The woman already has children, but it's the man's first and she is proud that he wants to know what to do 'when the time comes'. Sometimes Roberta gets the impression, from the way they look at each other, that these two are crazier about each other than most of the couples in the room. They give her an odd sort of confidence, because the woman *does* know what it's about, and she's in love and wants more of it, pain and all.

'Some women shouldn't be allowed to have children,' says Helen.

Roberta looks away quickly, smiling at the new couple on the other side of them. The woman is young, although she tries to make herself look older by using heavy foundation and bright lipstick. The pair have introduced themselves as Michelle and Sandy. They, too, are an unlikely couple, and Roberta feels that her labelling system is slipping. Sandy is at least thirty, with hair straggling over his collar. He has a long, bare upper lip, but beneath his lower one he grows a tiny vee-shaped wisp of hair. He wears a two-piece pink and green patterned outfit that looks like shortie pyjamas, and walk socks.

'All right,' says Ann Claude. 'Mother's going to have a contraction now. On to your sides, mothers. Now, pant, pant, blow, pant, pant, blow. Very good. Now, all you dads, glide your hand along her back and massage evenly and slowly, that's right, another little trial run. She's having the contraction *now*, okay, and now it's going off, so glide your hand *away* again.'

On Roberta's back, Paul's fingers feel like a bunch of wire spikes.

'You're hurting,' she whispers, but her voice sounds loud. He lets his hand drop. She cannot see his face but she knows she has embarrassed him. She reaches out for his hand, which feels like a surgical glove. Beside them, Michelle giggles. Roberta flicks a glance in her direction, thinking she will meet her eye and stare her down, but Michelle and Sandy's laughter is private.

'You're tickling me,' Michelle says to Sandy.

'All right,' croons Ann Claude, 'roll over on to the other side now.'

'I have to take a leak,' mutters Paul.

'Can't it wait?' Something in the air alarms Roberta. But already Paul has scrambled to his feet and is making his escape. She is left by herself among the monstrous women and their monstrous husbands.

Sandy directs his attention to her. 'Why did the beetroot blush?' he murmurs, his eyes flicking over Paul's empty space.

She pretends she has not heard him.

His voice is insidious, persistent. 'Go on, give it a go.'

'I don't know.'

'Because it saw Mr Green Pea,' says Sandy, with the remorseless insistence of a man who cannot let a joke pass. Roberta readies her label to paste on his file — a person who would crack jokes on his way to the gallows or in the middle of a tax audit. Somebody to watch out for.

Lying on her back, staring at the ceiling, she tells herself how lucky she is. A woman with a job and a husband, and a diamond engagement ring that sits snugly beside her wedding band, expecting a planned baby. At twenty-six, she is neither too old nor too young to be having her first child. She has had a scan because she goes to a specialist at her father's insistence, and specialists like scans; the baby looks fine. It's got all its fingers and toes, the woman in X-ray had said. She asked Roberta if she wanted to know about the other bits.

Roberta told her, no, she didn't want to know, and Paul agreed. But she has guessed, from the way the woman spoke, that there was another piece, the mysterious instrument, the little boy's penis. She has decided not to tell Paul, even though she knows she is right.

At Ann Claude's command, the group rolls sideways again, and this time she rolls with them, so it is not so obvious she is alone. She is facing Mr Blue Eyes' back. She closes her eyes so she does not have to watch what he is doing to Helen. With her eyes shut, Roberta feels comfortable and drowsy, suddenly quite sleepy, remembering what it is like to sleep on her own. In her warm womb, her baby floats and somersaults. Ann Claude has put on a soothing tape, and she thinks that it is good that she is not really on her own, that now she has Paul, whose hands are on her back, stroking gently but firmly, like a professional masseur, kneading deep into the muscles round the base of her spine where it aches.

'That's nice,' she says out loud, forgetting where she is. She hears Michelle's high whinnying giggle again and opens her eyes in a panic. Sandy has changed places with Michelle on the mat behind her, and it is his hands on her back, and Paul is walking towards them, his face blind with anger.

MOON SHADOWS

'YOU MUST HAVE known,' Paul says, as he puts the car away in the garage.

'I was asleep.'

'I'd only just walked out of the room.'

'I don't know why you're going on at me,' Roberta says. 'It didn't happen to you.'

'It's a violation,' states Paul. They turn the lights on in the house. 'I should probably call the police.'

The thought flicks through her mind, unbidden, that he is acting as if there has been a burglary. Someone has taken something that belongs to him.

'It was a joke,' she says. All she wants now, after the unpleasantly quiet drive home, is for the whole thing to be forgotten.

'Make up your mind. Now it's funny? Don't you care that he put his hand on you? Felt you up?'

'He'd say it was a mistake, an honest mistake.'

'He couldn't say that, he was facing your back. His wife was behind him.'

'Well, he probably would, wouldn't he? It's silly, you couldn't prove anything.'

'I saw it, Roberta.' His voice is pained with disappointment. 'Wouldn't you do anything if you were raped?'

This truly frightens her. Once, she had served on a jury for a rape trial.

'I saw what that woman went through,' she had told friends at a dinner party, one night when they had all been drinking wine too late. 'And yet we didn't convict the man because the evidence was faulty. There was a reasonable doubt. I lie awake at nights and think about that young woman. She was younger than me. I picked she was a street walker, or a sex worker of some kind. Like any other woman, she had the right to say no, and she had gone through all that, for what? For humiliation and more degradation and probably the pay-off of a good hiding from someone because she couldn't make her story stick.'

They had all looked away and Paul had wished Roberta would be quiet, because his section head was at the dinner, and the wives were clucking their tongues with disapproval. She could tell that they thought she was wrong.

He knows how she feels. What is he on about, she wonders, blurred with tiredness.

'We're not talking about rape,' she says. 'What we've got here is a prank, like a kid pulling his pants down in the playground.'

'You're passive, Roberta, that's what your trouble is.'

'I didn't know I had a trouble. You never told me before.' Though she is not sure about this; when she thinks about it, he may have been hinting for a while. 'I was asleep,' she explains again. 'Well half asleep anyway, thinking about you.'

'You often see it in the papers. Women in bed next to their husbands, and some joker comes sneaking in and gets into bed with the pair of them and does the wife over. Husband wakes up, wham bam, there goes this joker on top of his missus. Oh, I was just asleep, she says. There must be a lot of women who get fucked when they're asleep.'

'You're sick.' She is not just angry, but full of revulsion as well. They look at each other, shocked and bewildered. They do not quarrel as a rule, and now they are having this sudden outburst, saying disgusting and appalling things. Roberta has begun to cry and she would give anything not to be in tears. She does not like to give people that satisfaction. She stopped crying about things years ago. Paul shakes his head slowly, trying to clear the bad things he sees.

'Roberta, honey. What's the matter with us?'

He puts his arms around her and she is tempted to struggle, but, hating the way they have become instant strangers to each other, she longs more than ever for it be over. She lets him stroke her hair.

'I'm sorry,' he says, over and over again. 'Why don't you have a bath and get into bed? I love you.'

'It'll be funny,' she says, gulping for air. 'Some day we'll say, remember that night when the man who wore shortie pyjamas to ante-natal classes pretended to be you, and I fell for it. I promise we'll laugh about it.'

He starts to laugh, and soon they roll around, helpless in their mirth, reliving the moment. They touch each other in small, reassuring ways.

After she has had her bath and Paul has made her some Milo, Roberta sits on the edge of the bed, brushing her hair over her shoulders, letting the brush linger there, so that it catches the light for him. It's rough, corrugated hair but it shines with a fractured fire of its own. During the day she braids it into a sophisticated French plait. Roberta doesn't think of herself as pretty. She'll be handsome, she heard people tell her mother when she was young, which is a way of avoiding the truth: she has a steep nose and a long chin that rules out prettiness, dark eyes narrowing at the corners, skin which is as firm and smooth as a dish of clover honey. She has a habit of curling her bottom lip over her teeth, trying to make her face look shorter.

'Bess the innkeeper's daughter was brushing her long black hair,' Paul recites, and plunges his fingers into her thick, crinkly mane. 'You won't ever cut your hair, will you? You've got beautiful hair.'

'My hair's not black,' says Roberta, wanting to move her head away from the firmness of his grip.

'And the highwayman came riding, riding up to the old inn door.' His fingers tighten.

'I wouldn't exactly call Sandy a highwayman.'

'I didn't know his name was Sandy,' Paul says. He lets her hair fall. 'Are you ready to put out the light?'

I WAIT UNTIL his breathing seems even before I get up, though I am not sure. Our house is in the upper reaches of Ashton Fitchett Drive in Panorama Heights, a brand-new housing development beneath the experimental wind turbine. The turbine is what has drawn me to this place, the way it turns over and over, generating power with the breeze from the sea. Our house is new, three-bedroomed, two-storeyed, with pastel walls and blond pine timber, the nails neatly sealed so you can hardly tell they are there, double-glazed windows and deadlocks on the doors. This is what I wanted. Paul wanted to do up an old house in an established suburb, the way other young couples do, with a view to turning it over in a year or two's time and making some money. But I have lived in old houses all my life; sharemilkers' cottages that were never cleaned out properly by the last tenants, and later my grandparents' house which became ours. That house still makes me think of floral carpets and dark passages, although it is so different now. Then there was the student flat, where I met Paul.

'Actually, I don't think he's quite right for you,' my mother said.

Actually, I didn't care what my mother thought. I haven't cared much for a long time. Ours is an excellent match. Sometimes I wonder if we have done as many things together as we should, such as travelling more, before settling down like this. But then I think that a baby will fill up the spaces, and then the next one will come along and so on, until life itself is filled up, because that is what children do for you.

I expect to have more than one child. When I became engaged to Paul, my Aunt Dorothy, on my father's side, who lives in a resthome, sent me three crocheted milk covers weighted with beads round the edges. Normally I would have expected my mother to say something scornful, such as, 'Doesn't she know we've got refrigerators?', especially as the gift was from Aunt Dorothy. But three children, same as me, is what my mother said, quite casually, that's what that means. I'm more superstitious than I would ever let on to Paul and his parents. It must be the old Irish Catholic past that haunts my mother, haunts me. We try to pretend it isn't there, all that mystery and repression.

And Paul likes the smell of fresh paint after all. He has taken to the house and planted vegetables behind the trellis fence and built a barbecue out of old bricks. The curly numerals cut from copper on the letter-box are his handiwork. We meet in our lunch-hours to choose curtains and floor coverings that blend into our colour scheme of pale turquoise and old rose. The second bedroom is being brought to life with the addition of mobiles hanging from the ceiling, little giraffes, comic characters, brightly coloured numerals. Our baby will have all the right things, the proper sensory stimulation, from the outset.

I draw the curtain gently aside. Outside, the moon is bouncing over the harbour, huge, luminous and full. The sea is like an immense glittering lake with barely a ruffle on its surface.

I talk to my baby at nights. I'll love you, I say, I'll do my very best for you. I can't promise to get it right, but at least I'll try. I'll protect you. My hand lies on his head. He lies perfectly still inside me, and I know he is reassured by what I have told him.

When I first came here, I would have said that nothing goes on in the suburbs at this time of night. But I have begun to pick up on surprising things since my night vigils by the window. There is a youth who stumbles home with a guitar case under his arm; a man, once, who shifted house under cover of darkness; a woman who cries in a steady, rhythmic drone in a house I can never locate. The plaintive sound fills me with grief. In the weekends I watch the faces of women who push prams around the neighbourhood and I can't pick out anyone who appears to have spent the night in such a persistent state of desperation. Soon, like it or not, I will know all these people, when the baby arrives. Mothers' groups and play groups and school stretch before me. Does this mean that I will also come to know their secrets, or will they be hidden like those in my parents' house?

Another of those ripples of dread runs up my spine. I recognise it as dread, an old enemy that lurks at my shoulder. It was something I felt when I was still a young and promising gymnast poised on the beam, facing the space between me and the ground. Although I had been taught to fall without hurting myself, there were moments when I was not always convinced by my training and in the end that's what finished me. One evening, my father came to collect me from practice at the local gymnasium. He stood watching me; I rose on the ball of my foot, holding my head in the classical manner, so that it would move last and arrive first as I completed my turn. And, quite suddenly, I lost the centre of gravity. I froze, looking across the room at my father, and knew that I couldn't go on.

And again, called my coach's cheerful voice. But there was no again. Couldn't they see, I wondered, that my body was changing, that I would grow tall and that angles were developing. I'm sure they couldn't, I'm sure I looked like the cute little thing who'd been doing my stunts for years, but I could feel the changes going on, like an explosion inside me. I could feel my feet growing. I don't tell people I did gym — they wouldn't believe me. I'm too big, too lumpy and I have a habit of walking into things when I'm thinking, even though I can see perfectly well.

My father never once said how bad he felt that I didn't make the nationals. It's the killer instinct she lacks, my coach told him, the last time we saw him — either you have it or you don't. My father looked down at his hands, turning the car keys over in his fingers. That's okay, coach, that's my girl, he said, as if he were still proud of me. I didn't believe him.

The baby feels my disquiet and flips over in my womb.

I sing to myself, and to the baby, trying to make my voice soft and quiet. I know I'm in danger of driving Paul crazy, the way I can't sleep at nights, but he doesn't understand the way movement has lost control in my body. Some days it feels as if the baby's head is pushed into my pelvis, other times his toes are in my throat. Still, misery likes company, and although it is not exactly misery I am feeling, I keep needing to talk to Paul about this unaccountable fear, this void over which I am poised. It is no wonder, I suppose, that we fall to quarrelling so easily, the way I keep us both awake at nights. 'Moon shadow,' I sing, 'moon shadow, I'm being followed by a moon shadow . . .'

'Getting pneumonia won't help the baby much,' Paul says.

Of course, I knew he hadn't been asleep. And, all of a sudden, I think that the smell of fear in the room is not my own; it is his that has been infecting me, ever since we left the hospital.

I turn to the bed, where his shape, huddled under the duvet, is illuminated by the glow of the moon and the streetlight outside.

'You don't want to be in the delivery room when the baby's born, do you?'

'Yes, I do.' He responds so quickly that I know I'm right.

'You don't have to,' I say. 'I read in an article the other day that it's a modern fad. May be we've all been brainwashed into believing it's what's best for us. Some women like privacy when they're giving birth.'

'Are you saying you don't want me to be there?'

'Ann Claude said sometimes women shit themselves and it's really embarrassing. She told us that while you were out of the room.' It's a lie. She didn't say that. This was something I had read in a magazine.

'I can cope with shit,' says Paul. He sounds reassured, as if he can imagine shit and feel good about it.

'Well, if you should change your mind,' I say, trying to hide my doubt.

'Don't be so bloody silly,' says Paul.

'I'm sorry,' I tell him, which of course I should have said earlier in the evening. I slide into bed beside him and fall immediately into a deep and contrite sleep.

I dream. It must have been the man shifting house in the dark the other night that brings it back. My dream is lifted straight from life. We are shifting back to my grandfather's farm, which now belongs to my father. My brothers and I finish school one afternoon; it is a district high school where all the kids go together. Outside, my usually dependable father is waiting at the wheel of the family car, impatient fingers drumming up and down. My mother sits beside him. I remember thinking, something is going to change, nothing will ever be the same again. My brothers are called to hurry along, and I am bundled into the car, to make a rapid journey south, through the night, along the Desert Road. My brothers stare with apprehension through the windows of the car. My father stops the car so they can pee under frosty autumn stars, while the wind makes a rushing sound in the telephone lines overhead and over the vast, tussocky, dark land stretching away to the mountains, and for once they do not try to outdo each other in their arc.

I see them by the dim interior light of the car as they stand pointing at the night, two awkward boys in tight serge shorts. When they climb back in the car, we all settle down and are quiet, knowing that this is what is expected of us. Mike, Bernie and Rob, three farm kids in the back seat of a car, going they didn't know where. My mother's head is bent before me so that I see the pale nape of her neck, her dark and langorous curls escaping from a scarf tied roughly around her head. This naked neck seems vulnerable, as if it is arched for the executioner's stroke. When she lifts her head I see her profile, the narrow temples, the slender outline of her face, the shadows on her cheeks. She averts her gaze and is lost to me. My mother, my mother, my mother, I say.

It must be towards morning that I have this dream, because when I wake the room is full of pale light, the sea is an unearthly blue streaked with fog, the hills look as if they have been lifted from a Japanese painting and it's time for work again.

four

GLASS

BY THE TIME Glass follows Edith to the kitchen for his first cup of black Rio Gold, she is measuring blueberries in a jug for a muffin bake. Already she has mixed the first cup of flour, four raised teaspoons of baking powder, half a cup of sugar and a pinch of salt in a bowl. Edith doesn't like doubling quantities. It spoils the balance. Today she will show people through her garden, the first of her spring tours. Edith smiles to herself, whisking an egg with oil, and adding the mixture to the bowl, then the blueberries, lightly dusted with flour so they won't sink during baking.

'Did you put the chairs under the trees?' she asks.

'I was afraid they might blow away.' Mares' tails had appeared in the sky the evening before and, once, waking briefly in the night, he had heard wind over the house.

'Can you do it now?'

Glass thinks about forcibly taking her back to bed. The strength of his desire for her, all things considered, still astonishes him. From time to time, like this morning, he has flashes of her in his mind's eye as she was when she was young, with long, strong limbs and a boy's gait. He thought then that she looked like a farmer's wife, but he was wrong. He can see now that she wore her flesh too lightly, her chin too high. She was uncertain of herself, as might be expected, and perhaps she still is, only you can't tell any more with Edith. You can't know what she thinks, you can only watch what she does. If he were to take her back to the bedroom, she would not struggle or accuse him of some obscure violation. Instead, she would sigh with resignation, tighten her mouth and avert her face so slightly that, if he mentioned it, she would say he was imagining things.

On the radio, the forecast promises a sunny day, no wind or rain, just a light nor'-westerly turning to the south by evening. He decides to put the chairs out.

'It'll soon come round time for this baby,' he says. 'I wonder how Roberta's keeping.'

Edith's spoon flies round the bowl, mixing fast so the mixture will be light and elastic. Speed is what counts.

'Why don't you ring her?' she says. Her voice is distant. He sees the tumbler among the mixing bowls. She follows his glance; her hand closes quickly over the glass, and he knows it is going to be one of those days. He hopes that, by nightfall, Edith can still remember this morning.

'They won't be up. You know they sleep in in the city.'

'You don't like Paul, do you?' she says, as if he is the one sounding the warning.

'It's just a feeling I have sometimes.'

'You think he's a city slicker and he looks down on you. You think he's an educated know-it-all who, when push comes to shove, wouldn't know a bale of hay from a cow's backside, so actually you look down on him as well.'

'I see you're an expert on me this morning.'

'Oh no.' She begins to spoon mixture into the muffin trays. 'I wouldn't try that.' He recognises the old bitterness, but he can't help needling her.

'So you think Paul's all right?'

'I hardly know him.'

'What if this were Bernard and Orla's baby? You'd be racing round there checking up, out doing the milking for her, not baking cakes for strangers.'

Edith turns her response over carefully before answering him. They don't often talk these days, but she must understand that he expects a reply.

'It would be easier if it was theirs,' she says at last. 'I hate the way they're disappointed every month when it doesn't happen. Everyone asking them when they're going to have one. Or, nowadays, going out of their way not to mention babies. All those tests, the fertility drugs and all that stuff. Bernard jacking off in a bottle — can you imagine that? I can't bear it when I see it's not going to happen again. I don't know what to say. I don't even know how to say, "Hi Orla, how are you doing this morning?" because I know she's going to turn her face away from me, the same as if I was checking her bed for spots.'

'But that's not Roberta's fault.'

'Of course it's not. But they might not have a baby, not ever, and then what?'

'I don't think we should be less glad about Roberta's baby because of that,' he says in the heavy space between them. 'I'd like to see a kid round the place.'

'You should be so lucky. It'll be different, you see. You won't be able to own Roberta's baby.'

'You can't own anyone's baby,' he says, not following her logic.

'Go on, admit it,' says Edith, snapping the oven door shut. 'You've got it in for Paul because this baby will live in the city with him, and not out here on the farm. This is your problem too, matey.'

The kitchen feels too hot. He hears himself, flat and mean. 'You don't like Paul either.'

And he walks out of the room.

THE SKY IS marbled with a white-green light like the blown glass perfume bottle that stood on his mother's dressing table. When he took the stopper out he could smell tea roses. If he breathes deeply enough he might just catch their scent now. Above him the last of the moon is a disc like smooth candy. Then the sun lifts clear of the hills and the air is suddenly full of white hot sunlight, and excitement quickens in his veins. Another day, new promise, he is going to be a grandfather.

This land has been in Glass's family for four generations. The farm lies among rolling country burned out of the bush a century or more ago. Glass knows how to breed female animals to their maximum capacity, how to ensure that their fertility cycle continues year after year. The farm yields six hundred kilos of milk solids per hectare, high for the Wairarapa. He stands on the crest of the hill, holding his gun at his side. Edith is wrong — this is what ownership is about and he is proud of it. In the circle of light that surrounds the farm, all the trembling knee-high grass, the beautiful clover and rye, the cocksfoot and timothy lying before him is his. It is rich and luscious and soon it will be ready to cut for hay; it ripples and shimmers and billows; it surges with the day's early light, now purple and lavender in the shadow of a cloud, now flickering green like the feathers of a parrot. There will be a good crop of hay this year.

Glass is a big man who has never let himself run to fat. His fair hair is still thick and springy, neatly thatching his head although he is sixty. Running, down his cheek and into the corner of his mouth is an old, deep acne scar, which women find attractive. He has taken to reading glasses only recently. He is a well-spoken man; his mother was old money from up north and you can hear in his vowels her out-of-Walnut way of talking. If you ask people round about, they will say he is a strong man; if you ask his brothers-in-law they will go further, tell you he's a hard bastard. Close-mouthed, they say in the pub and down at the saleyards; understandable, he's got his troubles. Always, there is that underlying admiration — remember, the lad played for Wairarapa Bush.

Below Glass lies his farmhouse, a low white bay villa, formal in its symmetry, with a verandah running around it. Built early in the century, it has been softened and altered over the years, more recently by Edith, but this cannot hide its plain and stalwart origins. It looks to him like a ship lost at sea, surrounded by pergolas and gazebos, flowers and shrubs and peacocks on the lawn. Over twenty years his wife has transformed the garden from a staid and structured place to a wild welter of colour, a valley of roses, bearded irises, pentstemons, dianthus, mop-headed trees showering blossom, and all divided by curving paths and broad, stone-paved walks. The green tide of grass laps at the fence, a life-raft of roses spilling over the trellises towards it.

Behind him, a group of houses is clustered on the bank of a river edged with willows. They are roofed with tin, thinned by rust, and wooden planked, bare of paint. His father used to take him for walks on the farm when he was a boy. 'Did you know there's a white man living in there, boy? Now what would a white man want living amongst Maoris? It'll be women or drink. You watch out, boy, don't you go visiting down there.'

A car drifts along the road, a narrow strip of seal winding in a curve through the valley that divides the near home paddocks. You never know who will come up this quiet back road these days. On the corner, three white crosses mark the place where a car rolled and killed its occupants some months earlier. The crosses are garlanded with leis made of brilliant gold and purple artificial flowers. He wonders what Polynesians were doing driving at a mad pace through this part of the countryside. There was nowhere to go and nobody who knew them, so far as anyone can tell.

In the distance he sees Bernard and Orla, darting in the shadowy oasis of the milking shed, hears a dog bark as the first cows are returned to pasture. He can just discern their Friesian coats, like soft, stitched patchwork jumpers on their bodies.

When he left school, Bernard started work on the farm. The farm was to have gone to Glass's elder son, Michael, but he has a career in journalism and works in the press gallery in Canberra. He writes funny, tough columns that appear in different newspapers with his photograph over them, and don't reveal his own politics. His father cannot understand this. When Glass was a baby his mother said it was as clear as glass what he was thinking, and the name stuck. Glass. Through a glass darkly, Edith once said, but that is too poetic, too obscure for him, although he knows she understands that the name is not entirely true, that he deceives her and others around him if it suits him. But a man's politics are something you need to know, if you are to understand him. This is how you tell right from wrong, whether a man is for you or against you.

He doesn't like Bernard much, which is something he admits to nobody, and only rarely to himself. He tries harder with Bernard than with any of his children. Bernard and Orla have had a good start on the farm. When Orla arrived from Ireland she was pert and tricky and he could have sworn she would have babies. But why Orla, he wonders, acid-tongued, and now disappointed? He hears her across the paddock. 'Yo yo, get away back,' Orla calls to the dogs, from afar. The last cows are filing down the race. He hears the distant hiss of high-pressure hoses cleaning down the yard. She and Bernard have almost finished milking and soon she will return to the house.

Hearing her clear, bell-like voice echoing over the paddocks, he knows, with a pain that tightens his gut, that Edith would rather have a Catholic grandchild from Orla. She doesn't believe that Roberta and Paul are truly married, and although he has known it all along, it is not something he wants to admit to himself. He can see that she has not put aside one moment of their past. He remembers with painful clarity the time of his father's anger. It's like the banks hiring staff, boy, he had told Glass. No niggers, no queers, no Catholics. You have to learn the hard way, boy, his father had said, when he met Edith, the Catholic girl Glass had made pregnant.

'We don't need his money,' Edith had said, when he gave them the money to go sharemilking, 'we don't need anything from him.' But, not knowing anything else, and because there was a baby coming, he had taken it and gone. He had never seen his father again. Glass believes that what has happened to him has made him more tolerant; this is what he hopes.

He grips his rifle more tightly. The movement startles a rabbit, which leaps across his line of vision. Before his aim, the rabbit cartwheels, a tiny bolt of blood exploding in the morning sun.

The rabbit lies close to the perimeter of the far home paddock. Glass, setting off to retrieve it, is alerted by a familiar astringent smell, both smoky and floral, that puzzles him; it is the scent of crushed or perhaps freshly cut grass. Only as he stands from retrieving the rabbit does Glass's glance travel further.

This is the moment when he sees the circles. He does not understand how he missed them from the rise. It is as if they just happened, although that cannot be so, they must have come in the night. The pasture has been swirled flat in wide precise circles that overlap at their edges, with neat skewers at their centres. Outside the first circles lie narrower ones, like rows of embroidery on a doily, equally neat and exact in the way they are made.

ORLA

ORLA BEGINS BREAKFAST, but her mind is not on what she is doing. Yesterday a letter came and sooner or later she will have to tell Bernard about it. She picks up the pages from her mother again and sighs. These are not the usual complaints.

My dear Orla, Given that you are such a stubborn pig-headed daughter to me, I suppose I must think about coming to New Zealand, I am an old woman now and what is one more sacrifice more or less . . .

Orla lays the letter down. This is what she has desired for so long, but now that it looks as if it might happen she has not the faintest idea how she will cope. It should all have happened years ago. What will her mother think? She tries to see the farm and its occupants through her eyes. Wealth, to her, beyond her wildest dreams. Edith, flitting through her garden, among the pergolas and the roses, a glass poised between her forefinger and thumb, exclaiming at the beauty of the world, sniffing her gin between gulps of flowery air. Her son-in-law down at heel and ugly in his temper. Bernard has his mother's fondness for drink. At least she is likely to be spared the sight of her husband's brother, who hardly ever comes to the farm.

'What are you, queer?' Bernard had said to Michael, the last time they met.

Orla thought at the time that it was a cruel thing to say, even though in her heart she believes that Michael is as queer as water running up hill.

It is not just because he's single, she tells herself. Look at how he stands with his thumbs hooked in his trouser pockets, and the way he savours his food. Her mother would sense something different about him too, even if she couldn't put a name to it.

No doubt her mother will also see that, in spite of plenty, Orla's own housekeeping has become careless and frowsy. Her mother will behold her, in all her devastation.

When Bernard comes in, a few minutes later, she tests the idea on him. 'My mother's coming to stay,' she says, making it an accomplished fact.

'About time,' he says, as if her news is of no consequence. He sits down and stretches his stockinged feet in front of him, picking up yesterday's *Herald*, while he waits for her to serve breakfast. 'The dollar's down, thank Christ,' he says.

'You'll have to stop blaspheming,' Orla says.

He lowers his paper. 'I'll do what I like. This is my own house, isn't it?'

But Orla can swear there is relief in his voice. Perhaps he has guessed her plan. She rattles plates together and shoves them down on the table, as if her embarrassment is anger.

At this moment, Bernard's father knocks and enters without waiting for an answer. 'Someone's been playing funny buggers in the paddock.'

THE THIRD DAUGHTER OF THE EARL OF MAUDSLEY

SARAH'S MOTHER IS up and pouring muesli into bowls. I'm ready, she announces.

Sarah lies in bed and pulls the covers over her head. 'I'm temperamentally unsuited to early mornings,' she tells Wendy, when she comes to the door.

This does Sarah no good. Wendy stands with her arms akimbo. 'I always had trouble getting you out of bed.'

'I don't like getting up when I'm told.' Sarah hears herself behaving like a sulky child, and swings her feet on the floor. After all, she is at Ellie and Jack all the time to get up and go to school. This is regressive behaviour put on especially for Wendy's benefit.

Still she dawdles. Instead of taking a shower, she pours herself a long, slinky, oil-scented bath. Her breasts bob in the water. 'Great tits,' her husband, Tony, used to say. Tony, who manufactures barbecues for rich clients, considered himself a connoisseur of women's breasts and one of his clients had taken him seriously. She puts her hands beneath her breasts and watches them float, pinches her suckable nipples, and thinks about her lover. He used to like front-to-back sex so he could hold them while they made love. Sarah considers lying down in the water and drowning but she tried that when Tony left her and knows it does not work. Somewhere she has read that swallowing a banana skin will choke you. There are more obvious ways of killing yourself, and the fact that she does not review them tells her she is not quite ready for that.

'I don't believe in garden tours,' she announces, her hair under a damp towel. 'They're for geriatric greenies.'

Wendy does not reply. She is trying not to look as if she is hurrying or eager.

In the end, as Sarah has intended, they miss the bus. She parks the car, walks slowly to the bus terminal and checks. The bus has long gone. When she returns to the car, Wendy's hands lie in her lap. She looks down at them so Sarah will not see the unshed tears.

'I'm sorry,' says Wendy. 'It's my fault. I shouldn't try to organise you.'

'No, it's mine,' Sarah answers. 'Forgive me. I've got the route the bus has taken, and a map. We'll go in the car.'

Wendy brightens, and Sarah knows, inwardly, that it will only be a matter of time before she is in charge again.

THE BEST HOUSE Wendy and Mac and their daughter Sarah ever had was a little wooden Lockwood. They lived in it in the 1960s, not far from the seacoast, and within sight of the brooding white cone of the mountain. They watched the bright crimson and black-edged sunsets, and listened to the wooden house move in its joints on still nights. Together, in a sturdy but struggling Morris Minor, they travelled round the coastline, where the ink-blue sea lashes the black west coast rocks, and through the countryside. Mac and Wendy were always on the lookout for things they could turn into money.

Mac was an odd-job man who painted houses for pensioners, laid concrete paths and mowed lawns. He was also an inventor who sold patents on various agricultural implements, knowing that, if he could find the right buyer for his ideas, one day he would strike it rich. The work he did was so meticulous he was always in demand, but he charged so little, because he and Wendy believed in the principle of doing unto others as they would have done to them, that there was never any profit. So long as I have my health, we can make ends meet, he told Sarah, ruffling her hair, and smiling. Towards the end of the 1960s, Mac's health did begin to fail.

Wendy was full of ideas and optimism. 'We can live from the land,' she said. They collected bottles and tin cans for Wendy to sell, and in the summer they hunted for blackberries and wild japonica, so Wendy could make jelly and jam. Mac took a gun along in case they saw birds and rabbits. They even searched for fungus on fallen logs, like Chinese entrepreneurs at the turn of the century. For aphrodisiacs, no less. Sarah found some of the stuff one day; it looked like a frilly rubber diaphragm on a tree stump. Clever, clever Sarah. People knew them, waved out, shook their heads and smiled. A harmless bunch.

'What a dear little girl. Now which side of the family do her looks come from?' Farmers' wives asked this of Wendy when the family was seeking permission to pick mushrooms on their land, or gather pine cones.

And Wendy would say, with pride, 'She's our chosen one — you can't know things like that.'

'Well, who'd have thought it,' the wives remarked. 'She isn't exactly like either of you, I can see that, but goodness she certainly looks like one of the family.'

Sometimes the farmers' wives slipped Sarah a coin. 'Put it in your pinny pocket, and keep it fastened over,' they advised.

When she was ten, Sarah asked her parents if they must go on scavenging like this. They laughed gaily at her. 'Nobody has to do anything in this world, dear child,' Wendy had said. 'But it's such fun and it does bring in the little extras, doesn't it?'

'Well then, if nobody has to do it, I'm not going to any more.' Sarah can still see the way Wendy stood there, stung by her daughter's failure to understand.

'So we've got a little snob in our midst,' Wendy had said. 'I can't believe it. That's why I got away from England. From England and my father, the earl.'

Sarah often suspects Wendy of deliberately misunderstanding when it suits her, and also of untruths. Her father, the earl, is a variable whom she remembers with affection when it suits her and at other times disparages. But when Sarah thinks back over her life so far, that refusal feels like one of the cruellest things she has done to anyone; it was also a day that marked the beginning of something between Wendy and Sarah, a cycle of guilt and repentance from which neither of them has since been free.

That is why, on this lovely spring morning, Sarah is driving Wendy through the countryside in search of beautiful gardens, listening again to the story of the earl.

Her mother, as she tells it, was born the third daughter of the Earl of Maudsley, an unfortunate man without sons to whom he could bequeath things. One of Sarah's aunts had borne a son, and so now there was a cousin in England who was the Earl of Maudsley. This is the family mythology.

'I left England with a trunk of clothes,' the story begins. 'I had some kitchen utensils I'd saved up for from my monthly allowance. I went into my father's study one morning, and I said, "Father, I have packed my trunk and I am leaving." I'd been such a blow to him, his last hope of an heir, because the midwife had said to my mother, "That's enough. There'll be no more of this, or you'll be dead, and then where will the his lordship be?" '

'I can't believe people could go in for all that generational crap,' Sarah says. She is sure they have missed the turn-off to the first stop on the garden tour. 'It's as bad as Diana being measured up as breeding stock for Charlie, and look where it got her.'

'My father, the earl, was related to Diana's family,' says Wendy.

Sarah has heard this before. She sighs. 'So the earl didn't try and stop you from going?'

'Well, that's the funny part of it. He was furious. Loss of face, of course. He didn't believe me at first, but when he realised I meant business, he gave me a parting gift.' Sarah knows the parting gift as intimately as she knows her children's faces. The one last gift from the earl was a pair of pure silver birds mounted on filigreed stands. They have outstretched wings like fighting cocks, and a yellow sapphire in each eye. 'Took them off the bookcase by the fireplace and put them in my hands. Here, take these and don't come back moaning for more when they're gone, that's what he said to me.' Wherever the family lived, the silver birds held a place of honour. In the dingiest cottages, they stood shining on the mantelpiece, rubbed every day with a soft cloth.

'If I'd been a man, at least I might have got remittance money. But good Lord, look what I got in return for running off. Your father, bless him, and freedom.'

'Can't you sell the silver birds?' Sarah once asked, when things were particularly lean.

'Sell the silver birds? My dear, the birds are your inheritance. See, they have the earl's crest stamped beneath their stand.'

This is where truth comes unstuck. Sarah has long ago realised that, in her heart, Wendy is still the snob, the daughter of an aristocracy she claims to despise, and she cannot like this trait in her mother. Secretly, she describes her as a hypocrite. But Wendy also has an eye for what is beautiful and fine. The piano with the fire-eating dragons, the chiming clock and the pieces of china, delicate and rare, are not inheritances. They are items bargained and bartered for in old Taranaki homes; what others saw as junk, Wendy perceived as treasure, to put aside for Sarah.

So Sarah supposes she must love Wendy, in spite of everything for the energy and effort she puts into creating mirages, her boundless belief that things will turn out well. She thinks Wendy is foolish and vain, that her friends would be astonished if they met her, and would laugh behind her own and Wendy's back, but she is used to that. She has grown up with this woman. They will go on, she expects, being exasperated and affectionate, and she supposes that in the end she will not know Wendy much better than when they began. Certainly, she does not expect Wendy to understand her. Mac is dead, and the Lockwood house sold long ago to pay his debts. Wendy lives in her rented cottage by the sea where, as far as Sarah knows, the silver birds still gleam in the crowded space that doubles as a bedroom and a living room.

'Some day they'll be yours,' Wendy says. This has been a persistent refrain. 'You can take them now, if you like,' she had said, on the last of Sarah's infrequent visits. 'They'd be safer at your place than mine. Even if I'm out for an hour there's the risk of being burgled. They're only things, I don't need them.'

But, unlike the other gifts, Sarah will not take the birds. She wants to give Wendy some money from the barbecue manufacturer, but her mother won't hear of it.

Today, Wendy is oddly quiet about the birds; for the moment she has no more to say about them. She does not suggest that Sarah collects the birds, and Sarah finds herself unsettled by this omission, as if the last line has been left off a jingle.

'About your birth parents,' Wendy says.

This is what Sarah does *not* want to talk about, but it is this that has brought Wendy to see her. She is saved, for the moment, by the sight of a tour bus parked by a farm gate.

'Yes, that's the place,' says Wendy, with a certain satisfaction.

THE CAGE
I HAVE TO take tests for anaemia at the hospital, on the instructions of my gynaecologist, Mr Maitland, a short man with a pleated throat and a peppery disposition. I have been perfectly well up until now and I feel that he is simply justifying his existence and all the money my parents are paying him.

I get lost at the hospital, which is old and like a rabbit warren. You can as easily end up in the cancer ward when you have set off to visit an old lady with a broken ankle. I get into a lift. Lifts have never bothered me. Some people walk up six flights of stairs rather than get into an ageing lift, but I have always thought that, if a lift broke down, I would be calm and comforting to those less capable than myself.

It does not happen like this. As soon as the doors close, I realise that I should have turned left, back down the corridor, and I am headed for the wrong department. When the lift shudders to a halt, I am startled. There are six of us inside, two middle-aged women, an older man wearing a battered tweed cap, a smart young Asian woman and a sullen teenage boy. We stand apart from each other, the way people do, trying, in that compacted space, not to touch. When minutes have passed, we glance sideways at each other, our nervous smiles acknowledging that we are there. Only the Asian woman looks as if her self-control lies in being absolutely still. Nobody moves. It is surprising how quiet it is, even though we are trapped in the bowels of a huge and busy hospital.

'It'll probably start again in a minute,' says one of the women. An acrid smell of tobacco clings to the boy's clothing. I fight rising nausea.

And suddenly I'm up there again, with space beneath me, covered only by the flimsy floor of the lift cage. Don't be afraid, says my coach's voice, you haven't got far to fall. But I know it is a long way down.

'Shouldn't we ring for help?' I say, eyeing the little box on the wall, with the sign about it being for use only in an emergency.

Anything to take my mind off throwing up, off my own kind of high altitude sickness.

'No cause for a fuss,' says the second woman. Her breasts are like ledges of rock. I can't turn around properly without bumping into them.

There is a grinding lurch, and the lift slips downwards and stops again. I hear a thin scream that is mine but seems dissociated from me. A more palpable silence ensues.

'We should all sit down with our knees braced,' says the man in the tweed cap, after a minute or so. 'Like in an aeroplane when it's going to crash.'

I grab the phone, and a telephonist answers. 'Help us,' I shout. 'The lift's broken down.'

'Which department?' She doesn't sound very interested.

'I don't know. How the fuck do I know where I am?'

'All right, keep your hair on. What department were you heading for?'

'I'm in the wrong lift, I don't know.'

'Are you on your own?'

'Where are we going?' I ask the people in the lift.

'I was on my way to respiratory medicine,' mumbles the big woman.

I repeat the information to the woman on the telephone. The lift lurches again.

'Get me out, I'm pregnant.'

'For God's sake keep your hair on, you stupid cow.'

I put the phone down, not believing what I have heard. But it is true, this is what she said, and I am stuck here with these expressionless, apparently unmoved people.

I sit down on the floor of the lift, and try to bunch my knees up to my chin. Soon the man in the tweed cap sits down beside me. Glancing up, I see a glint of tears in the eyes of the boy, and am curiously comforted.

'Sit down beside me,' I say. The boy squats down, and suddenly, without a hiccup, a stream of vomit gushes out of him over the lift floor. Orange liquid mixed with fish and chips spills round our feet. I stand up again, and hold the side of the lift, gagging in the stench.

I grab the phone and shout down it. 'I'm the medical superintendent's daughter,' I say.

There is a hurried conversation. Another woman comes on. 'Ma'am, I'm sorry,' says the second telephonist, 'we're doing the very best we can.'

I hang up, and begin to sob. The Asian woman takes a Walkman and earphones out of her handbag and puts them over her ears. I wish I had some too.

'Stop it,' the big woman says to me. 'Think of your baby instead of yourself. If you go on like that I'll have to slap you.'

'Mother,' I say. 'MumMum.'

I SEE HER in another lift, a different hospital, some other time. My father has hit her with the back of his hand and she has fallen and hurt her shoulder. It is the only time I have ever seen him hit her, and I believe, though I have no way of knowing this, that he has never done it again. She has been screaming in incoherent rage, hurling all manner of objects, dinner plates, vases, a half-full bottle of whisky in his direction. He grabs her, holds her, while the boys and I look on. The farmhouse kitchen is splattered with scraps of food, shards of crockery, the rotten water from the vase. When she falls she lies among the mess before slowly rising to her knees.

'You've hurt me, you bastard,' she says to my father. 'Take me to the hospital.' Her arm dangles at her side.

I have to go with them. They try to leave me with my brothers, but I throw myself after my parents as they stumble out to the car.

'Take me with you, please take me,' I beg, clinging to my mother's jersey.

'I didn't mean to hurt your Mum,' says my father. I am lying on the grass of the lawn, beside the car. As my mother drags herself into the car, I seize my moment and tear the door out of her hand, so that I can jump inside too.

At the hospital we ride up in the lift to the X-ray department. My father, still angry, is tense and defensive as my mother cries messily in a loud, whining monotone. Her luxuriant hair is tousled and matted.

'I fell,' she says to the examining doctor.

'Easy, I should think,' says the doctor. 'You're not very steady on your feet now, are you?'

She stares right back at the doctor out of bloodshot eyes. But there is something defiant, even calculated, in her response. 'No, I'm not, am I?'

'It's lucky you were drunk,' says the doctor. 'You might have hurt yourself badly, mightn't you, if you hadn't had something to relax you.'

A look flashes between the doctor and my father.

'Give her an aspirin and put her to bed,' he says.

'Aren't you going to do anything for me?' my mother says, and her eyes are wide with a pleading I cannot interpret, although I guess she was trying to say that she does not want to go home with my father.

'I've got sick people to look after,' the doctor says coldly.

'I'm sick,' she says.

'You'll get better,' he says, and shows us the door. We ride in the lift in a silence broken only by more of my mother's muffled, hiccuppy weeping.

'I'm sorry, Glass,' she says, dull and exhausted. Neither of them looks at me. This is the same woman who imposes control on the chaos of nature. It would be easy to think that the difficulty has gone away.

'We won't say any more about this,' my father says, when we reach home. Michael and Bernard are nowhere to be seen. I agree with my father that I will never tell anyone.

THE LIFT GRINDS into action again and my fellow prisoners and I are swerved into another steep downwards dive, before we come to a halt. This time the doors open. A knot of people clusters below us. The lift is halfway between floors, which is as far as it will go. Someone has brought a chair for us to climb down on to. I see the dark space of the lift well at our backs as we slide over the lip of the lift floor.

A pert, confident woman, blonde hair piled up on her head, stands holding the chair. I look for kindness in the upturned faces, expecting someone to comfort me, a pregnant woman crawling out of a lift.

'You're not the medical superintendent's daughter,' says the blonde woman. 'We checked up.'

'Bitch,' I scream. 'Bitch, bitch, bitch, bitch.'

The woman holding the chair ducks, and someone goes to grab me. I am quicker than they expect, jumping with a gymnast's fluid leap towards the fire door, finding myself in a stairwell, running down, not looking back. I hear, among the voices behind me, someone calling, 'Mad as a maggot', but I don't care.

SCARLET RIBBONS

WENDY AND SARAH quarrel as they walk around Edith's garden. Wendy carries the floppy velvet bag over her arm. On her head she wears a huge sunhat, tied beneath her chin with a paisley scarf.

'It's a man, isn't it?' Wendy asks. 'You were expecting a man. I stood in the way of some fellow coming to slink into your bed after dark.'

'That's not true.'

'He's let you down, hasn't he?'

'Why do you say that?' Sarah knots and unknots her hands. They are too thin and her veins stand out.

'Ha.' It is more of a bark than a comment.

'I made a bad marriage — am I supposed to behave like a nun? Do penance?'

'A touch of classical Renaissance here,' says Wendy, looking around the garden. 'Interesting.'

The garden is laid out from the house in a rectangular lawn with low narrow walls down which erigeron and rock plants fall beneath Italian lavenders. A central middle path leads across the central axis to a gazebo and an organised cluster of rose gardens; it is only beyond this point that a certain wildness takes over, as the garden fans into serpentine grassed paths among brilliant displays of annuals. These walkways meander towards a large avenue of trees that lead to the paddocks beyond.

A spare, suntanned woman with dark hair turning white in slashes round the temples, is surrounded by day trippers to the garden. She wears a pale green silk shirt and severely tailored slacks, casually elegant in a way that those of her guests are not. They are a mixed lot: mothers and daughters like Sarah and Wendy, grateful for an interest they can share; a sprinkling of older men shambling behind wives with crimped blue hair, pearl button earrings and winged glasses, their angora cardigans buttoned across their stomachs; Japanese tourists taking photographs of each other in the swings beneath the trees, a small outing of the wheelchair-bound (to whom the organisation who has hired Edith's garden today will make a donation); a group of private school girls carrying notebooks and piping with excitement as they discover botanical labels on the plants.

'Who does your landscape design?' asks a visitor intensely, pen poised over a notebook.

The owner looks surprised, and raises her eyebrows. 'Nobody.'

'You must visit other gardens?'

'Never,' says the woman in the green shirt.

'Oh. Photographs, books, perhaps?'

'Perhaps.'

'Well.' The woman gestures helplessly. 'You do seem to have a painterly eye.'

'So what do you want, Wendy?' Sarah asks her mother.

'Ssh,' says Wendy, her fingers to her lips.

'Up here,' says the owner, tapping her forehead with her forefinger. 'It's all up here.' Finishing the conversation, she walks briskly to a long table where food is being set out.

'I want you to be happy,' says Wendy, as if there has been no interruption to the conversation.

'Well, let me get on with it.'

'Oh, I would, I would if you could. The trouble is, Sarah, you don't know who you are. How can you make choices?'

'I'm sick of all that, don't you understand?' Sarah says, more sharply than she intends.

'Don't be a baby, Sarah. How can anyone know anything if they don't ask questions?'

'That's your problem. You're the one who wants to know.'

There is a veto on the information in Sarah's adoption files. Her birth parents cannot be identified. It is a wound Sarah has failed to lick clean.

A group of madrigal singers in period costume is gathering beneath a central wrought iron dome covered with Mrs Herbert Stevens roses, their white petals like a fountain. The singers have attracted the day trippers around them.

'I have asked myself questions,' says Sarah. She hasn't intended to say anything, but the madrigal singers are humming softly to themselves, like an orchestra tuning for a performance, and the women in their absurd costumes, the high sweet buzz behind their closed lips and the scent of roses unleash an unintentional torrent of words. 'At night, when I was supposed to be asleep in whatever Godforsaken hole we happened to be in at the time, I would lie awake and ask myself what I would do if I was given away a second time. I was afraid of being on my own. I was scared of the dark, because people could hide in the shadows and take me away.'

'Oh Sarah, not now dear.' People around them are raising their fingers to their lips, signalling for them to be quiet.

'You started it. At least let me tell you what I think. Let me tell you the questions I've asked.'

The singers finish putting their song sheets in order. They begin to sing 'Scarlet Ribbons'. Wendy eyes widen with longing.

Sarah touches her own hair in a surprised way, as if she is discovering something, and begins to walk away, moving so quickly that Wendy has to lengthen her stride to keep up.

'I thought I was so lucky to be chosen by you,' says Sarah.

'And now you don't?' They continue through an avenue of elms planted closely together, their pleached branches forming an overhead tunnel.

'To tell you the truth, Wendy, the question I ask myself is, what authorities in the world would have given me to a barmy couple like you and Mac. That's the real question, isn't it?'

Wendy sits down abruptly on a woodland seat, looking out towards the rolling farmland, her face drained of colour. She begins to burrow in her bag, searching for something. Already, Sarah has begun to regret her thin tirade, even though she believes that she has said what she means, that the question has been lying there waiting to catch up with them both, sooner or later.

'Children think these things,' she says lamely. 'I've got kids of my own now.'

'But you're not a child, Sarah.' Wendy produces what she has been looking for, one of the silver birds. The sight of it silences Sarah. The singers' voices rise ever more sweetly in the summer afternoon: 'If I live to be a hundred, I will never know from where, came those lovely scarlet ribbons, scarlet ribbons for her hair . . . ' It is like the setting of a period movie — the rustic seats, the splendid backdrop of trees, the country women's pure voices soaring into the sunshine.

'Why have you brought those?'

'That, actually. I've only got one now. I want you to have it.'

'Where's the other one?' Sarah is becoming frightened.

'I sold it.'

'My inheritance?'

'Hardly important, by the sound of it.'

'I told you I could give you some money.'

'Tony's money. So you did. Pay your debts, eh? Get me off your back.'

'That's not true.'

'So what's true? You're the one telling all the truth, Sarah.' Wendy stares into the distance, her knotted hands clutching the bird, her face closed.

'Nothing's the truth. I've been left in the lurch and I'm unhappy and I just want to forget all this, okay?'

Wendy doesn't appear to hear her. In the distance something catches her eye and she almost rises to her feet.

'I needed the money,' Wendy tells Sarah in an offhand way.

'For what?'

'Oh for goodness' sake, Sarah,' says Wendy, 'you do go on about things.' She drops the bird back in her bag. 'I met a man from the Welfare Department on the beach up at home.'

'I don't understand.'

'No, no, why should you? Well, for a certain sum of money, he assured me he could find me the name of your birth mother. There are rotten apples in every basket, I suppose. It seems I was lucky enough to find one.'

A woman, short and wiry, walks across the paddocks with two men, heading in the direction where Wendy is gazing. All three appear to be carrying long-handled rakes, although one of the men could be holding a gun. The sound of the singing behind them is shattered by the arrival of a circling helicopter. The trio shake their rakes at the sky. A man with a camera hangs out of the helicopter as it hovers overhead. Sarah half-expects to hear gunfire, and she is not disappointed — only it comes from the ground and not from the chopper. The taller of the two men is firing his shotgun.

Then Sarah sees that the grass has been disturbed; from where she stands, it appears to be flattened in a pattern of sweeping circles and diagrams. 'Messages,' says Wendy, in a loud, excited voice.

Behind them, attracted by the sound of the helicopter, the members of the garden tour have begun to emerge through the trees. The owner strides ahead of them, her presence commanding. 'I'm sorry,' she says, 'I'm afraid that's all there is for today.'

Alarmed by the shots, tour bus operators are shepherding their clients away, and men are hurrying their wives down through the trees, although it is clear that most of them would like to stay.

Wendy begins to move towards the circles in the grass, following the three ahead.

'Wendy,' cries Sarah. She feels as if she has begun the most important conversation of her life and now it is being snatched away from her. Nothing can be heard over the deafening noise of the helicopter, now quivering like a giant beetle, a safe distance away from the action. There is a thin wind rushing through the air.

'Go home, Sarah,' calls Wendy, over her shoulder.

'Did you give the man the money?' Wendy doesn't turn back.

'Mother, did the man tell you who it was?'

Wendy walks on, drawing steadily abreast of the two men and the woman. The garden's owner peels away from the trees and follows her.

'Wendy, come back, you old fool,' calls Sarah. It is not clear whether her mother has heard this, although Sarah thinks she pauses. 'I don't want to see you again,' she shouts.

'I'M AFRAID YOU'LL have to go back,' says Edith, catching up with Wendy.

Wendy turns to her, eyes blazing. 'It's magic,' she cries. 'Pure magic.'

'Somebody smoking waccy baccy, more likely,' Edith says, her voice dry.

Wendy sees that, close at hand, Edith's face is mottled beneath her tan, and that her hands are work-worn and rough. But there is an irresistible air about her that convinces Wendy they are about to become friends.

'Oh come, don't you believe in spirits?'

'Madam,' Edith begins again, wanting to steer Wendy back to the garden.

'But don't you?'

Their eyes meet; Edith smiles a small sarcastic smile, but Wendy can see that it is at her own expense. 'Why not?' she says. 'All the same, it's a bit of a devil, all of this.'

Wendy closes her eyes and laughs out loud, her face turned towards the sun.

five

WALNUT

I HURRY THROUGH the hospital car park like a fugitive, certain that someone is going to apprehend me. This is irrational, I can see, because I have done nothing wrong. It is not a crime to call somebody a bitch, I am the injured party. But I am shaken, and nothing makes sense.

When I find my blue Honda Civic, I sit there for a few minutes, my hands shaking on the wheel, before I am able to start the car and drive away. I know I am not going back to work today, but I am not quite sure where I will go. I do not want to go home to Ashton Fitchett Drive, though I know that the sensible thing would be to lie down and put my feet up. I drift into a stream of traffic, down round the Basin Reserve, along past the carillon, and turn towards town. I think I will buy myself something, perhaps just some flowers, or fresh fruit, or perhaps I will go to a movie. But the traffic is heavy, and I pull left towards the motorway, and soon I am burning along beside the sea, heading north, driving towards the hill road that will take me to the farm.

At the foot of the hills I see a group of white horses at a riding school and lean down to make a cross on my shoe. This is what my brothers and I did when we were out driving. White horses, we would say, and we would lick our fingers, make a cross on our shoes and then cross our fingers. We made a wish and after that it was bad luck to speak until we saw a black dog. So the miles would pass, all of us shouting with relief because our fingers felt stuck to each other, black dog, black dog.

Travelling at speed, I make two more crosses, one for Bernard who has not returned my calls since my pregnancy began, and one for big brother Michael, whom I miss. I wish he had been around for me to call today. He would have known what to do. Well, maybe. At least Michael has survival skills, he got away.

It is then that I remember that I have a husband, and that it has not gone through my mind to phone Paul. It is still mid-afternoon; if I put my foot down I might almost get to the farm and back before he gets home from work. He has been working late the past few weeks. Or perhaps I won't go to the farm at all, maybe I'll just drive a little way and get the feel of the countryside around me, and then turn round and go back to town. But that's not true. I have never turned back from the farm, not once. I fumble with the radio, my linked fingers making me clumsy.

I hear my father's unmistakeable voice. 'Children probably did it,' he says.

Did what?

I turn the volume up, losing one of my crosses in my haste. Bernard's, I think.

'These circles are sophisticated and well planned,' says the reporter interviewing Glass.

'Look, I've got nothing to say about this. The Ag Department chaps are coming out here to have a look at what's been done to the pasture and then the grass will be raked over,' says my father. 'I don't know how you got hold of this garbage.'

'Well, as I think I explained, Mr Nichols, we had a call from a tour bus operator on his cellphone.'

'What are you paying him?'

'Have you heard the word pictograms, Mr Nichols?'

No, Glass has not.

'Well, let's say, do you think this is a natural phenomenon, or is it a sign?'

'What sort of a sign did you have in mind?' Glass asks, letting his guard down.

'Circles are sometimes ascribed to flying saucers and space men. Do you think this could be a sign from another galaxy?'

'Bugger off,' says Glass.

'These circles appeared at the Nichols' farm early this morning,' says the reporter, in summary. 'The formations appear to be about forty metres long, although the farmer is not keen on measurements being taken. Mr Nichols says that his cows are, quote, "all going haywire". Police are talking to Mr Nichols junior who was seen taking aim at a helicopter earlier in the day with a .22 rifle.' The reporter wraps up his story. 'An attempt is being made to photograph the crop circles for further analysis before they are destroyed.'

I have reached the far side of the hill and turn off down the road to Walnut. Walnut, where I grew up and went to school, is a market town situated north-east of the main line. The Tararua Ranges rear their blue spines to the west, the coast lies in the opposite direction. The sea is close enough to smell when the wind is right, and for seagulls to take shelter during storms, but too far to see from the farm, even from the hills where my father runs beef cattle. The market square has been built like an old English town around a group of walnut trees where the locals spread tarpaulins in the autumn to collect the nuts. The wide, leafy walnut branches are older than my father's father would have been. The village, for that is really what it is, used to be famous for an annual frog jumping championship but that was abandoned years ago when the animal rights people got to hear of it, and if they had seen the way my brother Bernard blew frogs up with a straw through their bums until they popped, they would have had even more to say about the matter. Now they have an annual cider tasting festival instead.

In Walnut, there is a garage, a Town and Country Farm Centre where you get everything from nails to pots and pans and gumboots, a coffee shop and takeaway bar, a supermarket and a hairdresser, and a police station. The fresh fruit shop has closed down, so has the post office, all but one of the banks and the jeweller's; the ladies' haberdashery is hanging on by the skin of its teeth. There are five churches — Catholic, Presbyterian, Anglican, Methodist and the Salvation Army — and the charismatics, who have the most worshippers anyway, use the gymnasium. The three pubs in town are not as old as you might expect because the Temperance Union held sway here for years, but they are well used. My grandfather belonged to the union, I think, but I don't know much about him. I never met him, not in the flesh at least. Correction, I met him when he was dead, but that hardly counts.

This is the area the settlers used to call the Widerup; my brother Michael used to call it that when we were children, a secret name, a corruption. I drive up a valley, past vineyards and new hacienda-style houses with arches and signs inviting people in to taste wine, past small, ugly, modern houses that have replaced some of the older, more picturesque cottages on the farms. But nothing really changes. Old mansions still stand behind avenues of trees. Sometimes I visited those places when I was a child, depending on my friends of the moment. Mostly, though, I spent my time with Pamela, whose family, I suspected, was hard up, although such matters were never mentioned. My family had moved from being poor to moderately wealthy, but I was taught to keep money to myself. Aunt Dorothy once said to me, before she went completely round the bend, 'Listen, young lady, old money makes out that wealth's not important. The women wear their sparklers in the garden and get them all dirty, so you can't see what they're worth. New money flashes them. We Nichols don't wear them at all except on our birthdays.'

A fire of tree stumps burns in a paddock. Spicy smoke filters through the air conditioning, and I am filled with an enormous longing, and a sense of loss that I don't live here any more, under the eggshell dome of the sky, among the remembered hills, the wide Widerup.

BERNARD AND ORLA'S house, which comes before my parents', is empty. I stand uneasily, listening to the ticking of an electric fence and a magpie shrieking like rusty iron from a macrocarpa. I breathe in the hot, acrid smell of the tree. Although the four-wheel drive is parked in the driveway of the top house, it, too, is empty. The remains of a picnic lie on tables under umbrellas; half-stacked cups and plates, leftover food on trays. An open blue bottle of Bombay Sapphire stands under the crab apple tree, its fragrant, ginny scent drifting through the leaves.

An agitated woman makes her way towards me through the lavender walk. Her eyes are teary behind big glasses and she pushes back reddish-brown hair growing out of a poodle perm, as if she is hot and tired.

'If you see my mother, would you tell her I've gone home?' she says, as if I am someone who has been there all the time. 'You'll know her, she's got long white hair and a mad look in her eye.'

'What have you done with your mother?' I ask.

'Nothing, really. We were late for the tour bus, so we took my car. I waited down the road for her, but the bus went hours ago. I expect she was on it. Oh well, I just thought I should check. Good luck,' she calls, as she gets into her car. I don't know why she thinks I am part of the establishment, standing there in my navy-blue maternity dress, dangling car keys in my hand. The air is warm and still, as she chugs down the road in a car that has seen better days.

I am thinking that I should go inside, leave a note, find somebody. This is when I see the woman's mother, or that's who I suppose it must be. She doesn't look well, but from what I can see her problem is not terminal. I feel like a cold-hearted bitch, but I've seen enough of this kind of thing in my life and I don't really care.

The Walnut coffee shop is about to close; I glance at my watch and discover the day nearly over, it's almost five o'clock.

Denise, who was two years behind me at school, is languidly wiping down the last table. I sit down and smile at her. 'Hi, Denise, I'll have a Devonshire tea. Please.'

'We've only got tomorrow's food left,' she says.

'Great, let's pretend we're getting ahead of ourselves,' I say, and because she is a subservient kind of person, and younger, and dying to ask me when my baby is due, she does what I say. I expect my mother treats her like this all the time.

I sit by the window and eat three scones and all the jam and none of the cream and, just as I hold the chrome pot over the cup for a second cup of tea, I see my bother Bernard coming out of the police station. He looks impatient and bad-tempered, and for a moment I think he won't see me. He is heading towards the European, the hairdressing salon. Just as he is about to turn in, he sees me and pauses. Calling out to someone I can't see, but I suppose it's Shelley de Witt who runs the salon, Bernard comes into the coffee shop.

'The cops took me in,' he says, leaning against the door frame.

'Shooting, eh?'

'People been talking?'

'I listen to the radio.'

'You've been to the farm.'

'Yes.'

'See Ma?'

'Nope.'

He pulls a chair out from the table and turns it back to front, straddling it and resting his chin on his arms.

'Want a cup of tea?'

'Nah. I might have a beer.' He nods in the direction of the nearest pub.

'Shouldn't you be home milking?'

'You thinking of running the farm?' His gaze takes in my stomach.

'Oh quit it, Bernard. I came in here for some peace and quiet. Are the cops laying charges against you?'

'Probably not. Depends on their evidence. Shit.'

'Who'd do a thing like that?' I say, meaning the circles. My brothers and I have always understood each other's shorthand, I'll say that about them. 'I mean, who could be bothered?

52

'Smart arses. Townies, I expect.' The old gulf yawns between us, but he is saved by the appearance of Shelley de Witt. You can tell, by the way people are herding together, that there is excitement in the air in Walnut this evening. A little knot of locals chatting in the middle of the road calls out to Shelley as she passes. I've never liked Shelley since she gave me a pudding-bowl haircut the week before I started high school. That was when I decided to let my hair grow long. I haven't had it cut since. Shelley's at least forty-five by my reckoning. Her fingernails are long and red, and she is deeply suntanned; I've heard she goes topless by the river. She calls her salon the European because she's travelled abroad. She says everyone in Walnut is a country hick, but she's stuck around so long it's hard to see her angle.

'I heard you were in the family way,' she says.

'Who told you that?' I don't like the way Shelley gossips either. She's great at playing both ends against the middle, while she snips and blow waves.

'Your Dad hasn't been in for a haircut for a while.' I know she is saying this for my benefit. There have been rumours about Shelley and she cultivates them; this is her back serve.

'I'll make him an appointment,' says Bernard. He turns a white grin on her, and though he's not much to look at, I can see a flash of the charm he had as a boy.

'How are the folks?' I ask, for something to say, though I only have to listen to the news to find out.

'The same. Dunno why they bother.'

I hadn't expected such major intimate stuff, here in the Walnut coffee shop. I had thought that he would say okay, great, they could do without this lot — something like that. But this is Walnut, not Lambton Quay.

'Marriage is marriage,' I say, and shrug.

'Yeah, well you're in on the secret these days, aren't you?'

He gets to his feet and I realise that Shelley has been waiting for him.

'Bloody cops took me in in their car. Shelley's dropping me home.'

'By the way,' I say, not getting up, 'speaking of mothers, somebody's left one under the camellias.'

His mouth drops open. 'Get to the point.'

I explain about the woman in the garden looking for her

mother. 'I think I found her. After she'd left. I saw some feet sticking out from under the hedge.'

'Jesus, Rob.'

'She'd been into the gin, she was passed out cold.' I feel pleased with myself, and I don't care that I have shocked him. The woman was alive, I could see that. I pick up my handbag and walk out ahead of them.

'Give my regards to Orla,' I remember to say, before I am out of earshot.

PAUL IS IN the front room watching television when I get back, which is something I hadn't bargained for. I realise that I have got into the habit of expecting him to be late.

'I recorded the news,' he says, pretending not to look at me. I don't like the edge in his voice. 'I'll wind it back if you like.'

I drop down on the couch and kick off my shoes.

'Paul, what's the matter with us?' Earlier, I'd wished for a happy life. I remember that I haven't seen a black dog all day.

'You've been to the farm, haven't you?' he says, ignoring my question. He rewinds the videotape so that everything happens backwards. I see Bernard fleetingly pointing a gun at a helicopter, in reverse, so that it looks as if he's shooting himself in the foot. 'You might have told me you were going.'

Suddenly I can't be bothered explaining how I started my journey to Walnut, that I didn't know about the circles until I was nearly there. I don't tell him that I've been trapped in a lift cage and almost out of my mind with fear.

six

LIFE IN THE COUNTRY

THE GRASS GREENS swiftly when unseasonable rain falls during summer heat so Edith and Wendy take a break from their ceaseless watering of the garden. Wendy is teaching Edith to make willow baskets. They gather branches from beside the gravelly river and boil them in old coppers that have been lying in the implement shed for years. The two of them are like witches round their cauldrons, the smoke curling from the open fires they light, the smell of the hot bark pungent and raw. The sun casts an idyllic pastoral glow over their labours. They wear their straw hats pushed back on their heads but both shun gloves, allowing their hands to become dry and cracked. Wendy's old, reptilian skin is covered with perspiration. She wears Edith's clothes — blue jeans and a checked cotton shirt that covers her baggy arms. Edith takes a strawberry blonde peach out of a hamper that contains water bottles and lunch.

'Not for me,' says Wendy, flinching. 'The feel of peach skin sets my teeth on edge.'

'I know what you mean,' cries Edith, 'my grandmother was just the same. As for me, it's the sound of a knife being drawn over paper. I feel as if I'm being sliced to the quick.'

'Astonishing.' Wendy leans back, still squatting. She means that it's astonishing that they understand each other so well. Her mouth and eyes are young, in spite of her skin and her long, tough teeth. She has allowed Edith to trim her hair. When Edith lifted the white mane and weighed it in her hand, Wendy gave a voluptuous sigh. 'Not too much, Edith. I don't want to look like mutton dressed up as lamb.' But her expression was pure pleasure at the human touch of Edith's hands. Now Wendy wraps her lips around the neck of the water bottle.

'This is the kind of scene I have dreamed of seeing many times,' she tells Edith, 'of walking through a vista of trees and seeing the light fall golden and mottled on women working in the landscape, like a painting by Monet. In my wildest dreams, I am coming upon my own self. And here it's come true. It takes me back to my childhood.'

'I remember when I was a child,' Edith tells Wendy, 'standing near the entrance to the mine at Roa, after I had taken food to my father one morning before he went to work, and the coal mountain was shrouded in a bright silver mist. The brightness came from the sun, and in a few moments, while I was watching it, the mist dissolved and the black point of the mountain emerged in a blaze of light.'

Edith and Wendy are high on their friendship, but now Edith is embarrassed; she doesn't know why she has told Wendy this apocalyptic story. 'I haven't thought of my childhood for years,' she says. 'It's not the kind you brag about round here. It must be you, it's like having a sister.'

'You don't have any?'

'I did have one, but she died when I was two.' Edith has brothers who live in coal mining towns down on the West Coast, but she can't remember when she last saw them. She feels the shadow of her sister across her life, although she has no recognisable memory of her. To have a friend like Wendy is to cast the shadow aside, and she supposes this is why the story of the mountain has come unbidden to her. Such dizzying pleasure is enchanted and absorbing, and Edith finds herself thinking of little else these days.

But Glass has said several times that there is no reason for Wendy to stay any longer. Who does she think she is, he asks of nobody in particular.

The morning after her collapse, Wendy had sat up in the guest room bed looking like death.

'I never drink,' she had gasped, her mouth parched and ugly.

'I do. It will pass,' Edith had said drily. It was she who had handed the bottle to Wendy in the first place. Wendy had stayed on in the garden, after the other visitors had left, stacking plates. Help yourself, Edith told her straggling guest, have a drink on me. Bernard had been at the police station, Glass fending off reporters. Somebody had to help Orla bring in the cows, although it was not something Edith would ordinarily do.

During the past month they have led near enough to sober lives, out here in the country. For Edith, that is not the whole truth — old habits die as hard as fleas on a dog — but she feels it is a beginning. She thinks that Glass should find plenty to appreciate in Wendy's continuing presence, although he doesn't seem forthcoming on the subject.

And if Wendy notes certain things about the household, she does not mention them: the habitual cleaning of the teeth, the discovery of a half-full (or half-empty, Wendy is never sure of the difference) bottle of gin under a silverbeet row, the telltale network of broken blood vessels in Edith's cheeks. Once she does say, 'My late father was something of a drinker, you know.'

Edith does not respond other than to say: 'How difficult for you.'

'He used to discuss his situation with Hardy, when they met. Thomas Hardy, you understand, the great novelist, who understood the perils of drink, as outlined in several of his novels about rural life. My father loved novels.'

'I don't read much these days. I leave that to my daughter. Life's complicated enough, without reading books about it.'

'I've learned a great deal about life through my reading,' Wendy observes.

Not that Wendy seems inclined to read while she is visiting. Instead, in the evenings she and Edith sit and pass the time in interesting domestic ways. Wendy is teaching Edith to quill. Their heads close together, they curl tiny strands of paper into patterns on cards. The trim little three-dimensional gardens they create out of paper are so pretty and perfect, replicating areas of Edith's own garden, that Edith is sure she can set Wendy up in business. Wendy smiles; she has tried that. She doesn't add to the story, simply basks in the room where they sit. It is full of deep-coloured rugs and old, glossy, dark furniture. Wendy runs her finger approvingly over the polished surfaces; it is another discovery, that they both haunt second-hand and antique shops. A high, horizontal window does not have curtains; the space is filled with the delicate leaves and setting fruit of a giant plum tree that allows filtered light into the room during the day and makes a flickering moonlit presence on all but the darkest nights. Another evening Wendy suggests they begin embroidering for Edith's grandchild. Edith looks vague and hesitant, as if she has forgotten about the forthcoming baby.

'Another night, perhaps.'

'I'd like to meet your daughter.' Wendy looks through the family albums, exclaiming over the children and admiring Roberta's wedding photographs, paying particular attention to Paul. Fine features, she says, but Edith shrugs. 'I'm sure you'll meet them.' Beside their lives here, the long anticipated birth now seems remote and unreal.

For the past month, Roberta hardly seems to have existed, although they talk on the phone once a week. Keep up the fluids, Roberta, remember not to drink alcohol (especially that, but it is unvoiced). When do you think you'll give up work? I've knitted some matinee jackets. My friend is going to embroider them for you — what colours shall we do them? Well, just a friend — you haven't met her, her name's Wendy, you'll have to meet her. Love to Paul, see you soon, oh and I bought a mobile for the spare bedroom the other day — felt animals, lime green and scarlet, with little bells that chime in the breeze. Yes, of course there'll be room for the baby. What's got into you Roberta?

Wendy studies her friend. 'I read somewhere that when friendship is just beginning it's like love — it wants to have everything at once. Colette, I think. Of course my father knew her. Admired her tremendously. What a woman.'

Edith looks puzzled.

'I mean,' says Wendy hurriedly, 'you mustn't let me come between you and your family. Perhaps it's time for me to move on.'

'Of course not. I don't want you to go,' says Edith. She stands; it is time to make the tea. Before they go to bed, they drink pale Ceylonese tea with a bitterish tang, accompanied by wafer-thin slices of lemon. Wendy's sigh of relief is almost audible.

'Perhaps we'll go to town at the weekend,' Edith offers. 'My daughter still works during the week. Or I could invite them over on Saturday.'

'That's the day you're giving the mulching demonstration,' Wendy reminds her.

'Of course, so it is. Well, we'll see Roberta some other time.'

So Wendy wears Edith's clothes and eats Glass's food, growing healthier looking by the day, if no less odd.

seven

BREAKING RULES
IF JOSH THWAITE is investigated perhaps he will go broke, maybe his kids will go hungry. His wife might have a nervous breakdown. Josh Thwaite could do himself an injury, or worse. People kill themselves over less than tax.

These things go through my head while I am waiting for Josh Thwaite to come to the phone. It has been answered by a woman, who sounded suspicious when I told her who I was. Well, I can understand that — I am the tax department, after all. Somehow she made it sound personal. I am fast going off the idea of helping Mr Thwaite, but I can't understand how he could have failed to get the message. I have sent his cheque back to him with a note pointing out the discrepancy. Now it has been returned, unaltered. I am surprised it has got past the sorting system a second time.

'I thought you might have shifted,' I say, when he finally picks up the telephone. He sounds young, puzzled.

'I'm sure I sent it all in.'

'You did,' I say, 'but the cheque was made out for the wrong amount. Look, it's okay, it happens all the time. I'm sure you didn't mean to do it.

'What would be the point?'

'Well,' I say, uncomfortably, 'a lot of people do it. You know, juggle figures. We know the way it is, you stall for time, but it doesn't work like that, we still charge the penalty.

'Hey, shit, I never sent nothing back.'

'We hear stories like this all the time. We realise when people do it on purpose that they're hoping to get more money in soon, but our officers are very thorough.'

'Look, I could do you for this. What are you accusing me of?'

'Nothing,' I say, as patiently as I can. I wish very much that I had minded my own business; soon I will draw attention to myself in the office. 'It doesn't matter, I just wanted to help.'

In the background, the woman who answered the phone yells at him. 'Tell them to stick their taxes up their arses. It's them that owe me.'

He says, uncertainly, his voice not properly guarded from the phone, 'Did you send a letter back to the tax department?'

'Wait,' he says to me.

There is total silence. While it lasts, I begin to imagine what these two are like. Josh, I decide, is a more sinister and difficult young man than I had first thought; he is red-necked and brutal and intractable, determined that he is right about everything; he sits in front of television, a beer in his hand, watching violent videos. His wife is a sullen, thick-waisted woman who hits their children with an open hand and changes the sheets once a month. I shudder, trying to imagine a language of love for this couple, and anticipate the self-righteous arguments I am about to have presented to me.

What he says, is: 'Why are you doing this for me?'

'I don't know,' I reply.

'Have you lost your nerve?' he asks, as if he knows what it is like.

'I'll post the cheque back to you,' I say. 'Just make sure it comes back right next time.'

'What about the penalty?'

'There's nothing I can do about that. But hey, you have a nice Christmas.'

'Happy Christmas to you too,' he says.

TURKEY

THERE WERE DISAPPOINTMENTS at the beginning, but once the wedding date was set, Fay and Milton had found plenty to please them.

'We're very liberal, of course,' Fay said doubtfully to her friends, after Paul first brought Roberta to meet them, 'but we're being positive.' What she meant was that people like Roberta's family, in the country, had a different kind of lifestyle from the Cooksleys. No opera, no nights at the theatre (although Fay has read about the madrigal singers on garden days — that's theatrical, she has to admit), no cappuccinos. 'They seem to have known each other for a while, although Paul didn't let on. Well, best for him to be sure this time, she seems very nice, this Roberta. Students together, she's an educated young woman.'

Fay Cooksley is small and fair and wears designer label clothes and is never seen without what she describes as her grooming in immaculate condition. She tinkles when she walks — her bracelets, her light laughter, her throwaway comments. Fay teaches English at a polytechnic, although this is not a financial necessity; she is known as a good sort, the life and soul of a party. More than this, she is the woman who generally organises the parties. If there is an occasion where people might be enticed to dress up in funny clothes, or make fools of themselves with idiotic speeches, Fay will ensure that they do it. I've got an effervescent kind of personality, I just can't help myself, Fay sometimes tells people. Fay has told her daughter-in-law Roberta this, and Roberta appears willing to believe her.

'I'm a person who doesn't look back,' Fay said. 'Let's get on with life.' The garden setting for the wedding had charmed them. They could ask as many guests as they liked. Edith was a wonderful hostess, although she did leave the wedding party earlier than Fay would have expected. She can still see Edith as she was that day; when Roberta walked into the garden with her father, wearing a simple Grecian gown and flowers in her hair, it was Edith whom Fay watched. Dressed in a burnt orange diaphanous gown that moved with her body, and a cloche hat with feathers sticking straight out behind, she was like a girl from the thirties, and Fay had felt positively vulgar.

But their friends complimented the Cooksleys long afterwards, as if it was they who had chosen the venue and made the arrangements. Fay still feels she doesn't know Roberta very well, although, it has to be said, Roberta does all the right things. She thinks she and her daughter-in-law will become closer after the baby.

All the same, it is mid-morning of Christmas Day and Fay is irritated to find herself being driven by Milton in the direction of Walnut. She had had every intention of putting on Christmas dinner, but she has been outmanoeuvred.

'Oh dear,' Edith had said, over the phone, 'but it's my turn to have Glass's family over. Oh, don't be offended if we don't come, but Glass is so, um, touchy, you could say, about things like that. If we change our minds now, I'd have a war on my hands.'

Fay has been inclined to bring her daughter and her husband into it, but she knows it's too late to summon them from Auckland. They have their own plans.

'It's not as if they come and visit us,' Fay complains to Milton, in the car.

'We'll just have to make a firm arrangement with them for next year,' says Milton. He is a placatory man with an instinct for survival. 'I expect it will be pleasant enough today.'

The dining room table is set for fourteen, with a long, snowy cloth and silver and a low arrangement of fresh roses and gypsophila from the garden. We'll soon be roasting in here, Fay thinks to herself, as the temperature soars outside. She can't imagine why Edith hasn't set out lunch in the garden.

'Kill a thirst, mate,' says Glass, unzipping a beer and thrusting it into Milton's hand. 'Make yourselves at home.' He and Paul have been for a walk around the farm, at Paul's request, so he can see where the circles have been, which doesn't seem to have pleased Glass.

'There's really nothing to see,' says Paul, to his parents, who had the same thing in mind. 'Just a sort of fuzzy outline.'

Fay expects to have met everyone before, at the wedding, but there is a stranger among the women around the silver punch bowl, whom she meets after she has kissed Roberta and Paul.

'This is my friend, Wendy,' says Edith.

Wendy stretches her hand straight out like a man and shakes Fay's hand vigorously. 'I'm so pleased to meet you,' she says, almost pulling Fay physically towards her. Fay, thinking Wendy is about to kiss her as well, withdraws as far as she can. The woman has a cultivated voice, but there is something nervous and excited about her, almost dangerous, Fay thinks. She is dressed rather rakishly in a blue denim jacket and a skirt that is too long for her.

'I hope you're enjoying the day so far,' Wendy says, her voice trembling and high.

'We went to church first thing.'

'Oh I thought you would. C of E, I take it?'

Fay finds this an odd thing for Wendy to say, but she nods. 'Anglican, yes. And you, Joan?' Joan Vance is Glass's sister, whom Edith surveys with barely disguised dislike. Yet they have interests in common. Joan and Arch are horticulturalists with a property further down the road. They supply Edith with her garden requirements, and she sends them clients.

'Press-buts,' says Edith.

Bernard says, 'Orla went to midnight mass. Catholic.' He grins at Joan.

'Oh, eeny meeny miney mo, churches are all the same.'

And Fay realises that she, of all people, is breaking one of the basic rules of polite talk, and finds herself at a loss as to how to switch the talk away from religion. Even Edith looks surprised by her friend's behaviour.

'Time to sit down,' she says loudly. Edith waves a glass in the direction of the table.

'Must dash,' says Wendy, 'got to earn my keep. You know, help with the dinner.' She vanishes to the kitchen, accompanied by Orla, the Nichols' daughter-in-law, whom Fay also thinks is odd.

They shuffle around finding chairs. Place names would have been a help, Fay thinks, pleased to have something to get her teeth into. It is hard to see how they will arrange themselves and, just as she expected, they are all sitting down according to couples. Joan and Arch's two children are a lumpy pair. Sally looks sullen; she has been seeing a young man with whom she had expected to spend Christmas, but his family haven't invited her. Her brother, John, looks simple, Fay thinks.

Finally, most of them are seated — the Nichols, the Cooksleys, the Vances, and Wendy. One place is unoccupied.

'Who's sitting there, Mum?' asks Roberta.

Edith looks perplexed. 'Well, for the life of me I can't think, dear. I must have set one place too many.'

'Shall I take it away?' Roberta asks. 'Make more room?'

'You do take up room enough for two,' cries Joan, and everyone laughs. Roberta is flushed and heavy, as if the baby is much closer than its expected arrival date in late February.

Orla and Wendy are bringing out dishes of roast vegetables — kumara and pumpkin and new potatoes — and small green peas, along with the accompaniments, as Orla calls them, the gravy and cranberry sauce, placing them around the table among the sprigs of holly. Real holly.

Now is the moment for Orla to appear with the turkey, so large that it looks more like a pig off a spit. It is garnished with chipolata sausages. Fay makes a mental note of this to describe to her friends.

'I'm glad it's your turn, Edith,' says Joan. 'Just you wait, girls,' she says, addressing Sally and Roberta, 'sooner or later every housewife and mother has to cook the Christmas turkey.'

There is a commotion outside, and voices on the verandah.

'That's Kaye,' says Glass. 'What's she doing here?'

'Oh my goodness, so it is,' says Edith. 'Well, it's just as well we hadn't started. She must have brought Dorothy.'

'I thought Dorothy was going to Kaye and Frank's,' says Glass sharply. Kaye and Frank are another Nichols sister and brother-in-law, a couple with whom they never share Christmas.

'No, I did ask her, I think.'

'There is a flurry as the men are ordered out to help bring up Dorothy's wheelchair. Dorothy tries to manoeuvre herself up the steps, but she can't lift her legs high enough. Eventually, somebody brings her a chair, and Bernard and John lift her, sitting up straight, into the dining room.

'Well,' says Edith, when they are all seated again, 'Fancy that. Happy Christmas, Dorothy. I knew I must have put that place there for somebody, but I'm blowed if I could think who it was.'

This is so calculated an insult that nobody can miss it except, mercifully, Dorothy herself. She is so pleased to be out of her resthome for the day that she doesn't seem to notice.

'The stuffing's made with chestnuts,' says Edith. She reaches over, picks at a small piece oozing from beneath the parson's nose and tries it. 'Mmmm,' she pronounces, 'you'll like this. Pass me the wine, someone, and let's drink to Christmas.'

Glass, his lips tight, picks up the knife, and begins to carve the turkey.

I HAVE THIS image of my family, the last time we were all together for Christmas.

My mother, indifferent and unreachable, sits leaning her head on one hand, thin silver bracelets dangling from her wrist, an empty glass hanging by its stem from her other hand. Michael is there, the brother I love best. My father, in an almost feminine way, is carving pieces of meat with the precision of a surgeon and laying them down so that the slivers fan out against the fine white plates, the same ones that are on the table today. He doesn't look at my mother or at Michael, who is in disgrace again, lonely and defiant.

'I won't come back again,' he said, that day, and he hasn't been back since, not even for my wedding. The strange thing is that my father and Michael are not unlike. What would my father have been like if he had not accepted, in the end, the weight of expectations that had been laid on him?

I look around the table and wonder if we are going to make it through today. Beside me, Paul is looking resigned. I see him catch his mother's eye across the table, and they each raise a brow, in a delicate fashion.

BERNARD HAS HAD little to say. His wife sits down beside him, at last. She is dressed in a white acrylic jersey and pants in honour of the day, but her top is splattered with grease from the turkey. He watches his father carving the bird, his hands itching to help, but he doesn't dare make the offer.

'What's this?' says his father, and holds up a little bubbling plastic bag on the tip of his knife.

'Oh my God,' says Edith, 'the giblets, how did I forget those?'

'Oh nooo,' shrieks Joan. 'It'll be tainted.'

Bernard is glad that it's not him who has discovered this; it almost makes him feel happy.

The turkey is edible, they all agree; really, if they hadn't known, they'd never have guessed. They pass the wine, they make jokes, they pull crackers and find treasures and funny hats, which they put on. Edith's Christmas pudding is what she describes as Very Old Christmas Pud, stiff with brandy and rum. It's the kind that can be fried up and eaten with ice cream for a week or more afterwards.

The heat is rising, and the fan that Edith has provided is working hard to keep the temperature bearable.

'Shouldn't we drink a toast to Paul and Roberta's baby?'

'We've drunk enough toasts, if you ask me,' says Glass.

'One more or less won't hurt,' says Bernard. 'Who votes on a toast for the baby?'

The room goes quiet, divided between father and son.

'I reckon we should have a toast,' says John Vance. 'Yeah, let's have a toast.'

Dorothy bangs her glass up and down on the table. Bernard fills her and John's glasses and then, because it would be churlish to refuse, they all allow him to top them up.

'To the baby,' says Bernard.

'To the baby,' they echo, all except Roberta, who is holding her hands against her stomach in a nervous way, as if to protect the child. Wendy, sitting beside her, pats her arm, as if they know each other well. Roberta recoils from her touch. She has had nothing to say to Wendy all day.

'You two can teach us a thing or two,' says Bernard. 'Eh, Orla? Have to tell us how it's done.'

Roberta's hand flutters to her throat.

'We wondered if you'd be godparents,' she says to Bernard and Orla, hoping that they will accept the compliment.

'So there is going to be a christening,' says Milton. There is another difficult silence.

Orla looks down at her plate. Milton laughs loudly to cover his embarrassment at his unintended gaffe.

'You could have one for us, eh, Rob?' Bernard says. 'If it's that easy.' He flashes her one of his rare white smiles.

'Stop it, Bernard,' Orla whispers. 'Please.'

'Yes, stop it, Bernard,' says Edith, 'you're embarrassing our guests.'

Orla pushes her chair back from the table, trying to escape, but she is hemmed in by Dorothy's wheelchair. Trembling with rage, Glass brings his fists down in front of him, spilling red wine across the bright white linen.

'That's enough,' he says. 'That's enough of all this.'

MILTON AND FAY leave when they think nobody will notice, but Wendy does, following them out, chattering about the garden, the heat, about the lovely dinner they have all had, trying to delay their departure. In a few moments, Paul sees that his parents are going and follows them out.

'It was nice of you to come,' he says, shaking hands with his father in a formal way.

Fay doesn't say, how did you get into this, son, but you can tell from her expression that this is what she is thinking. This has been quite a different gathering from any she has been to with Roberta's family before. She is reminding herself that Christmas is a bad time of year, but it's also a time when people have a tendency to say what they mean.

'It was nice for Roberta,' Paul says.

'She looks as if she needs a rest,' replies his mother.

'We'll get on the road soon.'

'Thank Edith for asking us, won't you?'

'We will go to your place next year.'

Wendy exclaims over a flower bed, as if she had planted it. 'I must do a bit of trimming and dead-heading here,' she says. She bends and breaks off some roses, handing them to Fay, so that she is forced to wait, while Paul and Milton walk on towards the BMW, parked in the shade.

'I'd like you to have this, too,' says Wendy, in a conspiratorial way. She slips a piece of paper out of a pocket in the denim skirt and hands it to Fay. 'I'm sure it will mean something to you, dear.'

Fay looks at the paper, on which Wendy has inscribed a date. An expression of astonishment crosses her face, followed by a flicker of fear.

'I don't know what this is about,' she says and stuffs the paper back into Wendy's hand. She walks swiftly away, and climbs into the car, without looking back. 'Goodbye dear,' Fay cries hurriedly to Paul, and slams the door shut.

As they speed back to town, Milton says, 'Don't let them bother you. The boy's made his bed and we don't have to see them that often.'

'I had no idea that family drank so much.' Fay stiffens her shoulders against the leather upholstery. 'And what a temper that man has.' She is talking about Glass.

THOUGHTS ABOUT LEAVING

GLASS SITS AT Orla's table drinking instant coffee. They are in the drawn-out, drained-of-emotion days between Christmas and New Year.

Bernard and Orla's house smells of boiled onions and baked puddings. She is a tidy enough woman but there is a bareness about the rooms. Lately, he has been seeking out her conversation. Her tea is too strong, but he drinks it any way. Bog standard Irish, says Edith. He hasn't felt Irish mist on his face, and he doubts that Orla has felt a great deal of it either, rather a cheek-by-jowl tenement house among streets streaming with children, and washing hanging limply across the yards. Her father is a welder in Belfast.

'I hope you don't mind me coming again,' he says. 'There's not much peace up there.'

Orla sits across from Glass, running a hand through her unruly hair. When Glass first knew his daughter-in-law she was small and pixie-like, with a chaste, unused expression, but hopeful — he would have called her eyes hopeful. Today there is something dull about her, dressed in baggy jeans and a loose T-shirt that hides her homely waist. A blowfly is beating itself to death on her windowpane. He wants to thrash it down. In the space of a few weeks he has become fretful, like an old dog. They are all sick of him talking about the circles, but the phenomenon, if that's what it was, has disturbed him, the tenor of their lives.

'You've still got your guest?' asks Orla, although she has seen Wendy only the day before.

This, more than anything, is what he blames on the circles, a third person in his household, who seems to have taken charge.

'I don't like it,' he says. Across the paddocks, Edith and Wendy can be seen at the back of the garden weeding the herbs.

'What's she up to now?' asks Orla, although her mind is not on the conversation; she's heard it all before.

'I found papers disturbed on my desk the other day,' he says.

'You should leave your doors closed.'

'I feel that she's looking for something. I hear her rustling round at night.'

'Perhaps she's just getting a snack from the kitchen,' says Orla thickly. She has begun to cry in a silent yet uncontained way, as if that is the whole object of his being here. Glass has never seen Orla cry.

'I wish I could make things better for you, Orla,' he says. 'D'you want me to speak to Bernard?'

She shakes her head. As she reaches above the sink for a paper towel to wipe her eyes, he stands and puts his arms around her, which is not what he had meant to do. Orla is not a woman for showing affection or allowing it to be shown to her. She has always kept herself to herself. Inside his embrace, he waits for her to tense, but instead she puts her face into his shoulder. She smells of carbolic soap and green apple shampoo.

'My Mam's sick,' she says. 'You'll remember, she said she was coming over here to see me. Well, it's not true.'

'She's a woman who changes her mind, as I recall.'

'She meant to come, she really did. But my sister rang for Christmas. It was all in her head. Mam's dying, Glass. I want to go home.'

'Well, of course you should go. What does Bernard say?'

'I haven't told him,' says Orla. 'Not yet.'

'How did we ever manage without each other?' Edith says. She and Wendy dust their knees down from the weeding and prepare to go inside. She means, of course, how did I ever do without you, but she feels certain that Wendy feels the same.

But Edith is more anxious than she appears. Christmas, she tells herself, was not a disaster. Really, it was not. I behaved better than usual, she tells herself, it was everyone else who was awful. She prefers not to think about Dorothy; she has pretty well forgotten why she enjoys putting her in her place. She has long ago decided that you can forget most things most of the time, when you get older, but Glass is not so sanguine. It's not what he has said, it's what is unsaid between them, even more so than usual. He avoids walking into rooms when Wendy is present, and when she comes into one where he already is, he goes out.

Finally, last night, he had spoken. 'I don't see you any more,' he says.

'I'm here all the time,' said Edith, surprised at this way of putting it, although she had been expecting an approach of some kind.

'So is she. It can't go on.'

'I don't see that she's doing any harm.'

'What does she want from us?' Glass said.

This, too, has taken Edith aback; it hasn't occurred to her that Wendy wants anything but the things she craves — companionship and a delicious intimacy that has been lacking in her life.

'I reckon she's a sponger,' Glass said. Afterwards, he had tossed and turned all night. Sooner or later, Edith knows she will have to deal with the matter.

The cellphone, lying among the garden tools, rings. The call is for Wendy. Edith is surprised; she had never considered whether anyone knew Wendy was here. How had she let them know? She has not seen her posting letters or making phone calls. There is a daughter, she remembers. Sarah, she thinks, although it is clear that Wendy has not seen her for years. Perhaps she lives in another country. Edith has never got round to asking; when she thinks about it, Wendy has never allowed it. But this is a man's voice, brisk and officious. Wendy starts when she hears it. Politely, Edith walks away while the conversation takes place.

When it is over, Wendy stands tapping the phone in the palm of her hand.

'I have to go,' she says. 'I'll leave in the morning.'

'When will you come back?' asks Edith, as if Wendy's home here is permanent.

'I'm not sure,' says Wendy. 'Perhaps I could come again next year?'

Edith realises that Wendy is talking about moving on for good.

'I don't want you to go,' she says, angry with some stranger claiming Wendy in this casual way, even though she can see that Wendy may be providing a solution to a difficulty of her own. 'How far do you have to travel?'

'Not far,' says Wendy vaguely. 'I might visit my daughter, I'm not sure.'

'So she does live in New Zealand?'

'Sarah lives in Palmerston North.'

Clearly, Wendy does not wish Edith to pursue the matter. 'Well, things are a bit up in the air, you see.'

But Edith is aghast. For all these weeks, and over Christmas, Wendy has had family just a short journey from here with whom, presumably, she could have stayed. She gets a glimpse of the matter from Glass's point of view.

'Can we run you to the bus?' Edith asks. 'Or, better still, I could drive you through. We could have a nice day, take a picnic. At least I could meet your daughter.' Straight away, she regrets what she has said — Wendy's daughter might have any manner of afflictions or deficiencies, she may have failed, or be in some way disappointing.

'I doubt if Sarah will be in the mood for visitors,' says Wendy. 'Besides, I've some business to do in the city. I'd be grateful if you could take me to the train in the morning.'

In the evening, she shows Edith a silver bird, which she produces from a large velvet bag she has been keeping in the wardrobe. Her possessions seem heart-rendingly small. The bird is beautiful, and the silverwork as fine as any Edith has seen. Wendy turns it over and shows her the Earl of Maudsley's crest. 'My family,' she comments. 'Of course, I could have bought it at any junk shop, couldn't I?' Her laugh is fleeting.

This could be true, but only a careless dealer would have let a treasure like this slip through at a price Wendy could afford. Though Edith has no doubt Wendy has seen better times.

She mentions this to Glass when they are in bed.

'So she's going,' he says, and touches her breast in a surprised and interested way. 'Be sure you check her bag when she leaves.'

AT THE END OF THE YEAR
MARISE ASKS PAUL and me over for a party on New Year's Eve, but neither of us wants to go.

'What would you like to do?' I ask, hoping he will say that we can just sit and look out at the sea. Last year, our first in the new house, we had had a party ourselves, and at midnight we could see firecrackers going off over the hills, and on the harbour, and from house to house people called out Happy New Year. A wonderful spot, our friends had agreed.

'I think we should go and see my parents,' he says. 'They're off to Fiji soon. We won't get a chance to see them again until they come back.'

So that's what we do. Fay and Milton live in a quiet cul de sac in an expensive neighbourhood. Their house is surrounded by velvet green lawns and magnolia trees and neatly weeded strips of garden. Doors open on to discreet balconies and nooks and a brick courtyard. Inside the house rolling cream carpet is broken by expensive rugs and heavy gold drapes. The look is designed to be both opulent and spacious. Look at our large, expensive house, it always seems to be saying. Perhaps this is unfair. In the beginning, when Paul first took me to visit his parents, this is not what I thought. But I sometimes feel that, in their house a vitality seems to be missing, which is at variance with the way Fay presents her personality. This is how it feels today; Fay looks distracted and drawn, not herself at all.

All the same, she makes an effort, as she always will. We all play croquet in the late afternoon, and Fay makes a warm smoked chicken and melon salad.

'You will finish work soon, won't you, dear?' Fay says, putting a cushion behind my back

'Yes,' I say. 'Can't wait, only another month.'

We don't talk about Christmas at all, for which I am grateful. I want to be forgiven, as if I am responsible. I am polite and compliant and think that I am lucky to be loved by them.

Paul pats my hand absent-mindedly.

eight

A LETTER TO ROBERTA

As soon as he opens his eyes, Glass knows something will happen today. In the half-light of dawn filtering between the heavy curtains that divide the bedroom from the verandah doors and the garden beyond, Glass Nichols sees his wife's face smoothed over with sleep, her mouth slightly open. She sleeps with a great stillness that he has always found restful, in spite of the cloud of gin and fertiliser which clings to her even in bed. Outside, birds are beginning to sing. He listens to his heartbeat, the sound of his mortality.

He wants to shake Edith awake. It is not sex he wants but something else, darker and more primitive, a knowledge of who she is. He wants to hold her and examine her feature by feature — the cool grey eyes, the long spine and the broadening hips, the small moles on her back, the crook of her arms where the flesh is softening, the whorls of pubic hair, the shape of her feet and ankles, the way the second toe is longer than all the rest. Form and shape are what interest him at the moment. When his children were born he had not considered their composition like this, but now it is as if his very life depends upon it, to know how these constellations of the body might merge and blend. He is thinking, what will my grandchild look like? An angry wafer-thin boy like Michael, or a solid meaty boy like Bernard? Or a delicate scrap of flesh like his daughter?

He tries his daughter's name aloud. 'Roberta,' he says, seeing her pale face and swelling body.

'What?' mutters Edith.

'I think the baby will come today.'

'It'd better not,' says Edith, sitting bolt upright. 'It's not due for a month.' It's as if she has spoken in a dream, and she lies straight down again and goes back to sleep.

Very quietly, so as not to disturb her, he slips out of bed and pulls on his clothes. He walks through the house, his house, that he has known since he was a boy, enjoying the quiet rooms. He stands in the doorway of the room, recently vacated by Wendy, which has been prepared for the baby when it comes to visit. He can see it, him, he corrects himself, because he, too, is certain of the sex, tucked up in the bassinet; later the boy will wake before them, demanding to be taken out on the farm by Glass. He smiles to himself.

In his head he starts to compose a letter.

My darling Roberta, he begins. And stops, embarrassed. This is like a love letter, not what he means at all. But he goes on with it anyway, in his imaginary handwriting. *I want to tell you about the time you were born. It was the craziest time of my life. Your mother and I were people cast adrift from responsibility. We didn't live on the farm then. Not our farm, anyway, just places we sharemilked on up north. Sure, we milked cows and were tired day after day, and the boys were growing up and we were responsible to the man who owned the farm, several of them as it happened, but the fact is, that for a long time, nobody noticed us. By that, I mean me. If I did well or badly, it meant nothing more than 'those Nichols down Ten Foot Road aren't up to much'. If we didn't like the farm, we could move on the 1st of June to another one, like sharemilkers do all over the place. My father never got in touch with us and I believed he had written me off for ever. I learned to play the fiddle and the washboard and sing blue grass country. We used to stay up all night till it was time to milk at dawn. We had a great time, though. Your mother was a different girl. Woman, is that what I'm supposed to say to young people? All right, she was a different woman.*

And beggar me, July 16, 1969, if we didn't get you, the same day the first man stepped on the moon. I looked out of the hospital window, and up at the moon. The television was on in the day room, and everyone who could get to it was there, although your mother was lying still and tired in her bed. Can I take her? I said to the nurses, which wasn't done in those days, to carry the baby around after it was born, but because they were excited they didn't notice that I held you, wrapped in your shawl. I walked down the corridor and saw another re-run of Aldrin and Armstrong planting their flag on the ghostly blue moon, as they had done earlier that day, and I said out loud, 'Yeah, fellas, good on you mates', but I don't need to travel through space to find the moon and stars, I've got her right here in my arms. I couldn't believe you were real. Now you wouldn't believe this, because all you Nichols kids are said to take after your mother, but I reckon you were the first one to look like my side of the family. I thought you were so pretty. I saw a look of my own mother, which is not in the others. This one's mine, I said to myself.

I went back to the ward. I want to call her Roberta, I told your mother. She looked up through a haze of pethidine. 'She's meant to be

Teresa,' she said. I said, 'You didn't know my mother, it wasn't her fault what happened to us', because I knew there was old history on her mind. 'Well, it's not a bad name,' your mother agreed, 'quite strong.' And we left it at that. And now you're having a baby of your own, and I don't know how to tell you how happy I am, and how much this will change things all over again.

Glass stops himself, embarrassed, and mentally consigns this unwritten letter to the dust bin.

RETURNS

JOSH THWAITE'S RETURN has appeared on my desk yet again. I cannot believe this. The system has collapsed. If there is one. Nobody really knows what the system is. We are just components of an organisation which is the sum of its parts, one department existing in a vacuum from the rest. The letter is unopened. 'Return to Sender' is scrawled across its face, in a tight, uneven hand. Josh's hand, or the woman called Leda? A wave of panic breaks over me on account of this stranger. Inside me, I feel the baby stirring, anchoring his foot under my rib cage as he shoves his head into the birth canal. All I want is to take a pee; Josh Thwaite, the spray painter, can fall off my computer into some never-never land, where responsibilities like tax and children are beyond reach, I tell myself. I have only three more days in this job and then none of it matters any more.

But there is something merciful and generous stirring in me, which I am fighting to resist. I have never tried to hide things in my work. Yet Josh's incorrect filing of his return seems like a coded message. What is it he said to me? Have I lost my nerve? How would he know?

A queue blocks the entrance to the toilet and I am too tired to stand. I come back into the office and sit down, trying to avoid Marise's eye.

'Are you all right?' she asks.

'Yes, why shouldn't I be?' I don't mean to sound so snappy — I know she is concerned about me — but I wonder if she has been watching me. Has she guessed that my work has become erratic? I wait until she is looking the other way, or at least I think she is, and slide Josh Thwaite's return into my handbag.

A few minutes later, when I have made it to the toilet, I begin to cry. My pants smell like old meat.

Back at my desk, I tell Marise that I can't stay at work. 'I'm feeling dizzy,' I say, 'I'm afraid I'll have to go home for the day.'

PRUDENCE DAVIES SITS in a street-side café on Lambton Quay. Once she would have pretended to read while she was waiting for a man. But Prudence has learned at assertiveness courses that this is child-like and immature, as is not travelling alone, or calling room service when you could go to a restaurant. You read if you want to read, and if you just want to wait for a man well, then you sit and gaze at the world in a cool, level kind of way, as if you have all the time in the world.

And Prudence *is* waiting for a man. 'I'll be out for a couple of hours,' she tells Florence, her secretary. Florence arches her eyebrows.

'Long lunch with Paul?' Florence is twice Prudence's age, with children of her own, and she has been a secretary for years. She can say what she likes and get away with it.

'I'm hoping he'll have come up with an answer to my problem today.'

'Your problem, dear,' says Florence, 'is that you want to get laid by Paul. On a regular basis, that is.'

'Our problem here is that we're short-staffed. Will you have that report done by the time I get back?' snaps Prudence. She has a pert face and small, even teeth and wears tinted, thin-rimmed spectacles for reading, but her reputation doesn't always run to a sense of humour.

Prudence is trying not to think about wretched old Flo and her vulgar remarks as she sits and waits on the Quay. The trouble is, she wants exactly what Flo has outlined. You don't forget old lovers as easily as all that.

And then he arrives, in that dashing, always slightly late style of his that she remembers from when they were students.

'Do you want to move upstairs?' she asks.

'We are doing business,' he reminds her, and her heart lifts. Prudence is an environmental policy analyst, with a budget of her own; she hires and fires staff. She has offered Paul a contract to find her a new office manager. Paul is quite right; they are civilised people, they have no need to hide out in back rooms, simply because of the past.

All the same, they can't help looking at each other, over their coffee, which spreads into lunch, and a glass of wine each. Just one, they say, we can handle that. They toast each other with a mock flourish. Prudence lowers her glass.

'What's the matter?' says Paul.

'I was thinking.'

'Don't.

'About out our twenty-firsts.'

Just a week apart. Fay held a fancy dress party and they all hired *Phantom of the Opera* costumes. Paul was the Phantom; he had lifted his mask and kissed her. 'Marry me,' he had said.

16 DIGGLIE STREET

IT IS ONE of those sprawling dormitory suburbs people call Nappy Valley, reached by way of a treacherous hill road. The houses sit in rows, oblong and multi-coloured, pre-cut and assembled on site, interlocking like pieces of Leggo. The residents say there is more to it than this; there are garden walks and squash clubs, churches and drop-in centres, just like everywhere else. No doubt this is true, but this is not what I see as I cruise through the area where my map tells me Digglie Street should be. Cars rust on the verges and young women dressed in black, with shaven skulls, prowl around the corner dairies. Roads lead to nowhere, except a long way out along a coastal road to a beach where waves shatter against ragged stones.

It was a stupid idea to come here. I am driving in a loop that leads me back to the beginning of the valley. Instead of looking for Josh Thwaite, perhaps I will head out to the coast, take a walk by the sea and clear my head. As I idle the motor, a couple walk towards me, quarrelling and bitter. The man turns in response to something she says and slaps her face hard. The sad, untidy woman falters and walks slowly on behind him, her head bowed.

Wildly, I wonder if this is Josh Thwaite, the brute of my imagination, already unhinged by his financial dilemmas. I gun the engine, taking off without looking where I am going, and suddenly I am at 16 Digglie Street without knowing how I got there. I have to look twice at the number, for the six has fallen upside down so that it looks like a nine. It swings on a post behind an old Bedford van splatter-painted green and brown like an army vehicle. A sign on it reads I GOT A HAIRCUT SO WHERE'S THE JOB?

Josh is in his painting gear when I walk down the path, or at least that's what I take it to be. His face is covered with a mask like a beekeeper's and he wears a once white overall, covered with infinite shades of bright, thick paint, a modern version of Joseph in his coat of many colours. As I push open the gate, the apparition advances down the path, the spray gun in his hand dripping glutinous purple paint. Behind him hang parts of car bodies hanging up to dry in an open shed, like fish ready to be smoked.

'This is the third time. Don't you fucking listen? We're not buying stuff.'

I put down my briefcase and hold out my hand. Even as I'm doing it, I wonder how I will explain a purple paw when I get home. It turns out not to be a problem. Josh Thwaite isn't shaking hands with anyone. He raises his spray gun and I duck.

'You must have me mixed up with someone else, I'm not selling anything.' I can hear how whimpery and apologetic I sound.

Josh lowers the gun. 'A woman in your condition shouldn't be out in the streets like this,' he says, in grudging recognition of my pregnancy.

'I'm not selling anything,' I repeat.

'Pull the other tit, it's benefit day. Everyone flogs off stuff round here on benefit day. I told Leda, nobody's putting a foot through this fucking door today, tomorrow or the next day. Not that she's on a benefit,' he corrects himself swiftly. 'I earn money.'

'I know that, Mr Thwaite. I'm from the Inland Revenue Department.'

Josh drops the gun and grape-purple paint showers the path. 'Fuck,' he says.

'Perhaps I've picked the wrong time.'

'Oh, fuck fuck fuck,' says Josh, and kicks the spray gun into a collapsed paddling pool.

'I was in the area so I thought I'd just introduce myself.'

Josh pushes the mask up off his face. Enter, the hero. Or the knave or the fool. He looks young. His features are rounded and generous, his skin olive; he regards me with large greenish eyes that slant upwards at the corners, under eyebrows which nearly meet across the bridge of his nose. His hair is cut in a straight line above his ears, and curls down his back in a swathe of thick ringlets pulled together with a rubber band. Now that my prey stands revealed in front of me, I am terrified. A royal stud, that's what he is; I should take him back to the office for Marise.

Josh Thwaite has had some bad luck in his life.
    His first car broke down the day that he bought it.
    He lost his Lotto ticket the night his numbers came up.
    And there is the question of the fishing boat that sank like a stone one night when he was out at sea, and all that it has meant for him since.
    He reckons his mother must have walked under a ladder when she was carrying him. Now, here is this Inland Revenue woman who looks like she's off her head, wandered in from the street. He doesn't have so much as a crock of shit at the bottom of the garden, and he wishes he did, just to fool them. He'd make sure they would never find it; bad luck doesn't mean he's not smart. But paperwork isn't the bean in his minestrone. They'll find something, because that's their job, to cause people like him misery and suffering. But it looks as if he's been chosen like a marble out of a jar, a random chance. Or perhaps the woman saw some flaw, something chipped, that he associates with himself and can't explain, can't see, but others do.

nine

CLEARING WRECKAGE
Josh's posture is threatening.

'Personal service, eh? Well, the introductions are over. You can go now. Anyway, I don't believe you, where's your ID?'

When I don't move, he says, 'This is harassment. You said you were going to post the cheque back.'

'I did.'

'No, you didn't.'

'So how come I got it in my in-tray again this morning?'

His shoulders slump as I stoop to open my briefcase.

'They must be crazy,' says Josh, while I fumble through the papers inside. 'They're taking a bit of a risk, sending you out here. Don't they know that?' His tone is unpleasant.

I try to measure the distance to my car but I find my legs are trembling so much I can hardly stand up. A huge weight bears down inside me, like a flower press on rose petals.

'I wanted to help,' I tell him, straightening up to hand him the cheque. 'If you could just correct the amount in the figures compartment and initial it, the problem's solved.'

I watch him hesitating before he accepts the cheque. When he has studied it, he looks at me with real and growing wonder. 'I see what you mean,' he says at last. 'But you came all the way out here to tell me this? What's happening, the Inland Revenue going broke?'

'No.' I am gasping for breath, beginning to pant with the exertion of trying to explain. A pain like a butter churn has developed in my abdomen.

'They'd notice you if I put it in the unclean box. Revenue Control would start to take an interest, can't you see?'

'Jesus.' Josh's bafflement is too much for him. He wipes his hand over his nose, smearing it with purple paint. 'I'm doing a perkie for a mate. Guy wants his Honda painted the colour of grapes. It's hard to get it right. Never painted grape before. Are you all right?'

I can't remember answering this. The sun is a bright lemon-coloured circle above my head, the world turned full of primary-colours. At my feet lies a bright red puddle which isn't part of Josh's artwork.

A woman's voice bellows from an open window. 'Hey dickhead, what d'you think you're up to?' The door crashes open and Leda comes flying down the path, her fists raised. She's thin, wiry and dark, wearing a headband, a black jacket even though the day's so hot, and tight jeans. Her hands are covered with heavy silver rings like knuckle-dusters.

'Another one of your girlfriends?' she snarls at Josh, assessing my condition.

'Never seen her in my life.'

'Some shit.' Leda's mouth is thin and mean. For all the fury, there is something cloudy and distant about her eyes.

'Help me, please.' I have fallen to my knees on the path.

'It's the tax department,' says Josh.

'I can see why she's been after you.' She is spitting contempt.

'Quit it, Leda, she's having her baby.'

'Tell her to have it somewhere else.'

'Call an ambulance,' says Josh. 'Hurry up, or I'll smack you in.' With a flounce, Leda disappears inside. He kneels beside me, taking my hand as he helps me to lie down on the grass beside the path. He cradles my head against his knee. 'What's your name, Mrs Inland Revenue?'

'Roberta.'

'Roberta who?'

I close my eyes, giving myself up to pain, partly because I have no choice, but also because I don't want to answer him. I have visions of him extracting information inch by inch, of phone calls, of Paul's discovery of where I am and of what I have done. Because, already, I am aware that I am involved in consequences. All I want is to get away safely, back to where I belong, without anyone knowing where I have been.

But my baby has his toes in my throat as if he is trying to push himself clear, like a swimmer freeing himself from a bank into midstream.

'Don't push,' Josh says, 'for Christ's sake, don't push. You'll tear yourself to bits if you do.'

Leda reappears from the house. 'There's been a truck and trailer crash on the hill,' she tells him. 'They can't get an ambulance here for at least twenty minutes.'

They look at each other. 'Take her,' says Leda. 'Go on, just get her out of here.' I can see, even from where I am, that she has shifted her position, that she accepts a responsibility she doesn't feel for me. Perhaps it is just self-preservation; what she has on her doorstep could cause a bigger problem for her than she needs — there is the question of tax, and of the way Josh looks at her when he is impatient, as he is now.

Already he is helping me on to my feet; Leda, smelling of dope and Napisan, holds me up while he opens the van. She digs her fingers into my arm so hard that it hurts.

'You'll have to lie down in the back,' he says. 'I'll drive slowly.' I am thinking that Leda will come with us, but children are emerging from the house and I see that either they will come with us, or Leda will have to leave them on their own. It will be Josh and me, the two of us.

'Just hold on and breathe nice and slow,' Josh says, 'you know about that?' Leda has produced a grey-looking pillow, which he arranges beneath my cheek. Very slowly, yet steadily, the van takes off along the road. I try to concentrate on the inside of the van, hoping to stave off another contraction; it is an interesting variation on thinking of England. The steering wheel is covered with tiger skin; crystals and a brass cross hang over the back window. The lights in the crystals are a distraction, dark eddies of fire and gold, like the forces at work in my body, shimmering and glowing above me. As much as I am able, I give myself over to this light.

'Bloody hell,' says Josh. We have arrived at the accident site near the crest of the hill. The ambulances have gone, but the road is still blocked by wrecked vehicles and police cars. We are caught in a build-up of traffic that stretches out of sight down the other side. Josh stops the van and comes round to me in the back seat.

'Roberta,' he says, as if I am an animal he is shepherding, 'I'm going to leave you for a minute.'

'Please don't.' I can remember clutching his hand, desperate for reassurance that I won't be alone. He leans over me and I smell mint, wild and clean, as if I am having my baby in the great outdoors.

Which, in a sense, I am. In a lucid second, before the pain grabs again, I recognise spearmint gum; Josh is close to me, taking on the same laboured breathing patterns as my own, as if he has become part of the action.

'I'm not going anywhere without you,' he tells me. 'There's a pile of traffic cops up there. I'll get them to clear a path through for us. They can phone ahead and tell Hutt Hospital we're on our way.'

'But I'm supposed to have my baby in town.'

He smoothes my face with the palm of his hand. 'It's too late for that.'

'Why did you come?' he says, while we are waiting for the police to come. 'Didn't you know it was going to happen?'

'It's my first,' I say. There is such a current of energy between us that it scares me. I search blindly for his hand.

'Who are you? What's your name?' he asks.

'I told you.'

'Yes, but the rest of it. This is crazy. I mean, man, it's fucking surreal.'

'I muster the strength to put my fingers on his lips. 'Don't keep asking questions,' I say. Though everything he is asking me is perfectly reasonable. How come I didn't know this morning? Or did I? I probably did. I want to explain to him the way I've watched animals go off on the farm to have their offspring. They don't want anyone around. Only this sounds precious and absurd. People want people, this is what we've been taught. It is clear to me that this is not Josh's first delivery and I guess he would find my reasoning unsound. It's not even reason, it's something more primitive and strange, the difficult side of my nature. If I look down off the beam I will fall. I am afraid that he will start massaging and prodding me, as Ann Claude has shown the men, but, also, I am terrified that he will leave me.

'I'll take her in my car, sonny,' says the policeman.

I shape a silent no at him, but I hope that it has the force of a scream.

'I don't think she can be shifted again,' says Josh. 'Too risky.'

The policeman hesitates; he's even younger than Josh, and nervous. You can see it running through his mind that he might be doing the wrong thing, but he doesn't want me in his car, because that might turn out to be a bigger mistake.

'Can you sit her up?'

'I'll try,' says Josh, and I find that, after all, I can sit up, with the belt looped across me. This seems to satisfy the policeman.

'Okay,' he says, 'let's go.'

'Ever been part of a car chase?' Josh asks. Sirens are wailing and lights flashing all the way across the hill, round the tortuous bends. There are police cars behind and ahead of the van. The young policeman talks into his radio; he turns to smile and nod encouragement as he leads us through the red lights.

As we sweep through the hospital gates, a huge pain bears down through my pelvis, grating me up as if my bones are caught in a vice.

'She could have done with an epidural but I think she's closer than that,' Josh tells the orderly who wheels me through the corridors. The sense of drama follows us on past afternoon visitors arriving with bunches of flowers and bags of grapes.

'You coming in with her?' the orderly says to Josh, as if there is really no question.

'What do you want, Mrs Inland Revenue?' he asks.

'I want you to be around, that's all,' I say, ' no big deal.'

ROBERTA'S BABY

A MIDWIFE HAS been hastily summoned as she dons her bike helmet to go home after a previous delivery, and she and an older nurse, also on relief, have taken charge of the delivery room. The ceiling is filled with luminous lights like flying saucer discs.

'She won't be long,' the midwife tells Josh, when he reappears wearing a gown. She has short-cropped hair and double-pierced ears. She shoots Josh a puzzled glance, as if she's seen him before. He holds a glass of water to my dry lips, wiping my burning face with a damp, cold cloth. Even my teeth have begun to ache, like people who get caught unexpectedly at very high altitudes.

'Shit,' I yell. I bite Josh's hand.

'Language,' says the older nurse.

'Leave off,' Josh says, his voice totally focused around me. He seems unfazed by my attack.

'Nearly there,' the midwife says. 'Look, you can see the crown, it's dark.'

Josh looks at me, and I look straight back at him. 'You can go now,' I say. I want to show him but I can't. I have an interior journey to make and he knows it's time for him to leave. If Paul were here he would be busy organising me and demanding that I have gas and pain relief and all that sort of thing, whether I wanted it or not. Paul would be scared.

'Just don't get too far away,' I tell him.

'Never mind,' says the midwife, whose name is Poppy, when he's gone, 'there was a time when all men did was fetch the hot water.'

I don't bother explaining to her that I'm happy about Josh Thwaite being a filler of water bowls — this is what I want.

I am handed a mirror and, in it, I see that the wide house of my body is opening, my flesh has turned raisin brown and in its centre is a growing sprout of hair. The huge disc-like lights hover above me, ebbing backwards and forwards. In a moment, like an exploding star, my son is born.

'Yes,' I say, triumphant, 'yess.' I have done it, all on my own.

And there is his cry, a thin little bark that grows louder and stronger.

'Tell Josh he can come in,' I say, when I have caught my breath, tasting his name for the first time.

In a few minutes, while the midwife works over me, the nurse hands my boy, clean and rolled in a white cotton blanket, to Josh.

'Have you got a name for him?' the nurse asks me.

'Nathan,' I tell her. I say it right off the top of my head, not a name I've thought of before. Josh nods his approval, doting over my son in a face-splitting way.

'Your first?' the midwife asks him, again with that quizzical expression.

'No,' says Josh, pushing the baby into her arms. The violence of his reply shocks everyone in the room. He starts to back away, his face now frozen in a kind of horror as he looks at me.

'Paul's the father,' I say weakly. 'We'll have to get Paul.'

'Oh dear,' says the relieving nurse. Her look indicates that I should count myself lucky to have anyone here at all, in the circumstances. She has seen us all, young women who have had sex with so many men that, science or no science, even DNA couldn't sort out who and when our babies have been conceived. She doesn't need to say it — a slut's a slut.

'I don't want any fights in here,' is what she does say.

'I'm not responsible,' says Josh.

'They all say that.'

'Paul's my husband,' I insist. 'He works in the city.'

'He won't like this then.'

'No,' I agree, 'he won't.'

Josh slides out the door.

'Somebody will be coming round to take your details soon,' the midwife says. 'I can't understand how you didn't book in. Haven't you been seeing a doctor?'

'Of course I have. Mr Maitland.' I note her surprise with satisfaction. 'The baby wasn't due for another month.'

'The midwife sits on the end of the bed. I can see her and the nurse reappraising me. The midwife's glance takes in my gold watch, which nobody has had time to remove, and the circle of diamonds beside my wedding band.

'Impossible. He's nearly eight pounds.'

'He'd probably have been an elephant if he'd waited any longer,' I say, looking down at him. I hold him gingerly as he looks for something in a blind, bunting way. His fists open and close, as if he is surprised to find himself where he is. I give him my finger to hold, so that he doesn't feel as if he has come into the world empty-handed.

'Monkey face,' I say.

He has fine delicate bones and a big pulsating fontanelle and eyes that are unmistakeably blue.

The midwife eases the hospital gown away from my breast, and pushes Nathan's head against it. He attaches himself to my nipple like a vigorous little suction pump. I look from one woman to the other, suddenly not knowing what to say.

'It wasn't meant to happen like this. Please find my husband. Did the man who brought me here leave any of my things?'

I am thinking that somebody will have to worry about my car later on but, for the moment, I need my handbag, which contains my credit cards, my library card, my tax number, my passport, my supermarket ID, our tickets for the last wine and food festival and, most important, a list of phone numbers. My bag and briefcase have been left at the desk. The staff are puzzled but courteous. They have become helpful.

Alone in the delivery room, I hear, through the wall, the voice of a very young girl whimpering like a cornered animal. Only thirteen, the nurses tell me. What is the world coming to? No, oh no, she says over and again. No, please stop it, please, oh no, please, I don't want to have a baby.

But I know now that nothing on earth will stop a baby once it is ready to come. I wonder if this girl is the one who came to antenatal classes, but of course that girl will end up in the hospital where she was meant to go. Everything will have gone wrong, her life, her illicit fumble with a class mate (for that is how I imagine it must have been), the hopes her mother has invested in her pathetic, pretty daughter, but at least she will be in the right place. The people surrounding her will be familiar, beloved. Not a stranger bearing a purple gun.

I feel Nathan slipping from my grasp and it would be the easiest thing simply to let go. Paul and I have planned a perfect birth for this baby, but Paul has not been there, is not even aware of his son's existence. And it's not his fault, it's mine. I have gone to a strange place, and been delivered of a child, as the Bible would have it, among strangers, braying in the arms of a man I have never seen in my life. My elation has drained away.

Very carefully, I lower Nathan on to the bed beside me, and lie back against the pillows.

ten

BIRTH NOTICES

MARISE IS THE first to reach Roberta. 'Don't tell them where I was,' Roberta says, when Marise arrives at the delivery suite.

'What did you think you were doing?' Marise is no fool; there is no point in trying to hide what she has already worked out anyway. She had left her computer on at Josh Thwaite's file.

'Don't make it worse.'

'What will you tell them?'

'Nothing.'

'Okay, so what will I tell them?'

'Anything, make something up, you're good at that.

Marise smiles in a malicious, thoughtful way. Roberta closes her eyes.

FOXING, GLASS THINKS, watching his daughter. He knows when creatures are absenting themselves from their situation. It is like dying animals, often it seems as if they have entered the realm of death while their limbs are still twitching. Not that he thinks his daughter is dying, not that exactly, but something has changed in her, something that frightens him. She is like a war casualty.

Edith and Glass and Fay and Milton cluster round the bed. Edith and Glass have come in a hurry, Edith's face naked, except for the broken red veins that bloom in her cheeks when she hasn't had time to cover them with make-up. Fay is a woman good at carrying things off, but her composure is badly shaken. Milton's smile is sheepish and engaging. What was it someone down at the yards had said to Glass, after meeting Milton? He remembers. A man who interviews well and changes jobs often. He'd spat in a pen of Herefords. Top jobs, he's a club man, mark my word. There is more to his smile than meets the eye.

His daughter's crime is to have had her baby in the wrong place, at the wrong time. She should never have been where she was. *She has brought it on herself.* The accusation hangs unspoken but heavy in the air.

'It could have happened anywhere,' Marise says. 'You could tell by the way Roberta was prowling about that something was wrong.'

'Then why didn't she go home? Any . . . ' Paul stops himself. He had been going to say any normal person. 'Anyone else would have gone home.'

'She doesn't have experience at having babies,' says Marise, adopting the role of expert.

'This man who delivered her baby on the back seat of his car, who is he?' Paul asks, his voice cold.

Roberta opens her mouth as if to speak and changes her mind. Nobody except Glass notices. She wants to argue with him, he thinks, tell him it wasn't like that, which he already knows. But she won't.

As much as possible, with so many people crammed in the small room, Marise looks Paul up and down. 'I wouldn't have a clue,' she says.

'You must know who she was going to see.'

'She didn't tell me.'

'Hadn't she talked about any of the cases she was dealing with?'

'Don't you know about the Privacy Act?' Marise produces a nail file from her handbag, and begins to shape her nails with elaborate care.

'This is a little different,' Paul snaps.

In a way, he is speaking for each of them. They are all trying to picture this stranger who has taken over the role of father, and disappeared now, like an odd mirage, a flicker in their collective imagination.

Roberta is looking for the stranger too, Glass thinks. He is shocked by the realisation, but he can tell that it is true. Paul, standing beside her, looking foolish and embarrassed, when he might have been proud, is not who she wants. He wonders where Paul was; it has taken hours for his parents to track him down. Glass tries to ignore the sharpness of the voices and the tension in the air, and concentrates on the baby. He sees perfection, the child smooth and unmarked from his rapid transit into the world, but perhaps that is what all grandparents see. The child is fairer than he had expected, but he can't see himself in the little sleeping face.

'So who do you think he looks like?' Edith asks, bending over the bassinet. Her voice is thickened like lemon honey, a dangerous sign, her eyelids swollen.

'Oh, he's Paul's double,' says Fay, 'and he's always looked like his father, right from the start.'

'Shall I hold him?,' Edith says. 'I am his grandmother.'
'Be careful,' says Paul.

'I'll lift him,' Fay says smoothly. This is how Fay gets to be the first grandmother to hold the baby. She and Milton stand side by side, smiling and comparing the shape of his face with both of their own.

'He's a dear wee man,' says Fay, relinquishing him to Edith.

'Just a few more minutes,' says a nurse, putting her head round the door. 'Mum and Dad need some time to get to know their new baby. And mother needs a rest by the look of things.'

Edith broods over the baby. 'Not a Nichols,' she says, with satisfaction. 'So what's his name?'

'Paul shifts uncomfortably. 'The nurse says she's going to call him Nathan.'

'Darling, I thought you'd chosen Adrian,' Fay says.

Paul shrugs uncomfortably. 'Whatever.'

Edith stands up, her voice calm and crisp, as if she has suddenly woken refreshed from a nap. 'Nathan. Excellent. A gift from God. Old Testament.'

'Really,' Fay murmurs, 'must we always bring religion into it?'

'Jewish, isn't it?' murmurs Milton. 'I hadn't realised.' He has continued to hover like a good public servant.

'We're not.' Glass stops himself, astonished at how easily he is drawn into taking sides in what is, after all, only sniper fire. But this knowledge, too, horrifies him, because it tells him that, in the space of a few minutes, battle lines have developed between these civilised and ordinary families.

'Well, as long as you've got it decided for the birth notice.' This, from Fay.

'We don't need a birth notice,' says Roberta, opening her eyes.

'Don't be silly, dear,' says Fay, as if Roberta has been part of the conversation all along. 'My friends at work are dying to know all about it. You have to have a birth notice.'

'I don't,' says Roberta. 'People put such stupid rot in the papers.'

'We've got nothing to be ashamed of, Roberta,' Paul blurts.

There is another of those unpleasant silences.

'We don't have to put in any details,' says Paul, compounding the embarrassment.

'I'm sorry to bring it up,' says Fay, 'but we are booked in for Fiji this week. Should I cancel my bookings?'

'We've paid for them,' says Milton.

'Do Bernard and Orla know about the baby?' Roberta asks Glass, without answering her in-laws.

'Yes,' says Edith, too quickly.

'What did they say? Are they pleased?'

'Why don't we let Roberta have a rest?' Marise encourages them. As she takes the baby from Edith's unresisting arms, he curls his fingers around her thumb, looking for his mother. Marise's face is fierce with concentration as she lays Nathan down in his bassinet. She, Fay and Milton prepare to leave.

'You go too, Paul,' says Roberta.

'For God's sake, Roberta.'

'I need some sleep. They won't keep me in here for long.'

'We were entitled to two weeks by law when I had you children,' Edith says.

'It all depended,' says Fay.

'Depended on what?' Milton asks.

Fay shakes her head as if she's forgotten where she is and bites her lip.

They move towards the exit sign but Glass hangs back. 'I'll catch you up,' he tells them. Paul hesitates before he picks up his jacket and walks out. Later, Roberta will think that this was when things were decided between them.

Glass takes her hand in his.

'I never met Josh Thwaite before, Dad. The man who came with me to the hospital.'

'It doesn't matter,' says Glass.

'But it's true.'

'I know,' says Glass.

'Dad,' says Roberta. 'I don't want this baby. He's nothing but trouble.'

Glass feels himself go cold and quiet inside. He has to find a nurse, get something to settle his daughter down. Their proximity to each other feels dangerous and mad. He doesn't want to know her secrets. The trouble is, he knows her, sees in her his own divided self.

'You don't mean that,' he says. 'You'll love him.'

'I do,' says Roberta. 'That's not the point.'

'Paul will get over this.'

'I'm frightened,' she says.'

Sometimes we have to learn to do the things we're most scared of.' He is seeing her, of course, up in space, looking down.

'Then what happens?'

He puts her hand carefully under the cover and straightens the sheet, desperate to reassure her.

'You can pretend you're not scared,' he says. 'It's a start.'

eleven

REGRETS

INSTEAD OF GOING home, the next morning Roberta and Nathan are transferred by ambulance to the hospital in town.

'What's wrong with me?' Roberta asks. The birth has been so swift, she feels so fit, that she expects to be sent home the next day.

'Nothing,' says Mr Maitland, smoothly. 'You're in very good health.'

'Mr Maitland wants to keep an eye on you,' says a nurse when she enquires further. 'Just for observation.'

Paul travels in the ambulance with Roberta. He arrives, ready for the journey, looking quiet and apologetic.

'We'll have to arrange to get my car back,' says Roberta, for something to say.

'It was parked in our driveway with the keys under the mat when I got home last night,' Paul tells her.

'Well, that settles that.'

'Um, I did find the guy.'

'You what?'

'The hospital gave me his name.'

'You didn't go and see him?'

'Well, of course I did.'

'He wasn't very friendly,' Paul says, holding her hand as they trundle at a sedate pace down the motorway. She has always thought that you would travel fast in an ambulance, with flashing lights and a siren. Though, come to think of it, she has had enough of that lately.

'I could have told you that,' Roberta says.

'You didn't, though. You didn't tell me anything about him.'

She doesn't reply. It seems pointless explaining to Paul how obnoxious his behaviour had been the previous day.

'Don't hold it against me,' Paul says. 'It was a shock for me. I can see that you weren't yourself, everybody's reminded me that your hormones were out of kilter. I guess something just clicked in your brain when you went into labour.'

'Well, thank you,' she says. 'It's good to get a diagnosis.'

'I just wanted to put things right with that guy. Let him know we were grateful.'

'What did he say?'

'Fuck off.'

'Well, he would, wouldn't he?'

She is mortified by her mental picture of Paul turning up on Josh's doorstep. And, worse in a way, what Paul will have made of the circumstances.

'I could see he was on the bones of his backside. I offered him a hundred bucks.'

'No!'

'Okay, bad move. Day full of bad moves. Let's just start again, shall we? We've got the rest of our lives. We've got our baby.'

'I'm sorry, Paul,' Roberta says, and she is. She is full of contrition and a longing to put things right, to return to some distant time when it seemed that they had perfect understanding. 'I'm truly sorry about all this.'

'Oh, hon.' He puts his arm around her as nearly as he is able, because they are strapped sideways on the bench in the back of the ambulance. She knows that he is pleased with this admission of impropriety; people don't say sorry unless they must. He hopes his pleasure is secret, but she knows better.

'This has been a hideous experience for you. Let's just put it behind us,' he says, magnanimous.

'I CAN'T BELIEVE she'd do that,' Prudence says. 'I mean, it's really irresponsible.'

'I still can't understand it, either,' agrees Paul. They are eating asparagus rolls in Kirkcaldie and Stains' tearooms. It's Fay's birthday tomorrow, and Paul hasn't had a clue what to buy her before she leaves for her holiday. He is grateful that Prudence has offered to help. They have settled for a perfume which Prudence remembers Fay has always liked, and then a cup of coffee and a snack seemed in order.

'It seems quite, well, um, if you don't mind me saying so, pretty odd.'

'I know, don't spell it out to me.'

'But the baby *is* all right?' says Prudence.

'Oh yeah, he's a neat little guy,' Paul says. 'Kind of cute.'

'I guess babies always are.'

'No really, Prue, he's nice. Quite smooth, you know, not all scrunched up like some of them are.'

'Does he cry a lot?'

'Wait till he gets home and I'll let you know.'

'Ah me,' says Prudence with a dramatic little sigh. 'Some are born to responsibility, Paul.' She gathers her handbag up with a display of organising its contents and checking her diary. 'The rest of us just have a good time. I really should be getting back to work.'

'I'm sorry, I didn't realise you were in a rush.'

'Mistakes happen, Paul,' says Prudence. 'That's the way it is, people just make mistakes.'

'So that's it?'

'We're both pretty busy, I guess. Spot you, Paul.'

He watches Prudence's neat little bottom disappearing through kitchenware.

THE WATER BEARER

PAUL BRINGS FRESH fruit and flowers every day, which add to the growing profusion of floral arrangements around her bed. The obligatory birth notice appeared the very next day after Nathan's birth. Roberta hadn't realised she knew so many people, but when she begins to count up her family, all aunts and uncles and cousins, they are, well, countless. At first, the nurses lift Nathan into her arms every time they pass. She notices they don't do this with the other women, for whom it is assumed that feeding comes naturally. As Mr Maitland has instructed, she is being watched.

'Your milk's coming in well,' says one of the nurses, encouragingly. But she doesn't need encouragement. Nathan's lips around her nipple give her an odd sensation; she thinks of cows letting down their milk when the cups are put on, and supposes this must be the same. The milk is drawn as if from a deep well and it surprises her how distinctly she can chart its course. She has never believed that people can feel blood coursing through their veins, but milk seems different, a separate force, as tangible as the movements of a baby before it is born. Sometimes she looks in disbelief at Nathan's shock of hair lying in her hand, as she manoeuvres him on to a swollen breast. He is so complete, so ready to launch himself into life.

Between feeds and bathing and changing Nathan, she shows him to visitors bearing gifts which she unwraps and exclaims over.

There are blue stretch-and-grows and blue booties, blue mittens and blue matinee jackets, bundles and bundles of Treasures (which Paul says are environmentally unfriendly and they should use only in an emergency; at the rate she is accumulating them it looks as though they are set for a lifetime of crisis), Buzzy Bees, Bunnykin plates and mugs, a nappy changing board, vouchers for baby shops from people who believe that they already have just about everything. Edith brings a silver spoon. 'You couldn't exactly say he had an auspicious start,' she says, 'a bit like Jesus born in a manger, really. I thought we could give him a silver spoon and pretend he was born with it in his mouth.'

'Gee, thanks, Mum,' says Roberta. She guesses that Edith is waiting for her to say more, but she doesn't.

An arrangement of flowers arrives with a card from Bernard and Orla, although she has heard that Orla has gone away. It is an overly extravagant bunch of flowers with little chocolate bars piled inside the cellophane wrappings. The wrappers have things like 'I Love You' and 'You're So Cute' printed on them. *I'll see you soon as I can,* Bernard has written on the card, *but you know what it's like with cows, and all,* and she does know. Now that Orla's gone — done a vanishing act, as her mother puts it — Glass can't come to see Roberta either because he has to work in the cowshed.

Marise brings still more flowers, a designer composition of sunflowers and willow branches and snapdragons, jewel colours wrapped up in brilliant layers of tissue, turquoise and magenta and gold. There is something anarchical about them; they make Roberta feel strong and dazzling, and at the same time they are so beautiful that she is transported back into that endless mythical summer of childhood, before she believed anything could go wrong in her life.

A card comes from Helen, she of the gloomy pronouncements and the burnished, well-to-do husband, saying how lovely to have it over earlier than expected.

A lumpy envelope, delivered to the hospital and not sent through the mail, also arrives. It contains a lucky charm bracelet, hung with a crooked star and a water bearer, the Aquarius symbol, which, she realises for the first time, is Nathan's. There is no card. She can't think who has sent her this, perhaps one of the very young women from work . . .

On the evening of the second day, she is joined in the ward by Michelle, who had been due to have her baby before Roberta. She and Sandy, of the pink and green lounging suit, have a daughter. Sandy buys her spectacular presents: a porcelain music box shaped like the Madonna that plays 'Ave Maria', and a fourteen-carat gold eternity ring studded with sapphires and diamonds, with hooped earrings to match. Roberta pretends to be asleep when he comes to visit. When he has left, Michelle stretches out her chubby little hand bearing the new ring.

'Did your husband buy you some jewellery?' she asks.

'Yes,' Roberta lies. 'he gave me this.' She shows Michelle the charm bracelet, without letting her linger over it.

GRIEF

ON THE THIRD day after Nathan's birth, Roberta begins to cry. It starts as quiet weeping, which she hopes other people won't notice. Especially, she doesn't want Michelle to notice. When she has been crying for a few minutes, something worse overtakes her, a dark wretchedness, which emerges as sobbing she can't control.

Staff come running to her side.

Third day blues. It will pass, they say.

A nurse sits on the bed, the curtains drawn around them. She is a well-scrubbed young woman, ingrained with antiseptic. She has not long finished smoking a cigarette. 'Heaps of new mothers cry like this. It's hormonal. Didn't they tell you about this at antenatal?'

Roberta stares in disbelief at the curtains. Nobody else shares her despair. Michelle and she have been to the same lectures, but she is not howling like this. And yes, she does remember being told that this could happen, but it was hard to imagine then what it might be like. She would be so pleased and happy when her baby was born that sorrow like this would be impossible.

The nurse is patient and kind, eager to explain in the best textbook way. 'When you're pregnant you have a really high hormonal output. When you go into labour your oestrogen and progesterone levels are fifty times higher than before you got pregnant. So then, when you have the baby, they drop right back to where they were before. It's enough to make anybody cry, like drug withdrawal.'

Roberta is grateful that she is being treated like a real person who can understand and follow this, and she stops crying long enough to ask the nurse if this has ever happened to her.

'No way, thanks, babies aren't for me.' She laughs, but not unkindly. Her fingernails are bitten.

'I know I should be happy,' Roberta says. She wants to explain the dark mood which has overtaken her, but it's impossible. She thinks of what her father has told her. I must believe that I am happy, she tells herself — if I believe, it will come true. Nathan lies asleep beside her, unconscious of how his unscheduled appearance, his existence, have made her body feel as if it's hit a solid object, and turned her head into something resembling the contents of a scrambled computer.

There is concern in the way that the nurse looks at her. 'I'm going to get your doctor,' she says.

'Oh, he mightn't like to be disturbed.'

'We'll take a chance on that.'

'You said this was just normal.'

'I was forgetting,' she says, with a tactful hesitation. Roberta knows they are back at the episode of Nathan's birth; it points to the possibility of her being unhinged. Women who have babies in the street are unreliable. They may be mad. She can tell that the stories around her are multiplying.

'I'm not suicidal,' she says. 'You won't find me hanging from the shower rail.'

'I still think he should come.'

And crotchety Mr Maitland does come, rubbing his hands together with a sound like chamois leather on the side of a damp car.

'Well, my dear,' he says. His attitude is friendlier. He can't have made much money out of her, not even his delivery fee, Roberta thinks. Perhaps he can add this to the bill.

Mr Maitland scratches his index finger back and forth over his upper lip. Whatever he thinks, it demands his deepest concentration. 'I think that you would be better off at home.'

'Thank you,' Roberta whispers. She wants to get away from the hospital, away from all this normality and cheerfulness, and women who have perfected the process of childbirth.

'Good, that's settled. It might be an idea if you had a few sleeping tablets to help you through the first few nights. Mothers need sleep.'

Although Roberta's instincts are against this suggestion, it has a certain appeal. She realises she is so tired that she cannot think. The last sleep she remembers having is a strange deep slumber after Nathan's birth.

'What if I don't hear Nathan wake up when I go home?'

'That's what husbands are for,' he says, with a return of the fatherly smiles he gave her when she had first begun attending him. 'You're lucky you have a husband.'

RECOGNITION

THE HOUSE IS clean and bright when they get home, everything in its place. The sea is blue and shiny, the pot plants in the courtyard have been kept watered; they glow with summer flowers.

'Welcome home, hon,' says Paul. He is carrying Nathan as if he were a dish of eggs.

They stand by the window, still awkward with each other, not knowing what to say.

'What do you think?' Roberta says.

'I think it's time he and I got to know each other.' Nathan opens his sleepy eyes and, if she hadn't known better, Roberta would have sworn he looked at Paul like a kid who's just seen a rock star.

'It'll be okay,' Roberta tells herself. 'It'll be all right.'

twelve

POULTICES

FOR THE FIRST week Roberta is home, the hospital picks up the napkins and delivers them back, fresh and still warm from the hospital driers. The Plunket nurse visits. 'What a gorgeous house,' she says. 'He's a lucky little boy to come home to a place like this. You should see some places.' But her look indicates that people like Roberta could not imagine houses too awful for the human spirit to flourish.

Roberta develops mastitis. Her nipples harden and crack and she thinks she looks like a cow with swollen udders. Paul seems almost relieved, as if this visible illness is something he can comprehend. He rings Edith, who recommends hot packs, and binding of the breasts. She sounds harassed and distant when Paul hands the phone over to Roberta.

Nathan cries all one night. Paul walks up and down with him. 'Don't panic,' he says. 'Wind, I expect. Isn't that what babies get?' He rubs Nathan's back and for a while the baby sleeps on his shoulder. 'There,' he says, as if it is easy. But when he puts him down, Nathan is away again. 'If you could just feed him again.'

Her milk won't let down because she is afraid the child will hurt her when he suckles.

'Try,' says Paul, 'or I'll have to ring the doctor.' It is three o' clock in the morning and she cannot imagine Mr Maitland's response if he were to be phoned up now.

'I'll call him first thing in the morning,' she promises. 'Go back to sleep and I'll look after him.' Paul has to go to work; she knows she has to learn to cope.

'All right then,' he says, and buries his head under the covers. He sighs and tosses in a dramatic kind of way. It is the first time he has been irritable with her in the month that she has been home.

Roberta takes Nathan downstairs to sit in the bright kitchen with its rimu trim and marble-topped benches. Somehow she must feed him. She pushes him back on to her breast and shuts her eyes, as if not seeing him there will block out the pain. It is so bad that she screams and looks. Her milk is stained with blood.

'Great,' says Roberta. Talking to herself is becoming a habit, but it's good to have someone around. 'I am feeding my baby my own blood.' She lets him suckle and it actually helps. Nathan is quiet, perhaps because he is less hungry, or perhaps he is too exhausted to scream any more. But in the morning the pain is just as bad.

Paul has an early appointment. 'You ring the doctor straight away,' he calls as he leaves. Nobody could tell what a bad night he has had; he looks as smart as ever.

The phone rings when he is barely out of sight. Marise. When Roberta hears her voice, she doesn't say anything at first.

'Roberta,' Marise says anxiously. 'Roberta.'

Roberta begins to cry, this never-ending weeping which is becoming her constant companion, and tries to explain that it is absolutely nothing at all. Quickly, Marise extracts the truth.

'Stay right where you are,' she says, although Roberta has not planned to go anywhere.

In next to no time, Marise walks through the back door, carrying a large shiny plastic shopping bag. 'My sister has a cure,' she announces. 'It's either very new or very old, but it can't hurt you to try.'

She produces a large firm cabbage from her bag.

'Yuck.'

'You don't have to eat it, you wear it.'

When she thinks about it later, Roberta realises there is something shy and excited about Marise that she cannot quite place.

Taking a sharp knife, Marise begins stripping the cabbage until she finds two large, veined leaves, smooth and curling inward like giant shells.

'Take your gear off,' she orders. Roberta unbinds herself and her breasts roll forward like big red turnips. 'Put these on,' she says, when she has recovered herself. She places the leaves on Roberta's burning skin, pulling her maternity bra up, to hold the leaves in place. 'Just sit and relax, okay?'

'But what are they supposed to do?'

'Your body temperature cooks the cabbage. Cooking cabbage releases enzymes that draw the swelling. Well, that's what my sister says.'

Roberta is past caring how ridiculous things might look. Everything looks absurd. Marise lights a cigarette while they wait for something to happen, then crushes it out, looking guilty.

In a few minutes the smell of cooking cabbage fills the room. The leaves wilt, turning a sharper shade of green. Marise peels them off Roberta's breasts, replacing them with two more. This time they cook more slowly. Roberta feels the pain shifting, drawing towards the surface.

'It's working,' she says, smiling for the first time in a week.

Marise grins. 'Wearable cuisine.'

That is the moment Paul chooses to return to the house for papers he has forgotten, his sleepless night catching up with him after all.

He stands looking at the scene in the kitchen with distaste. 'Early dinner?' he says. He picks up the saucer where Marise has stubbed out her cigarette and looks at her accusingly. Marise gathers her belongings and walks out, without saying a word.

'I thought you were going to call the doctor?' he says to Roberta.

'I will.'

But she doesn't. She uses the cabbage leaves several times during the day, and by evening she is able to feed Nathan again.

When he comes home, Paul doesn't ask whether she has rung the doctor again.

'I hope you've taken a shower,' he says, as she gets into bed.

Roberta lies beside him; he lays his hand on her. 'They're softer,' he says, grudgingly.

'It's a relief,' she says.

Paul leans over her and lowers his mouth to her breast. He sucks her nipple hard, dragging on the sour soup of her milk.

Roberta hears a quiet voice in her brain. This is not what I want, it says to her. She lies quietly beside him and lets it talk.

thirteen

ROBERTA

Her days are quiet, punctuated by the wind. Young mothers in her street walk by wheeling prams, skirts whipping around their knees. She looks at them for signs, trying to gauge their happiness, their capabilities, whether they are coping with the world. Some of them look tired, but none of them is distraught, although on once a week visits to the supermarket she sometimes hears women shouting at their children when they have done nothing wrong. It is not anger that she feels. Roberta does not want to shout at Nathan. She is not sure that she feels anything.

Even if she is lucky, as the Plunket nurse says, the dark mood she experienced in the hospital grows deeper. In the mornings when she wakes, her eyelids won't open straight away, glued together by dread. She rubs them to get rid of the sticky substance beneath, but there's nothing there, just remorseless light when finally she begins to face each day. The person she remembers being, before this, before pregnancy, before Nathan, has gone. The waviness in her hair disappears, the small curling fronds around her face. The weeping returns.

Bernard comes to visit one day, unexpectedly.

'It's time I saw this baby of yours,' he says, standing framed in the doorway, almost having to bend his head.

'He's asleep,' says Roberta, as if she doesn't want to show him to her brother. 'I mean, it's great to see you. He does cry quite a bit, so if you could just not wake him up.'

Bernard walks up the stairs behind her, awkwardly trying to tiptoe.

Nathan is asleep, his face peaceful and smooth. 'You'd better hold him,' she says.

'Well, if you're sure.'

She lifts him out of his bassinet and places him in Bernard's arms. He stands quietly for a long time, looking at Nathan. She wishes he would say something.

'Stop looking so scared,' he says. 'I'm not going to run off with him.'

But she sees the covetous, stealthy look in his eyes, the brother she has never altogether trusted.

'I'll make you a cuppa,' she says, just so he will give Nathan back.

'Sounds good,' he says, but when Nathan is down again, and they have returned to the kitchen, he says, 'Well, I'll be off now.'

'But you've only just come.' Roberta is afraid that she has offended him; he is family, after all.

Other days, she sits idly, when there are things she could be doing. She catches herself examining her love for Paul in minute detail. Anyone might be forgiven for wondering whether she ever saw anything good in him at all, she tells herself sternly. But that is not the way it has been. She believes that what they have experienced is love. Isn't it?

Paul and Roberta lived in a university flat together. The arrangement was not by design; there was simply a vacancy in the flat Roberta shared with two other people and he answered their advertisement. These women held a house meeting. 'Do we want any more men?' they asked each other.

They had all but given up on admitting men into the flat after a succession of boors who smoked more dope than they thought safe, mixed up whites and coloured in the washing machine and missed the lavatory bowl — all that kind of stuff.

Then Paul turned up on the doorstep. He was well-spoken, seemed quiet. 'I only need a place until the end of the year, then my girlfriend and I will probably get married.' They were impressed.

They held another house meeting. 'If he doesn't work out it's only a few months to the end of the year,' said one of the flatmates.

We can probably cope for that long, if he's awful.

But he did work out, beautifully. He was clean, tidy and a great cook. He knew the difference between good wine and bad, not as something learned and ostentatious, but as knowledge taken for granted. Roberta remembers the way the pattern of life in the flat became more mature, their behaviour like that of grown-up people. They sat down for meals, and took proper turns at shopping so that there was always food in the house, and, without being asked, took to playing the stereo at levels which they had all secretly yearned for.

Paul didn't bring Prudence, his girlfriend, to sleep over, which was a relief. The couple went to her place, or his family's, at the weekends, and during the week they both studied. Prudence wore a neat sapphire engagement ring, which was unusual for a student. Her father was a doctor up north. At the end of the year there was a shock announcement: Prudence had been awarded a scholarship to study abroad.

'I told her she had to take it,' Paul explained to them. They were impressed by that, too, though one of them, whom the others secretly thought was going off the rails anyway, groaned and said, 'Do we really trust a SNAG?'

'Our commitment could never be in d oubt,' Paul said. 'Of course I'll wait for her.' He was quiet for a week or so, and the women asked him to stay on in the flat.

Towards the end of the following academic year, Prudence wrote him a dear John letter, to say she had fallen in love with a ski instructor in the French Alps. Everyone felt furious with her. Paul was just about to complete honours in psychology, and he looked so awful that they all took turns sitting with him in the evenings just to be sure he kept studying. When it was Roberta's turn, she sat very still, reading and hardly daring to breathe lest she break his concentration.

Her own study was lumbering along; she was studying accountancy because she was considered good at mathematics, which only meant she had stayed the course at high school when everyone else had dropped out. Secretly she wished she had done arts. She wanted something that took her nowhere, as her mother said, although what she knew about it Roberta wasn't certain. Edith sometimes suggested she might go back for the winter balls at Walnut. There was Grant, who had always fancied her. Grant wore cable-knit sweaters and kept his hands in his pockets, and her cousin Sally had wanted to marry him for years. Roberta wondered if her mother's desire to match them up might be in order to put one over her in-laws, but that seemed too uncharitable a thought, even for Edith. At other times, she wondered if her mother wanted her home to be her friend. A friend for the rest of Edith's life, when all else failed. Some hope.

One evening, Paul said, 'I can't go on like this, I just can't. Come out and have a drink with me, Roberta.'

At the pub he looked at her across gin and tonics. 'You keep me going, Roberta.'

'It's not just me, the other girls care about you too,' she said, because that is the way she has always been, wanting to share praise as well as blame. Her brother Bernard used to jeer and call her the peacemaker, as if it was an insult, because she wanted to bring about harmony where none was possible.

'No, it's you. I wait for it be your turn to sit with me. So I thought today, how silly this is, that I'm waiting for it to be your turn, and what a sap you must think me, needing a nanny every night. The truth is, I don't want to think about Prudence any more. I'd like to spend some time with you.'

Thinking back, she does not remember him telling her that he loved her, though she is sure that she said this to him. After he passed his exams, the two of them went on a working holiday to Australia. Roberta worked as a waitress on the Gold Coast, and Paul got a job relief teaching for a while. The beginning of the university year started and they should have gone back so Roberta could return to varsity, but they didn't. They became a couple, and now they have been one for six years, married for the past four. They are generally kind to one another; they have had some fun together.

So she finds herself going back over that time, trying to decide when she began to love Paul, and she finds that she can't, what ever she may have said; it's like a stitch in a piece of embroidery, already so smooth and worn that it does not bear close examination because then the whole picture is open to question. At first it is shocking to consider that she might not love him in the way she believes, a kind of an unfaithfulness in itself. But once she has begun, she cannot stop; it's like scooping sweet crumbs from behind her teeth with the tip of her tongue. She catches herself in the act again, and asks herself again and again, what sort of a person am I? What sort of a monster?

She glimpses her reflection in odd corners of the house, not in the mirrors, because she cannot bear to look at herself, but, depending on the light against the windows, sometimes she sees herself there, or in the glass of a picture, another time in the polish of the sunlit table.

This time last year, she was a pretty young woman who wore well-cut suits with padded shoulders, and softly draped blouses so that she wouldn't appear mannish, the clothes sprinkled with fine gold jewellery. She visited restaurants with her husband, and had begun to hold dinner parties. Now, she is a gaunt-eyed creature with dry hair springing out of her scalp. She feels as if she has flu all the time.

One day, when the wind is quiet, she stands outside and studies the wind turbine, turning over very quietly in the gentler air. What do women really want, she asks herself. Did I ever ask for this? Thinking about this sends a shudder through her. She goes back inside and puts another pile of washing into the machine, but continues to shiver. She wonders if she is feeling one of the earthquake tremors which often strike Wellington. People wait for the big one.

But the earth below hasn't moved, like a bad joke about sex. What she feels is inexplicable sorrow. She has not been given to phobias, except for her sudden fear of heights, nor does she consider herself foolish or ignorant. As well as the half-finished degree in accountancy, she reads books. After she stopped gymnastics, she took up reading in a big way, not as a brainy or ostentatious occupation. Some girls read when they are small and give it all up when they reach adolescence. They don't want to be geeks or swots, they say, and so it is one thing or the other. But Roberta was different. She read her way steadily through many books, in a private, interested way, just for the pleasure of it.

In spring she went to the women's book festival, standing shyly but firmly in the queue so that visiting authors could sign the books she bought. One year she got Fay Weldon, companionable and motherly, another time Barbara Trapido, with raining grey hair and a raw friendly face, and once A1 zipless fuck Erica Jong, in this day of Aids. Would you please sign my mother's name, it's to Edith, thank you, thank you, she loves your books so much, she lives in the country, couldn't make it herself, oh I'm sorry to hold up the queue, thank you, thank you.

She never gives the books to her mother. Edith doesn't read. She gardens with a ruthless quixotic artistry, and she drinks.

fourteen

EDITH

EDITH IS LOOKING for a bottle of gin. She thinks she left it in the trough in the top paddock, but she can't find it. The arms of her jacket are soaking and slimy from several unsuccessful sweeps of the trough. Perhaps she left it in the blackberry bush near the stream bank. But the blackberry has been cleared, something she had forgotten. May be the toolshed, though that's a dangerous one; Glass knows most of the spots in there.

She hiccups and sighs. Anyone would think Glass never took a drink himself, which is rubbish. Glass gets pissed as a fart if he gets half a chance. Give me a night off, old girl, your turn to drive home. As if I don't know he's trying to put the brakes on me. As if he can stop me if I really want to.

But I do want to. I always want to stop. I want tomorrow to be a better day. But there is that first sweet slide, the lovely burn at the back of the throat, the small sunburst in my head; it is always new, like love. What would I do without that? And the last mouthful of the day, when you know you can't go on because the walls are shaky, and words are like stones, that's a nice one, holding it in on the tongue, slowly rolling it around like mouthwash, so that it lingers on.

A warm night. Mulching to do in the morning. Hot roots. And mildew on the Michaelmas daisies. Yes. We must have a party for the baby before autumn grows late. My grandson. My little boy. No, Roberta's little boy. Tomorrow, I need to see Roberta and the boy. What is the matter with Glass and me? I need Wendy, she'd sort me out. Yes. Bitch. Where have you gone? I was doing fine until you walked out on me. This is because of you.

A patchwork of stars between the clouds. Might be rain tomorrow. How good it would be if it rained. And here is the gin she has salted away, carefully placed in the old hidey hole, the filled-in rabbit hole by the third post of the home paddock. Out of gin, are we, Glass? Up your poo hole.

Edith gives a little hiss of pleasure and sits down beside the post. Very carefully now, Edith, she tells herself. Go easy, just a capful, neat like that. Neat. Yes. Oh, God. Oh Mary, mother of Jesus. Thank you.

And where is Glass? Glass is prowling, gun in hand, as far as he can by night around the perimeter of his property. Above him a white moon shifts across the sky, briefly illuminating the bowed heads of his cattle. When a light pierces the darkness he shoots at it, causing a paddock of yearlings to stampede. The light may be nothing more than the milky moonbeams caught on the river. Or a reflection from a distant car light glinting off the window of a barn.

ONLY THE LONELY

BERNARD TRIES TO write a letter to Orla. Writing letters is painful for him, not because he is bad at writing itself — it's just that the words won't come to him. When he thinks of writing words about love and longing he can only think of romantic song titles, and he sees that that won't do. Dear Orla, love me tender, blowin' in the wind (that's me, Orla), only fools fall in love (yeah, yeah, yeah), if you're going to San Francisco (or any other damn place in the world but here), I'll follow the sun (tomorrow: maybe). These songs that spring to his mind date back to some time in the past, as if they mark a point where something in his life was arrested, or even ended.

Just once since she left, Bernard has rung Orla in Ireland.

'And what do you want?' his mother-in-law asked when she answered.

'Well,' he said, and hesitated.

'Not much use for a well if you don't have the water.' Bernard thought how healthy she sounded.

'I want Orla.'

'I'll get her to ring you,' the old bat said, 'always assuming you can afford for us to transfer the charges back to you.'

When Orla doesn't ring (and, of course, he had understood that she wouldn't from the start, because she wouldn't have been given the message), he promises himself he will write her a letter, but he doesn't. The dreams don't go away.

THE WOMAN IN THE PADDOCK

SARAH HUNTS THROUGH the advertisements of the garden tours until she finds a cellphone number in Walnut. She is answered by a woman who is clearly very drunk.

'Wendy Mullen? Never heard of her in my life. Who is this woman?'

'My mother. Well, I was given your number and it just seemed possible. We visited your garden on a tour a while ago.'

The line has a crackle on it as if the phone is out of range, behind hills or something. A sound like a cow moving and lowing quietly in the night interrupts the conversation. Sarah has the odd impression that the woman to whom she is speaking is out in the countryside on her own. Not so odd, really; Sarah, too, is used to listening to the night by herself.

'What would I be doing with your mother?' The woman coughs, or heaves; it's hard to tell either way. 'No good talking to me, I'm just a drunken old rat.'

'I'm sorry, it's just that she's disappeared.'

'Disappeared mother, eh? Who have you told about this?'

'Well, nobody really. She goes walkabout — my mother, I mean. I suppose I should advise the authorities. I'm really sorry to have troubled you.'

'Goes walkabout does she? Sounds pretty odd.'

'Well, she stays with people. She's always liked shifting around.'

The woman at the other end sighs. 'I might bump into her.'

'You do know where she is, don't you?' Sarah demands.

'No, as a matter of fact, I don't, not right now.'

'But if you did know?'

The woman groans. 'Fools rise all the time. Tell me the number and I'll write it down if I remember. What did you say your name was?'

Sarah doesn't believe the woman will remember the number. But she decides to leave it a week or so longer before she goes to the police.

fifteen

WAR WOMAN

ONE MORNING, ROBERTA receives two phone calls. One is from her mother and the other from Marise. Summer is cruising rapidly into autumn. She can smell the brown, dusty winds that will be blowing on the farm, even though she can't feel them on her skin. Her nose and eyes water sometimes and so she guesses it must be the nor'-westers that are causing it; they can do strange things to a person. Everything can be put down to the wind, this is the best way to look at it. Her hair is falling out and she is tired all the time.

When her mother rings, the first question Roberta asks her is what is the wind like?

'Don't worry,' Edith says, 'the garden is looking fine. Have you set a date?'

'What for?'

'I was just thinking about the baptism.' Roberta notes this, because when Edith had talked earlier of this occasion she had spoken of a christening, as Protestants do. Now she is talking like a Catholic.

'I don't want any of that stuff,' she tells her mother.

'I can't stop you being a heathen, I suppose, but this is different — you've got the baby to consider.' She is talking as if it's a decision like choosing fluoride.

'When are you coming to see me?' Roberta asks, trying to change the subject.

'Really, Roberta', Edith says, 'I don't know what's got into you since you had this baby. It's hopeless trying to talk to you.'

'I don't get much sleep.'

'Oh, that. Well, nobody does.'

'He's got diarrhoea.'

'What have you been eating? Chocolate? Grapes?'

'How come it's my fault?'

'I didn't say it was. Oh for goodness' sake, after three months you must know that what you put in your mouth is what comes out Nathan's other end.'

'Thanks,' Roberta says. 'My milk's drying up anyway. I'm going to give him a bottle.'

'You can't do that.'

'Oh, can't I just.' Roberta hangs up. Nathan loves his bottle. So does she; quickly and secretly she is letting her milk dry up. Doubled his weight, the Plunket nurse had said, approvingly. Roberta sees no need to tell her the truth.

When Marise rings she tries not to reveal how she is feeling, endeavouring to sound light and airy. 'I'm busy, really must go,' she says, the bright housewife.

'He came to see me,' says Marise.

'Who?'

'Josh.'

Roberta's heart seems to have stopped above the telephone. 'I do have to dash,' she says.

'He's got something for you.'

'I can't think what. All my stuff was accounted for. Paul made sure of that.'

'Not the placenta.'

'What?'

'He's got Nathan's placenta in the freezer. He thought you might want to bury it.'

'I don't believe this. You're being disgusting. I mean, this isn't very funny, Marise.'

'It's not meant to be. His girlfriend's family do it. He just thinks everyone does it.'

Robert's mind flicks back to the day of the birth. She can see Josh speaking to the midwife, a transaction taking place. She believes Marise, but it is hard to comprehend that this thing, this part of Nathan — part of her, if it comes to that — is in a stranger's house, tucked up with the cat's meat and fish fingers.

'What shall I tell him?'

She laughs, in what she hopes is a merry, clever way. 'Tell him anything you like.' For the second time that morning, she hangs up without saying goodbye.

Actually, she has no answer. She has no idea what Marise should say to Josh. She decides that she won't talk to Marise again. It's better to keep herself to herself.

I've got to get it together, she resolves, I've got to get myself together. She sees the way Paul looks at her sideways in the evenings, well, the evenings when he is at home. He works very long hours. Human resources are, of course, endless. He can afford to be choosy, he says, his firm has a good reputation. They prefer people who are in jobs, and looking for some sort of improvement in their salary packages and status, to people who have no jobs. We upskill, not sideways skill, he explains.

What if someone wants something less important, she asks. What if they just want to take life easier? He looks as if Roberta has taken leave of her senses.

'I'm just trying to take an interest,' she says. 'Unemployment's on the rise again, if you can believe the newspapers.'

'It'll sort itself out,' he says, without raising his eyes from the work he has brought home.

'I see,' she says. 'Yes, of course.' There was a time when her views on employment would have been of value; it's been her business too. She folds a pile of napkins, flicking them so they snap, full of clean sunshine and windy air.

'Couldn't you have done that earlier?' he says.

All the same, even if he is being a jerk, she thinks she may need to change. Some people might say Paul has been very patient. They might say things haven't been easy for him, and she would have to agree with that.

After these phone calls, Roberta gets her car out of the double garage and straps Nathan's carrycot into the back seat. Since Nathan's arrival, she has ventured only as far as the supermarket, but today she will go out like other mothers do. If she could think of someone to visit she would. Her best friend, Pamela, has gone on a working holiday. Roberta still calls her my best friend and she can't think of anyone else she likes better. At school they spent every day in earnest consultation about boys and music and their lives. She has become a big-busted, cheerful, capable person who worked for a vet until she went away, and she still calls men boys. All the women from the flat have gone, dispersed to high-powered careers or marriage in other towns.

Roberta thinks longingly of Marise, and puts the thought firmly out of her mind. She can take a walk in the Botanic Gardens, with Nathan in his backpack, letting the sun warm them both. In the end, nobody has bought them a stroller, and she hasn't seen the need so far to go out and buy one herself.

Her car has had so little use that the battery is flat and she has to roll it down Ashton Fitchett Drive in order to start it. The engine clucks and falters into life. It's like her, she thinks, too hard to start.

By the time she does begin something, she doesn't want to do it. She doesn't stick at things; she has heard this before. Like today. The car park at the gardens is full and when she has driven up and down the line of parked cars twice, she turns round and leaves. Driving home, she loses her way, crossing into the wrong lane on a roundabout. It is so silly, as if she is a stranger. Instead of going up the hill, she has turned down to Newtown. It is here that the car engine dies altogether, giving her just enough warning to pull into a parking space.

For some minutes she sits in the car while Nathan whimpers in the back seat. She is responsible for all of this — her broken-down car, Nathan crying. She has run out of prepared bottles. Her milk is dry, or so nearly that it makes little difference, and she has a raging thirst. Autumn sun simmers on the pavement outside the car. It would be easier to die than to make the effort to go on any further.

'I'm responsible,' she says. It means she has to go on. She decides that, if she can get a drink and something to eat, she might be able to feed Nathan. Point to you, Edith. She extracts Nathan from the car and puts him in the backpack. Walking soothes him until they arrive at a milkbar cum restaurant full of chipped formica tables and school chairs. When she sits down Nathan whimpers again. An attendant waving a fan over a row of sandwiches stops to bring her a tray of tea.

This is the moment when the War Woman comes in to the shop. This is what Roberta comes to call her. Her language sounds guttural and coarse, although maybe it is beautiful; her huge face has wide planes and spaces on it, like that of a woman in one of those documentaries where people tear each other apart in snowy wastelands and die in blood on plains, in the streets, before the camera's eye.

Her eyes are small in relation to the rest of her face, glittering and dark in sunken hollows, her big, loose mouth reveals a black gap where one of her upper front teeth is missing. In her arms she carries a big boy, the size of most children of two or three, although clearly still an infant, to whom she is shouting a song. Behind the counter, the attendant pours a cup of coffee, without being asked, and hands it to the War Woman, who puts money on the counter.

The boy, on this warm afternoon, wears a green and white fake fur hat with ear muffs. His mother tugs them down, as if to keep his ears warm. The child returns a look it is difficult to interpret: a smile, a crooked leer, a vast indifference to her attention. She shouts with pleasure and drinks some coffee, standing up at a table. Every muscle of her face is contorted into an attentive adoration of the child. She extracts a baby's dummy from the pocket of her baggy, bibbed overalls (perhaps this is what makes Roberta think she could be Russian? She has seen pictures of women in labour camps wearing clothes like this) and puts it in her mouth. She sucks hard on the dummy and then, with a cry of glee, plunges it into the baby's mouth, singing her loud song, and looking to see whether the attendant and Roberta are watching.

Nathan starts to scream, reminding Roberta of his presence. She lifts her blouse and offers Nathan her breast, which he nuzzles fretfully. The War Woman roars and drags the dummy from her son's mouth and for a moment it appears that she will thrust it into Nathan's. Instead, she casts a look of contemptuous pity on Roberta and bestows lavish kisses on her son's face. Aaaah, she cries. Aah.

Ah ha ha, her laughter follows Roberta down the street. Roberta runs, because she must save Nathan. She does not adore him in that way. She cannot be consumed by him, or by Paul. Her running footsteps take her to a bus stop, and, for the moment, she believes she can save him. When she is on the bus she realises he is not safe, because he is still with her.

SNOT
As ROBERTA STANDS at the bench the next morning, something astonishing happens. The feeling of having the flu has persisted. She has told Mr Maitland about this at her six-week check-up, when he assures her that everything is fine, she can have sex again — all the stuff that women wait to hear, or their husbands do, although she hasn't been in the mood and Paul doesn't seem anxious. Once or twice it has happened. It has occurred to her before that Paul is a very directional kind of lover. I like it like that and that and that, he says lately, sounding like an advertisement for fried chicken.

'I don't want to give you antibiotics,' Mr Maitland said, 'not when you're feeding. It doesn't look like flu to me.'

'But I have a runny nose,' she said.

'Mention it to your regular doctor next time you see him, if it persists.' He was signing her off, getting rid of her, she felt. A bit of a neurotic, she fancied him writing in his notes. That was nearly two months ago. She has tried ignoring her symptoms.

This morning, as she measures mix into bottles, she sneezes and something slips inside her head. It is like a clot moving under her eye. Roberta blows her nose into a strip of paper towel and finds she is holding something solid. When she pulls it, she feels the thing drawn down out of her sinus cavity, creating a trail of emptiness and relief. In the paper towel lies an angry green piece of mucus, the length of her little finger and nearly as round. Livid and putrid, it is encased in a skin of its own, separate and seemingly alive. She wouldn't be surprised if it wriggled.

She lays this thing on the bench and studies it with the fear one reserves for unexpected reptiles. But it looks more like a little green haggis than anything. From the open knife drawer, she takes a vegetable knife, and stabs it, but already it is shrivelling in the sun into something smaller and less excessive than the green creature that has emerged from her head. The tip of the knife pierces its skin and it is just another piece of snot.

BUT MY HEAD is clear, and I see what I must do. I go to a mirror and look at my face. I don't like what I see but I hold my own eye.

ROCKIN' ROLLIN'
THE TRAIN RATTLES and slides, entering gullies where ngaio and gorse jostle for space, and rushes up the other side. The back fences of neat houses flash by, with just enough time to glimpse napkins on the lines and paddling pools and women chatting over fences. One of the stops is alongside a garden centre, the parking lot crammed with cars. Women push trolley-loads of plants and bags of manure towards their cars in the lot, mostly two by two with their friends. I imagine my mother, seeing her through the fine mist of water sprinklers. Only Edith was always on her own. The women laugh and call to their children, shout see you soon. Their hair shines and their teeth sparkle, their tight jeans cling to their sensual hips as they walk. This is how mothers ought to look. The women don't look up and see me watching from the window of the train.

I look down at Nathan in my arms. The train sways into a curve in the hill, Rockin' rollin', I sing to him, quietly, so nobody will hear. I am War Woman, I do what I must. I kiss Nathan's sleeping face, his forehead, the tip of his nose, each small ear. My darling darling little boy, my beloved son, I say to him, my incantation, my song, my sleeping memory.

sixteen

RENUNCIATION

'Why ever didn't you tell me you were coming?' Fay says, when she sees Roberta coming up the path. 'You're lucky to catch me in. They cancelled staff meeting this afternoon, so many people are away on courses. I don't usually get home until five on a Tuesday, and then we often have drinks after work that day. It is lovely to see you, though,' she thinks to exclaim, and reaches for Nathan.

The Cooksleys have seen little of Nathan so far. Fay is still shocked by the manner of his arrival. She doesn't say I told you so to Paul, or that Roberta is at fault or disorganised, but Roberta feels that she might think these things. And who can blame Fay?

'Life hurries on by,' Fay says, as she is fond of saying.

'How was Fiji?' asks Roberta, although she thinks that it is a long time now since Fay and Milton had their trip. Perhaps they have already talked about this. Had she seen some photographs of lagoons and palm trees and Fay and Milton sitting on a beach wearing silly hats and goofy grins?

'Fine,' says Fay, glancing at her oddly. 'Just fine. Where did you leave your car? Oh look, he's smiling at me.'

'I didn't feel like driving,' says Roberta. 'Well, I thought it would be good for Nathan to try out the train. I used to love trains when I was a child.'

'Oh, what a good idea.' Fay sounds doubtful. 'I suppose he'll remember, like reading to babies in the womb.'

'He's growing,' Roberta says. 'He's put on six kilos.'

'Wonderful. Tell me, did you check the train timetable for getting back? Well, dear, I'd love to run you back to town, but I've got a meeting tonight. Or Paul? Is Paul coming to pick you up? Oh well, he knows where to find things in the fridge. He and Daddy could put a meal together, couldn't they? How are you managing, by the way?'

'I'm really fine.'

'That's our girl.'

A shadow has crossed the lawn. There is no sound, but both women are aware of it. They glance up and see an older woman standing near the gate, her back turned to them. Fay's hands flutter to her throat.

'Who is she?' asks Roberta.

'I don't know,' says Fay, handing Nathan back. All the same, Roberta feels there is something familiar about the woman. Another time, she might have cared to think about it.

Fay walks outside, trying to look brisk, but there is nervousness in her manner.

'I've told you not to come here,' Roberta hears her say. Fay closes the courtyard gate behind her and the two women are obscured from her view.

'It would be better if we talked about it,' says the visitor.

'We really don't have anything to talk about. If you don't go away I'll call the police.' Fay speaks in a loud, bossy voice.

'It'll be on your conscience.'

'I'm going to write to the authorities about you, ' says Fay. 'You're a public nuisance.'

Fay can manage anything, Roberta thinks, and places Nathan on his rug, in a patch of sunlight by the door. Beside him she places two letters. The back door is open and she closes it quietly behind her when she leaves.

EDITH'S EYES ARE puffy and tired. Teacups scatter the kitchen table among the litter of farm mail and accounts Glass has been working on during the evening. Bernard notices how speckled his mother's hair has become; tonight he sees that it is nearly white in the wings above her ears. Edith holds a letter, and as soon as he is seated she begins to read it aloud to him.

'Now comes the moment of truth, when I must tell you what I have decided.'

'It's from Orla,' says Bernard dully.

Edith blinks. 'No, it's from Roberta. Milton Cooksley faxed it to us an hour ago.' The Nichols have moved into the world of technology as Glass keeps up with dairy company politics and now that Edith, herself, runs a business.

'Go on,' Bernard says, but his heart has lifted a fraction.

'I know you have done up a room for Nathan, and made plans, but it isn't going to be like that. When you get this letter, I won't be looking after Nathan any more. It's not because I don't love him, it's because I want to do the best I can for him. I am planning to leave him with Fay and Milton this afternoon, because I am sure they will help Paul to look after him. I'm not worthy of a beautiful son like Nathan. There has been too much trouble and unhappiness over his birth, and I am sure Paul will be a good father.'

'Where is she?' asks Bernard.

'We don't know.'

'She'll be dead, I expect. That's what people do.'

Edith lowers her head into her hands.

'What do the police say?'

'They haven't been in touch with them yet. They're hoping she'll turn up.'

'That's ridiculous — they should be out looking for her.'

Edith turns her haggard face towards her son. 'It's not a crime to leave your baby at your mother-in-law's house. Besides, what difference does it make? If she's dead it can't be undone, and if she's not we can deal with it.'

'They could stop her from doing something to herself.'

'You go to the police then,' says Glass, with more than a touch of malice. 'You go right over and have a chat with them.'

'Mate, is that all you've got to say?' Bernard says.

'Perhaps she'll come here.' Glass ignores the bitterness in his son's voice. He tastes cold stones under his tongue.

'Clearly that's not what she had in mind,' says Edith, 'or she wouldn't have written to us.'

'She might, though.' Bernard reasserts himself. 'I could start looking around the barns and places like that. If she's still alive, she'll change her mind about this.'

Edith reads again from the letter. 'I know I am right, so please do not think that I will have some sudden change of heart. You know me, if I say I can't do it, well I just can't.'

'She always was a dropout,' says Bernard.

PAUL FINDS ROBERTA at dawn, sitting in a bus shelter. Roberta is cold, because rain is falling over the city, and she has walked through it; sitting down in the shelter with her clothes dripping.

'I meant to go further,' she says, 'but I was too tired. I wanted to have a rest first.'

'Come home, Roberta,' says Paul. 'We can talk about it there.'

'I don't want to. Please don't make me see Nathan.'

'He's at my mother's place. Remember, you left him there yesterday?'

'I left him there for you.'

'I can't look after him on my own.'

'It'll work out for the best. You'll see, Paul, it will.'

'Are you leaving me, Roberta?'

Roberta looks confused. 'I suppose I must be, I hadn't thought about that.'

'But hon, you said just a minute ago . . . well, I don't know what you mean.'

'I suppose I must mean that. Silly, I hadn't thought about it like that.'

'Roberta, you can't stay here.' People stream past them, walking from the railway station towards the city and work. His wife looks shabby and abandoned, and he looks like someone trying to pick her up. 'Please, the car's just round the corner. We can go somewhere and talk about it.'

'Where will you take me?' Even in her distracted state, Roberta can see that it won't do, sitting here arguing like this. If she makes a run for it he will catch her and it will all get much worse.

A bus completely covered with an advertisement for house movers pulls up alongside them. The windows are painted over to look like curtains. The driver is one of those fast ones who veers into the kerb, barely waiting for people to leap on.

Roberta steps on to the bus and the driver pulls out while she is still taking money from her wallet. She can see Paul behind the curtains, but she doesn't think he can see her, as she makes her way to the exit near the back and takes a seat.

She stares at the inside of the bus. On the wall, a poem is written in big letters. It is by a young poet whose photograph she has seen in the papers and it is called 'Instructions for how to get ahead of yourself while the light still shines' — about riding a bike at night from the top of Brooklyn Hill. It might have been written for her, if she had had the nerve to do something like that; she would like to have been as daring. Especially, she likes the way the poem draws to a close:

> *As you come to each light*
> *you will notice a figure*
> *racing up behind.*
> *Don't be scared*
> *this is you creeping up on yourself . . .*

But she is scared and before she has completed a section, she gets off the bus and shelters inside a hat shop that is just opening its doors. The last two lines of the poem stay with her:

> *As you pass under the light*
> *you will sail past yourself into the night.*

Even though it's morning. Although the racing day will soon be night again and, in the meantime, she doesn't know where she will be when darkness comes. She likes the idea of sailing past herself. She buys a dull, grape-coloured cloche hat made of a woollen felt material with a small brim that can be slouched down over her forehead, or curled up or down all the way round. She puts it on, pulling it over her hair and, when she is sure she is not being followed by Paul, she makes her way up the street.

I BOOK MYSELF into into a bed and breakfast at the top end of town.
'I've been on the train all night,' I tell the woman at the desk. 'My luggage is down at the station, it's being dropped off later.' She doesn't give me a second glance.
It is not too late for breakfast; her husband, the proprietor, a man with a limp and soft hands, serves me sausages and eggs and hot coffee in the square little dining room. The table is covered with a green and white striped cloth. I trace the stripes up and down, and try not to show how hungry I am. Around me, travellers make plans for the day, calling out to each other, asking for routes and destinations and possibilities.
Where are you going? they ask me. I tell them I am still deciding, and try to disarm them with a smile. Normal behaviour.
When I have finished breakfast, I carry the key lovingly up to my room; my new home, as I am thinking of it even before I open the door. The room has plain deal furniture and a floral duvet, just as I imagined. I've cleaned rooms like this in my student days, put my hand down the loos, pulled hair out of the shower ducts. As a matter of routine, I check the sheets and run my finger along a ledge; I find it very clean. I unlace my damp sneakers and lie down on the bed without taking off any more clothes.

PAUL PULLS THE single chair across the room and sits down with his back to the door. He crosses his arms and dozes. When he wakes up,

Roberta's position is exactly the same as it was when he arrived; her breathing, if anything, is deeper. He checks her pulse and the fineness of the bones in her hand touches him, reminds him of his son.

They stay like this all day. The room is on the second storey of the bed and breakfast, close to the iron roof. Rain has begun to fall in earnest over the city, making a loud metallic rattle, and with it comes a humid, rising heat, so stifling that he feels he cannot breathe.

He has followed her progress through the city. When she turned into the boarding house his head was filled with silly ideas. Sitting here, like this, he sees how foolish they are, because Roberta is not the kind of woman whom he expects to have a lover. He has never thought about her in this way before. He doesn't see her as being ravished by Josh Thwaite; he regards her only as peculiar. He can't remember when he wanted, really wanted, Roberta and it is difficult to imagine anyone else feeling the same. And yet, he had thought her beautiful.

'I'm looking for my wife,' he had said at the reception desk. 'Medium height — wearing a hat.'

In another, less casual, hotel, they might not have told him. 'Second floor, two on the right,' the woman had said. 'She's expecting her luggage.' He hadn't even had to knock; the key was still in the door.

He wants to shake her awake and tell her how irresponsible she has been, but he doesn't. He sits here and studies her, and wonders what to do. He leaves the room only once, to slip down to the lobby and make a phone call to his mother.

He wants to get away from the dazed air of the room, but he is held there, hoping that if he just sits it out, answers will come. He might escape in the end. Other couples must do more than he and Roberta do, which is sleep — or she seems to sleep and sleep and when he nods off she is awake, so that their lives never quite coincide. This is what happens when she does wake up, towards five o'clock in the afternoon. Roberta turns wide, barely surprised eyes on him as if she has hardly been asleep at all, and speaks to him when he is half stupefied with drowsiness.

'What are you thinking?'

'Nothing,' he says. 'What about you?'

'I was wondering,' Roberta says, choosing her words with care, 'if people could go on like this. If it could be enough to go to sleep and wake up and not ask anything of each other.'

'Of course it's not,' he says. 'You know it's not. We've got Nathan to think about.'

'You've got Nathan,' says Roberta.

'Come home,' Paul urges her.

'I'd like to stay here another night.'

'I can't leave Nathan with my mother any longer. She's already out of her mind.'

'Poor Fay.'

'You don't have to be like that — it's not her fault.'

'I'll go down town soon and get Kentucky Fried and a drink and come back here and sleep some more,' Roberta says. 'I like it here.'

'You won't go away?'

'Not tonight.'

Leaving her here is practically the last kind thing Paul does for Roberta, and soon he will regret it.

FAY RINGS EDITH to let her know that Roberta is safe for the moment.

'We'll come down and collect Roberta and Nathan straight away,' Edith says.

'Roberta's with Paul and we're not sure, exactly, where they are.'

'Then we'll come and get Nathan.'

'You can't,' Fay says, in alarm. 'I can't give him to you without Paul's say so.'

'You'll have to hand him over sooner or later. Roberta obviously needs help.'

This is altogether the wrong thing to say to Fay. 'I don't know how you've got the nerve, Edith. How many times have you seen Roberta lately?'

This causes Edith to pause. 'Well, you have to go to work, don't you?' she says.

'I can take leave.' Nathan screams in the background, pausing only to hiccup. 'Look, Edith, I'll catch you later.

And then the phone rings again, and this time it is Wendy. Glass and Bernard are trying to eat lunch at the kitchen table. They all experience a rush of hope, that Roberta is found, that she is on her way to them.

'Yes, do come, Wendy,' Edith says. 'I'd be glad to have you here for a while.'

'You can't let her come,' says Glass, when she comes back to the table. 'What are you thinking of?' He means, are you drunk?

'She'll help,' Edith answers, with conviction.'

'What if Roberta brings the baby here?'

'Then Wendy can stay with Bernard. There's plenty of room over there.'

'Forget it,' says Bernard. He and his father glance at each other, suddenly united.

'You're not fit to drive,' Glass tells Edith, 'and I'm not going to town to pick her up.'

'JOSH, I DON'T know where she is any more,' says Marise, over the phone. 'I've been to the house again, but there's nobody there, not even a nappy on the line.'

'Leda says she'll throw out the placenta. I guess I can't really blame her.'

'Can you stop her?'

'She thinks I'm soft on that woman. Shit, I only saw her once. That's crazy.'

'Bring it round to my place. I can put it in my freezer.'

'Are you sure about this?'

'Yes, of course.'

'D'you believe in all that stuff?'

'I don't know. The Egyptians buried them too.'

'Did they?'

'So I'm told. It's supposed to be the baby's twin. We'd better be on the safe side.'

'Yeah, I reckon,' says Josh Thwaite, relieved.

'YOU DIDN'T LEAVE her alone in that room, Paul? How could you?'

'She promised, Mum, she said she'd be okay.'

'Promises, Paul. For goodness' sake, they're getting the mental patients to sign bits of paper these days, promising not to kill themselves. What's the very first thing they do when they get out the door? Don't shake your head at me like that, son. They kill themselves, that's what they do, with their useless pieces of paper folded up in their pockets right next to their hearts. I thought you would have known better.'

And she does say what's been on her mind for years. 'I don't know how you ever got yourself into this mess in the beginning.'

EDITH WALKS OUT into the garden where she can't hear the voices of the men. She stands and surveys the central rose garden with savage distaste. Her Old Blush Chinas are planted behind pink verbena which have developed rust in the overnight rain. She ought to do something about it, but she can't be bothered. Instead, she tears a verbena plant from the damp soft ground, leaving a yawning gap in the garden layout. She pulls out another plant, then another, flinging them behind her as she crawls along the ground on all fours.

This is where Wendy finds her. She has hitched a ride from town on the rural delivery van.

'Did they tell you I was drunk?' says Edith, when she sees her.

But Edith has not been drinking; Wendy can see this. Today, although Edith looks harrowed by life, she is sober. 'They found her,' she says, sitting back on her heels. 'They found Roberta.' Because she is so tired she has forgotten that Wendy doesn't know what's happened. So, having begun this way, she has to tell her all the story, as much as anything to explain the destruction she is wreaking on her garden, although at first Wendy cannot see the connection.

'We should never have come back to the farm,' says Edith, crouched on her heels, her hands covered with plant stains.

'This is paradise,' says Wendy. 'How can you say that?'

'Paradise, huh?' Edith rocks backwards and forwards, her head in her arms. 'Wendy, you're always on about art.'

'Ye-es?'

'This was mine. Not books or paintings or willow baskets or paper quilling or embroidery, although each might serve as a statement, but a garden. Perfection among the wreckage, if you want to be literary, Wendy.'

Wendy is silent.

'Get drunk with me, Wendy. Let's get rotten.'

'No,' says Wendy.

'Scared bitch. I thought we were supposed to be sisters.'

'Why do you do it?' asks Wendy.

OF COURSE THEY don't leave Roberta in the boarding house room alone. Unasked, an assortment of people become involved in her life: Paul, his mother and father, Paul's sister Laura, who flies down from Auckland to help with the situation, the police. They won't leave her to eat Kentucky Fried and stare into the sweetness of silence. She cannot be allowed to abandon her son this easily. She'll be sorry, is what they say, and, naturally, they are right.

I don't want a mess, Paul tells his family and friends. New baby, good job, beautiful house. To this list he tentatively adds a pretty wife who could make something of herself if she felt like it. At the moment she is not very well adjusted but he can see they will have to work on this. Life can be too perfect.

The policewoman is not unkind when she knocks on Roberta's door. 'I have to talk to you,' she says. 'There's so much on the news about people, y'know, injuring themselves when they're depressed.'

'I won't,' says Roberta.

'People say that. You have got some pills, haven't you?'

Roberta is silent. 'I didn't ask for them,' she says, finally.

'We can't just ignore it when families report things like this.'

'I explained to my parents.'

'Well, actually, dear, it was your mother-in-law. We haven't talked to your parents yet. Would you like us to get in touch?'

'I don't want to speak to them.'

'Would you like to go to a women's refuge?' asks the policewoman.

'No, I wouldn't,' says Roberta, backing away.

'I'll be back in the morning,' says the policewoman, looking grim.

After she has gone, the proprietor bangs on her door. 'You'll have to be out in the morning,' he says.

'You said I could have a week.'

'A mistake in the bookings. Sorry,' he says. She hears the uneven tread of his limp on the stairs.

CORRESPONDENCE
The Registrar
Births, Deaths and Marriages
Lower Hutt

Dear Sir/Madam

I am concerned that a matter concerning my privacy may have been released to unauthorised people. I would like you to obtain my file and I will phone you shortly to discuss this matter.

Yours faithfully
(Mrs) Fay Cooksley

seventeen

THE COUNSEL OF FOOLS

FAY KNOWS A counsellor. She knows several. She and her daughter Laura discuss their relative merits.

'Stress management,' states Laura. 'She definitely needs that.' Laura is a health communications officer so she has some special insight.

'Yes, obvious. Very anxious, too. Paul says she doesn't sleep well,' Fay says.

'She lacks motivation,' Laura says. 'I mean she hasn't really got anywhere much, has she?' Laura is wearing an old candlewick dressing gown of Fay's that they have found at the back of her wardrobe. It is three o' clock in the morning, and they have drunk several pots of tea. 'This thing really can't go on, Mummy, it's too big a toll on you.'

'One does what one has to,' says Fay.

'When you think what he could have had. Well, he's messed up his life — Paul has to be responsible too.'

'Well, you can't blame him too much,' Fay says. 'She's a deceitful girl.'

'Really?'

'Didn't I tell you? Paul found a cupboard full of feeding formula.'

'Oh my God, no.' Then Laura shrugs. 'Perhaps it's just as well. I mean how would you have managed these last few days?'

'Yes, but don't you see? She's been planning this for a while.'

TINA AND ULRIC'S rooms are situated in an elegant old house with polished wooden floors and high ceilings. The furnishings in the waiting room include glass-topped tables, bright Scandinavian rugs and leather-covered couches.

Laura crosses her legs at the ankles and bends her knees so that she sits in a graceful S-shaped line, settling herself in with a copy of *Vogue*. 'I thought you might like a woman to come with you,' Laura says. She was waiting in the car when Paul picked her up.

'I don't care,' says Roberta.

Roberta has never known exactly what Laura communicates about which aspects of health. She asked once. Laura had responded with a list of outcomes and probabilities and dividends for the future. There's a lot of unsubstantiated claptrap around in people's minds, Laura said, which leads Roberta to the view that she works for the government on cost-cutting measures in hospitals.

'I don't actually need to see anyone,' Roberta says.

'Well,' says Laura, in a sweet, reasonable voice, 'if you see Tina and Ulric and have a chat to them, you'll make us feel better about things. You could do that for us, and then it'll be over.'

And then I'll be free to go, Roberta thinks. She has never realised how like her mother Laura is, and suddenly she thinks that they are equally detestable. No, it's not sudden — she has always suspected that she doesn't like Fay. But how can you justify not liking someone who is beyond reproach? She doesn't speak to Paul and Laura again until they reach the counsellors' rooms.

The three of them, Tina, Ulric and Roberta, sit in deep chairs in what might pass for a circle, although Roberta has the impression that the others have their backs towards the door.

Tina clicks her fingers at Ulric in a jazzy way. 'Let's go,' she says. Roberta sees how she perceives herself as switched on, understands why Fay is convinced of her suitability for the task ahead. Ulric is a short, nuggety man with brushed-in dye through his hair and tobacco-stained fingers.

'Yeah, let's shoot,' says Ulric, exuding a challenge that says we'll-have-no-nonsense-here. His accent is slightly American. 'This is a pretty funny thing to have done to your family.' Direct approach.

'They're Paul's family,' says Roberta. She hopes she sounds patient and respectful.

'Roberta.' Tina leans forward, speaking as if to a child. 'Fay and Milton are a very loving, forgiving couple. You're a lucky young woman to have married into a family like theirs.'

'Am I?' says Roberta.

'They don't find it easy to relate to you. I've heard that you don't relate easily to people.'

'Have you? What a bummer.' She pulls herself up; they're needling her and she's walking straight into it.

'Look, you can't just go around leaving your baby the way you did on Tuesday.'

'I thought they'd look after Nathan.'

'That's hardly the point.'

'What *is* the point?' says Roberta wearily. The enormity of her mistake is beginning to hit her. She should never have given Nathan to Fay. But who else, that's the whole problem. She can't explain this to them.

'Well, don't you think it's a bit of a slap in the face?'

'No,' says Roberta. 'Giving them their grandson isn't a slap in the face. It's hardly denying relationship, if that's what's important.'

'It's an odd idea wanting to give your baby away to anyone.' Tina has a silly, vain face, Roberta decides.

'Sometimes people just have to.' But she is aware how uncertain she sounds.

'And live to regret it.' This from Ulric. Roberta sees he's playing the fall guy.

'Do you think I wanted to give him up?' Roberta allows a note of surprise to creep into her voice.

'Then why didn't you give him to your parents?' Ulric snaps. He is definitely letting her know he won't take any bullshit.

Roberta doesn't reply.

'Perhaps,' says Tina, ' you don't trust your parents with Nathan?'

In the silence that follows, Roberta pulls her sleeves down over her hands, and fiddles with the cuffs.

'Perhaps you'd like to tell us a bit about your background?'

'No, I wouldn't. Thank you. I wouldn't want to do that.'

'Uh huh. Have you ever considered psychotherapy?'

'No.'

'Pity. You might find it helpful.'

'There's nothing wrong with my family,' Roberta shouts.

'I see.' Ulric makes a note.

Tina pushes a box of tissues towards Roberta.

'It's all right, thank you.' Her hands are trembling so violently she can hardly hold the cup of coffee they have given her, but she is not crying, will not cry, not this time.

Tina tries again. 'Tell us about your interests, Roberta. What do you do with your spare time?'

'I read.'

'What sort of books?'

'Oh, novels and things.'

'Made-up stories, eh? What about non-fiction? Real things?'

'No, not much. I used to be a gymnast.'

'Ah.' Tina sits up. 'Gym? Aerobics, that sort of thing?'

'Not really. Competitions. Well, you can't keep that up forever, can you?' She is trying to ingratiate herself.

'It might be a good idea for you to join up for an aerobics class,' says Tina, 'get your confidence back, self-esteem. Lots of people to meet.'

'I don't want to meet people,' says Roberta.

'Why not?'

'That's the problem.' Tina and Ulric have spoken at the same time.

'I know enough people,' she says too quickly.

Ulric puts down his pen. 'So you think you're different do you, a cut above other people?'

'I didn't say that.'

'Thousands of people enjoy aerobics,' says Tina. 'Do you think there's something wrong with enjoying aerobics?'

'Who taught you to be a counsellor?' Roberta asks.

Tina pushes herself back in her cushion. 'I don't think we're making much progress here, Ulric.'

Ulric scratches his chin. 'So how *is* your marriage, Mrs Cooksley?' he says.

'I beg your pardon?'

'Paul says you have been rather indifferent lately. Your sex life, I'm talking about. Cold, he says you're cold.'

Roberta's eyes fill with unbidden tears. 'I'm sorry about Paul,' she says. 'I knew it wasn't enough. He and I talked about it.'

'Oh, you talked about it. And when did you talk about it?'

'At the bed and breakfast place. I woke up, and I said to him, would it be enough, the way we were. Of course, I knew it wasn't.'

'You actually talked about sex?'

'I don't think that's any of your business.'

'You see, Mrs Cooksley,' says Ulric, pursuing his distancing act, 'it seems to me that you haven't exactly told us the truth.'

'I haven't told you any lies, either.'

'You have some odd distortions of what truth really is. You're hardly a straightforward kind of person, are you?'

'Why do you say that?'

Ulric appears to have had enough of her too. 'Fancy footwork, young lady, I'll give you that.' He leans back and swivels in his chair, so that he can look out the window past her head. 'The circumstances of Nathan's birth were hardly, what would you say, normal?'

'Is that what this is about?'

'Well, were they normal or not?'

Roberta stands up. 'If you'll excuse me.'

Tina and Ulric stand quickly with her. Tina says, 'Roberta, we want to help. Let's have another go at understanding each other. If the three of us could just try and all get in touch with our feelings. Do you go to church?'

'I've been,' Roberta tells Tina, her teeth gritted.

'Then you'll know how people turn to one another and say God be with you, and give their hands to each other. Why don't we just try that, the three of us? Or give each other a big hug.'

'I don't believe you people are for real,' Roberta says.

Tina extends a look of heavy pity. 'Paul and his family wanted to keep this within the family. They wanted to save your face.'

'From whom?'

'People.'

'People. Always people. I'm not going to tell people, are you?'

'Roberta, you don't understand. Paul is going to take you to the doctor. This will get much worse for you before it gets better.'

Such is punishment. Tina did not offer hope with her diagnosis and Roberta was suddenly too weary to argue.

ROBERTA

FOR I AM ill. In the end, I have to admit this to myself. I have made plans, carried them through, even asserted myself a little, or so I think. But the effort has worn me out. I abandon myself to sleep again, on the downstairs couch of the house in Ashton Fitchett Drive, where, when I was in my plain room under the guest house roof, I had sworn I would never go again. This time when I wake up, my doctor looks down at me. He isn't carrying a strait-jacket, but he might as well. I decide to go quietly.

HOW MANY PEOPLE think about being admitted to a psychiatric hospital? I'll tell you what I think; there is nobody who doesn't say to themselves, it could as easily have been me. Somewhere, just inside our consciousness, we have this small mechanism that ticks over and over like one of my father's electric fences, beep beep beep, and one day somebody hits it the wrong way, and that's it, the trigger's gone off.

Show me the person who hasn't seen darkness. Who hasn't walked up to the edge and tiptoed away empty-mouthed from the sweet taste of madness and death? It could be anything: a bad-tempered teacher; an indifferent salesperson who refuses to allow you to return a garment you never meant to buy; the refrigerator repair man who doesn't turn up on time and makes you late for work; your supervisor who bawls you out when you do get to work; the woman who beats you to a car park on a hot day; the mechanic who fails the car for its warrant of fitness; getting your period; getting your period again. I'm getting into women's stuff here. Well, perhaps women have more reasons to go mad than men.

You might survive in the world, or again you might not. You might end up like I did, saying well, yes, that's not such a bad option. Yes thank you, I will allow myself to be driven to hospital. Oh, take whatever you like, I don't expect I'll care what I wear. Can't I just put on one of those nightgowns or something? No, don't bother about my make-up, I know I'm ugly and nothing will never make me look right again. It's okay, I understand. Don't pretend you think any differently.

And then you will walk through the doors and see them closing behind you, and you won't even think, Are they locked? Can I get out of here? Because you just won't care. If you have never thought about these things, then you haven't lived in the world.

I AM ADMITTED into an acute ward, lined by four beds made up with light yellow covers. The walls are painted cream, there is a lot of varnished wood around. The day room is a combination of dark blues and browns, colours meant to be harmonious but deliberately unexciting. The open-plan ward has windows through which the staff can observe us from the main office station at all times.

The nurse who helps me put away my things is kind. I like her right away, in spite of myself.

'You've got a little boy, haven't you?' she says.

'I did have, but I've given him to my husband. Well, his mother actually. It's much the same thing.'

'Really,' she says, 'and when did you do that?'

I have trouble remembering. 'Yesterday? Perhaps it was the day before.'

'Was it Tuesday?' she asks encouragingly.

'Yes, I think it was.'

'She'd be pleased to have a little boy?'

I'm warming to her more and more. 'Surprised, I think.'

The nurse grins. 'Mothers-in-law need a little tickle up now and then.'

'They don't get a good press,' I say, 'though some are better than others. I think mine's a really capable person.'

'What's her name?'

I have to think about that, too. The odd thing is, I really have forgotten all sorts of things, as if my memory is a white board that's just been wiped. 'Fa-ay,' I enunciate, giving it two syllables. Giving Fay heaps.

I collapse on the bed, suddenly weak round the knees. 'I don't want this to be happening,' I say. 'I wish I was dead.'

The nurse sits down beside me. 'Do you think about dying?'

'I don't know.' I feel her waiting beside me. It's such an enormous fraught question and one I have been avoiding, although people seem intent on investing me with death wishes. I think of the fresh-faced policewoman and her anxiety. My hands look like two rabbits sitting in my lap. I wiggle my fingers as if they are ears. I think of my father shooting rabbits. I remember a calf I reared getting sent off to the works.

'Yeah, I think about dying. I mean, as a general sort of topic.'

'Do you want to be dead?'

'That's a pretty loaded question.'

'Yup. But you brought the subject up.'

I have to think back over the conversation. I'm scared shitless because already I can't remember what I said to bring on this line of questioning. But because I like this peachy nurse with her calm fingers resting on the cover beside me, I want to give her something back for her efforts. Nurse Peach, I mentally dub her.

'Yeah, well. I want to be dead if it changes things.'

'Have you thought what it would be like to be dead?'

'Empty,' I say.

'Yup. It could be. Do you want that?'

I find I am thinking about an open grave. 'Empty is as empty does.' This is the kind of thing my aunts would have said.

'What does that mean?'

'I still want to be able to feel pins in my flesh.'

'Okay.' Am I imagining it, or does she approve of my answer? I scratch my fingernails hard along my arm, leaving a trail of scarlet welts. I don't feel anything, though I've drawn blood. I look at the nurse, appalled.

'I didn't feel that,' I say. This is the moment I decide I'm sick. I can't even hurt myself.

'Perhaps we could cut those nails,' she says. She takes my hand in hers and holds it, and I begin to sob against her shoulder.

'It's okay,' she says. 'It'll be all right.'

'How?'

'We're going to give you something to help bring you up. Lift your spirits.'

'Medicine?'

'The doctors are planning on giving you Prozac. It's an antidepressant.'

'Will it make me sick?'

'I can't promise that it won't. But it works for a lot of people. It's the Princess Di drug.'

'It hasn't done her much good, has it?'

'It depends on how she was before,' says the nurse.

She leaves me, though I feel the watching eyes. While I am sitting there, a cheerful man bounds down the corridor. This is something I am not prepared for. I had not thought of men roaming around the place. He has blazing eyes and a shock of fair, spiky hair.

'Hey sweetheart,' he says. 'What are you doing here? A pretty girl like you in a place like this?'

'I'm sick,' I say.

'No, you're not. Who's been feeding you that line? Come on, tell me about it. A lovely kid like you should be out enjoying life, not moping around here. I'm Jedediah, by the way, bet you've never heard that one before, eh? Means friend of God. I'll see you right, Roberta.' His eyes have already travelled to my name printed above my bed.

'Come on, out of here, Jed,' says the nurse, materialising from the corridor.

'What's the matter with him?'

'Nothing we can't take care of.' Soon I will learn to recognise the manic depressives for myself.

THE ANTI-CHOLINERGIC effects of Prozac are a dry mouth and constipation, not that there is much for me to get constipated on. I don't eat for the first five days in hospital. Within hours of beginning Prozac my head starts to feel as if it is bursting. I don't tell anyone because I think that it is part of my illness and the medication will make it better. The headache persists, flaring and waning from time to time like a deflated balloon suddenly filling with air and collapsing. I begin to vomit, kneeling on the floor, hanging on to the edge of the bowl.

My mother and father find me like this, a few days after my admission. I look up and see my mother's startled eyes above me.

When I have finished heaving, for the moment, I say, 'Looks great doesn't it, Ma? Good scene, wouldn't you say?'

After that, they have to lock me up in a room which has bare walls and an uncovered mattress lying on the floor and a two-way mirror in the ceiling, up where I can't reach it, can't shut them out. I feel as if I am flying through fog on a very small, very noisy aeroplane when you can see only a nimbus of light around the propellers and shapes that may be mountains. There is giggling outside the door which can be heard as mad laughter and I want to join in. The drug ebbs slowly from my system and I am back where I was at the beginning.

I sit with my knees drawn up under my chin, feeling sorry for myself. I sing, erratically, in a small depressed voice:

Moon
shadow moon
shadow
I'm being followed . . .
. . . by a moon . . .

They feed me Clonazepam, which brings me back down to earth. Weeks pass that I don't remember. There is no room for memory, fabrication, books, although I try to read them but cannot recall what they are about when I put them down; no room for the elaboration of an idea, or for imagination. For this I am grateful. They ask me, can Paul come to see you today? He has asked us to ask you. I say, no, no thank you with a chirrup and what I hope is a bright and pleasing smile. Do you want to see Nathan? Nurse Peach asks me on other days. No, I say, scowling, so that she will not pursue the matter.

Then there is a day when my spirits lift, just a fraction, like light fanning over the hills at daybreak. Walking down the corridor, I aim to avoid Jed, dispensing haphazard words like pearls before him, but as usual it is impossible.

'I want to pray for you,' says Jed. 'Why don't we just get down on our knees together?'

'In your face, Jed,' I say, and laugh at his expression, the sudden respect.

WALLFLOWERS

DR Q'S ROOM is across a courtyard. Dr Q is not his name, it's another name I've invented. The doctor from Hell, I thought of him, before we met, although he turns out not to be like that. He can disarm me, as Nurse Peach does. He has glinting, merry eyes behind half-spectacles, and wears a gaily coloured cravat. All the same, I am careful. Behind every Dr Q there lurks a Tina and Ulric, I tell myself. He has the same motives as the rest of them, I am sure. In the end I must return to being Roberta Cooksley, wife and mother.

I have told him this. The first time I saw him, I said, 'I can see what you're up to.'

'Well, it's your choice whether you want to be a wife or not; it's more difficult to stop being a mother. It's a status that giving birth bestows on you, like it or not.' I notice that his bright brown eyes fade at the edge of the pupil so that there is a pale milky line within the circle before it shifts to a different shade of white. 'Perhaps it's the way you deal with motherhood that's the issue here,' says Dr Q.

I am impressed with the way he opens up an option to me right away. What he says does make sense. But he wants me to talk to him, rather than the other way round, and, so far, and for the most part, this is too much effort. Sometimes I ask questions in a desultory kind of way.

'This is post-natal depression?' I say one day, part question, part statement.

'I hesitate to put labels on things,' he says. 'Why do you think that?'

'They told me in hospital, when I had Nathan, that my hormones had probably gone wrong.'

'Did they tell you that PND is rarely isolated to hormonal dysfunction on its own?'

'No, they didn't. Is that why I'm here?'

'I don't know why you're here,' he says. 'You need to help me on that one.'

'So what's another reason for this whatever you call it?'

'Syndrome? Well, a lot of women who suffer from one form or another of PND are what you might call high achievers.'

'That's not me,' I say, relieved.

'Or they have very high expectations of themselves.'

'So I may not have managed this disaster all on my own?'

He looks at me keenly. 'Possible.'

'You want me to talk about my family,' I say, turning away.

As I am leaving, he says mildly, 'You know about ripples in a pond?'

'Of course. Doesn't everybody?'

'Sometimes circles go on replicating themselves inside a group. Or a family. That's another way of looking at it.'

At other sessions, we often just sit for a long time. Once, he said, 'Can you explain why this is so difficult for you?'

But I can't. I sense I am losing him, patient though he is. It's just a small thing that tells me this. One day there is a new aide in his department. We are near the end of another hour of my silences, time for morning tea. 'How do you take your tea, doctor?' the aide asks.

'In a cup,' he snaps. Then he corrects himself and apologises. But I know, I can tell how he feels.

When the aide leaves the room, he says, 'You don't have to go on with this.'

'It's all right,' I say, suddenly afraid that I am going to lose him altogether. I will have to settle for his imperfections.

So THIS MORNING we must find a way to please each other. I dawdle across the yard, stopping to look at flowers. They are mostly tough, ragged old wallflowers with a sharp, lingering perfume.

'Well then, how have things been going since the last time I saw you?' he asks, when I am seated.

'Okay.'

'Been passing the time all right?'

'Bit like watching paint dry,' I tell him.

He barks with sudden laughter. We look at each other, both with a sense of hope. I see that his thick grey hair has been cut into a boyish mop-top. It pleases me, oddly, as if his vanity, his transformation, has been performed for me, although I know that's not true. He will have done it for himself, for an image he perceives when he shaves in the morning, for facing the day and people like me, and perhaps to convince some other person in his life that he is unpredictable and charming and youthful. I realise his advantage; I will never ask him for whom he has his hair cut, but he will ask me everything.

'You were looking at the flowers on the way over here,' he comments.

'Yep.'

'You like flowers?'

'My mother does.'

'Uh huh.'

'She would have pruned those wallflowers out there.'

'She's a pretty good gardener, huh?'

'Brilliant. Her garden's been in lots of magazines. She has walls of flowers.'

'Wall flower. Walls of flowers.'

I flick him a glance to see whether he's taking the piss, but he's not.

'Wall of flowers, flowers to the wall,' I say.

'Yeah?'

'Flowers flowing.'

'Ye-ess.'

'Flow wolf.'

He slides a piece of paper towards me.

'Can you remember what you've just said?' I take the paper and write swiftly:

wall of flowers
    flowers to the wall
flowers flowing
    flow
  wolf
   wolf flower
lower wolf
    flow
  flowers re-wall
  flowers flowers flowers

I hand it back, and he studies it for a long time, without saying anything.

'What frightens you about your mother's garden?'
'I knew you'd say something like that,' I shout.
'Okay. So, you're not disappointed. Do you want to go now?'
'No.'
'All right then.' He sits back with his eyes half-closed.
'She gave up,' I say.
'Being a brilliant gardener doesn't sound like giving up.'
'You don't understand.'
'Help me then. I could try.'
'Everything she thought and felt, she put there in the garden. If she felt anything.'
'Don't you know?'
I try to contain my distress by shaking my head.
'Your mother had secrets?'
'Perhaps. It's hard to tell.'
'Or you've forgotten?'

I nod. In a way this knowledge is something else I don't want happening to me, but it is better than wishing to die. I can tell that I am going to feel the pin in my flesh very soon.

AT THE END of the drive to the farm at Walnut, on that faraway night, I was hurried away to bed amid quiet voices and soft footfalls. All the next day I was told to go out and play in the garden. The weather was overcast and dull and I felt lost among the green-grey shapes of the rhododendrons. The garden was large, laid out in parterres and knot gardens containing lavender and sprinkles of late-flowering cosmos left over from the summer, like flecks of flesh in the cold foliage.

Towards the end of the afternoon I was called inside by my father's sisters and told that my grandfather was about to leave for the funeral parlour. My father stood at the head of the casket, looking sombre and responsible. The casket was piled high with flowers. My brothers stood at attention beside him, dressed in white shirts and grey flannel trousers. The aunts and their husbands, except for Dorothy who had never married, were ranged along the room: Joan and Arch, Dorothy, Kaye and Jack. My mother stood behind her husband's family so that she could avoid the envious glances her sisters-in-law were casting at her, whenever they could see her. Behind their backs, she crossed herself.

'Isn't that beautiful?' one of the aunts said, and I guessed that my grandfather lay inside the casket, covered up with petals and vines. I remember wondering how he could breathe inside all that. The tall wardrobes reflected back images of myself, half the size of my awkward brothers. A day or so later my mother would sell the wardrobes for ten dollars each. My mother was different, once we moved house that last time.

What I didn't know at the time was what she wanted to be different from. I thought, at first, from our old lives, but I can see now that she wanted to be different from the Walnut people. You could see why at the funeral, in the way they dressed their solid, bosomy frames. Joan wore a rust-coloured suit with padded shoulders and matching patent leather shoes; Dorothy had a shapeless three-quarter coat over a murky pink dress that might have come from a jumble sale; Kaye appeared in a cream mix and match angora outfit, decorated with paisley whorls.

And my mother? She was dressed in a beautiful dark blue dress, cut high round her white throat. Her hair was brushed back and held simply with a single, unadorned comb.

It had come on to rain when we walked through the cemetery behind the coffin, my father and mother leading the way. Although hats were not in fashion at the time, my mother wore a dark felt trilby like a man's, only more stylish, with the front brim slouched over her left eye. The aunts whipped out stubby umbrellas and, stumbled along, trying to keep hold of them and sniffle into their handkerchiefs at the same time. They took their husbands' arms (Arch had to have Joan and Dorothy on either side, and they kept bumping him in the eye with their umbrellas). My older brother, Michael, was a pall-bearer, his knees almost buckling, along with Kaye and Jack's son — the two eldest grandsons. The other four were Freemasons, as my grandfather had been.

My mother kept on walking, with the rain streaming off the brim of her hat and down her shoulders; she appeared not to notice. As the minister, a Presbyterian with an old, cold face and white bristly hair, read the service, my mother stared straight ahead, as she had in the car the night before, her chin tilted upwards slightly. Dorothy, who had nursed my grandfather through his final illness, was bubbling away incoherently; Arch had to hold her up. We turned and walked back the way we had come, surrounded by stone angels.

It was then, walking through the cemetery, that we came upon another group at the far end. Two men, who stood checking a newly dug grave for another service, looked up as we approached and stood still, watching us. When my mother drew near, one of the men walked forward, his hand extended to her. She stopped beside my father, and the whole entourage had to halt behind her.

'Father Bird,' she said, taking his hand. 'How very nice to see you.'

'And you, Edith. Will we see you in church?' He was a slightly stooped man with tired, kind eyes.

'I'd like that.' It was neither a promise nor a commitment, but it was clear for all of us to see, that my mother would like it very much indeed.

'That's not little Michael?' he asked, his eyes following the casket, now being placed in the hearse.

'It is,' she said.

'How he's grown. A credit to you, Edith.'

While they were speaking, the other man looked on, with nothing more than a nod in my mother's direction. She did not know Alec McNulty at this stage. It would have been their first meeting.

My father turned away, as if to walk on without her. She smiled at Father Bird and resumed her walk with my father, her eyes full of tears that the rain could not disguise. The aunts and uncles followed, shocked into watery silence.

The days immediately following the funeral felt very long. There was decent mourning to be observed, and the family could not hurry away, or so they thought. Kaye and Jack owned some land they had been breaking in a few kilometres away and Joan and Arch did market gardening down the road, so the four of them, and Dorothy, were able to 'come and sit' as they called it.

Sitting meant just that, sitting in the sitting room darkened with half-drawn blinds, exchanging sad little comments, and saying, 'Well, do you remember this?' or 'When we were children, we did such and such.' The tedium threatened to stifle everyone in the stale, lifeless room. The heavy lounge suite covered with fawn moquette crouched on the old rose-splattered carpet, crowding us into corners. How our mother loved this room, exclaimed Joan, during one of their interminable dialogues. Yes, they murmured, our mother had style. For her time. How Dad missed Mum. Yes, they sighed, I guess it was what killed him in the end.

Occasionally, they noticed me. My brothers had vanished, to explore the farm, they said, meaning that they were getting the hell out of it, so they could find a place to go and smoke. It was difficult to find a place for myself, because Dorothy still occupied my bedroom. At nights she tossed and turned in the bed opposite, and when she did go to sleep she snored in deep, stentorian honks. With all her things there, it no longer felt like a room that I could go and sit in on my own. My mother made endless cups of tea and delivered them to the mourners. I could see that it gave her something to do. Later in the day, they would have two whiskies each, out of crystal glasses. No thank *you*, the Presbyterian minister had said, with a frosty smile, at the wake, reminding them of grandfather's days in the Temperance Union. Just as well times change, Dorothy commented later. Still, when you get down to tin tacks, said the sisters, it's better to have a minister of the old school.

My father appeared at a loss; he could see, on the one hand, that Edith was contemptuous of the wake, and of him, each time he joined it, but it was equally clear that he perceived it as a duty to be present. So I sat near him, and maintained my own silence unless I was spoken too. My hair was plaited in a single long braid that I could almost sit on. I sat on the floor with my back to the wall, curling the end of my plait around and around in my fingers.

'What a dear little girl,' Joan commented, now and then. 'So like the Nichols family.'

My father flushed with pride.

'Yes, a real Nichols,' Kaye said.

'No, she's not,' my mother said, passing with another tray of tea.

'Do you let her have sweeties, Glass?'

'Oh, one or two, Kaye.'

'Well, here you are, dear.' And another paper bag of jubes slid my way.

They had children of their own, but most of my cousins were older, except Sally, Joan and Arch's late bonus baby, as they described her. She was being minded while they sat. My aunts had already forgotten how to deal with a seven-year-old.

I searched in vain for some conversation that would reward them for their sweets and their uncertain overtures. I lit on my autograph book among the bag of treasures my mother had hastily packed on the night we fled to Walnut. Michael had given it to me the Christmas before; it was almost empty because my friends were still barely old enough to sign their names.

'Would you sign my book?' I asked.

'Autograph book,' they enthused. 'Oh yes, now there's an idea.'

Joan wrote the first autograph:

You ask me for something original
I scarcely know where to begin
For there's nothing original about me
Except original sin.

They rocked with laughter when she read this out, their moods lightening at last.

'Give it here,' said Kaye. She paused for a moment before scribbling down her verse; when she finished she blew on what she had written as if the ballpoint pen were real ink. Handing the book back to me, she read aloud over my shoulder while I studied it.

God made little niggers
He made them in the night
He made them in a hurry
and so forgot to paint them white.

Her audience was helpless with mirth.

'I think you can put that away now,' said my mother, who had returned to wipe up a spilt ashtray.

Kaye flushed. 'I suppose we'll be having the priest round here now, will we, Glass?' she said, with a mean edge to her voice.

My father didn't answer, and it was left to Arch to intervene. Arch had helped the old man with the milking, earning extra income while he and Joan were getting established in the market garden, or that's what Arch said, as if the establishment were now a fact.

'D'you reckon you'll be needing a hand, mate?'

At this time of year the cows were dried off, so the question was not one that required an immediate answer. But it marked a turning point in this process of mourning. It was time to plan the future, and already some of the boundaries were being staked out.

'We just wondered,' Joan said, unable to keep the anxiety out of her voice. 'I mean we're not quite sure where things stand.'

What they meant was, what was in it for them, now that the farm had slipped out of their grasp. The sisters had all been left money, but the real treasure lay in the land.

'Well, I guess Edith's a pretty handy milker,' said Jack, nastily.

'She's a good milker all right, faster than me,' said my father.

My mother was standing at the door. 'I won't be milking on this farm,' she said. 'I've finished with milking.'

There was one of those palpable awful moments that you wish you didn't have to live through.

My father said, evenly, 'I've got two sons, Arch. Thanks anyway.'

Everyone packed up soon after that, except Dorothy, who slipped off to the room she and I shared. My mother didn't leave the kitchen while they said goodbye to my father and me. I felt guilty because I had stayed with him, and not gone to her, yet, I understood that he didn't want to be on his own.

'You didn't say,' my father said, standing at the door of the kitchen when the last car had pulled out of the driveway. 'I thought you were in this with me.'

'You didn't ask,' said my mother.

'I did.'

'No, you didn't. You asked me if I would come with you, Glass Nichols. It's less than a week — have you forgotten that quickly? The choice is mine, you said.'

'So what are we arguing about?'

My mother picked up another overflowing ashtray and tipped its contents into a rubbish tin.

'You told me there was no choice for you. That you had to come.'

'How could I go anywhere without you?' my father said. 'I couldn't live without you.'

They looked at each other, full of painful yearning that I already knew would end in their entwined limbs and lush breathing on a double bed, wherever that room might be. They were like two creatures locked into an embrace that you sensed they would like to break out of, but never could. You could say, Dr Q, that it passed for a kind of happiness. Or, perhaps, that to be outside it was unhappiness. But I don't know the difference, because I don't know about passion.

'You don't?'

'Not really, no, I've never experienced that.'

'Does it bother you?'

'I'd like there to be some kind of hormone injection so that I could get it over with. You know, a shot of experience rushing through my veins.'

'Nothing long-term?'

'It causes a lot of bother.'

'But you'd like to try it?'

'Sometimes I feel caught in the middle, you know? It's like I know and I don't know.'

MY GRANDFATHER HAD not forgiven my father for a hasty marriage, one summer, to my mother, when Michael was on the way. But he allowed the couple to stay on the farm, provided my mother stayed clear of the church. There was a baby coming, and he felt it his Christian duty to ensure that his grandchildren were brought up in a proper way. This child, as his son's child, was all that would be left of the Nichols name.

But my mother is my mother, and of course she didn't stay away from the church. Her father had died in the mines down south, not long before she met my father; she lit candles for him. Everyone knew she was skiving off to mass from the word go, except for my grandfather. He found out when Michael was a baby. She took Michael to town to have him baptised, because you couldn't hold a baptism in secret, at least not in Walnut. What was worse, she took the old Nichols family christening gown with her and had him done in that, and his picture taken. Grandfather heard about it, anyway, which was when he told them to pack their bags and go.

You would wonder how he got away with it. But this was 1959, the world was a different place. Grandfather Nichols was never spoken of when I was small. His photograph was still on the wall when we returned to the farm from which my parents had been banished, although I didn't get long to study it. It disappeared in the purge. As I recall, his was a dour face, pinched around the mouth beneath a narrow moustache. I looked for a gleam of gentleness in his eyes but I couldn't see it.

Perhaps Edith swore to herself that she would never come back. We've never talked about it, she and I, but she told my brother, Michael, who is her favourite child. Me? Oh, I don't know where I come in the list. Why did she weaken? Was my father an addiction that she would, later, replace with others?

These are the things I ask myself now, not then. At the time, my mother made a great to-do of cleaning up after the relatives, banging dishes noisily and vacuuming out the room where they had sat. When she finished, she walked down the dark passage with its flower-infested walls and carpets, and threw open the door where Dorothy sat on a bed.

'You. Time for you to pack,' said my mother, her chin in the air.

'I looked after Glass's father,' said Dorothy. 'You can't just throw me out like this.'

'Glass will write you a cheque,' said my mother. 'Ten thousand dollars, take it or leave it.'

On top of what Dorothy had already been bequeathed by her father, I guess this was a generous offer. Dorothy left that night.

In the morning, all the furniture in the house left too, taken away by a local trucking company my mother had hired. I don't know when she had had time to order furniture, but that same night, the trucks came back to the farm, loaded with new beds and chairs and a table. The decorators moved in the following week. My father didn't say a word, or not that I heard.

But that was only the beginning. Shortly afterwards, she tore out the existing garden, all except a stand of magnolias and an avenue of old and graceful trees. In the spring, she began a new garden, and all through that summer, and every summer since then, although mostly it is piped now, she carried water from the river at night, until her garden became a miraculous profusion of colour. It was not a riot of colour, as they say, because my mother has always known where she would put every plant in her garden, and she has followed their progress, in the same way that my father appears to know every stem and blade of grass on his farm.

'SHE MUST BE quite something, this mother of yours.'

I shrug my shoulders.

'Did you admire the way she went at things?'

'I don't remember.'

'Come on now, you've just told me all this stuff. She didn't take things lying down, did she?'

'Yeah. Well, I'd forgotten about it.' My voice is rougher, wilder.

'You just remembered, eh?'

'Yeah.'
'How did your father feel about all the changes?'
'I don't remember. I want to go now, okay?'

eighteen

MILKING
THROUGH THE CRUSH of steaming animal bodies, Glass watches his son at work in the shed, the practised way he changes the cows over, his sure handling of the machinery, as if each action was second nature. He works much more quickly than his father these days. Glass hadn't expected it to be so hard to come back to the shed. It hadn't been so bad at the end of the season, but now it has begun again, and the cows are coming in so fast he finds it hard to keep up. His joints are full of unusual aches as if he is coming down with something. In the mornings his knees crackle in an alarming way when he bends over to put on his socks. This is it, he thinks, the beginning of age.

The cow he is supposed to be milking shifts uncomfortably; her milk has begun to let down in anticipation, creating a foamy puddle on the floor. He sees Bernard glance at him, and grins as if it's nothing. He and Bernard have always had this in common, if little else — their love for the warm, leathery flanks of the cows, the flood of their milk, the pulse of the machines. Now he wonders how long it can go on, or why it should. It's not just the work that's bothering him, it's the intolerable emptiness of the farm, a sense of loss that permeates every action he takes. It's there behind his eyes first thing when he wakes, and his heart aches with it when he lies hoping for sleep at nights.

'Any word of Orla?' he says, when they are hosing down.

'She's doing well enough,' Bernard says.

'I wondered if she might be back in time for the beginning of milking.' Although, clearly, this is not so.

'We could take on some labour,' says Bernard.

'I can manage,' says Glass.

'Well, then,' says Bernard, directing a high-pressure jet on the shed walls.

'About this baby,' Glass says. He almost has to shout to make himself heard.

Bernard turns the hose off. 'What about this baby?'

'I wondered. Bernard, Nathan ought to be here on the farm.'

'Yeah, well, you'd think so, wouldn't you?'

'If Orla was here.'

'Yeah?'

'Perhaps she could help out with the baby until Roberta's finished at the hospital.' There, he's said it, but as soon as the words are out he knows he shouldn't have said them. He has known all along they would be wrong, but still he had to try.

Bernard's face is bleak. 'On loan, d'you mean?'

'Well, never mind.'

'Listen,' says Bernard, 'nut cases like Rob can stay locked up for years, and then they come out and make trouble. You see if I'm not right.'

'She's your sister.' But it's just something to say.

'Let's get something straight,' says Bernard. 'Orla'll come back in her own good time.'

TRUE VIRGINS

THROUGH THE TREES, he sees Edith, and for once there is no sign of Wendy. Sometimes he feels that their incessant conversation will drive him crazy. Their talk is meaningless to him; when he approaches, they look up with slight irritation, as if he is intruding. Wendy has moved in again like one of those aunts who come for a week and stay forever. There is a worryingly permanent feel about this visit, as if she is more sure of herself than the first time. She makes herself useful in a multitude of ways that are difficult to argue with. Glass sometimes wonders what makes her so different from his sister Dorothy, whom Edith had so summarily dispatched. Several times, lately, he has prepared himself to tell Wendy she must go. As if sensing this, Wendy slips out of sight when Edith is not at hand.

Through the still bare branches of deciduous trees Glass watches Edith dividing up perennials, ready to plant them out in borders for the coming summer. He sees young Edith Murphy, and his eyes mist behind his glasses.

You work backwards, if you dare.

It is 1957, or thereabouts. They have been vague to their children about the dates when they met. He, too, has lost sight of the facts.

There is a line of ragged fruit trees along the driveway that have since been replaced. He looks up and sees Edith walking down through the trees towards him, although he is with her too. He's scared and he doesn't know how to look his father in the eye.

And yet there is the feeling, as well, of being somehow proud and excited. As if the world were full of surprises and one of them had just caught up with him.

He'd been looking for a true virgin when he met Edith, but he soon found there weren't many around. There were plenty of girls who said yes after dances at the Walnut community hall, for which he was grateful, but he had more than that in mind. Of the possible virgins he did meet, he didn't care much for what was on offer.

Edith Murphy was different. They met at the Majestic Cabaret when he was down in Wellington to play football one weekend. The night after the game, at which he had scored the team's only try, he had been out to score again. He remembers the beer, and the dancing that followed, the streamers and balloons that they leapt up to burst with their cigarettes, the excuse-me dance when he was left at a loose end after a team-mate prised him away from the girl he was dancing with, cheek to cheek, just for the hell of it, to remind him he wasn't the only guy in town.

That's when he saw her, sitting in a shadow of the room, wearing a blue dress with a sash at the waist, like a kid, and shoes with straps. Straps, for God's sake.

'Like a turn?' he said, as if he was conferring a favour.

When she stood up, she was much taller than she appeared sitting down, and too thin. But she danced as though her blood were on fire, without speaking, barely following him, almost as if she were dancing on her own.

He danced the next two dances with her. When his mates looked over at him, he grinned and shrugged his shoulders, as if to say, a bit of a novelty.

'Walk you home?' he asked, when it was over. 'Unless you live on the other side of town, because I came here on the train, and I'm skint.'

'Just along the street,' she said.

She led him up Boulcott Street, past St Mary of the Angels, and he saw her head kind of bob as they passed the church. He could see it then, the Catholic look of her, and he nearly turned around on the spot, but he was holding her hand and he liked the feel of her fingers linked with his. Halfway up the hill that climbs towards The Terrace, she turned off towards the back of the Grand, where a frail wooden bridge over a gully connected the street with the rear of the hotel.

'I've got a room here,' she said. Christ, he hadn't thought of her as rich; she looked as if she was on the bones of her arse.

'I work here,' she explained, leading him towards the staff quarters.

'You'd better go now,' she said, dropping her voice in the passageway. 'I'll get the sack if they catch you inside the building.'

They had paused by a doorway. 'Is this your room?' he said, as she slipped a key out of the cloth bag that hung on her wrist.

She nodded, her eyes full of sudden apprehension and a new appraisal of him. He could see that she had never meant him to come as far as this, but she hadn't wanted to let go any more than he had. Her look turned to terror when he took the key from her hand and slipped it in the lock.

Inside the room, he pushed her against the bed, confident now that she wouldn't scream. He'd guessed by now that the hotel was her first job. Did he force Edith Murphy? He would say that he didn't. He would tell himself, even now, that she wanted it.

He still had his trousers on when they started; he remembers with pleasure the resistance he found inside her; with shame, he remembers the blood on his fly he couldn't hide when he returned to his own hotel, and the rest of the team still up and partying as he walked into the lobby.

'Guess she had her monthly,' he said, and laughed.

In the morning, the team climbed on to the train, which was hissing steam down the station, their scarves floating behind them in a dawning southerly wind. He didn't know why he looked over his shoulder, but when he did she was there, dressed in a thin white jersey and a red skirt, shivering in the wind. He caught the glint of a cross on a gold thread of chain round her neck. He didn't wave out to her, or let on that he knew her, even though they were looking straight at each other. He could sense the trouble of her. All the same, he was touched by her image, like an insubstantial figure in a grainy old movie.

Glass thought he would never see her again — you could say that he prayed he wouldn't. But he did, one morning in late spring, when he called at the box for the mail after the rural delivery van had passed.

'Hullo,' she said, from where she sat by the letter-box, a suitcase by her side. Even before she stood up, he could tell that he had been right about the trouble. Her stomach was a bump under her skimpy dress, the same one she had been wearing at the dance, without the sash.

'I'll look after you,' Glass said, after an awkward silence. 'You'd better come and meet the family.' For the first time, he was grateful that his mother was dead.

She nodded and took his hand. They walked up the driveway together, petals scattering down on them from the flowering trees. That was the closest they came to celebration.

'Those were the trees you tore out,' Glass says to himself, 'in that one giant day of bulldozing. You remember, Edith, I never said a word. I understood why, although it wasn't what I wanted. At least, I think I understood, but my father was dead, and I had stood by you, and I thought it was enough. I thought I didn't have to give everything up. Not everything.'

He doesn't think about the day he told her to give up the church, just as his father had done (no, he's too hard on himself, it wasn't like that, he had right on his side). And Edith said, carelessly, 'Oh, it's not really the church — who cares about the church. I've given up God, which could be a problem. We'll just have to see.'

He's hoping she will look up and see him. He'll signal across the space between them — Hi, Edith Murphy, how's it going — but she works away without seeming to see him, a weather-beaten woman kneeling to trim her end-of-winter garden.

'Edith, we need to talk,' he says. He speaks quietly so as not to startle her.

She stands, dusting down her jeans, and he has the impression that she has known he was there all the time.

'I keep meaning to pull it all out,' she says, gesturing around the garden. 'I don't know that it's worth the effort.'

'You need peat on that garden,' he says. 'Bring things on nicely in the summer, the same as last year.' He has been sparse with his praise in the past.

'Wendy persuaded me to leave it a little longer.'

'Edith, I think we should see the lawyer. I've had a letter.' The envelope has been burning a hole in his pocket for the last two days. 'The Cooksleys are taking a court order to get permanent custody of Nathan.'

'Well, that was to be expected.'

'We can't let them do that.'

'Can't we?'

They stand glaring at each other.

'Let's get something straight,' she says, pocketing her pruning secateurs. 'Why are we doing this? Exactly why are we planning to hang out for Nathan?'

He studies her for a few minutes, looking hard for Edith Murphy. Knock knock, he wants to say, like the kids do, anyone home? He thinks he sees her there, that scared and scary girl.

'I mean,' says Edith, 'do we just want to make him a gift he can't wait to resist? Like this?' She sweeps her arm towards the skyline beyond the farm.

'History,' he says. 'I don't care who gets the farm when I'm dead.'

'Don't you, Glass?'

'Not really. The kids can do what they like with it. What about Roberta?'

'Ah,' she says, 'that's different.'

This is the moment Wendy picks to walk out of the potting shed.

Glass's face freezes. 'I thought you were inside.'

'I'm sorry,' she says, with a deprecating smile. 'I didn't realise you were still here.'

'Glass thinks we should be putting up a fight for Nathan,' says Edith.

'Edith,' says Glass, his voice full of warning.

'Personally,' says Edith, 'I think it's time our daughter pulled her socks up.'

'You don't believe that,' Wendy says.

'You don't know what I believe,' says Edith rudely. 'You're both being ridiculous. If the girl had wanted her baby that would be one thing. But you can hardly fight to make her keep it.'

'It's not her fault,' says Wendy.

'What do you know about it?'

'Sometimes I think you're quite narrow,' their visitor says. It's as if Glass isn't present.

He turns and walks slowly between the trees, feeling, again, the bone-aching creak of his knees. It gives him little satisfaction that these women have fallen to quarrelling.

A MANDELBROT SET

HE SEES A small bus, one of those mini-vans, parked near the road. He should have known as soon as he saw them, a bunch of weird-looking jokers with binoculars strung around their necks, and walk-shorts and socks and sandals — you could spot them for crazies, a mile off. But Glass can't believe he's seeing right. At first he starts running towards the men, then he slows down and recrosses the paddock, in the direction of the house. He enters by the back door and quietly picks up his gun.

One of the men stands at the front of the group, waving his arms.

'Do any of you recognise this pictogram?' he cries out to the others.

Glass had believed the circles long gone. Yet, in the pasture, he sees that the shadow of them, a fuzzy outline of the peculiar formations, can still be perceived. Perhaps it is the new season's regrowth that has thrown them into relief again.

'Yeah, Norm, if it's what I think it is. It's a very exciting find.'

'I tell you, we're looking at a Mandelbrot set.'

'Okay,' says Glass. 'You've had your fun, you can get on your way now.'

'Mr Nichols, is it?'

'That's me, but you can forget the ceremony. Just go,' says Glass, his hand instinctively tightening round the gun.

The man is insensitive or a fool or both. He doesn't appear to understand the danger he is in. 'I beg your pardon, Mr Nichols, but what you are looking at here is the expression of a higher form of intelligence. Surely you wouldn't deny access to one of the great mysteries of the galaxy.'

'There's no spacemen here. Now bugger off.'

'What we're looking at is a mathematical formula denoting infinite chaos, which may relate to the pattern of worlds beyond ours. You see, these circles, they just keep going on and on multiplying. There's no knowing where they might go next.'

'Infinite chaos, is it?' says Glass, lifting the gun a fraction higher.

The man called Norm says, 'You don't need to worry. They only seem unpredictable, like earthquakes. But that's because we don't have the correct mathematical equations to describe the dynamics of their system. Once we know that we'll be closer to understanding how chaos is generated. You see?' His face gleams with perspiration and what Glass perceives as mad, moist eyes glistening behind his spectacles.

'I'm going to shoot you bastards.' Glass raises the gun.

'I think he means it,' says one of the men, and most of the group begin to climb back into the van. After a moment, Norm decides to join the retreat. A very old man, wearing a raincoat over his shorts, takes longer than the rest. 'Don't shoot me,' he says, putting his hands up, as Glass takes aim.

Glass meets the eye of the old man, and lowers the gun. When they're gone he sits down in the paddock, his head on his knees, and weeps. He, Glass Nichols.

nineteen

SARAH

SARAH AND ELLIE and Jack begin to eat dinner together again. Once more she prepares food every night, her recipe books strewn around the kitchen. Her job in advertising is going well; she has a promotion and hasn't had to ask the barbecue manufacturer and his new wife for extra money for some time. She has passed through her crisis, she has moved on. The children's school reports have improved already. One evening, Sarah makes spinach quiche and tossed salad, which the children eat without asking for McDonald's. Ellie, who is doing a genealogical table for homework, wants details about her grandmother's family.

'I'm afraid I didn't know them,' says Sarah.

'Don't you want to know?' asks Ellie.

'I guess so.'

'I want to know everything about Wendy,' Ellie says. She has a tremble in her voice, and Sarah thinks, damn, why is there always just one more thing to solve. Except that lovers and husbands and disputes go away, but mothers don't. 'I miss her,' says Ellie, 'and you don't even care.'

Sarah tries to ring Wendy at the camping ground the next day. It is hard to remember clearly why they quarrelled in the first place but now this amorphous disagreement has escalated. Sarah dismisses Wendy in her head as a vain, interfering old woman, a lifelong misfortune she has to endure. While she had felt injured and bereft about matters in general, she had written Wendy a letter she has since regretted. There has been no reply and she is ashamed.

'Your mother hasn't been here for months,' the camp proprietor tells her. 'There's a big pile of mail sitting here waiting for her, but we don't know where to send it. Will I redirect it to you?'

'I suppose so,' says Sarah, with the old impatience. Her mother is as irresponsible as ever; it isn't all her fault that they have quarrelled. When she hangs up there is a moment of unease, but then she tells herself, Wendy has shifted so many times, at such short notice, that it's no cause for immediate alarm. All the same, she thinks she will soon make some enquiries.

When the mail arrives, in a bundle held together with a rubber band, the envelopes are brittle and discoloured where damp teacups have sat on them in the camping ground proprietor's office. Sarah thinks of herself as a principled person in this respect. Whatever her failings, she has never opened other people's mail.

She rolls the rubber band off the half dozen or so envelopes. There is a renewal form from the electoral office, two unpaid bills — one for a veterinary account for a seagull with a broken wing, the other for the repair of a heater. And there is a letter addressed in her own handwriting which causes her to gasp with relief. She rips it in two without looking inside, and shoves it in the rubbish bin. There is also an official-looking letter from a government department:

Dear Mrs Mullen

We have had a complaint laid with us which suggests that you may be in receipt of certain information, the use of which contravenes the Privacy Act. You should be aware that the breach of confidential documents is a serious matter and will be treated accordingly.

Yours faithfully
Office of the Registrar of Births, Deaths and Marriages

This makes no sense at all to Sarah. Finally, there is a letter with a pawnbroker's sign of three gilded balls above the return address:

Dear Mrs Mullen

We wish to advise that if we do not receive a payment for the loan you have taken from us within seven days, the goods you deposited as security will be sold.

Yours faithfully
G. Sterling
Proprietor, Certainties Pawn Shop

'Actually,' says Sarah, 'I believe I know the owner of this piece, I've seen it before.' The Earl of Maudsley's silver bird lies gleaming cold fire as Gunther Sterling wraps it in tissue paper for her. 'Funny, I could have sworn it was part of a pair. You couldn't let me have the name of the person you got it from?'

Gunther has fair, smooth features and a spiky haircut. He bunches up his mouth over his secrets.

'I couldn't divulge information like that,' he says.

Sarah eyes light on a gold sovereign chain. The price label says five hundred and ninety dollars.

'Just what I've been looking for,' she exclaims.

Their eyes lock. Sarah's mouth is open and excited, as she holds the chain in her hand. The tip of her tongue hovers on her upper lip. Gunther reaches for her credit card again.

'I think I have a recent address for the lady,' he says. 'She rang the other day to see if it was sold.'

Sarah is certain, as soon as she sees it, that this is a number she has rung before. She is at once disconcerted and reassured.

'SO WHERE IS she?' Ellie asks that night.

'She's staying with some friends.'

'I don't believe you,' says Ellie.

Sarah points to the bird on the mantelpiece. 'I expect she'll come and see us when she's good and ready.'

twenty

ROBERTA

NURSE PEACH WAYLAYS me to report that I have a visitor. I have refused so many visitors that she is concerned about how I will react. 'I'm sorry, she's really insistent,' says Nurse Peach. 'I told her you didn't have to see her if you don't want to.'

'Who is it?' My first thought is to go and look for Jed and see if he wants to bite some ears off. This is what he does to people who get in his way.

But before Nurse Peach has a chance to answer we are at the day room door, and I can tell that she has been charmed by my visitor and wants to give it a chance. Marise has her back to me when I walk in. From the way she stands, I can see she is nervous. I would be, too. A commotion is in progress down the corridor where a man is being committed. You might think you are voluntary in here, but it can be an illusion if you start causing problems. He wails and shouts for help; the doors have been temporarily locked. Nurse Peach has to leave me alone with Marise.

When she turns round I see she is more beautiful than ever, the butterfly wings of her grey silk hair cupped under her chin, an uncertain smile illuminating her face. She has put on weight. Marise is pregnant.

Whatever unpleasant thing I was going to say dies on my lips. I hurry towards her and we are in each other's arms, embracing. Then I hold her from me so I can examine properly the interesting bump of her stomach.

'Three months,' she tells me, proudly. 'I'm showing early, aren't I?'

'You were always so thin, you'd show a pea in five minutes. Is Derek pleased?' I don't ask aloud if it's Derek's baby.

'Yes,' she says, answering the spoken and unspoken questions at once. 'I think he's pleased, but scared as hell, at our age.'

'Yes, I can understand that.'

'Oh sweetie.' She is still holding me, the first person who I've allowed to touch me like this in months. 'I reckon it was you and Nathan that did it. Rush of hormones, you know?'

158

I don't really. She always thought I knew things like this, but I didn't; Nathan just happened, like part of a programme.

'When are you going to see him?' Marise asks.

'Is that what you're here for? Did they send you?'

'Who's they?'

'Look, Marise, I'm right into therapy now, and it's working.'

'He's only a little baby,' says Marise.

'Have you seen him?'

She avoids my eye. 'Not for a while. Roberta, please listen to me.'

'Don't start lecturing me, Marise. They'll throw you out of here, if you do.'

'Well, it's quite a little hidey-hole you've got here, isn't it?' She looks mean and calculating, just the way she does when somebody is telling her obvious lies about their tax evasion. I really hate her at moments like that. 'Why don't I just leave now?'

I sit down in one of the big dark blue chairs and stare at the notice board on which we wrote at the last group meeting: I Want to Have a Happy Life. No Nuclear Bombs in the Pacific This Week. I Want My Little Girl to Get New Friends Who Don't Know Where Her Mummy Is. May Nurse Peach Burn in Hell. This last, added after the meeting, has been clumsily half-erased. Lucky for them I don't know who did it.

'Quit staring over my shoulder,' Marise says.

'I thought you were leaving.' I've learned a few tricks of my own in here.

'Now you just listen to me,' she says. I can tell that she has worked out that she has to get this in quickly, while the staff are preoccupied. 'I've got the placenta of your baby in my freezer.'

I sit up, appalled.

'Yes, well actually I'm not very keen on it, either. To tell you the truth, it makes me sick looking at it. I thought it was kind of sweet when your friend Josh rang me up about it, and I agreed to take it from him. But I can understand why his wife didn't want it — it gives me the creeps too.'

'I didn't ask you to keep it. Get rid of it.'

But while I am sitting there, within shouting distance of the insane and our keepers, something is boiling up inside me. It is feeling. It is the look of Nathan when he was born and the milky smell of him when I held him. It is the way he lay in my arms in the train and trusted me, rockin', rollin' all the way, and I betrayed him.

'I'll tell them I'm going out.'

'Now? With me?'

'Yes.'

'Won't they stop you?'

'I doubt it.'

Marise looks agitated. 'Roberta, Josh Thwaite is with me.'

'Why? What are you up to?'

'Nothing. I'm not up to anything, you silly, self-centred bitch. He rang me to see what I'd done about it, and I told him I wouldn't do anything without telling you. So he said if you didn't want it, he'd fix it for me. The guy's responsible, even if he's a bit off the planet.' She glances around. 'Well, you've got kinkier friends than Josh Thwaite, if you don't mind me saying so.'

We stand glaring at each other. Marise doesn't seem phased that she has just abused me in these surroundings, as if she's stopped noticing them. She even looks pleased with herself. 'He said I shouldn't have to do it on my own, so we agreed to drop by and tell you before we buried the thing.'

'Okay, I'm still coming.'

Things have died down in the corridor. I go along and find Nurse Peach. 'I'm off out with my friend.'

She is startled. 'Are you sure this is a good idea, Roberta?'

Marise appears behind me, looking ethereal, and totally trustworthy. 'We'll only be an hour. It's such a lovely day, I thought Roberta might like a drive around the bays. We might go for a little walk.'

'I'd love that,' I say, like a child pleading for an outing, and Nurse Peach looks reassured and pleased for me.

'Take a jersey,' she advises, as if she is my mother.

When Josh Thwaite first sees me, I think he is going to jump out of Marise's car and run away. His brown, shining curls have grown longer, gripped in their pony-tail with one of those coloured elastic bands that girls buy from the supermarket. There is black stubble on his chin.

Marise hesitates, then throws him the car keys. 'I'll get in the back,' she says, before either of us can argue. A faint bitterish smell of sweat clings to him. I like it.

It is a still, translucent day, more than a year since my family had celebrated the coming of Nathan, and here I am, riding along beside Josh Thwaite in Marise's sleek red Porsche to collect his placenta. This strikes me as so peculiar and funny that I throw my head back and laugh. The sound startles me as much as it does my companions. I don't remember when I last laughed out loud. I try it again. Ha ha ha.

'It's all right, I'm nuts,' I say.

Josh glances at Marise in the rear vision mirror.

'No, you're not,' replies Marise sharply. Josh gives an almost imperceptible nod.

Simmer down, I tell myself. If you don't shut up, they'll take you back.

At her house, Marise orders Josh to pull into the driveway. 'I won't be long,' she says, disappearing through her shrubbery.

Josh and I are left sitting alone, side by side. He rests his hands over the leather steering wheel. I look for signs of paint under his nails and see none.

'I'm on ACC right now,' he says, and shows me the scar of a healing cut on the palm of his hand. I touch it briefly, brushing my fingers over his. We smile at each other nervously and glance away.

This is unfinished business; some day I will want to reflect, in tranquillity, what it was like the day Nathan was born, the way Josh kept me safe. I'm not ready for it yet, but I guess this will be the last time I see him.

'Why did you do it?' he asks.

'Please don't you start.'

'Was it because of me? I mean, did you get in that much trouble?'

'It was my trouble, not yours.' I can see he doesn't believe me. 'I couldn't look after Nathan. I couldn't keep him safe.'

'Are you sorry?'

I shake my head back and forth. 'Don't ask,' I tell him, hearing a quake in my voice that threatens to get out of control.

'Do you dream about him?'

'Why should I do that?'

'Because I do,' he says.

'Josh, I don't dream about anything. I take medicine.'

He sighs. 'What would you like to do with the baby's placenta?'

'What did you have in mind?' I had thought that perhaps we should just get rid of it at the tip, but now I'm not so sure.

'Leda buried hers and we planted a tree over it.' This reminder of Leda brings me back to reality; I definitely won't see him again. But in a way, this knowledge makes me bold.

'Did you have a boy or a girl?'

'She had a boy. She's got one of each now.'

This is an odd way to put it, as if Josh is disclaiming the children. He runs his fingers nervously through a strand of his rich hair, and for a moment I think he is going to tell me something, but then Marise appears, a plastic shopping bag and a spade balanced in one hand, a picnic basket in the other. Josh gets out to help her put the last two in the boot. She holds on to the bag.

'Can I look at it?'

'I wouldn't if I were you,' says Marise, but I do anyway. The contents of the bag are a shrunken, livery-looking bundle.

'Where to?' asks Josh.

I CHOOSE A hill covered by pine trees at the back of the zoo where it is quiet. The hilltop is reached by a rough road and walking tracks that peel off from its edge. Sunlight slants through the trees on to the merry scarlet car.

'Remember what you said about shadows on the sun, that time?' I say to Marise.

She smiles at me, in acknowledgement, and nods her head. It feels right, that this part of me should be laid under a soft coating of needles illuminated by fractured sunlight, where nobody is likely to disturb it.

As Josh points out, it is important we that bury the placenta deeply, safe from marauding animals. We choose a young, straight sapling. Marise and I sit among the pine needles while Josh starts digging beneath it, protecting his injured left hand as well as he can. Soon I take over, enjoying the swing of the spade and the earth turning in the cool, damp air. They seem surprised by my strength.

When the hole is dug, I lay the placenta in its bag in the ground. We look at each other uncertainly.

'Should we say something?' says Marise. 'You know, sing, or anything like that?'

'It's not a funeral,' says Josh. What he means is, we shouldn't get too solemn and ritualistic.

But then I remember the way my mother used to sing to me under her coat and, without looking at them, I begin to sing the first thing that comes into my head, some lines from 'Morning Has Broken'. 'Morning has broken/like the first morning,' I sing. 'Blackbird has spoken/like the first bird.' They begin to hum quietly along behind me. 'Praise for the singing, praise for the morning . . . ' And that's all I can remember.

I ask Josh if he has a pocket knife. He doesn't but Marise has a fruit knife in her picnic basket. I want to make a nick in the bark of the tree so that I will remember the spot. I can't make much of an impression on the wood, but I think to myself that Dr Q would approve. The placenta is buried deep in the woods but I have instilled the memory within myself: I am not ready to slide into oblivion.

CAT TWISTS

DR Q HAS tripped and fallen as he was running for the bus this morning. He looks pale and out of sorts.

'Look,' he says, in that slightly accusing way men have, when they have hurt themselves. He shows me the mud on his jacket, the place where he has grazed himself. I don't touch him, the way I did Josh, but I am pleased he has shown me. I take it as a small sign that he sees me as a real human being with whom he can share his discomforts, rather than someone for whose needs he must always cater.

'You never believe it'll hurt so much when you fall,' I tell him. I explain how I used to be a gymnast.

'Do you remember the worst fall you ever had?' he asks with interest.

'Yes,' I say, 'only don't try and analyse it, okay?'

Taking his silence as agreement, I recall for him the last night I went to the gymnasium. 'I tried to do a cat twist. You know how a cat lands on its feet when it's dropped?'

'Yes, I do, but you're not a cat. I mean, human beings aren't cats.'

'No, but it's possible to learn the same principles of motion. This is to do with Newton's Third Law of Motion. For every action force there's a simultaneous force, equal in magnitude but opposite in direction. By varying the moments of inertia, a body changes its resistance to motion. That's what a cat does when it's in the air, and ends up on its feet.'

'Hmm, that's interesting. I had a cat that never used to land on its feet. It worried me.'

'You need more than one trick to be a gymnast,' I tell him. 'Amplitude, that was a word my coach used. It means breadth and abundance, so that for every jump and swing you take you have enough range to complete it. And courage. You have to have courage to perform. You can't have amplitude without courage.'

'Quite so. I can see that.'

'Do you think I lack courage, doctor?'

'That's not the way I see you.'

'But I didn't complete the jumps.'

'You lived in the country. Who took you to gym?'

'My father, as a rule. My mother made me all the fancy outfits, made sure I had the snazzy leotards. She's clever like that. I think she was trying to make up for my communion dress.'

'Oh yes?'

'Doctor, we had a deal.'

'Yes, so we did, Roberta. I apologise.'

I can't hold it against him. I've got here on my own. In a way, I don't care whether he listens or not.

SOME ASPECTS OF SEXUAL DESIRE

IT WAS AT church that my mother got to know Alec McNulty, the man who was with Father Bird in the cemetery on the day of my grandfather's funeral. This is the man I call my mother's prince of darkness. Alec was the church organist, although you wouldn't have thought so if you'd seen him. I think he once played in a dance band. At some time he turned up in Walnut as a farm labourer and, finding himself the only man around who could tickle a tune out of the church organ, he was persuaded to play on a regular basis. Alec, who was about fifty, had close-cropped hair and heavy wrists, and eyes that looked at young girls. My mother wasn't young when they became friendly; she was in her late thirties.

Why have I spoken so little of my mother? I've told you what she looked like, and the things she did, but, actually, I haven't much idea about the kind of person she is. She is so elusive, with her erratic charm, her sudden black moods, that I find it impossible to pin down her nature in a way I can describe. Her past feels dark and impenetrable. One night, a few years ago, we were watching television together at the farm when the Pope was visiting the country. Pictures appeared on the screen of sick people being taken to see him at an outdoor rally. A woman was wheeled out in a bed, her gaunt expression like a death mask, her eyes staring into space. The camera lights were trained on her scraggy neck and her thin pathetic arms struggled to lift themselves in acknowledgement of a blessing. It made me feel ill to watch, but my mother suddenly sat forward in her chair, focusing all her attention on the woman.

'My God,' she said, 'That's Nellie Civil meeting the Pope. Fancy.' She used the remote to flick the image off the screen.

'Who was Nellie Civil?' I enquired.

'Oh, a nobody. I mean, like a nobody. I went to school with her. She used to walk backwards round corners so she wouldn't meet strangers.'

'Down the West Coast?'

'I can't remember,' she said, because she had been drinking. I have never been to the West Coast, but I did go to church for a long time. I have more than a passing knowledge of the Pope's ways.

When I was small, before our return to the farm, my mother took us children to church, wherever we were staying at the time. The boys kept an eye on me while she went up to the communion rail and bobbed before the altar, and sometimes, depending on how strict a church it was, I would be allowed to run and dip my hands in the baptismal font and splash water over myself. My father didn't seem to mind, but then I don't recall him minding anything in those days.

It was after we came back that everything changed. There was a tension in the air when Sunday came around. My mother couldn't avoid the relatives who lived all about us. They called to visit, their faces stiff with disapproval at everything she did, but this new mother of mine, so determined to do what she wanted, in return for going back, never missed church. She got in the car and drove down the road. I suppose it got to my father, torn between her and his sisters.

When we got to church, she would act very devout, sitting up near the front and not taking her eyes off Father Bird during the sermon, or Alec McNulty while he belted out the hymns. It was a sound that made you want to tap your toes rather than incline yourself to God. His eyes sparkled when we sang and his shoulders moved up and down. He often smiled in our direction; my mother had a soaring soprano voice, one of those that others use as an instrument to follow.

My brothers, who had both practised the faith until then, were also torn apart over this. But they were teenagers; they shrugged it off and, before long, they stayed home. Soon Michael left the Widerup, went to boarding school and never really came back to the farm. He found friends, and often stayed with them through the breaks. His visits home, since then, have been rare. Bernard elected to stay at school in Walnut, and I guess that would have suited my father; Bernard had to work hard enough to make up for Michael.

My mother began to help with work around the church, doing flowers, that kind of thing. She had started taking a night class in floral art, driving into town one evening a week.

The day was drawing near for my First Communion. I should have taken it earlier, but with all the shifts we'd made I was behind with my religious instruction. I was very mystical and spiritual, the way little girls are. At the convent school I went to, we used to sing 'O Mary, we crown you with blossoms today, Queen of the Angels, Queen of the May', for the May procession, marching around with angelic expressions on our faces. I thought a lot about the Virgin Mary.

But my day never happened. At dinner, one evening, my mother said she thought perhaps I should leave it for a year. I couldn't believe she would say this to me.

'I'm not sure that you're ready, Roberta,' she said, sitting and patching a sheet in a virtuous way. My father was reading the newspaper. I saw the pages become still.

The material for the white dress had been bought. I began to scream with rage and frustration. 'I don't care what Dad wants,' I shouted.

'It's nothing to do with me,' said my father.

'Yes it is, it is. You always growl at Mum for going to church.'

'Well, I haven't growled this time,' my father said.

'It's true, darling,' said my mother. 'It's not your Dad's fault. Father Bird and I have decided it would be better if we took our time over this decision.'

'I'm not going to church any more,' I raged at her.

'Well dear, we'll have to see about that.' Only there was a look of satisfaction in her eyes which I didn't understand at the time. I can see it now that I'm grown up. This was what she wanted from me. My father folded his paper and went outside into the dusk of evening. I saw him walking towards the paddocks, not looking back. My mother went to the window and watched him for a moment.

I don't remember any abatement of the cries which echoed from their bedroom in the weeks that followed. But it astonishes me that she imagined my father would not work it out. I suppose this is what lovers are like when they are so obsessed by their passion that they think can get away with anything.

One Friday, that summer, my father was away, as he always was; that's the day farmers go to town to do their business. You could bank on him being gone for several hours.

It was the school holidays. Bernard and I were hanging around the house, his chores finished until evening. My mother had worked in the garden all morning, and had just taken a shower; a cloud of perfume seemed to billow around her. 'Would you like to take my car and go for a drive with Roberta?' she said to Bernard, with a lovely big smile. Bernard was fourteen at the time, and practising to get his licence the day he turned fifteen. He was big for his age — he'd just begun to shave fluff off his face — but he went bright red with pleasure when she made him this offer, even though I could see that having me along took the shine off it.

So we set off, Bernard and I, driving towards nowhere in particular, although my mother had given us money for ice creams when we got to the store. We were thinking of driving out to the coast. Before we had gone very far, though, the car's engine began to splutter and miss.

'We're going to have to turn back,' he said. I saw that he was frightened. There would have been a penalty if we'd been caught. I imagine he was worrying that we would break down and have to be rescued, and then it would come out, ending his hopes for a licence.

The house, when we returned, was very quiet. My mother was nowhere to be seen. Bernard went around calling.

'I suppose she can't be very far away. D'you want to make some lunch?'

'No thanks, I might go for a walk.' I didn't feel hungry at all, just uneasy.

'Don't go too far away,' he said, cast in the role of reluctant baby-sitter. He sat down in front of the television; there wasn't much on in the daytime then, but he found a panel of women giving advice to people with problems and settled himself in to watch.

By the river, I saw my mother and Alec McNulty. There were buttercups out by the river, and sun shining through the willow branches. My mother was naked, lying back in the grass with light falling about her, so that her cream skin glowed gold-yellow. Alec McNulty's fingers trickled over her breasts, and the look on her face was pure exultation, closer to ecstasy than anything I had seen in church. She lay back in the grass, her hands behind her head, her knees pulled up, while he continued to stroke intimate places, first where you could see, and then so his fingers disappeared inside her. She kept her hands away, as if to prolong what he was doing, as if, were she to touch him, he might stop. Her spine arched over and again.

Alec did stop after a little while, saying something with which she agreed, and she seemed to spread herself even wider on the grass, while he slid his shorts down over his backside. I thought his face looked like that of a giant bullfrog, his throat working, as he lowered himself on to her. She reached up then and touched his face, as if it were beloved to her. I watched her shuddering pleasure in him, and heard her voice, harsh and unmusical. I thought that she, too, looked like a frog, a little buttery-coloured frog.

EVERYTHING IN THE house changed, now that I knew my mother loved somebody else. And although I didn't know exactly what for, I was waiting. Everybody would have known, one of the men would have told him, perhaps one of the brothers-in-law. I can see the scene, four or five men leaning on the rails at the saleyard, prodding the rumps of the beasts in the pen.

'Flighty creature,' one of them might have said. 'Drives the boys wild. How's the missus, Glass? Settling in, is she?' All the time needling the animal so that it jostled the other cattle. 'Causes a bit of trouble when she's put to the bull, if you ask me.'

And my father, his face flaming would have understood the crude shorthand. Then one of the older men would have taken him aside. 'Take no notice, lad, you're the only one who knows whether your hearth's clean or not.' This was how they talked.

I sit there, looking at the scene for myself, inspecting it.

'You don't have to go on with this,' says Dr Q.

I start, feeling guilty, seeing how tired he is today. I had forgotten his fall, his paleness.

'Unless you want to,' he says, and smiles at me. His concern has been for me, rather than himself. I am exhausted, too, but it feels as if we're in a relay race that has to be completed.

'There's not much more.'

WE WAITED IN the hotel for my mother to come. She was supposed to be meeting us there after shopping in the city. My aunts and uncles were there, at the end of a market day in Walnut. The dining room in the Walnut Hotel is exactly the same now as it was then, lined with maroon and gold embossed wallpaper.

Dinner was served on the ringing of a brass bell. There were no menus and no orders were taken; we all lined up to be served or went without. The chef stood and carved the meat off the legs of lamb, the haunches of beef and pork. The vegetables lay in four large stainless-steel dishes alongside. Dessert was pavlova and fruit salads arranged on a separate wagon.

'We'd better begin,' said Auntie Kaye. She had developed leather pouches under her eyes this last year or so, perhaps from all the cigarettes she smoked. She helped herself to two slices of beef, three of pork, one of lamb, all four vegetables, brown gravy and horseradish sauce. We held back.

'She'll be here soon,' said my father, with stubborn patience.

'The child's starving,' said my aunt, looking at me.

'Yes, all right. Go on, Roberta,' said my father, 'help yourself.' But he didn't take any for himself.

When I had finished what was on my plate, he urged, 'Go on, have some more, it's a treat. Hurry up, before your mother comes.' All the while, he kept glancing at his watch.

But she didn't come. She was upstairs, with Alec McNulty, up the crumbling stucco-lined staircase, in a room with cheap crumpled turquoise curtains and orange-checked blankets, and she'd forgotten what time it was. My father saw Alec trying to slide out the side door of the Walnut Hotel's Barracuda Restaurant, and the next moment, he was bolting up the stairs.

I see it over and again. I think she's putting on lipstick when he comes into the bathroom. The towels are fresh on the rail and the clean glasses still wrapped in their paper. She wears the stain of

Alec McNulty unwashed upon her skin. They walk down the staircase, his fingers on her wrist, and the piano player is playing 'Drunk with Love'. I remember this last part very clearly. The rest is something I see when I am in old seedy hotels, like the kind of places I worked in, and the boarding house where I went after I'd said goodbye to Nathan.

If you weren't part of it, you could say there was an element of farce about the end of my mother's affair — in one door and out the other, all those frozen moments that can still pull a laugh. But if you're in it, it's all pain. They brawled their way through months of shouting and pleading.

'You may stay if you wish,' he told her one morning, his voice cold.

Did she have a choice about leaving? I suppose so, but if she did, she didn't take it. I guess some women want to taste variety without its consequences. I'm sure the outcome was more than she had bargained for. And I think there was more to it than simply my father's discovery of her treachery; there was his grief too, his look of having been totally abandoned. Yes, I am partial to my father, though I am not blind to his weaknesses.

The outward signs of their fury stopped quite suddenly. Late one night I heard her screaming but he was silent; after a while, I understood that she and I were alone in the house. Later, she came into my room and lay down on the bed where Aunt Dorothy had been and soon she slept. I smelled the harsh odour of straight liquor.

When I speak of her prince of darkness, you may say that he had operated in exceptionally broad daylight, but what I mean is that a darkness entered her soul. Perhaps it was already there, just waiting for its moment. She became an alcoholic as soon as she began to drink. I read somewhere that alcohol is linked to the memory of sexual violence. Now, I suppose that would have come from Alec McNulty. Wouldn't it, Dr Q?

But strangely, they continued with a violence of their own. Michael came home for a time that year, and then he left, more or less for good. Sometimes I think that it's their lust that drove Michael away, beyond reach, and also, that it's what's held Bernard there, mesmerised, as if by two snakes devouring each other. I think Bernard was looking for someone like my mother, a saintly, Catholic woman who turned into a whore, but of course, Orla would never be like that.

The power within the house shifted. My mother never went to church again. Religion wasn't mentioned and I avoided it at school, standing stony-faced when prayers were read at assembly, my eyes straight ahead. My mother's garden flourished as she worked in it every day. Around five in the evening she took her first drink. In the summer she carried it outside, walking around looking at the roses; in the winter, she merely propped herself beside the stove where she was cooking dinner and drank. Sometimes it made a difference to the way she behaved; at other times you would scarcely notice it.

I became their perfect child, the centre of their lives and the conversation they had with each other.

'DID YOU EXPECT Nathan to be perfect?' asked Dr Q.

'I don't know. I didn't think about that. At least I don't think I did. I expected more of myself, I can tell you that. But then I always do.'

'You weren't disappointed in him?'

'No, not at all. Only in myself. When I saw Nathan he was all I could have imagined, but . . . '

'Yes?'

'Nothing really. That's all there is to it.'

'There's a saying we doctors have. Listen to everything that comes before the but.'

I feel like crying. I think I've been protecting myself with all this talk, but he can see through me all the time.

So I tell him. 'But when I took him home, he seemed like a doll.'

'Uh huh.'

'You don't seem very surprised.'

'Nothing much surprises me much any more, Roberta.'

'I felt like a doll who'd been put in charge of another doll. Big dolls and little dolls. What do you make of that?'

'I think we've probably made enough of things today.'

'You regard this as a breakthrough?'

'What do you think?'

'I want to see Nathan again.'

'Ah.' He rubs his sore elbow and his stomach grumbles. It's way past lunchtime.

'I want to see him properly, you know, a real person.'
'Good.'
'So we're finished then, you and me?'
'I think we've hardly begun. We can start on the work now.'
More work. Always, Dr Q has more work for me to do.

twenty-one

MRS BLUE EYES

AGAIN, WHEN I return to the ward, I have a visitor. I don't recognise her at first, a trim woman in early middle age, wearing a high-throated blouse and a severe jacket and skirt of very good cut.

She puts her arms out to me, but I am wary of strangers, especially those who want to embrace me. I am not sure whether she is a new patient and, if so, she may be a strangler, for all I know.

'It's He-*len*,' she cries.

Helen Blue Eyes.

'Dear Roberta,' she says. 'I came as soon as I heard. Well almost, because I had to get someone to care for our little girl.' She glances nervously at her surroundings, the way they all do. 'She's such a darling baby, just a few weeks younger than your little man.'

'Who told you I was here?'

'Well now, that would be telling, wouldn't it? I just heard you weren't so well.'

I rack my brains, trying to think who we know in common.

'Paul?' I hazard. She shuffles and I know I am right.

'How is he?'

She looks scared then; I can tell she doesn't know the half of it.

'Why don't we sit down?' I suggest. I steer her towards the courtyard. She looks over her shoulder, as if looking for someone to reassure her that she is not going to be knifed. It is cold outside, a sharp wind rattling the bamboos that edge the yard. I wear a heavy tamarillo-coloured jersey sent to me by Auntie Kaye, but Helen shivers in the wind. Jed sits smoking at a table with another patient, dressed only in a singlet over his trousers. He has lost some weight, his eyes look sunken. He comes and goes inside his electrically charged brain. I think they will be moving him on from here soon.

'Come and help us save the world, darling,' he calls to me.

'Not today,' I say. I motion for Helen to sit down. She leans towards me, her manner confidential.

'He's right,' she says. 'We should make plans to save the world. We have to save the children.'

I have forgotten what she is like; I glance around, wondering if Nurse Peach is handy, but she is nowhere to be seen, which is probably my own fault. I have been avoiding her since my excursion with Marise and Josh. I have not told anyone what we did.

Helen says, 'Did you know that a couple left their little girl in the middle of a freeway in America?'

'No,' I said.

'Terrible. A terrible thing. They had a pact to kill themselves and the little girl didn't want to do it with them, so they left her there. Now isn't that a dreadful story?'

'Dreadful,' I agree.

'You see, dear,' she says, leaning even closer towards me, 'when I heard that story, I thought, poor darling, I should have seen her mind was going.'

'Are you talking about me?'

'You did leave him, didn't you, dear?'

'Not like that.'

Her eyes shine with fervour. It occurs to me that she really has been admitted, and that when it comes eight thirty tonight the gates are going to be locked and I will be shut up here with her.

'Your little boy's doing really well.'

'He is?'

'You'll be proud of him when you see him, smiling and laughing all the time. I'm sure they'll let you see him soon.'

'I can see him whenever I want,' I say.

She smiles at me pityingly. 'Of course, dear,' she says.

'As a matter of fact, I'm going to see him tomorrow.'

'Yes, of course you are.'

'I really must say goodbye,' I say, in what I hope is my most engaging social tone. 'I'm late for lunch already, and you kind of look forward to things like that in here.' I know that in her inexorable way, she is going to tell me something horrible.

She gathers herself tidily together. 'Now, when they let you out of here, you mustn't mind what people say to you.'

'I won't.'

I can't stop what comes next, short of putting my hands over my ears and causing a scene.

'That little girl Michelle, who we did classes with, well, she's very young, she doesn't understand illness like more mature people do. She just blew up and said the nastiest things when I told her what had happened. You mustn't think that way, dear, I said to her, she can't help it, poor girl. Look, I said to her, having children simply drives some women mad. I told her it wouldn't happen to you again, they don't let it, do they? She'll have her tubes tied, I told her. Will they do it soon, dear?'

HOME TIME

'WELL,' I SAY to Nurse Peach, 'I'm off now. I'm going home.'

'Roberta,' she exclaims, with alarm. 'You can't go home yet.'

'Why not?'

'Where would you go?' I guess she is asking if I have a home to go to, but I am past having pride.

'I've got plenty of places to go.'

'Yes, but are you expected? Has someone arranged to pick you up?'

She knows she has me on the run. 'Are you going to detain me?' I ask.

'No-o. I don't think so. But we need to talk this through.'

'I've done enough talking.' And it's true, in a way, because this morning I have been so drained of words that I have none left for her.

'Have you talked about it with your psychiatrist?'

'He said we'd made a breakthrough.' I don't like being devious with Nurse Peach and, as I suspect, she is not going to let me get away with this.

'We'll have a talk to him about this,' she says.

'You can.'

'But, as I had half-expected, she is in for disappointment in that quarter. Dr Q has taken the rest of the day off sick by the time she gets through.

'If you're not going to detain me, I'm going to leave anyway.'

'He'll be disappointed about this.' When I have nothing to say, she asks again, 'Who will I ring to come and get you?' I have a suspicion she knows something I don't.

'Nobody. I can get a taxi.'

'I'll have to get some staff,' she says.

'What for?'

'So you can sign the form.'

'What kind of a form?'

'An A1. 9/94.'

175

I have no idea what this means, and I am not surprised when she leaves me waiting for a long time, hoping I will cool off. I tell myself to stay calm, not to let anyone provoke me, although it is one of those days when there is a tense, edgy feel about the ward, as if there is a northerly blowing outside. Eventually she comes back, followed by another doctor whom I hardly know. He is a pleasant man, flustered with overwork.

'You're sure about this, Roberta?' he says.

'Yep.' I've fallen into the ways of my companions in here.

Nurse Peach hands me a card with an appointment for a psychiatric out-patients' clinic. 'I hope you'll keep this appointment,' she says.

I nod in a businesslike way. The doctor is trying to assess my state of mind on the spot but I'm not giving him any openings. I smile and nod when he tries to engage me in conversation. He looks at Nurse Peach and shrugs.

'Well then, if you've made up your mind.' She hands me one of her forms, which is for discharge against medical advice. I fill in the gaps: I, Roberta Cooksley, hereby discharge myself from hospital.

When I have finished this task, she hands me my bag of clothes and I sign for my rings and some cash I have in safe custody.

'There's a bed here if you need it,' she says.

FAY, JUST HOME from her aerobics class, wears a fluorescent tracksuit and a matching headband with her Reeboks. Standing by the twin roller doors of her garage, she glows in the cool afternoon, until she sees me.

'What are you doing here?' she whispers, her manicured hand at her mouth.

'Where's Nathan?' I ask.

'They said they'd let me know if you were released.'

'They wouldn't have used that word, Fay. I was a voluntary patient.'

'Well, whatever.' Fay gestures impatiently as if I am playing a wilful game of semantics. She stands massaging her soft throat in a nervous way, and I realise with pleasure that she is afraid, as momentarily I was afraid of Helen, in the presence of someone she regards as a dangerous lunatic on the loose.

'I gave him to you, where is he?'

'Well dear, that was months ago, things change.'

'Nobody told me.'

'I gather you didn't ask.' I make her nervous, standing and looking at her. 'You didn't really think I'd turn in my job, did you?'

'I thought you'd look after him for me. I thought you'd want to.' But as I say it, that sounds like nonsense. The enormity of what I have done to Fay is something I've only just grasped; it is true she has a life of her own. I see how mad I was when I gave him to her. And worse, how could I ever have thought Nathan would be happy with her? This moment of enlightenment reassures me that I must be well, able, at last, to understand cause and consequence.

'So where is Nathan?'

I see Fay turning over in her mind whether to tell me, but it is a question she can hardly avoid. 'With his father, of course, where did you think he'd be? A child should be with its parents.'

'I know,' I tell her. 'I realise that now. I'm sorry for the trouble I've caused. I'll go and see him right away.'

'It's a bit late in the day for that, I'd have thought.' She is still nervous but a shift occurs; something about the nature of her fear changes. 'Well, I hope you've got somewhere to stay.' By late in the day, I think Fay means this particular day, this afternoon. For although I believe I am well, I have been in hospital a long time. Words have a literal meaning and I am not ready to translate their nuances, at least not here, not out in the world. As I turn away it does not occur to me that she is not talking of an hour or so here and there; she is talking about time for once and for all.

ROBERTA WALKS UP the hill along Ashton Fitchett Drive, pulling her patterned woollen jacket around her, the bag of clothes bumping her knees as she walks. The houses look different from when she was last here. This is not a place to be frightened of, she tells herself. She has been a scared stranger in this world of newness and development, this suburban landscape with the giant windmill turning its arms overhead. It is like settling in another country, and now she is ready to discover its topography, its surfaces and tributaries, until it is hers. She will be friendly and outgoing and invite people over. What has happened will pass into memory. It will be part of her history, but other people will forget.

A police car cruises slowly along the street. A safe place to live.

The house has a comfortable familiarity. She raises her hand to knock, thinking how odd it is to have to knock at your own door.

The two of them, Paul and Prudence, have been watching out for her. They have heard the news: Roberta is out.

As Paul opens the door, Roberta sees Prudence's face at the window, and recognises her at once. Nathan is in her arms.

'I'm home, Paul,' she says, the words thick in her mouth, like medicine.

'Go away, Roberta,' he says. 'We don't want any trouble.'

The police car just happens to be idling past the gate. Only Roberta sees that it is no coincidence.

Prudence, wearing a skirt printed with an ethnic design, wrapped gracefully around her slender waist, walks through from the kitchen into the hallway behind him. Just as Helen had said, Nathan is doing well, chuckling in Prudence's arms. Roberta reaches out to him, but he buries his face shyly against Prudence's shoulder.

'You brought it on yourself, Roberta,' says Paul and closes the door.

twenty-two

JOSH
THERE IS AN art theatre and coffee bar within walking distance of Ashton Fitchett Drive. All my money has gone on the taxi and I have no phone card. But the staff at the cinema remember me, a woman who sometimes, at the weekends, watched a movie by herself. As a rule, it is a crowded place, but towards the end of a movie's run you strike sessions when there is hardly a soul in the place. I would wait until the last day before the film was withdrawn, so I could sit in splendid isolation with only the cat that lives at the theatre on my lap, a couple of loners like myself and the screen filled with images for company.

Oh, the seeds of my destruction were there for all to see, long ago. How could Paul have made a mistake like me?

'Bit of a problem,' I tell the woman at the counter. 'Especially bad day at the office. Could I possibly use your phone?'

'Yeah, it'll be okay this time.' She knows I haven't been at the office. Have they heard about me, I wonder. They are showing *The Madness of King George*, and today is one of their rushed-off-their feet times. Madness is hot. 'I expected it to be funny,' says one woman to another as they leave a session. 'But it was pitiful, really. Didn't you think it was sad when he went round the twist?'

I clutch the phone, praying Marise hasn't given up work yet. It is more than a month since I saw her.

'God, what are you doing on the loose?' says Marise when I get through. It's meant to be a joke, but it falls flat. She sounds harassed. 'I'm in a case meeting,' she says, when I explain. 'Wait outside the theatre and don't move till I get there, okay?'

'You won't send the cops, will you?' I am surprised they have not followed me down Ashton Fitchett Drive, but perhaps their only brief is the maintenance of order in the street.

'Don't be ridiculous,' she says, and hangs up.

Now an hour has passed. Evening approaches as I wait for the red Porsche. But in the end it is Josh Thwaite in his battered Bedford van who sits in rush-hour traffic, honking the horn to attract my attention. I don't hesitate about getting in beside him, but once I have, I can't think how I could do this to myself — as if I'm not in enough trouble already. And it is only an afternoon since I left the hospital.

'Why did you come?'

'Marise couldn't make it. You put the shits up her, phoning like that. Did you run away?'

'No, I explained to her.'

'Well, she was in a bit of a rush when she spoke to me.' He looks rough, wearing a baseball cap and a Swanndri as if he, too, has come out in a hurry.

'You didn't have to come. You'd be best to keep away from me.'

'Don't tell me, I know that already.'

It seems as if the whole world is against me. The last time I saw Josh we had spoken to each other with great kindness. And it is certainly true that I have not asked him to come; I feel nettled by his attitude.

We head toward the sea, the bare, windswept bays where waves break in green shards of water on this cool, breezy evening. He pulls into a parking bay and we sit looking across the black needle-point rocks, the gap-toothed, barbaric coastline. His fingers drum on the steering wheel.

'Your old man doesn't want you back?'

'That's one way of putting it. You're not responsible for me.'

'We've been through that. Where am I taking you?'

I explain how I had wanted to see Marise and borrow some money. Tomorrow the idea is to go to my parents' farm. This is a plan I've worked out on the spot. I am seething with rage towards Marise, who has landed me in this, like a corny matchmaker who hasn't got her facts right.

'I'll take you to the farm now,' he tells me. 'The old girl's just had a rebore — she should get us there.'

I am provoked into an immediate argument with him. It's a long way and I haven't got money for petrol or for us to get anything to eat, and yes, I can get my parents to give me some money when we get there, because, yes, I do have it right, he hasn't got much cash on him either, but what about his wife?

'I'm not married,' he says.

'Partner. Who cares? What's a marriage licence these days?'

'It's different from what you think.'

'But you live with Leda.'

'Yeah, yeah, okay.'

'Like, really live with her?'

'I guess so.' He hunches his shoulders forward, edging his body away from mine, watches a gull dive for a fish beneath the waves. 'I didn't ask for this any more than you did. I didn't ask you to start having your baby on my doorstep.'

'So stop trying to rescue me.'

'I'm not,' he says, looking straight out to sea. 'It's just that I've always thought about meeting someone like you.'

'You don't know me.' He has never seen me except in childbirth, or when I'm on the loose from a psychiatric ward. My mind flicks quickly over the manics I've been around in the last few months, but Josh doesn't fit that mould.

'You don't know me either,' he says, turning towards me. We look at each other warily. I see what he means. I want to jump his bones, yet there is little I know about him.

He is idly fingering the sleeve of my jersey. 'You look pretty in that colour.'

'I look like a tomato.'

'Nah, better than that. It warms the colour of your eyes. You've got really nice eyes.'

'Thank you.'

'So why don't we start again?' he says. 'I thought you were a rich bitch and you think I'm married.'

'I'm probably still not hard up. Even now,' I say, wanting at once to keep the record straight. I'm thinking about his income tax problems and the spare little house in the suburbs.

'It's not the same thing,' he says, as if I'll understand his shorthand approach.

'So what about you?'

'I used to be a fisherman,' he tells me, still looking out to sea. 'My boat went down and I'm too scared to go back to sea.'

'That must be hard.'

'It is, because I love the sea.'

'What happened?'

'I was on this fishing boat. It just sank like a stone one night, well, pretty close to it — we only had a few minutes' warning. Three hands lost, but two of us stayed afloat on the life-raft. It was a cloudy, windy night. You could sort of see the stars now and then, know what I mean?'

I do know; I've been out on the farm often enough on nights when you look up at the sky and see faint streams of stars between ragged banks of cloud.

'It was choppy, but it wasn't the weather, the fish were loaded all wrong. The person that done that's dead. Yeah, nothing you can say about that really.'

'A mate of yours?'

'Yeah.' His hand finds mine and he grips it tightly, as if he has to hold on to someone while he is telling this story.

'We didn't fight or shove for a place, nothing like that. But fuck, y'know, it was scary. It was dark, and the sea was like a big black mountain. Bloody cold. We got in a line, two of us holding the boat on the deck for the others. We were the best swimmers, so we go shoving and shouting at them to get in. But then the boat tilts over real fast, and all of a sudden they're in the drink, and me and my mate are left hanging on to the lifeboat. We heard their voices calling out against the wind for a few minutes. Yeah.' He twists my hand so that it hurts. 'I still hear them sometimes, y'know?'

'I guess I would too.'

'Then we're in a flat patch of water, and we could launch ourselves off. Next thing, there's just the suck of the boat going down.'

I can't speak for a while and I see that he is crying. I touch the side of his face.

'Haven't told anyone else about this,' in answer to my unspoken question. 'Not all of it, not like this. What you've gotta know, though, one of those fishermen who went down was married to Leda.'

'Aah.' I suck my breath in, but I have already guessed this. 'She was having a baby?'

'Yeah. She's tough on the outside, and kind of mean in her ways,' he says, as if to excuse her. 'But she didn't have anyone. Well, me neither.'

'You've no family?'

He shifts again. 'Not that you'd want to know.'

'I might.'

'Take it from me, they're a bunch of arseholes.'

'Do you care for her?' I have to ask him, and he has to tell me the truth.

'I care for her,' he says and part of me breathes a sigh of relief. 'I wouldn't do the dirty on her.'

'Aren't you doing that now?'

'I mean, like walking out without telling her. Look, she knows where I am. She doesn't like it, but she's got no claim on me. See what I mean?'

'But you care for her, you said so.'

'Give over, eh.' He drops my hand.

'But if you love someone . . . ' Probably I sound like a schoolgirl. And anyway, what do I know about love?

'I didn't say that.'

'Well, do you?' Now that I've started, I can't stop. It is past time for my medication.

'I dunno,' he says wearily. 'I'm in the shit, just like you.'

'What are you going to do about Nathan?' he asks.

'I've got to get him back. But I can't think straight tonight. My father might know what to do.'

'Then I'll take you to your folks, okay?' When the Bedford roars into life, he says, 'I reckon you'll dream about him tonight.'

'Nathan? I have been already. It started weeks ago.' I don't need to tell him that the dreams began after he and Marise and I buried the placenta.

'Look in the glove compartment,' he says, 'you might find something to eat.'

There are two squashed Moro bars. I offer one to him. 'You have them,' he says, 'you probably need some sugar.'

'GLASS,' SAYS EDITH, urgently. 'There's someone outside.'

Glass is preparing to go to bed, even though it's only nine o'clock. His back is so painful he doesn't know how he will get up in the morning. He wonders about finding the liniment in the bathroom cupboard and asking Edith to rub it. Wendy, for once, has gone to her room. Unfair comment: of late, Wendy frequently goes to her room soon after dinner. He can't understand why she doesn't just leave. She and Edith have begun a small business packaging seeds for sale, which seems to keep them occupied, but the conversation is more sparse. Edith hasn't mentioned Roberta in weeks. Tomorrow he has decided he will take a run into town on his own and see if he can find out from the doctors how things are going. 'Let the treatment run its course,' they have told him.

He looks at Edith, with impatience, as if she is seeing things. But her gaze is so intent that he pulls himself to his feet. He sees them, Roberta and Josh, walking up through the avenue of trees, holding hands in the moonlight.

At first, seeing his own life before him, he finds it hard to believe what he sees. He wipes his eyes with the back of his hand. But Edith is already out the door and flying down the path to meet them. When she reaches the couple she slows down, as if she doesn't know how she got there. At first Glass, following more slowly behind, thinks Edith might strike Roberta, the way she holds up her hands blindly before her. Then she reaches for Roberta, holding her in an awkward clasp, pulling her daughter's unresisting head close to hers. Roberta allows herself to be held in this embrace, although she doesn't respond.

The young man stands to one side. When he sees Glass, he holds out his hand.

'I'm Josh,' he says, and Glass knows that something else has changed, and perhaps it will be for the better. 'I'll leave her with you.' He nods in Roberta's direction, turning back to a van you could only call a heap. Glass can't see how it would get a warrant of fitness.

twenty-three

FAMILY REMAINS

GLASS SHOWS ROBERTA a picture of her grandmother. They are sitting in the implement shed where Roberta has taken her father a thermos of tea. His hands are covered with grease from working on a tractor.

'Under there,' he says, pointing to a pile of old stock registers, 'something for you.'

Unsuspecting, she lifts the hard-covered exercise books. Her grandmother's face stares back at her.

'Came across it,' he says. 'Thought it had gone.' He means, she understands, that it has survived the purge.

Her grandmother's dark hair is parted straight down the middle and coiled in a shiny, low bun that balloons behind her head. Her eyes are surrounded by a strong fringe of lashes, her skin fair. Like Roberta's, her chin is long and almost jutting. There is no hint of resignation in her expression. She wears a a light-coloured dress with stripes running vertically from the shoulders to her waist; four bold buttons stud the centre of the bodice. An embossed gold locket lies in the hollow of her throat.

'She died just before I met your mother,' says Glass. 'We had that in common — her father had just recently died too.'

'Has Mum seen this?' asks Roberta.

'No, not yet.' She guesses he is not planning on showing it to Edith.

He wipes his hands on a piece of rag, itching to pick the photograph up, but then he decides against it. She sees how he has carried this image through the years, bearing the death of his mother away from the farm, like a slow, unhealing scar.

'You're like her,' says Glass.

'No,' says Roberta. 'Don't saddle me with that.'

'But it's true.'

'Don't try and suck me into all this,' she says. She tries to make her voice as tough as she can.

Roberta walks slowly back to the house. She has an image of her own. It is the day of her grandfather's funeral. Her aunts have written in her autograph book and she hands it to her father. 'Will you write one too, Dad?' she says.

And suddenly his face colours. He takes the pen from her and scrawls over the page. The words he writes are 'This land is my land', and he signs his name underneath.

AN APPLICATION
I, PAUL VAUGHAN Cooksley, hereby make application to the Family Court, under Section 10 of the Guardianship Act, to be appointed guardian of my son Nathan Cooksley.

From careful reading of the Act, I understand that, in certain circumstances, the Court may deprive a parent of guardianship of a child and award it to the other parent.

I am aware that this will not take place unless the Court is satisfied this parent is for some grave reason unfit to be a guardian of the child or is unwilling to exercise the responsibilities of a guardian.

I believe my wife, Roberta, from whom I have recently separated (refer attached document) is not in a fit mental state to be the guardian of our child. Roberta abandoned our son at my mother's home, and shortly afterwards became a voluntary patient in a psychiatric hospital.

She responded very slowly to treatment for post-natal depression and refused communication with me and other family members. Although of great support to me, my mother works, and has been unable to assist in Nathan's care. Being Nathan's sole care-giver has been at great inconvenience, as I had to take considerable amounts of time away from my work, until I was able to find a person who could help me with Nathan. This person is Prudence Davies, currently residing at my home in order to assist with part-time nannying duties. Nathan is now nine months old. He attends a well-run day care centre chosen by Ms Davies. He is a contented child and has formed a close attachment to Ms Davies and myself.

I request full guardianship of Nathan with limited visiting rights for his mother, if she recovers her health. To tell you the truth, your Honour, I am worried out of my mind about this situation.

Roberta hands a copy of this letter to her mother.

'He's got all the jargon,' says Edith. 'And a touch of pathos as well.' She turns the pot three times before she pours herself fresh tea, her fourth cup of the morning. Edith finds it thirsty work being dry; she smiles to herself. If anyone has noticed her new state, they haven't mentioned it. Edith has been to see a doctor in the city. She has not told anyone this. Since the first of what the doctor describes as her alcohol-free days, the first in twenty years, there has been an odd clarity about her vision. The first day was a novelty, like a diet, and then she worried that it would become tedious. But mostly she feels so light-headed that it's as dizzying as being drunk. She still hasn't got used to the area of her brain that is free of pain in the mornings. And she smells the foliage in her garden, so sharp and poignant that her senses are overcome, the freesias, which smell like incense beneath the kitchen windowsill.

'Don't worry,' Edith tells Roberta. 'It'll be all right, he can't get away with that.' She, who has never cared for Paul, hopes she is right. Her daughter is puffy round the eyes and has put on weight.

'Does this mean you will have to go to court?' asks Wendy of Roberta.

Roberta shrugs; she always avoids speaking to Wendy unless she has to. The table is cleared to make room for the three of them, Wendy, Roberta and Edith, to work on the latest venture. They sit close together, measuring out seeds, although Roberta's heart is not in the task.

'Have you taken your pills, dear?' asks Edith. She finds it odd feeding substances to Roberta while she spends so much energy avoiding them herself. Roberta's doctor at the hospital says she may have to take Amitriptyline for months. That, alone, is a thought to sober her. All the same, she has moments of joyous certainty when she tells Roberta that things will work out. Since she began her own experiment with sobriety, Edith has remembered all manner of things about her daughter when she was small. She remembers, in particular, holding her close under her coat, and singing to her in the wind. What would happen if she were to tell Roberta that, she wonders. Perhaps she would embarrass her. She feels she must move slowly and carefully. Even so, she rests her hand on Roberta's shoulder for just a moment as she leaves the room. There is no reaction at first, then Roberta pulls away.

UNEASE

WHEN EDITH LEAVES, Wendy sidles towards the door, as if she doesn't want to be alone in the room with Roberta. Their unease with each other is mutual.

'Your mother's only trying to help,' Wendy says.

'Well, I guess we'll sort it out.'

Wendy says, 'You remind me of my own daughter.'

'I didn't know you had one,' Roberta replies.

'She's your kind of person,' says Wendy.
'What kind of person is that?'
'Independent. Rather prickly. Clever.'
'I'm not clever.'
'Yes you are, you don't want people to know. We could be friends, Roberta, you and I.'
'Why would we want to do that?'
'I saw from your room that you liked books.' Wendy has been displaced from Roberta's old room. She lives, for the moment, in the obdurate silence of Bernard's house. It is not that the Nichols have no other spare room in their farmstead, but it is filled with a cot, a highchair, mobiles hanging from the ceiling, and a size nought pair of gumboots at the door. Get rid of that stuff, Roberta said, on her return. But Edith had not. Instead, she has closed the door. So Wendy sleeps in the bare room which Orla had intended to decorate for her mother and listens to Bernard through the wall tossing and turning at nights.

'You know, I've seen you somewhere else,' says Roberta.

Wendy backs closer to the door. 'I'm sure you haven't, dear. Only that time when we met at Christmas.'

'Oh, never mind.' Roberta stands up from the table, pushing her fingers through her hair. 'It must be the drugs — you think all kinds of things. You're not on the run from the tax department, by any chance?'

Wendy's mouth drops open.

'Sorry, old habits die hard. I wanted to be an income tax inspector at one stage of my life. An uncomplicated ambition, wouldn't you say? Everything in black and white, right or wrong. Pity it didn't work out.'

Wendy turns into the shadow of the door and Roberta sees her in profile.

'I know where I saw you,' she says. 'Why would you follow us?'

Wendy is spared Roberta's interrogation by the arrival of Josh.

'HAVE A BEER, son?'

Roberta winces at her father's choice of words.
'Bit early in the day for me,' says Josh.
'Yeah, me too,' says Glass.
'I'll make you a cup of coffee,' says Roberta. 'How d'you take it?'
Glass glances from one to another. Roberta blushes; it's like

asking your husband on your honeymoon — a dead giveaway that they hardly know each other.

'I'll make it,' says Edith, hurriedly. The three of them are left in the room to make conversation.

'What do you think of the team?' Glass asks Josh.

'Uh.' Josh is uncertain.

'Our boys need to sharpen up in the line-out, don't you reckon?'

'Yeah, maybe. I'm a league man myself.'

'Yeah?' Glass looks uncomfortable. 'Well. Yes. Things are a bit different nowadays.'

Roberta wonders why he bothers. Michael and Bernard never gave him the satisfaction of a good try in their lives.

'I hear butterfat's doing well at present,' says Josh in a polite voice.

'Bloody terrible,' says Glass. 'You chaps don't know what a rough time we're having out here.

Roberta longs to quieten the two of them. Glass is glaring at Josh as if he is asking for a loan; Josh is embarrassed by his gaffe. She can imagine that he has been practising all the things he might say, on the way over the hill — butterfat, cows, the weather. It's no better than it was with Paul.

'Why don't we go out for a bit?' she says, standing up.

Edith appears with a tray. 'I thought you were staying for coffee.'

'I'M SORRY,' SAYS Josh.

'It's not your fault. I guess fathers are like that. What d'you want to do?' They are driving away from the farm.

'Is there somewhere we can have a drink?'

'Yeah, the Walnut pub.'

'You don't sound too keen.'

'I'm not,' says Roberta. 'It's a dump. As a matter of fact, I want to get my hair cut.'

'You can do that any time, can't you?'

'Not what I had in mind.' Roberta is warming to her idea. 'I don't drive right now,' she explains. 'Because of the pills. I'd kind of like to be independent about this.'

'So you're a grown-up, you can do what you like.'

'It doesn't feel like that at the moment.'

'How much are you going to get cut off?'

'I'm planning a serious kind of haircut.' They have reached Walnut; Roberta signals for him to pull in alongside the European. And it's true, she doesn't want the worry of being even faintly pretty any more, she doesn't want to remind people of her ancestors. 'You're not going to try and stop me, are you?'

Josh touches her hair. 'You might be sorry for this.'

'I've got a father, thanks. I had a husband who sounded just like you, too. What is it with you men?' She is unwinding her hair from the rough braid over her shoulder. Josh lifts a rope of it to his face. 'It smells like apples,' he says.

'Shampoo, that's all it is.'

'Perhaps you should get it cut,' he says. 'Perhaps it's just as well.'

Shelley de Witt is between clients. She sits smoking in one of the empty chairs, stretching her red-nailed fingers and blowing a plume of blue smoke into the air.

'So,' she says, 'I didn't expect to see you back in here.'

'Just think of all the scores you can settle with the Nichols,' says Roberta, settling into a chair. 'Clippers all over.'

'You're joking.'

'Just cut it.'

'How much do you want for your hair? I am ethical, you know.'

'Ooh, la, la, Shelley,' says Roberta, inhaling some of the lingering cigarette smoke. 'You can have it. Put it in the museum or something. Put it under your pillow and pretend it's Bernard's. Or who ever.' She can't bring herself to say, my father's.

'Sure your friend doesn't want it?' she says, looking out the window at where Josh is sitting in the van.

'Do it.'

Without another word, Shelley picks up Roberta's hair and slices through it, her scissors making a squelching sound as if cutting a length of shiny material.

In twenty minutes it is all done and her head is covered with a furry mat of spikes. At once, she feels lighter, freer, without having to support the weight of her hair. Her eyes look enormous in the mirror, luminous and strange, her eyebrows like neat brown feathers laid above them. Shelley runs a slick of gel over the spikes and Roberta thinks the dark feathery tufts look like a blackbird that's been in the rain.

Josh, waiting by the van, stares in disbelief as she steps into the town's broad, stucco-fronted street.

'You look like a stroppy dyke,' Josh says.
'You don't mind?'
He laughs. 'I don't care, anarchy rules — you look great.'
'Yeah?'
'Yee-ha.' He touches her face with his fingertips, kissing her in the street where people can see them.
'That's the first time you've kissed me,' says Roberta.
'You're so beautiful,' he says. 'I can't believe how gorgeous you are.'
'I'm meant to be plain — it doesn't matter what I look like.' She cups her hands round his face and kisses him back, tastes the gum on his breath.

ANOTHER LETTER COMES for Roberta:

Children & Young Persons Services
A Division of Social Welfare

Dear Ms Cooksley

In the Matter of Nathan Cooksley COOKSLEY v COOKSLEY

Your attendance at a Family Group Conference, as directed by the Family Court, is required. The date has been set down for October 12. To facilitate ease of attendance for as many of your family members as possible, the venue appointed is the Presbyterian Church Hall in Walnut. A lawyer has been appointed to represent Nathan. A list of Nathan's relatives has been drawn up. We have invited these people to attend this conference.

Yours faithfully, etc
Mary Mason
Care & Protection Officer

CONVERSATIONS ABROAD

'SO WHAT'S THE weather like over there, Orla?' Bernard asks.
'Oh it's a grand soft day, you know how it is.'
'Yeah, autumn and wet. I thought you were coming home, Orla.'
'Well, yes, of course I am, and all, but I want to see that my mother's mended first.'

Orla stands in the hallway of the house in Belfast, the receiver pressed hard against her ear, her hand over the mouthpiece, in an effort to conceal her conversation. Bernard shouts, as if hoping his voice will carry all the way from New Zealand without the aid of the phone.

'I thought she was dying.'

'Well, that's what I thought too.'

'So what's happened? Another miracle?'

'I wish you'd keep your voice down, Bernard.'

'You got my letter?'

'Yes.'

'And the picture of the baby?'

'Yes, oh I did. He's a fine little man, that nephew of yours. Poor wee boy.' Orla has looked at Nathan's picture many times. She longs to trace the curve of his eyelids with the tip of her finger.

'You and me, we could look after him, perhaps.'

'Oh, and what does Roberta think about that?'

'Roberta's daft.'

'Bernard,' she says, 'they wouldn't give us Roberta's baby? Not for keeps?'

He is too slow to answer.

'She's a bad girl, that Roberta of yours. All airs and graces and now look what she's up and done to her parents.'

'We need you here,' he says. 'If we had him for a bit. Well. You know what I mean.'

Yes, I know all too well what you mean, Orla says to herself, when she hangs up. If you and I have to face each other again, Bernard, a baby would soften the view. But perhaps he is right, it might be a place to begin. Only when Nathan was gone, because she knows this is what would happen, they would be right back where they left off, staring at blank walls rather than at each other.

'If you're thinking of going back to New Zealand, I'd advise against it,' says her mother, when Orla returns to the front parlour. It is a little room, crowded with chairs covered with antimacassars, small tables stacked with framed photographs of family, and a tea trolley bearing china cups that never get used from one year to the next, except the first two on the right-hand side which are brought into service when the priest comes to visit, and a couch where her mother lies, a peggy-square rug pulled up to her chin, while she watches the television in the corner.

'But my husband's over there, Mam,' says Orla.

'Exactly,' her mother replies. 'What's he doing over there, when he should be by your side? There's nothing but harm and grief can come to you out there amongst those savages.'

'IT'S AS IF she's living in a dream,' says Glass to Edith, as they climb into bed. 'Doesn't she realise that she's going to lose that baby for good?'

'It mightn't come to that,' says Edith.

'Oh come on, just take a look at her.' Since Roberta's hair has gone, it feels to Glass as if there is not much more he can lose. Just when he felt hope, everything has become confused again. And there is something different about Edith that he can't put his finger on.

'MICHAEL,' I SAY, 'couldn't you come home? Just for a couple of days?'

'You don't know what you're asking,' my brother says, from his terrace house in Sydney. I can see him now, although it is some years since Paul and I visited him there. The houses are small and close together but they have delicate verandahs trimmed with curly wrought iron. They have become smart and expensive. Michael's walls and furniture are white, his pictures extravagant

'You don't know what my in-laws are like, they'll run rings round our family.'

'What about our father, the saint?'

I am silent. My father hasn't spoken to me in days.

'Have you got a good lawyer?'

'Dad's hired Tom Dunsford. Remember him?'

Michael groans. 'Didn't you tell him you wanted somebody flash? The old man can afford it.'

'You know that's not the way things work round here. Please Michael, I don't ask much. This is about my son.'

For a moment I think he is going to weaken.

One day, I came in from school and my mother and Michael were sitting in the kitchen, their hands entwined across the table. Michael had been crying. I was shocked because, in places like Walnut, the saying big boys don't cry still holds good. But he looked exhausted with weeping, as if it had been going on for some time.

'Michael's going off to university,' my mother said. I was still quite young, and I didn't really know what this meant, but I recall being surprised that Michael was so upset, now that he had his heart's desire. Something major had happened. My father took phone calls in the evening. He spoke in a quiet voice; I heard him assuring callers that his son was leaving and wouldn't be back for some time.

'It's not his fault,' I heard my mother say, later that night. 'He didn't start it.' This was in the worst days of her drinking, when she couldn't put arguments together at all.

'That's his story,' my father said. 'The bugger.'

'It won't happen again,' my mother said, 'he promised.'

'We'll see,' said my father, and I suppose he is still waiting to see, to be convinced one way or another, or perhaps he doesn't think about it any more, I don't know.

'It would do more harm than good,' says Michael.

'So I'm on my own?'

'I hear you've got a bloke.'

'No,' I say, 'not like that. What about you?'

He doesn't reply. He's right, I am on my own.

twenty-four

INFINITE CHAOS

As ROBERTA WALKS into the church hall the first person she sees is Prudence holding Nathan. Her face bare of make-up, hair pulled back behind her ears, Prudence looks at once intense and vulnerable. She wears a simple yellow wool tunic over black leggings. Roberta is glad she can't see herself. The previous day she and Edith visited Miss Millie's Haberdashery in Walnut to buy clothes that fit, to tide her over until she's back to her usual weight. They are baggy round the middle. Edith suggested she wear a scarf over her cropped hair.

'It's not a court,' Roberta reminded her.

'You just don't know what they get up to,' Edith said grimly. 'From what I've heard of these family conferences.'

Roberta has just guessed her mother's secret, if secret it is intended to be. Her mother is wholly sober. She is astonished that she hadn't noticed sooner. In the end, Roberta wears her felt hat with the turned-up brim. It makes her feel jauntier when she puts it on, but she sees her mistake mirrored in the expressions around her.

Not that it is her appearance which preoccupies her; it is Nathan, casually held on Prudence's hip. Roberta lifts her arms involuntarily towards him, and puts them down again. Nathan shows no sign of recognition; she will be ignored, and these people will know. Don't let the bastards see what you're thinking, had been Marise's last advice over the phone. Play it cool. She wishes she could see Marise with her swinging grey hair in the throng of people jostling to get inside the hall, but Marise's baby is due soon, and the doctor is concerned about her travelling. Besides, as Marise isn't family, she didn't think she could ask her. So what is Prudence doing here?

When she sees Roberta, Prudence kisses the end of Nathan's nose. Nathan claps his hands. 'We're just staying a little while,' Prudence murmurs as she passes.

'She didn't need to do that,' Edith says. 'She didn't need to say anything.'

The hall, normally bare except for a battered piano in the corner, has been prepared for the occasion. Chairs are artfully laid out to look as if everyone will sit in a big circle. Roberta is familiar with this layout by now. A small table is laden with plastic cups, a jar of instant coffee, a box of tea bags, a litre of milk, a screw-top jar containing hardened sugar.

Roberta has little idea how most of the people come to be present. In all, she counts twenty-four people in the room, including Nathan and herself. A group of officials, practising professional ease, stand on one side of the room. Mary Mason, the care and protection officer who sent Roberta the letter, is a tall woman with frizzy red hair and a stern, freckled face. She wears a no-nonsense tweed suit which makes her look hot in the spring afternoon. She is flanked by two social workers, the Plunket nurse who came to see Nathan when Roberta first brought him home and three lawyers — a young one appointed by the court, Brian Adams, who has been hired by the Cooksleys, and Tom Dunsford, who has acted for the Nichols since Glass was a child. Nurse Peach and Dr Q are seated already. Roberta doesn't look at either of them.

The rest are family, more or less, their names and relationship to Nathan listed on a sheet of paper she has been handed. They are:

Roberta Cooksley, mother
Paul Cooksley, father
Fay Cooksley, paternal grandmother
Milton Cooksley, paternal grandfather
Laura Monteith, aunt
Prudence Davies, care-giver   (the terminology makes Roberta want to puke)
Edith Nichols, maternal grandmother
Bruce (also known as Glass) Nichols, maternal grandfather
Bernard Nichols, uncle
Orla Nichols, aunt   (only Orla hasn't shown up — she's supposed to be on her way from Ireland, the plane last heard of delayed in Los Angeles)
Dorothy Nichols, great-aunt   (Dorothy is in her wheelchair, propped up by three pillows, a line of spittle running down her chin)
Joan Vance, great-aunt   (Joan's work-roughened hands display their displeasure, the

Arch Vance, great-uncle
Sally Vance, second cousin

John Vance, second cousin

way they're folded in her lap, her thumbs rotating around each other)

(Sally, who has just become engaged to Grant, casts Roberta sly looks beneath lowered lids)
(a strong back is an asset in the gardens, his mother reminds Edith)

Apologies: Kaye and Frank Drury, Michael Nichols

    The Cooksley family stand together, looking well groomed and complete. It comes as a shock to Roberta to see that today, with the exception of Edith, who looks rakish rather than smart in a battered linen suit, her family seem such a motley bunch lined up against the Cooksleys. Fay and Laura are becoming more and more like each other, she thinks, both wearing long, straight, dark skirts with slits and matching jackets, that make them look, at once, both elegant and out of place in the Walnut Presbyterian Church Hall. Milton, taking an afternoon off from work, is especially suave. Roberta allows herself to reflect, with a moment of bitterness, on Michael's absence.

    Mary Mason, clears her throat and looks round the room. Roberta wonders if she is going to say something like, dearly beloved, we are gathered together in the sight of this congregation.

    'Well, people,' says Mary Mason. 'Welcome to Nathan's family.' Bernard, who has been glancing surreptitiously at his watch, gives a start; he looks out of the window when he catches people looking at him.

    'We're here to discuss Nathan's future. As most of you will be aware, two applications have been made for Nathan's custody. It's the court's job to decide the best arrangements for him. We hope, in cases like this, that families can get together and sort things out between them, keeping in mind the best interests of the child. It's clear that Nathan is a lucky little boy to have so many people who care about him here to discuss his future.' She smiles in a way that doesn't invite comment.

'We'll begin with a professional overview of Nathan's situation, then we're going to leave you all together so you can talk things through on your own.'

The court-appointed lawyer is first. He hopes, he tells them, for an outcome in which Nathan continues to know both his parents in a loving and supporting environment. 'Nathan appears very well cared for at the moment,' he says, turning to Prudence. The Nichols family draw in their breaths. Roberta realises that Prudence has the status of a professional in this matter. 'Could you tell us about his milestones, Ms Davies?'

'Well,' says Prudence, with a bright, sweet smile. 'Nathan can say Dad Dad, can't you, sweetheart? And he's crawling everywhere, when he's in the mood. He's got five teeth, and another one coming. He sleeps through every night.' Her hand smoothes Nathan's hair. 'He's a bit shy with strangers.' Nathan ducks his head against her chest.

The Plunket nurse is next.

'I do realise that Roberta's birth experience was very traumatic,' she says doubtfully. 'But her house was always very clean. Still, it was a pretty new house, so I suppose that's fairly easy to keep up to scratch. There was never anything like unwrapped nappies around the house, nothing like that. I mean, I'd have to say, Nathan was very well provided for in the material sense.' Leaning forward, she allows her doubt full rein. 'I did wonder if there was just that something lacking. It was hard to put my finger on the problem.' She looks at Roberta with regret. 'He does seem very contented these days. Prue's been doing a great job.'

'Prue Pooh,' says John Vance.

'M . . . ,' Mary Mason glances at her file. 'Mr Vance, please.'

The social workers say much the same thing as the Plunket nurse. Nathan is doing very well with Paul and Prue, not that it's their job to influence the outcome. Brian Adams makes some notes.

'What about, what about, er-um, what about the farm?' says Dorothy, spittle flying in all directions. 'He'll get the farm from the Nichols, you know.' She shoots Edith a look of hatred, as fresh as if it was baked yesterday.

'Yes, perhaps,' says Glass, leaning over and taking her hand. 'But this isn't what it's about, Dorothy.'

'I mean, it's not going to the Car-tholic church, is it, Glass?'

Glass pats her hand held between his. 'Don't worry, Dotty dear,' he says.

Mary Mason gives Glass a clear, icy smile. 'Perhaps if your family could just let us finish,' she says. 'You'll all have your turn soon.' She turns to Nurse Peach.

Roberta knows she has to look at her and at Dr Q, who gives her a slow wink, as Nurse Peach prepares to speak. Roberta opens and closes her mouth in surprise. Everyone is looking at her, so she composes herself.

'Roberta is a feisty, independent person at heart,' Nurse Peach is saying. 'Today she is with her family but you should remember that at present she has no other choice. She wanted to go home to Paul, but she couldn't. We didn't impose a meeting like this on Roberta — you need to be sure you're not forcing issues on people before they're ready. It doesn't mean Roberta will not be a very good mother when the time is right for her. In the ward, the other patients really liked her. She's a caring person, with a sense of her own identity which keeps getting stronger all the time. Something has affected her confidence and that's her difficulty. We consider the depression she suffered after Nathan's birth to be clinically overcome. She needs your love and support, not your criticism.'

'Hey, wait a minute,' says Paul, looking injured.

'You'll have your turn, Mr Cooksley,' says Mary Mason. 'Doctor, what is your view?'

Dr Q has a sardonic smile hovering at the corner of his mouth. 'If you're asking my opinion, I see that Roberta may have difficulties to face.' His eyes travel round the room. 'I'd relish the opportunity to work further with her.'

For a moment she had thought him on her side. She looks Dr Q in the eye, and he looks straight back at her.

Brian Adams shuffles paper to attract attention to himself. Preparing himself to get down to tin tacks, they say to each other afterwards. He is a fresh-faced man, youthful in appearance despite his grey hair. He has an engaging cleft in his chin. He and Milton look like two out of the same mould.

'I am afraid,' he says, after a meaningful hesitation, 'that Mr Cooksley, Paul that is, was in despair, even before Nathan was born. He loved Roberta. But sadly, he has to accept that there's something seriously amiss with his wife's approach to motherhood. Nathan's birth, on the doorstep of a total stranger — well that's what we're told — came as a dreadful shock to him. This concern about Roberta's emotional health is all very well, but what about Paul?'

'He's got the baby,' says Joan.

'Paul did everything he could to provide support and understanding for his wife. Look at it this way — she wouldn't see Paul or Nathan for months and then she walks in off the street, expecting to pick up where she left off.' Brian Adams bestows a glimmer of a smile on the circle to remind them that this is a chat. 'Well, Roberta may be well again, I'm delighted to hear it, but you did discharge yourself from the hospital, didn't you? It seems to me that you do make all the decisions, Roberta.'

'I thought you said this wasn't a court,' says Bernard.

'Mr Adams, may I remind you that this is a family conference,' says Mary Mason. 'I'll have to ask you to withdraw if this goes any further.'

'Of course, Madam Chair,' says the lawyer. 'Forgive me, I just thought that before the family began their discussions they should be aware that these matters will be raised in court next week. I wouldn't want it to come as a shock to them. I had hoped to open the way for the Cooksley family to say what is really on their minds. It could be embarrassing for them, otherwise.'

'That kid should just be at home with his mother,' says Joan Vance, nodding in Nathan's direction. Nathan gives a breathy contented sigh against Prudence.

'Well, the question of where Roberta might give Nathan a home would be a good place to begin, perhaps,' says Mary Mason.

'The country's a damn fine place to bring up children.' Joan looks proudly at John and Sally. The Cooksleys' eyes follow hers. Roberta knows their worldly, half-suppressed grins of old.

'Mr Dunsford?' enquires Mary Mason.

But Tom Dunsford, in his loose three-piece suit with egg stains down the front, is fast asleep, his mouth open.

'Tee hee,' says Dorothy. 'Dunsford always did sleep through everything. He writes lousy wills.'

Mary chooses to ignore Dorothy this time. Even the Cooksleys look as if they think it's gone far enough.

Nathan stirs in his sleep.

'Ms Davies has advised us that she doesn't wish to add to the family conference. Thank you, Prue, you're excused.'

Prudence rises gracefully. For a moment she hesitates, as if considering whether to take Nathan over to Roberta to say goodbye, then pulls a regretful face, before disappearing out the door. Paul's eyes follow her all the way.

'There's a whiteboard available for you to write up your ideas as they come to you,' continues Mary Mason, 'and it might be useful to appoint a spokesperson who can sum up at the end when we return.'

'Is that like a foreman of the jury?' asks young John Vance.

'Not at all,' says Mary, trying to control her impatience. 'It's just a list of recommendations for the court when it sits.'

'So what if you don't agree with us?' asks Joan. 'Are we all wasting our time?'

Edith and Glass glance uneasily at each other. Roberta thinks, if I get up now and tell the Vances to shut up, we could all go home.

As they mill around over cups of tea, Fay walks over to Edith.

'And how are you, Edith? The garden doing well?'

'Yes, thank you,' says Edith, turning away.

Bernard strolls to the window and gazes outside.

'This is kind of like *Oprah* or the *Ricki Lake Show*, isn't it?' Sally says to Roberta. 'Everybody slagging each other off. I'm quite looking forward to the next bit.'

ONLY THE COOKSLEYS haven't slagged anyone off, at least not directly. They have paid good money to have that done for them, sitting, all the while, with their remote smiles fixed in place. But now the Cooksleys and the Nichols are locked in silence, looking at each other.

'So who's going to start?' says Edith. It's the first thing she has said.

'Wouldn't it be best if we did what Mary suggested? Just fling a few ideas up on the board?' Laura says.

'Who's going to write on the board?' asks Sally. Roberta sees that she hopes it will be her.

But already Fay has seized a felt pen and is standing in front of the whiteboard. 'I guess I get to do a lot of this,' she cries. Standing there in her pretty clothes, she makes it seem like a party game they are about to embark upon. She draws a line down the centre of the board, and heads one column 'For' and the other 'Against'.

'For and against what?' says Glass.

'I would have thought that was obvious. For and against Nathan living with Roberta.'

201

Quickly, under 'For' she jots, Roberta Is Nathan's Birth Mother. 'Anyone think of anything else? Okay, let's move on to the other side. I think Brian's already made a couple of observations on this.'

More writing, this time in the 'Against' column. Nathan Is Well Cared For In Present Situation.

'Orla and me could help look after him.'

'I beg your pardon?'

Glass is the only person in the room who doesn't look surprised. 'If you just stopped all this shit,' Bernard says. 'Soon as Orla gets here we'll look after him okay. Till Roberta's ready, of course,' he adds hurriedly.

Fay's nostrils flare, as if he hasn't spoken. Developing Well, she writes in the lengthening column under 'Against'. Much Loved.

'Put that in the other column too,' says Edith.

Fay obliges, and continues with her own list. She says the words aloud as if some people present may not be able to read. Roberta Has Not Been Well. Roberta Possibly Needs More Treatment. Conditions At Home Are Not Ideal.

'Who says they're not?' Edith says.

'Oh come on,' says Laura, 'you're into the grog all the time. I've heard about that.' The refinement in her voice has slipped.

'It's not true,' says Edith.

'Liar,' says Fay, the chalk stopping in mid-air. 'You were totally inebriated last Christmas Day.'

'Pissed as a newt,' says Dorothy.

'You old bitch,' shouts Edith.

'Lost her rag, wouldn't you say?' Laura says. 'Really, you don't need to say anything to these people — they do it all to themselves.'

'Well, what do we all think?' smiles Fay.

'I think that sums things up pretty well, dear,' says Milton, straightening the crease in his trousers.

Glass stands up, his face cold with fury. 'Not one of you has asked my daughter what she thinks.'

Paul shrugs his shoulders. 'Okay, Roberta,' he says. 'So what do you think?'

'We could manage.' whispers Roberta.

'You and your boyfriend?'

Roberta sits bolt upright. 'I haven't got a boyfriend.'

'Oh come on, some bloody unemployed fisherman, doing

under the counter spray painting out in the wops. You're as big a liar as your mother.' He pulls a disgusted face in the direction of Edith, who has sunk into an angry silence.

'What about your girlfriend?'

'Yeah, what about her? Showing up here,' says cousin Sally. 'Cheeky little cow.'

'Prudence isn't my girlfriend.'

'Well, she was,' says Roberta. 'That's how I got landed with you, between shifts.'

'That's enough, Roberta,' says Fay.

They all begin to shout then. This is a family conference, hasn't anybody remembered that? They all get to have their say, okay?

Roberta's head drops to her knees, as if her neck is a stem holding up a dying flower. Her hands curl over the top of her head and clasp it, under the felt hat. A pulse throbs in her swollen temples.

'I want Nathan,' she says, her voice muffled in the rayon and cotton mix skirt from Miss Millie's. 'I never meant to give him away.'

Glass kneels beside his daughter, desolate in the face of her inconsolable grief. 'Dad,' she says. 'Oh Dad, I never meant it. You don't know, you just don't know what it was like.'

'Yes, I do,' says Glass.

Bernard, standing by the window, suddenly bangs his fists down on the keyboard of the old piano, causing a sullen, meowing stream of noise to echo round the room. Roberta lifts her face. Surely, someone will come. But nobody does. This is it. This is a family conference. They are getting on with things.

IT IS HOURS before it is done, the recommendations delivered to the reconvened group, headed by Mary Mason. The Nichols mostly remain silent.

The families leave ahead of the social workers and doctors. As Roberta passes Dr Q, her eyes firmly before her, he speaks to her. 'I'd like to see your hair,' he says.

The pupils of his eyes are the same tired, friendly brown, surrounded by their faded white rims. She takes off her hat, shaking her head, marvelling again that it is so light.

He gives her both thumbs up. She waits for more.

'Your move, Roberta.'

twenty-five

EXODUS

ORLA IS NOT on the plane; he knew it all the time that he sat in that room. Bernard had sent her the money for the ticket. Did she get as far as Heathrow, he wonders, and then turn around and go home? Or did she simply go out shopping in Belfast in the morning, and pretend to herself, while she was having tea in a café, that it was not the day she was booked to fly to New Zealand?

Bernard sits outside the Walnut Presbyterian Church Hall and thinks for a few minutes. He is tempted to go to the hotel for a pint, but it is nearly time for milking, and he always goes to the shed.

He starts the wagon and pulls out of the parking lot while the rest of the family is still clustered around looking distracted and unhappy. He drives slowly towards the crest of the hill and looks down on the valley where the farm lies. He sees the Maori houses, which is what Orla called them. He loved Orla. He doesn't know whether he does any longer, or whether he still does but has been conquered by his failure to love anyone well.

His gun rests on the seat beside him. Bernard never travels without that lovely, living piece of wood. Nobody's safe in this world without fire in their hand, he has always believed. But what is he to do with it, and who can he save except himself? He runs his hand longingly over the barrel.

Down at his own house, he sees movement. Wendy at the clothesline, he thinks, though it is too far away for him to be sure. Oddly, he hasn't been unhappy with the peculiar old woman who has been living in the house with him these past few weeks. He has found himself laughing, on the quiet, at some of the weird things she says. Perhaps his mother has known that what he most needs in life is someone to pick up his socks and have a few laughs.

He lets the clutch out and rolls on down the hill towards the farm.

WENDY KNOWS, FROM the way they walk into the house, how badly things have gone. She has made a frosted lemon cake and left it in the kitchen for Edith, but without a note.

The young man she thinks of as the courting gentleman is waiting in the gazebo by the central rose garden where the verbena used to bloom and where Wendy first heard the madrigal singers, not far from the spot where she last saw Sarah. He has been there for more than an hour. She watches Roberta alight from her parents' car and walk towards him, sees the way they cling together. Glass, looking stooped, comes out of the house again, heading towards the milking shed.

And here, at last, is Bernard, pulling up in his driveway. She sighs with relief, although she doesn't know why she was so worried about him.

'Going somewhere?' he asks, when he sees her. She has packed her velvet bag and some plastic bags of odds and ends she has accumulated over the last months.

'I'm hoping to catch a ride from the neighbours in a few minutes,' she says. 'I'm going to catch the train.'

'I'll run you to the station,' says Bernard.

'You can't do that, it's time for milking.'

'I'll worry about that.'

'You must be in a hurry to get rid of me,' she laughs, trying to make a joke of it as she does up her seat belt.

'You weren't as bad as I expected,' he admits.

'Have they sorted it out about the baby?' Although, really, she knows the answer.

'I don't reckon.' He lights a cigarette with one hand and inhales in a long, thoughtful way.

'Bernard, what are you going to do?' There is something different about him that she can't read.

He blows the smoke out, filling up the cabin of the wagon. 'Stop worrying about life,' he says, with a white grin. 'Your stop, ma'am.' He pulls in at the station and lets her out. 'Don't do anything I wouldn't do.'

When he gets back to the house, Bernard begins to pack. He doesn't take much: a couple of changes of clothes, a few photographs, stuffed into a red backpack with a plastic tartan stripe down the side, the guitar his parents bought him as a child, some faded sheet music from the days when he tried to learn the instrument, his wallet and credit cards. There is pain in the collection of some of these items, but he can bear it, he tells himself. The only way to deal with it is to take it with him.

Looking round the house, he considers the evidence of Orla that is left behind. An apron hanging on the laundry door, her scuffed slippers at the bottom of the broom cupboard. Why she would leave them in the broom cupboard he can't imagine, but that's Orla. The wardrobes contain some of her clothes, the towelling dressing gown still grubby round the cuffs. There are ornaments sent to them by her mother for Christmas, mostly beer mugs with daft Irish sayings inscribed on them. Each of these items he carries into the room where they slept together, placing them in a neat pile. He is disappointed to discover that there is no cash lying around the house in the places where he stored it. He guesses that Wendy's velvet bag carries a comfortably fat roll of his money.

'COME AWAY WITH me,' says Josh.
'I can't,' I say.
'What can you do here?'
'Nothing, but what will they think?'
'They'll think we're having it off together, I expect.'
'Just walk out like this?'
'Bring a jacket. Tell them you're off.'
In the house, my mother sits gazing into space. 'I have to go,' I say to her. She is holding a clean glass in her hands, turning it round and round.
'That won't bring your baby back,' she says. She has noticed Josh's van. I expect she has seen us in the garden.
'I'm in love with him,' I tell her.
'Love,' she says, 'oh, love, is it?'
'Mum, please.'
She looks at me, her eyes dark with a mixture of anger and grief. 'It's hardly the time.'
'What's a good time, Mum?' I say. Perhaps she wants to tell me there is some grace and happiness that will tell me when the time is right, but I know she can't do that. She wouldn't know happiness if she fell over it. I want him now, I could tell her, right now, when everything about it is wrong, and I'm bereft. But I don't speak. There is nothing inside me except hollow space and maybe that is a state of grace, which can be filled only with desire and its outcome. There has to be something to put in its place or I'll die. An extreme way of looking at it, but this is how I feel. I can't sink any lower than I have gone this afternoon; there has to

be some way up. I think of stopping to explain, to remind her that I am an adult, that I know about sex and its consequences, but in a way we would both know that wasn't true. I know only a version of it all, Paul's version. Besides, she is familiar with all this; she understands the way I'm compelled to go after Josh, but she can't admit it to me.

'Don't worry about it, Mum,' I say, heading off to my room to pick up a jacket.

'Roberta,' she calls after me.

'Yes?' I am determined not to go back.

'Why did you leave him?'

I can't help it, I go back to the kitchen. 'What are you talking about?'

'Paul. People can work on their marriages. You never gave yours a chance.'

'Haven't you ever wanted to leave?'

'I had children,' she says, her voice virtuous. 'So did you.'

'Don't hand me that crap,' I answer. 'You stayed for yourself.'

'This Josh.'

'What about him?'

'He'll be a one-night stand, you see if I'm not right,' she says.

This is about as nasty as it can get without us coming to blows. I walk out of the house without saying goodbye.

Inside, I know my mother is thinking about drinking, if she hasn't already begun. A twinge of guilt nearly makes me turn back. Then I think that it's up to her whether she drinks or not. I didn't ask her to stop on my account.

WE DRIVE SOUTH to the coast, to an old fisherman's cottage at Ngawi, in a landscape of giant rocks and tall cliffs. The village is perched hard up against the sea, the beach festooned with orange-red craypot buoys. Dark blue echiums with massed stems of flowers flourish in the windswept gardens. The cottage belongs to a friend of Josh's. The key is behind the fencepost, although the door is so loose on its hinges we can just about push our way in.

We have bought food on the way at a remote store near the crossroads, tins of corned beef and mangoes and a loaf of bread. He has a six of beer in the back of the van. He opens one and hands it to me when we are inside the cottage. It is a gloomy little place with a naked bulb in the kitchen, and a dim shade above the bed.

The air is heavy, with a dark wind. He is nervous, I can see that now, more than he was before, when he thought that he would have to persuade me, or that I might walk away from him. I run my hands over my stubbly head and feel a total absence of desire, shivering, both from real cold and from fear. Night has fallen, and there is an open fireplace but no wood.

'I'll gather some driftwood from the beach,' Josh offers. It is an excuse for us not to go to bed.

'It's all right,' I say. 'It's just that my feet are cold.'

He hesitates. 'Take your shoes off,' he says softly.

I slip off my tidy sling-backs. He kneels and holds my instep.

'Wait,' I say, and unpeel my pantyhose, turning away from him. Remember, I have been to a family group conference this afternoon; I wear my plain, cheap clothes; I have tried to look respectable.

'Lie on the bed,' he says, 'I won't do anything else.'

I lie down on the bunk, while he sits at the end, warming my feet with his hands. He strokes them with a long, slow, deliberate motion, caressing my arches, kissing my heels and ankles. Heat rises through me, travelling up through my body.

'Let me look at you,' I say, as we begin to undress each other. We begin our inspection, the slow exploration of one another's skin. I find the word 'Alys' tattooed on his hip. 'Who is she?'

'My wife,' he says.

'You said you weren't married.'

'I'm not. I was. Does it matter?'

I consider this; I don't know how many more women I'm going to find. Josh unleashes his hair from its pony-tail, letting it fall about my face, my shorn head inside the tent of his hair. 'I love you,' he says.

I kiss him on his face, his cheeks, his mouth. 'I love you, Josh,' I say, 'I love you, I love you too.' I can't bear to wait for him any more.

An electrical storm passes over the coastline in the night, and between waking and sleeping and making love we fumble for the candles in the darkness. Their light smoulders on the walls.

'I want something to eat,' I tell him.

'You've got an appetite,' he says, but he gets up and opens the tins of food and carries them over to the bed. I let him feed me morsels of meat and fruit, like a bird with its young, sucking the pink beef in its gelatinous mass.

'Do you want a joint?'

I haven't smoked for years. It's long past time for my medicine and I've got no idea what it will do to me.

'I don't mind if you do.'

He shakes his head. 'It's okay.'

Josh seems as nearly perfect as it is possible for any human being to be; the flickering light ripples over his strong shoulders and torso, his pubic hair rising in a dark line up the centre of his belly towards his navel. I can't keep my hands away from it, from him, although I'm exhausted by my discoveries and by passion. I can see that he is tired, too.

While we eat, and drink more beer, I hold the soles of my feet together, my knees apart, and in the candlelight I see that I look like a large golden frog. It seems I have learned the mysterious truth: about happiness and need and depravity, the way each insatiably feeds off the next. I haven't thought about Nathan for several hours, but remembering him now — the curve of his cheek, the mop of curls I wasn't allowed to touch — I begin to cry. Josh holds me in his arms, rocking me to and fro, and I think of what my mother said, earlier in the afternoon: this won't bring your baby back. Outside the storm has cleared, blown out to sea by the harsh winds.

'Look,' he says. I follow the direction of his gaze, beyond the uncurtained window. Stars sweep down in rivers and fields of light, close to the horizon.

'Scorpius rising. Fishermen know stars. If we don't, we get lost.'

'Will you go back to sea?' I've stopped crying, calmed by his voice and by the sight of the sky.

'I don't know,' he says. 'It might happen.'

'I don't want you to.' Immediately, I feel his body tense.

'We'll see.'

'What's going to happen about Leda?' As soon as I have said this, I regret it.

Very carefully, he lays me back on the bed, disentangling himself from me, and pulls the blanket up. 'It'll start to get light soon. D'you want to get some sleep?'

'Josh,' I say. 'Please, I'm sorry.'

'I know you are,' he says.

'But you did say you loved me.'

'So I do. But I told you I wouldn't leave Leda in the lurch, didn't I?'

'You're not going to leave her?'

'Not just like that.' He is dragging his clothes on, in a hurry. 'Look,' he says, when he has tucked his shirt into his jeans, 'you're not ready for this.'

'Yeah, sure,' I say, turning my face to the wall. 'Blame it on me.'

We glare at each other. Electricity lights the room again, so that we are caught, suddenly, in blue light. Gently, he touches the side of my face, in the way he has. 'I wanted this to be a good time.'

'It is,' I say, and hold his hand. But I feel older, cold again and drained. He offers to sleep on the chair in the kitchen, but I tell him not to be silly, and, after a while, he climbs under the blanket beside me, still in his clothes, and we sleep together. When I wake he has unzipped his clothes and we begin again. I see that desire and possession are not far apart. I am possessed by him; I can't see how he can resist my need to possess him, to have him all for myself.

JOSH DROPS ME off at the farm gate soon after dawn. Always coming home. My father is walking to the cowshed alone.

'Shall I come in with you?' Josh says, although I can tell that he is hoping I will say no.

'It's okay,' I say.

'When will I see you again?'

'I don't know.'

'Are you still shitty with me?'

'Not really. I guess the answer is when I feel like it.' I climb down out of the now familiar van. 'I had a good time,' I add.

There are no lights on at Bernard's house. I remember that my father had been heading for the shed on his own the evening before. My parents' house, when I go inside, is very still. Their bedroom door stands open and I see that my mother is sleeping heavily.

Pulling on jeans and gumboots at the back door, I race over the paddocks to join my father. His look is distant. 'Where's Bernard?' I ask.

'Buggered off.'

'You're joking, Dad.'

'Every other bugger's gone off, why shouldn't Bernard?'

He doesn't speak while we milk. I'm not very experienced. The boys have always been there to do the milking so I have to really concentrate on what I am doing. But we get through the job together, he and I

'Thanks,' he says, when we're through hosing down the shed. He walks off, without waiting for me. I guess it's written all over me. Well fucked.

Which is true. I watch his disappearing back, and turn back towards the shed. Is this how far I've come? The wooden fence stretches round a territory in which, if I'm not careful, I will be trapped for life. A grazing wind, the remnants of last night's storm, has curled over the hills and I stand there on my own, wondering what will happen to me, holding my jacket around my middle. I don't want to let go of what's happened to me overnight, this sensation that's like flying. At least I am back inside my own skin.

twenty-six

MORE RECIPES FOR DISASTER

AN AFTERNOON WHEN the queues stretch interminably. The checkout operators are wilting and there are not enough packers to go round. Prudence joins the shortest queue, although experience tells her that this is not always the fastest route out of the shop.

For Prudence, supermarket shopping is like an adventure. Once she is inside that hall of food, the aisles buzzing with bargain hunters, she feels truly alive. The Christmas decorations are up already, the speakers relay a carol. Her heart skips a beat, because she feels on top of it all. She smiles at raw-handed men behind the meat counters, selects fruit with a judicious eye, tests items like cheese by the weight in her hand, as well as the colour. Other women chat to her when they see Nathan sitting in the trolley with his legs through the holes. Isn't he gorgeous, they say. Love the curls. Ten months, that's amazing, you'd have thought he was older. He really is the cutest thing. Your first, is he?

And Prudence smiles at them, saying yes, he's my first, he's good like this all the time. Once or twice Nathan has put his arms up to another woman as if he wants to be picked up, a habit he has just recently acquired, and it embarrasses her, but they don't seem to notice. So friendly, they say, and pass on, tossing tinned apricots and eggs and cleaning fluid into their trolleys.

The woman ahead of her in the queue turns out to have two hundred and forty-five dollars worth of groceries to be put through and her EFTPOS is playing up and the tired woman on the checkout keeps putting up her hand for assistance but nobody comes near. Be patient, Prudence tells herself; Nathan is starting to nod off. She has taken a half-day off to spend with him, which she often does now. When she and Paul have got things sorted out, she will have a brother or sister for Nathan. He won't be any different from the new baby, she could never love another kid any better than this one.

She is sorry for Nathan's mother, nutty as a fruitcake, and not very bright, she's decided. She's surprised that Paul had turned to Roberta, the last person she would have expected he might choose in her place. You wouldn't pick his mother's problems in Nathan, he's so well adjusted. She gives him her finger to hold while she reads a magazine. Nathan clings sleepily to her. Behind them, an older woman clucks at him. He puts up his arms for an instant, and then, to Prudence's relief, he changes his mind, returning his attention to her.

The woman looks vaguely familiar; perhaps Prudence has seen her at the shop before. Quite recently even. Her grey hair straggles from a bun, her hands are calloused as if she is used to hard work. But she is fresh-faced and wholesome, the kind of woman you would seek in a nanny. A recipe catches Prudence's eye. She has been paying attention to new things to cook. Paul has mentioned that Roberta was not half bad in the kitchen. She supposes Roberta had to be good at something; she understands she was hopeless in bed. Her eyes light on a recipe for asparagus wrapped in thin omelettes. She has already bought asparagus, but the recipe calls for leeks and fresh ginger, neither of which she has. She is trying not to mind the delay, but the troublesome shopper is still taking time. The manager has been called to check her card.

The grey-haired woman behind her seems unfazed by the delay. Prudence wonders if she knows there is a ten-item fast queue; she is person who might come from the country.

'You've only got a couple of things,' Prudence says to her, 'd'you want to go on ahead?'

'I've got all the time in the world,' the woman says, with a smile.

'It doesn't usually bother me, but I'm starting to get niggly.'

'All the queues are quite long,' says the woman. 'I wouldn't give up on this one.'

'Maybe I've got time to duck over and grab a couple of things from the vegie department?' Prudence says. She hasn't been meaning to do this, but the woman seems friendly.

'Poor girl looks as if she'll be a while,' the woman replies, nodding towards the checkout operator. 'Why don't you pop over? I'll keep an eye on the little boy — he won't mind, will he?'

'No, he seems to like you, thanks a million.'

'I'll just squeeze past your trolley so I'm closer to him,' says the woman.

And there goes Prudence, bouncing along in her artful, cheerful, shopping clothes, her comfortable canvas espadrilles, in the direction of fruit and vegetables. A packer finally appears at the checkout counter and speeds up the service. The woman wheels Nathan and the groceries alongside the counter.

'His Mum won't be a moment,' says the woman, and picks Nathan up out of the trolley. He squirms with the delight of freedom. 'Come to Granny, sweetheart.'

The operator looks impatiently over her shoulder, trying to decide what to do with Prudence's laden trolley, grateful that the woman is at least dealing with the child. 'Next please,' she says, pushing the groceries aside

The woman's step is firm and quick as she walks towards the exit.

twenty-seven

EXPOSURE

HOLMES, TELEVISION JOURNALIST, is lunching in a restaurant off High Street in Auckland, when his cellphone rings. 'Haul your arse out, mate,' says his producer. 'We've got a child abduction on the wire.'

'Whereabouts?'

'The Wairarapa. Place called Walnut. The chopper's on stand-by, we can take off as soon as we get confirmation.'

'Blah. What's the weather like?'

'Choppy.'

Holmes groans. 'Any leads?'

'Only a description of the abductor.'

'Any ransom?'

'No, no contact with the family.'

'So who've we got?'

'Hopefully, the mother. The baby was in a snatch and grab from a Wellington supermarket yesterday afternoon.'

'What's the Mum doing in Walnut?' Holmes is halfway down High Street, on the run.

'Lives there. Baby was out with hubby's girlfriend.'

'Fantastic,' says the talk host. 'Sounds like a good story.'

MARISE COMES, SO pale since Tamsin's early Caesarean birth that her face and hair almost merge together. She looks waif-like and frail and has copious supplies of milk. Her face, when she looks at Tamsin, is absorbed and secretive, as if nobody else exists. But she's here for me, when she shouldn't be, and Derek is furious that she has come, and I am fussing over her the way she did over me. I bring her a milky cup of tea and freshly cut brown bread sandwiches filled with mashed eggs, and this is a good distraction, although somebody, I think it's my cousin Sally, says in a hushed voice, 'It's too bad, her bringing her baby here. How's Roberta going to feel?'

'I feel like death,' I say, 'but I want Nathan back more than that.'

Grief confers a certain status, as if somehow the bereaved can do and say anything. I remember the time my friend Pamela's brother was killed in a riding accident, the way she was no longer responsible for our friendship, how it was all over to me to make sure that she coped with her crisis. Not that this is a death, but it has the same aura around it, the same kind of terror. People are treating me with wary respect.

The phone rings again.

'If it's Josh, tell him I'm not here,' I mouth to Marise who has taken over answering the phone as if it were her job. The police have been to see him and we argued when he last phoned. Nathan is nothing to do with you, I said to him and he had shouted back at me that he is, Nathan is his business too.

But it's not Josh.

'It's television,' Marise says. 'The *Holmes* show.'

'No.' This is from my father. 'I've had enough television on this place.'

'I'm sorry,' says Marise, 'there's nobody here wants to talk to you.' Her eyes widen. 'Roberta, I've got Holmes himself on the line.'

'Give him to me,' I say.

'You can't,' shouts Glass.

'I'll do anything it takes to find Nathan,' I say. 'Yes, it's Roberta speaking. Am I okay? No, I wouldn't exactly say that. I want my baby back. Can you help?'

THE CHECKOUT OPERATOR says, 'The baby's Mum is called Prudence. She comes in here quite often with him. I think she must live round here somewhere.'

'She drives a little blue Honda Civic,' says the young man who packs the groceries. 'I heard she wasn't the real Mum.'

'Oh God, don't tell anyone. The boss said we're not to talk about it.'

The packer is alarmed. 'But I just did. There's a woman from television out there in aisle number five. She's chatting to everyone.'

'I'M SORRY, ROBERTA,' Prudence says, and I guess she must be. Her voice is as thick with tears as my own. Two of us have mislaid Nathan.

'What does Paul say?'

'He says you must be even crazier than he thought. But I don't believe that.'

'He thinks I took Nathan?'

'Um, well something like that, yes. Look, I'm not supposed to be talking to you, but I'm worried about the *Holmes* show.'

'They've been in touch with you too?'

'I know they're after me. We could both just say we're not interested. I don't want to go on it, do you?'

'Too late, Prudence. I'm doing it.'

'So what are you going to say?' A shrillness has crept into her voice. 'I mean, we need to get our stories straight, don't we?'

'I don't know, Prudence,' I say slowly. Prudence is frightened of what dirt might be thrown up about her and Paul. For a moment, when she first rang, I'd had respect for her, that she would go against Fay and Paul, and Milton and Laura, and call me. Now I am remembering the times when she has held Nathan in her arms, and denied me the warmth of his skin against mine, and his right to know me as his mother.

'My grandmother always watches that programme. I don't of course, but, you know, she's not very well at present,' Prudence burbles.

I hand the phone to Marise, my hands shaking.

'Piss off,' says Marise to Prudence, and puts the phone down.

'HAVE WE GOT a landing spot sorted out?'

'Yeah,' says the pilot. He consults his references, listening to instructions though his headphones. The weather is a little gusty, a little dodgy, and the crew is mildly on edge. 'Hell, I know that place,' the cameraman says. 'I reckon we'd better go round again. I got shot up last time I was over that farm. I knew we should have pressed charges.'

'Nobody's going to shoot them,' says Marise, a few minutes later, speaking to television news on the phone. 'Hey, don't worry about it, Bernard's gone to Ireland. Last heard of boarding an Air New Zealand flight bound for Sydney; the international police have already checked him out. Well, no, he's not actually in Ireland, yet, but the police know he landed in Oz.'

'More and more weird,' says Holmes. 'Watch out for sharp shooters in the hills.'

'We're landing on the lawn, alongside the rose garden,' says the director. 'Aim for the patch by the gazebo.'

HOLMES ALREADY wears make-up when he comes into the house. I hadn't expected that. He is solicitous but professionally unobtrusive.

'Just tell me where you'd feel most comfortable talking to me,' he says. 'Out in Mum's garden?'

'No,' I say.

'We got a room ready for Nathan,' Edith is telling him.

'Excellent,' says the director. 'How would you feel about that?'

'I don't want to go in there.' The room is like a mausoleum in the middle of the house that we all tiptoe around. The door hasn't been opened since I came here to live.

'Okay,' says Holmes, 'have you got any other suggestions? We just need a glimpse of the wee chap's personality, something to make the viewers relate to your loss.'

Marise is handing make-up to the director. 'You don't have to have it,' the director says, 'but a little touch-up might help.' I know my face looks scrubbed and raw. I've got the fading evidence of one of Josh's love bites on my neck, like a kid. Marise gives me a sidelong glance. I haven't told her that I have been to bed with Josh. She slaps pancake stick over it before the other woman sees. The director looks mildly nettled at this interference, although I am being treated with almost exaggerated care.

'Any photos of little Nathan?' asks Holmes.

I have several, one of him taken in the hospital, and another of him at three months, when he was still with me, and one that Paul had sent to the psychiatric unit. I can't bring myself to look at them. Marise lines the photos up on the table: Nathan with his fists curled up by his sleeping face, Nathan in my arms (I'm glad of that one now, even though I'm ten kilos overweight and my hair looks like straw) outside the house at Ashton Fitchett Drive, Nathan sitting up in his high chair banging the tray with a spoon, and laughing.

'All right,' I say, 'We'll do it in the bedroom.'

JACK IS AT soccer practice, and Ellie is visiting a friend, so Sarah Lord eats her meal sitting in front of television.

As the news finishes the face of a young woman comes up on screen. 'I just want my baby back,' says the woman, in a ten-second grab, and then there is a tracking shot across a beautiful garden to a farm homestead. Sarah sits bolt upright. She knows the garden, she has met the woman.

'Tonight,' says Paul Holmes, 'we have the case of a young woman who has had her baby stolen, brutally snatched in a supermarket.' The camera pans to a close-up of Roberta's swollen, unhappy face. There is something desperate about the bruised space beneath her eyes. She has a welt on her throat.

'No story, tell us what happened.'

Roberta's eyes are fixed straight ahead. 'I wasn't actually with him,' she says, in a halting voice. 'He was in a supermarket with . . . with a friend of my husband's.'

'A close friend?'

'Yes, they've known eath other for a long time.' She goes on to relate the story as it has been told to her, then she describes her baby's appearance, while the cameras zoom over photographs and cut back to her face, framing her anguish.

'I've been sick, and I haven't looked after Nathan for a while. But he's still my baby.'

Holmes speaks gently, on a small rising inflection. 'This friend of your husband's, you get along all right with her?'

'I wouldn't say that. Paul and I were going to go to court about Nathan this week.'

'Hmm. So Prudence and Paul want custody of little Nathan, and so do you?'

'I guess that's about it.'

'You see, I'm a bit concerned . . . '

'I didn't take Nathan,' says Roberta, before he can finish. 'They're the ones who had him.'

'Yes, well all right, they had him, so they're not the ones who've run off with him.' Holmes cups his chin in one hand, a pencil point side out, held like a cigarette between two fingers. A baby mobile hovers in the background.

'Unless they wanted to hide him from me.'

'Do you think that's what happened?'

On national television, Roberta begins to cry. Sarah wishes it would stop, she can't bear to watch this woman's pain.

'No,' says Roberta, 'I don't think they would have done that. But I haven't got him, and I can't think why anyone else would want to take him. It just goes to show that Prudence can't look after him though, doesn't it?'

'Tell me about the woman who took him,' says Holmes.

'Well, apparently, she was a woman with kind of straggly white hair and an English accent.'

'And you don't know anyone like that?'

'Roberta shakes her head, massaging her cheekbones with her fingertips.

'Nobody been round, having a bit of a look about the farm or anything like that?'

'Lots of peoople come here to look at Mum's garden. I suppose there's Wendy.'

'Who's Wendy?'

'She's a friend of Mum's.'

'No,' says a voice off-camera. The angle is widened to reveal a woman sitting on a low bed, beside a teddy bear. Sarah knows her, too, even though she looks hunched and blowsy. The last time she saw her, she had been striding through her garden, giving orders. Now her expression is startled and disbelieving.

'So Wendy looks a bit like this person you've described?' Holmes says, glancing from mother to daughter; Sarah can tell he is treading a fine line.

'Yes, I guess she does. But, that's crazy. She wouldn't do that. At least, I don't think so.' Roberta glances sideways at her mother.

'Where's Wendy now?'

'I don't know,' says Roberta. 'Look, I just want Nathan. If anybody knows where my little boy is, please, please let me know. I can't bear this.' Her shoulders start to shake, there is a soft fadeout to black.

In the studio, Holmes turns to his audience. 'The very sad case of Roberta Cooksley whose little boy has gone missing, somewhere, we don't know where, don't know why, one of those apparently senseless crimes. And police will be following up new information as it comes to hand. If you have information ring this toll-free number.' The numbers roll across the screen.

Sarah writes the numbers down, her hands shaking, and sits staring at the television without seeing the rest of the programme. When she thinks about it, she hasn't actually got any information. She doesn't know where her mother is. She thought she was at the farm, but Roberta has just said she isn't.

Ellie comes while she is still sitting there. The *Holmes* show is ending; there is another shot of Roberta's tear-ravaged face.

'What happened to her?' asks Ellie.

'Somebody took her baby.'

'Who?'

'Well, I don't know. They wouldn't put it on television if they knew.' She is thankful Ellie hasn't come in earlier.

'Spare a thought for Roberta Cooksley,' Holmes reminds them, 'a bereft mother, pleading for the return of her son. Somebody out there has Nathan. If you have any information which might lead police to him, phone now. We all want to find him. Those were our people today, that's *Holmes* tonight.'

Sarah reaches for the remote control and changes channels. She should get up, go to the telephone. It has taken her such a long time to arrive at this point of equilibrium in her life. The Earl of Maudsley's silver bird glares from her mantelpiece with a baleful eye.

CHOOSING TRUTH

EDITH IS SITTING in the shadows of the barn. Glass has been looking for her.

'Going somewhere, Mr Nichols?' the policeman asks, as if it's not his own property. As if he is a suspect.

'Just to the barn.'

'Looking for company?' The inference is clear.

Edith is propped on the floor with her back to the timber wall, her eyes unfocused, a bottle in her hand. She has been drinking neat gin. There is something confusing going on in her brain. She is fighting for her memory. Already, the time of lightness and clear thinking has receded, an interlude she cannot imagine having achieved. She believes that if she could retrieve that clarity for just an instant she could work out the key to a problem.

Glass wants to kick her when he sees her.

'Where's the woman's family?' he says. 'Come on, I want to hear it.'

'I told you, the same as I told the police — she's got a daughter in Palmerston North.'

'They need more than that.'

'Wendy never told me,' says Edith.

Glass studies her. 'She must have let something drop, all that talk, all the time you spent together.'

'It's the truth,' she says, closing her eyes.

'I should kick you out, you old soak.'

'Why don't you then?' Daring him.

And for a moment, he almost does. Instead he picks up her feverish hand, and drops down beside her. 'I'm thinking about leaving the farm,' he says, after a silence. 'Whatever happens. I reckon I've had enough.'

'You're just saying that, Glass. Expediency. You want something.'

He drops her hand back into her lap.

'I mean, it's a bit late, isn't it?'

He doesn't answer her; probably she's right, the accumulation of wreckage between them is hard to believe.

'I do love you, Glass,' she says, inconsequentially.

'Yes,' he says, 'of course. I know that.'

'I never cared about anyone else. Know what I mean?'

'Well, then, it's all right, isn't it?'

'Glass, I don't know where Wendy is. Cross my heart.'

'Her daughter? You can't think of a name?'

'It might have been Sarah.'

The door swings open. Their daughter looks down at them, full of rage and contempt.

'Roberta,' says Glass.

'What the fuck do you two think you're doing?'

Roberta stands in front of her mother. 'Get up,' she says.

'That's enough,' says Glass. But Edith is clutching at the wall behind her, pulling herself to her feet. Mother and daughter stand glaring at each other.

Roberta turns on Edith. 'You and your crazies. Where is she?'

'Don't know. Just told your father.'

'Is that the best you can do?'

'What do you want me to do?'

'Stop hiding behind all this crap. Tell the truth for a change.'

'Sorry. Wish I knew.' Edith hiccups and wipes her mouth on her sleeve.

'You do,' says Roberta. 'For Christ's sake, remember. I mean, for *Christ's sake*, Mum.'

Edith crosses herself, swaying. Her eyes lock with Roberta's, in and out of focus. Father and daughter hold their breaths.

'Perhaps in the kitchen? Might be something there.'

They take off their gumboots at the back door, habit overriding their haste. The policeman seems to have gone home, or perhaps he is asleep in the car. Nothing stirs. The house feels still and close.

Edith opens the drawer of the dresser, rummaging among bits of string and plastic bags and corkscrews and preserving jar lids, old shopping lists and the draft of her seed catalogue.

'Yes,' she mutters. 'Daughter. Sarah Lord. I have the number. She rang me one night.'

Glass is dizzy with relief. 'I'll ring the police.'

'No,' says Roberta, snatching the paper from her mother's hand. She picks up a set of keys from the ledge above the bench, the keys to Bernard's wagon, recovered from the airport. It stands in the driveway of his deserted house.

twenty-eight

ROBERTA AND SARAH

It is surprising how calm Sarah Lord sounds, as if she has been expecting my phone call. I ring from the phone box near the general store out in the middle of nowhere, praying that my ancient Telecom card is still operational. As I dial, I am raking the landscape for approaching headlights, ready to make a run for it if I see a police car. My card has a dollar left on it. Sarah answers straight away.

'It's Roberta, isn't?' she says.

'Can I come and see you?'

'Of course.'

She may think I'm deranged. I don't know what she will know about me, whether her mother has been in touch with her, talked about me. I half-expect the police to be parked outside, although I have broken no laws, am free to come and go. But they will expect me to lead them to Nathan. They have no reason to trust me. I park Bernard's four-wheel drive around the corner from her house.

'I've just made some tea,' Sarah says. Although it is spring, she has an open fire burning in the grate. She hands me a toasting fork with a crumpet on the end of it.

'You've had an amazingly long day,' she says. 'What time did you talk to Holmes?'

I tell her how he came out of the sky in a chopper and took away my image and my fears, leaving me to wonder what on earth I'd done.

'You were good,' she says, 'really straight up and down.'

'You didn't think I sounded vindictive?'

'About your ex and his girlfriend? It's nothing to what I would have said.'

'Really?' When I had met her in the garden for those few minutes, the day of Wendy's appearance at the farm, I would have said she was scatty, but I'm liking her more and more by the minute.

'I expect she's in love with him, all the same,' she says reflectively. 'It happens.'

There doesn't seem any proper response to this.

Sarah has made tea in a pot shaped like a pumpkin with a stalk to lift the lid. I know this is chic kitsch — some of Paul's and my friends in the city used to specialise in it — but Sarah's unconventional house doesn't seem contrived, just put together with a touch of fun and drama and a fair bit of romanticism. I look at the books, the kooky china, the artwork, roll my finger over the dragon on the piano. Kids' stuff is thrown around, roller blades and tapedecks and posters. I feel a kind of envy for Sarah.

'I wouldn't mind this,' I say.

Sarah sits down with her hands around a mug. 'It has its moments. I get lonely. Now what about your baby?'

'That's what I'm hoping you can tell me. Where d'you think Wendy's taken her?'

'You're quite sure it's Wendy?' says Sarah.

I stare at her. 'I thought this is what it was all about.'

'She hasn't been in touch with me,' says Sarah.

'I wondered if you didn't get on.'

'Not exactly that. We'd just cast each other off, if you see what I mean. Well, maybe you don't. I'm adopted, actually. I'm still trying to sort it out in my head. She'd left me to it, I think. I did tell her to.'

'But it's not sorted?'

'No, I don't think so. But I miss her, you see.'

'She's pretty weird.'

'Yeah, I know, but she's what I've got.'

'So possibly you think I can live without my baby?'

'I didn't say that. I don't know whether my natural mother could or not. In a way I don't want to know.' Her look is harder, more penetrating than I expect. And I can see what is going through her mind — I can give my baby away and go on television and drive around in the middle of the night and look at the things in her house. I'm still alive. I'm a sort of living proof that she doesn't have to seek out her history and live all its pain.

'I've been in hospital,' I say abruptly. 'Psych ward.'

Sarah is still. 'Shit,' she says. 'Why didn't you say?'

'On television?'

She gives a half-hearted grin. 'Okay,' she says. 'Let's look at what we've got. Look, you'd better see this.' She unfurls a letter and hands it to me. 'What do you make of that?' The letter is about Wendy invading someone's privacy, the likelihood of her having information which she is using to the detriment of others.

'Is there any way that this affects you?'

'It doesn't make any sense at all. I can't think how it's anything to do with me. Perhaps I should have rung and asked them.'

'I don't expect they'd tell you, if it was for real.'

'You think it's phony? Look, it's on letterhead.'

'That doesn't make it real. People can get access to letterheads, copy them, all sorts of things. The technology's changed things like that. Even the officialese doesn't sound quite right.'

'Don't you think so?' Sarah is curious about how I know all these things.

'I worked for the Inland Revenue Department.'

'I don't believe it. You don't look the part.'

'We're mostly pretty normal, just like real people.' I smile for the first time in days.

'Okay, so wouldn't you send a letter like this?'

'Not up front like this. It's not very subtle. Somebody wants her to shut up, that's all.'

'But whatever they were on to her about, Wendy wouldn't know, would she, because she never got the letter.'

'Look,' I say, 'there's something I should tell you. When I left Nathan, I left him with my mother-in-law. I went to her house and simply walked out on him. I hate what I did, but I couldn't help myself.'

'She didn't try and stop you?'

'I'm sure she would have, but she didn't know what I was going to do. Somebody came to the house and made it easy for me. A woman who frightened her. I'm sure it was Wendy. Is she a blackmailer or something?'

'No,' says Sarah, her head in her hands. 'She's not like that.'

'I don't know what she's like,' I say. 'She wanted to be friends, but I couldn't let myself. You know, she was my mother's friend, she seemed to get between her and everyone else.'

'Really?'

'Yes, really. But perhaps I wasn't fair, because I can see my mother's never had a friend.'

'Wendy lives in a world of make-believe. I've got no real idea of her personal history — some of it's true, and some of it's fantasy. She sees herself as the heroines in the books she reads, some of it I think she makes up as she goes along.' Sarah, with a distracted air, walks to her bookshelf and takes down *Brewer's Dictionary of Phrase*

226

and Fable, opening the volume at a marked page. 'This was one of my mother's books. I found this entry ringed, a long time ago. I've never thought of it again.'

In astonishment, I read: DOMIDUCA: *the goddess who brought young children safe home, and kept guard over them when out of their parents' sight.*

'She wouldn't hurt Nathan,' Sarah says.

'Where would she have taken him?'

'To her cottage by the sea, up the north of Taranaki. It's near a camping ground. If she's not there already, I'm fairly certain that's the direction she'll be heading. I could take you there if you like.'

'Could you?'

'Yes, but I'll have to get someone to look after my kids. Their father, I suppose, although I wouldn't want him to know where we were going.'

'How soon could we go?'

Sarah looks worried. 'Not before morning. But we need some sleep. It's a long way.'

I know I can't go much further without collapsing. All the same, I don't want to stay around here, now that I have a lead.

Sarah is thinking. 'One of us should wait here, in case she turns up. If I gave you directions, would you stay here till dawn, have a kip first?'

'This isn't a brush-off?'

'Why should you trust me?' says Sarah. 'Well, I can see that you mightn't, but what else have you got?'

I know I have to go on my own. That is, if I want to see Nathan again. If I have any chance of restaking my claim upon him. I have no idea how it might turn out, or what I will have to do when I get there, but I must go. First, before anything, I have to know that he is alive and safe.

SARAH WAKES ME at dawn, just as she promised. She is still wearing the same sweater and jeans that she wore the night before, so I guess she has sat up and kept watch. I hadn't expected to sleep but as soon as I lay down on the comfortable mattress on the floor of her room, I went straight into the deepest and most dreamless sleep I can recall since long before Nathan was born.

We sit on either side of her drop-leaf kitchen table, snatching a quick cup of fresh coffee. We talk very quietly because her children will wake soon and we don't want them to know I have been here. I am beginning to see Wendy in a new light — a woman missed by grandchildren, a provider, of sorts, for her daughter, a strange, passionate lost creature.

'Have you got a boyfriend?' I ask. Boyfriend sounds juvenile, but lover feels presumptuous.

'I did,' says Sarah, 'but it turned to shit. I'd like another one but there's not much going that hasn't got a return-by date. What about you?'

'I don't know,' I say. 'Sort of. He doesn't know what he wants.'

'Do you want to marry him or something?'

'I don't want to share him,' I say. It's not the time to explain all of this, but I have come to the conclusion, in the past few strange days of my life, that I want more than my mother seemed to want: to be wooed, corrupted and defiled, and then, contrite, return to the life she had lived before, without responsibility for her absence, without the need to make decisions about change. I see how that has failed her. Besides, Paul was never like my father. He was never half as good, and I couldn't have him back even if I wanted to. But I want Josh for myself, not just as an interlude in my life. I feel that we could sit here talking for days, two serious, quiet young women, interested in books and men . . .

'It's time for me to push off,' I say. Sarah hugs me in a fierce, affectionate embrace, as if we have known each other much longer. It feels lonely setting off on my own, driving through the quiet streets of the town.

AN ORDINARY GRAN

NATHAN IS WELL, as it happens, although he is fretful and as tired, in his way, as his minder. He has been travelling, so Wendy tells people, with his English grandmother, who looks, at the moment, like other people's ordinary grandmothers. Wendy had a haircut in the first hours after she took Nathan from the supermarket. Cut above her ears, and shaped up the back of her head, her hair now looks like that of other perky elderly women. The hairdresser's assistant held him during the haircut, feeding him morsels of flaky chocolate. Wendy was sure it was bad for him, but she hadn't wanted to draw attention to herself.

'What a good gran you are,' said the hairdresser, handing him back.

'Oh, no more than most,' replied Wendy. She wore a sensible floral dress and a cardigan.

Nathan sat up in his new stroller and smiled. The first night they were together, the pair stayed in a good hotel on The Terrace in the city. Wendy sent for room service to bring soft-boiled eggs and fresh bread for them both. Nathan had a new bottle which she filled with milk or juice. She gave generous tips. In the morning she paid with cash when she left.

The second night was not so easy. She had started the day with the intention of going to Sarah's, but the bus had been booked out, and the train had already left. Later in the day there would be another bus, but Nathan was showing signs of wear and tear, and she couldn't duck and dive out of shops any more. She had half-expected Nathan's photograph to be on the front page of the paper, but the story must have broken too late, or it hasn't been picked up by the papers yet. They went to the library, where Wendy scribbled a letter, then they set off for the bus station again, but she became afraid. A stream of people was heading towards the railway station and, on an impulse, she decided to go back there. A unit was about to leave and she boarded it without seeing its destination. The reason for this excursion was becoming difficult to remember.

On the train, she rested her head against the window and watched the sea rushing past, while the child wriggled and struggled in her arms. She thought about her father, the tall man wearing a waistcoat, properly buttoned, and plus-fours. The rough landscape, the baby, the end of the line when the train stops, wer e not what she saw. She regarded the boy with positive dislike as she got out of the train and walked him, in his stroller, to a motel. She paid cash up front at the desk and asked that she and the child not be disturbed.

Nathan sleeps, wakes, she feeds him a tin of baby food and a mashed banana. It is not his fault, she decides, recovering a little of her affection for him. In the evening they watch television together, or she thinks he is watching, his eyes overbright, his cheeks flushed.

Wendy sees Roberta on television. She sees Nathan's picture. And there is Edith's garden, not as manicured as it was when she had first visited it a year earlier, but still opulent with spring blooms, still the beautiful place she has left days before. It would be possible to leave the child here; he would be safe enough until they found him in the morning.

She rings reception. 'Please give me an early morning wake-up call,' she says, 'and order me a taxi for seven a.m.'

GOING ON

I HAVE TRAVELLED some hours. I pass police cars, think I'm being watched. I am erratic and unstable, I have that on expert authority. A little madness goes a long way. It can haunt you for the rest of your life.

The country towns trickle past me: Waverley, Patea, Kakaramea, the names roll off my tongue as I say them to myself. I turn the radio on, Melissa Etheridge is singing. Will she love you, I ask myself, dancing in my head. Will anyone love you the way I do? I catch sight of myself in the mirror when I look up to observe the car behind me. You look like a dyke, Josh had said, a woman with huge eyes and a furry matt of spikes on my skull. My heart hurts so much it feels as if it will burst my chest. Will Leda love Josh the way I do? Does Prudence love Nathan? What's happened to me? I've become a different person. I have, in my mind's eye, a snapshot image of us three kids — Mike, Bernie and Rob. What's happened to us all?

The detour carries me past Hawera, and I think about stopping to eat, but I can't stop now. I gun on up through the wide, flat, grass-drenched landscape, through Normanby and Eltham and Ngaere. I drive past the high, white mountain, through more towns and over a long hill.

WENDY

DEAREST SARAH,

I have something I must tell you immediately. You will know soon enough, but I would like you to learn it from me.

For some time, I believed I knew the identity of your birth mother. I was sure that if I told her about you, and what a delightful person you were, she would at once want to know you. I took every step I could to track her down and tell her what I knew.

I had made a mistake, she told me, it couldn't be true. I am not the woman you are looking for, she said, over and again. Finally, I understood that she wouldn't come round to my way of thinking. So I took her grandson instead. A real living relative for you, I believed. Blood ties.

Well, it seems that, as she said, this is not the woman and I have made a grievous error. Perhaps that is what you have expected of me, all along. You will see it as another obsession of mine.
There it is. I have the child — to tell you the truth, I don't quite know what to do with him.

With my love, as always,
Wendy

Wendy is right, as it happens. An obsession is how Sarah will come to describe it, when she talks about it later.

NATHAN
NOW THEY SIT in a fur-padded InterCity bus heading north-west. Because she is tired, Wendy is afraid people will offer to help with the child. Nathan wants to crawl through the bus and she hasn't the strength to hold on to him much longer. She had forgotten babies were so strong and so wilful. Perhaps it is because he is a boy.

In the interval between changing buses at the depot in New Plymouth, she almost turns herself and Nathan in. She is surprised that there is nobody there to apprehend her. The child has pulled himself up on a seat and looks around with a calculating eye. He staggers and falls, and crawls again.

SARAH HAS GIVEN me a key to Wendy's cottage near the camping ground, and careful instructions on how to get there. And at last I am there, finding a huddle of rickety baches squatting on the seafront, a streaming green sea pounding on the rocks, flax bushes stirring before a gathering ocean wind. The wind whistles under the eaves of the tiny, steep-roofed cabin where Wendy once lived. I am full of trepidation as I walk down the rough path towards it.

I am terrified of what I will find. I don't know what I will do if she is there, nor what I will do if she is not. Outside, wash tubs appear to have served as a garden. A cluster of wild marigolds fill the corner of one, and nasturtiums trail down another in defiance of the salt wind. Shells and driftwood have been placed in a rough boundary around the place. Nobody answers the door, and it is so quiet I know there is nobody even breathing inside. Perhaps this is not the place, I tell myself; somewhere up the road there is another house just like this, where Wendy will be waiting with Nathan. But the key slides into the lock and turns.

Order of a kind prevails inside, although the cabin is crammed with all manner of strange objects: an old copper, driftwood, coils of wire, a hand-driven sewing machine with a storage pouch that bellies beneath it, more pots and pans than one person could need, a plaster bust of Mozart, a faded Pink Panther hanging from the ceiling, a painting signed by McCahon, the blade off a windmill, books standing on top of each other on the floor. A bench with a tin sink and a wooden drawer filled with worn, bone-handled cutlery, and no cupboards beneath, runs down one side of the cabin, and, through the clutter can be seen a bunk with a musty but neatly folded pile of blankets.

I sit down, weak around the knees, overwhelmed by the futility of my journey. Through the open door, I see the sea. Muddy waves swirl around an ochre-brown rock that looks like a temple, or a flower pot overturned. This is where I'm always ending up, somewhere at the edge of things, on the margins, looking back to where I've come from. I've never felt more empty, more futile in my ambitions. I am far away and on my own, and I've lost Nathan in a void as big as the ocean.

This is where Wendy finds me, late in the afternoon. It is not until later that I find out I have been caught up in something random and incidental, that what has happened to me could have happened to anyone. There is less symmetry than I had supposed.

NATHAN, MY BEAUTIFUL, tousle-headed son, looks right through me at first.

I kneel in front of him. 'Darling,' I say, willing him to like me. No, more than that, I am desperate for him to love me, as if my presence is a reward that he should immediately understand. I put my finger on his lips, his nose; I wiggle it and laugh. He stares stonily at me.

'Perhaps if you were to feed him,' says Wendy, taking him out of the stroller.

'You feed him,' I say, throwing myself down on one of her rickety chairs. 'Really,' I say, 'I should just fuck off and leave you to him, if you want him that badly.'

And then it happens. Nathan, who has been sitting on the floor where I have left him, pulls himself up on the leg of the bunk. Turning and measuring the distance between us, he takes two steps, sits down again and smiles.

'How long has he been able to walk?'

'That's it, his first steps,' says Wendy.

'Are you sure?'

She nods, her face alight.

'Little show-off, you've done it for me, haven't you?' I exclaim over him.

Nathan repeats his new achievement, this time with three steps. I grab him and hug him and only now he doesn't pull away from me.

Wendy has a spare camp stretcher that she sleeps on. We go to bed very early and again I sleep well, only it's more lightly than the night before, because this time Nathan lies beside me, his face pressed against my neck, his fingers clenched in my flesh.

'Monkey face,' I murmur when he stirs against me, 'my little sweet potato,' and we go back to sleep again, my baby and I. It is hard to believe that I have ever known despair. All the same, I dream, towards morning, that Josh Thwaite is beside us. I remember the way he used to ask me about my dreams.

Wendy looks at me over breakfast. 'What are you going to do?' she asks.

'You know what I have to do,' I say. 'I won't tell them where I found him.'

'But you must.' She looks alarmed. 'It would be such a waste.'

'Wendy . . . ' I begin.

'No,' she says, 'don't you see, it doesn't matter what we say, they'll never be convinced that we didn't do it together.'

'All right, all right then. But we'll go for a walk first.'

'You should go quite soon,' she says, 'otherwise they'll find us.' The camp proprietor is back at the grounds; his absence must have been brief. Soon, she tells me, he will notice her, even if nobody else does.

'Half an hour.' I am not ready yet to let Nathan go. I have a hazy idea that this is the day the court hearing is set down for, not that it was ever intended that I be present. I leave Wendy sitting outside her cabin weeding her tubs and planting out seedlings, as if she is going to be there for ever, an unlikely goddess. She gives us a wave as we set off down the beach together.

I carry Nathan for a while, but every now and then he wants to get down and show off again. He stumbles and laughs, turning to be picked up when the going gets rough. The sand turns to unstable dunes, and I carry him on my shoulders. We walk in a circle, away from the beach and around the houses, coming to a park of sorts, with a swing and a see-saw. A wooden fence runs past it.

'Hey,' I tell Nathan, 'you don't know what I can do, do you?' Climbing up on on the fence rail, I test my weight on it. Shoulder height, it is not as stable as the beam in a gymnasium, but it will do. Squaring my hips, I relax my shoulders, my head held erect. I turn my feet in order to feel the edge of the rail as I traverse it. First I walk backwards and forwards two or three times until I am certain my balance is under control. I poise, ready for take-off, my back arching. Then I stretch and somersault backwards through the air. My feet land in perfect position.

'Nothing to it,' I tell him.

I AM SURPRISED at my competence in dealing with authority again, although once I would have taken it for granted.

'There is a custody case pending over this child,' I say to the court registrar, when we have presented ourselves at the courthouse.

'We're aware of that,' he says, turning a fish-eye on me and tapping away at his computer screen.

'I'm Nathan's mother. Now just find me a place where I can change and feed him, and leave us in peace, while you sort it all out.'

Sarah comes and she holds Wendy's hand for as long as they are allowed, before her mother is led away and locked in a cell. I don't want to be a witness to this.

Nor do I wish to hand Nathan over to frightened, pasty-faced Paul, whose job is on the line because of the scandal and all the time he has taken off work, and Prudence, who looks underweight and ill, but when they come I don't demur, although it breaks me up all over again to see him go ricocheting off again. But I am hopeful that, because I have found him, and because he doesn't want to leave me, it won't be quite the open and shut case they had thought.

I don't say anything much, just study them with slow contempt, and I see that the new person I am frightens both of them. I don't say goodbye to Nathan, I say, see you soon sweetheart, and kiss him on the forehead and walk away quickly.

twenty-nine

INSIDE

Sarah Lord turns off the motorway at Tawa, and then left again at the prison gates. She has never been inside a prison before and she doesn't expect to be stopped at the entrance. It will, she supposes, be like hospital visiting. She carries flowers and a variety of fruit in her basket.

'You'll have to leave those outside,' says the guard.

'But these are for my mother.'

'Sorry,' says the guard, 'you can get them on the way out.'

The smell of disinfectant and boiled cabbage engulfs her. It is not an odour that masks dirt, simply the despair of women who have reached the end of the line; yet it is thick and congealing. Sarah gags as she waits in the visiting room, the barred doors closing behind her. She glances behind her, as if seeking escape.

'You're not meant to get out,' says the guard.

The visiting room is crowded: young women with tattoos on their faces holding hands with men in black leather jackets; middle-aged women talking to their children; girls who look as if they have just finished library school. It is impossible to tell the difference between murderers and child bashers and thieves. Or kidnappers, for that matter. Sarah sits still, with her hands between her knees, until Wendy, dressed in a shapeless green dress, appears at a warder's side. Her smart haircut has grown out; now the white hair is blunt cut across the bottom and pegged to the side of her head with hair clips, allowed during visiting hour only.

'Is there somewhere we can talk in private?' Sarah asks.

Wendy smiles in a distracted way. 'Nobody's going to listen to us — they've got their own problems to worry about.'

'How are you?' says Sarah, when they have found a corner.

'I've got some arthritis but I'm seeing the doctor,' Wendy replies. 'Things aren't too bad. I'm allowed to read. It could be worse. I can't imagine what my father would think.'

'Never mind,' says Sarah, 'never mind. I'll get you out of here soon.'

'Like the Scarlet Pimpernel?' says Wendy, her eyes gleaming.

'Oh Mum.'

'Did I ever tell you that the Baroness Orczy came to stay with us when I was a child? Her real name was Mrs Montagu Barstow, a great friend of the family's.'

'I guess she'd have worked out a plot for you, Mum,' says Sarah.

'Did you ring Edith?'

'Yes, I did.'

'And is she going to come?'

'I don't know, Mum. She sounded busy.'

Wendy's eyes cloud. 'Well, she does lead a busy life.'

'Mullen,' calls the guard at the door. 'Visitor.'

'That'll be her now, I expect,' says Wendy.

But it is Fay Cooksley, pallid and frightened, clutching her Italian leather handbag.

'Well,' says Wendy. 'Goodness me. It's all right, Mrs Cooksley, they've got me, I'm all locked up.'

Sarah looks from one woman to another.

'Sarah?' says Fay quietly.

'That's me.' Sarah doesn't put out her hand. 'Shall I stay?' she asks her mother.

'No, dear. It's all right.'

'Well, it doesn't matter.' Fay is flummoxed, groping for appropriate small talk. 'I'll only be a few minutes,' she tells Sarah.

'I DID HAVE a child before I met Milton,' Fay explains. 'A little girl who died soon after birth. The same day Sarah was born, it seems. You were sold bad information, that's all — the wrong mother of the wrong child.'

'You don't need to tell me this,' says Wendy.

'Well, of course I don't. I didn't need to come here.' There is a touch of asperity in Fay's voice. 'But I wanted to tell someone. I've never told anyone, you see, not even my mother.

'Perhaps the baby didn't die,' says Sarah, with sudden bewilderment, and something like hope. Wendy glances at her. 'You hear of things like that.'

'The baby did die,' says Fay firmly. 'I could show you the death certificate.'

'No,' says Wendy, 'I believe you. I knew ages ago, I just didn't want to believe it. I'm a silly old fool.'

'I didn't feel anything for years,' said Fay. 'I pretended it didn't happen. But you don't forget.' Her eyes fill with tears.

Wendy regards her with some sympathy — a middle-class woman, a good girl, caught out.

'I won't tell anyone.'

'I don't expect you will,' Fay replies. 'No, I didn't think you would. But that's not what I came about. There's something else.' She hesitates — 'I've asked my son to work something out with Roberta over Nathan.'

'Shouldn't you be telling Roberta that?'

'She'll find out. I just wanted you to know. My husband thinks I'm insane.'

'Roberta's fighting for Nathan anyway,' Wendy says.

'All the same, it might make things easier for her.'

'Thank you.'

'Well,' says Fay, 'I'd better make tracks. We've got a staff do tonight.'

'Goodbye, Fay.' Wendy sits very still, her eyes resting on Sarah.

thirty

ROBERTA

I HAVE A new lawyer now. Her name is Mildred Dombey, a woman who has come to the law in middle life. She and I and Paul sit around a long, oval, highly polished table in Brian Adams' office. There are oil paintings on the wall and thick shagpile on the floor.

'We don't think court battles do anyone any good,' Adams is saying. 'Reconciliation of Nathan's interests seems more appropriate.'

'Quite,' says Mildred. 'So we can agree to joint custody?'

'I think that's going a bit fast,' says Adams.

'Where would Roberta take Nathan when she had him?' asks Paul.

'Ask her,' says Mildred. 'She's right here.'

Paul turns to me. 'So, Roberta,' he says, when I don't say anything, 'where would you take Nathan?'

'I've bought a house,' I tell him. 'My very own.'

AT FIRST IT hadn't felt like my own, because my parents had put money into it, and so, for that matter, had Paul — through the money from my settlement that I spent on the deposit. It's a long, narrow terrace house in Newtown, not the kind of place my father had in mind for me when he offered the money. I am not quite sure, myself, why I chose it, except that the dark hollow of its interior feels like a place I understand.

Built at the turn of the century, its foundations are crumbling and I know it will need all the money I have saved by not buying a smarter house. On either side, just a couple of metres separate me from my neighbours; you could land spit balls on either of them without walking further than the front door. I don't mind this, only when they are tuned into a different television channel at night. If I lie still, I imagine I can hear them breathing through the walls.

The more I live in it, the more I know it is right.

The back of the house opens on to a courtyard of ragged and badly laid bricks where the sun shines until about lunchtime. When I first move in, I do little more than sit outside making friends with a ginger cat from next door. One day I think that if some branches of the big silver birch in the yard were cut, the sun would last longer. I go down to the hardware shop and buy a saw. While I am up in the branches, my mother arrives. Edith nods approvingly, without saying anything much.

'You could put a little seat down there, make a garden round it,' she ventures.

'I'm not into all that garden stuff,' I say. I have visions of being like her.

Not that everything has stayed exactly the same for my parents. I see them holding hands with the dry, bony ardour of sexless affection, blindly turning their faces from the past.

'I said to your father, you and me growing old in the suburbs, don't see it,' she had reported to me.

When he said that he was finished with the farm, she had not believed him, or perhaps, that difficult night, she had not really heard him. But he tells her that she can stay there on her own, if she likes, but he is up and off. Once they decide to move there is a lot to be done and the organisation of the shift takes her months. My mother has relaxed her love affair with drink, though perhaps it will come back. I think she has gone back to God, as they say, but we don't talk about that.

'I keep meaning to visit Wendy,' she says.

'Then why don't you?'

'I don't know what I would say, to tell you the truth.' And I can see how it is for her, remembering their conversations on the farm, the endless private delights of Wendy's fantasies and bookish half-truths. It wouldn't be the same behind bars.

'No garden,' she tells Glass, when they buy their new house on the outskirts of town. It is a brick bungalow with a rectangular blue swimming pool. A forsythia grows at the front; Edith has never given garden space to forsythia — a common shade of yellow, she has said in the past.

'You'll have to have something,' Glass says.

'Then you do it,' she replies. 'You just plant out the stuff and keep it weeded, but don't expect me to do it.' But, in the spring, Edith talks about putting a bed of cream polyanthus under the forsythia to tone it down a bit. And now she is sniffing around in my garden, getting ready to organise me.

As if she is reading my mind, she sits down on the step, seeming to let well alone. She scratches in the earth at a crumbling brick, levering it from its base. I see then what I haven't noticed before, that there is some kind of design underneath. The next week, when she comes back, she carries a pick, spade and some trowels in the back of her car. Without saying anything, we both set to work, clearing away silt and rubbish, until the pattern becomes clearer: bricks set in an ever-expanding circle. I have found my father's story about the circles and how he nearly killed a man over them oddly heartening; I mean, that he had made something out of it important enough to tell me. I like the idea of circles exploding from the centre, caught in endless multiplication, but at least erratic, not conforming all the time to the common view of a circle, not meeting expectations. I can live with that.

When I go down the street, I look for the War Woman, but I never see her again. I recall her passionate possession of her child and I think that she was probably wrong. Do people own children? How can I answer that? Nathan is my son, but I relinquished him through a time of terror and despair. A part of me says that children grow and become less and less their parents' children; another part of me says that we are never free of each other, but bound up in indissoluble strands, in which possession has no place.

On a morning when I can put it off no longer, I pull on a jersey and some leggings, wind a cheerful scarf around my neck, and set off along the street, as if I am not going anywhere special. When I get to the hospital, I keep walking up through the grounds, and turn left at a small building. I walk down the corridor, intending only to make an appointment. I can always change my mind.

But his door is open. Dr Q sits at his desk, gazing out the window, eating peppermints. He is wearing a dark denim shirt and a hairy brown jacket.

'Business a bit quiet today,' I say.

He holds out the bag of peppermints. 'What kept you so long?' he says. 'I've been expecting you.'

'I want to get a job sooner or later,' I say.

'Well, I haven't got one for you.'

'No, but you'll find work for me.'

'Yes,' he says, pushing his spectacles up on his nose. 'There's always work to be done. Why don't you sit down?'

And then there is Nathan, who comes to me every second weekend at the start. But it has been agreed that the time will increase if things go well between us. I think that they are, though

I am nervous when Paul brings him round to me, and it is worse when I take him back to them. I can almost see Prudence inspecting him for dirt. Prudence and Paul have begun their new family in the house that was mine. When Nathan gets older, he will be able to choose whether he lives with me all the time and I feel sure that he will, though that's a long way off.

One day, Josh Thwaite comes to visit. I make that sound as if it is especially significant, but it is not. Josh calls often. I've left Leda, he told me a long time ago.

'That's fine,' I said at the time, 'if it's what's right for you.'

'So when can I move in?' he had asked.

'Later, not just yet.'

'Don't you want me?' he had enquired, in an injured way, although all the evidence was in favour of me wanting him a great deal. He is back fishing, on Italian boats down at Island Bay.

'When you're sure you're sorted out, we can think about it.' I have experienced some serious grief over Josh Thwaite; I do even now, when he leaves me. But I am not ready for all that commitment and routine again, and I want him to be quite sure he knows what he is letting himself in for when he gets me, because, once it's decided, I don't plan to let him go.

This day, when he comes, I am working in the back yard, digging a little trench to lay stones round the edge of the narrow garden. 'I could build a swing for Nathan,' he says. 'I reckon he'd like that.' He pulls himself up on a branch of the silver birch tree. 'It's really strong. Or I could make a frame for it, if you're worried about the tree.'

'That sounds like a good idea,' I tell him.

We stand in my patch of sunlight, watching the sky, and although it's not in place yet, we both see the swing, flying higher and higher, backwards and forwards, with Nathan holding on.